A TALE OF THE HIDDEN ISLE

MORE FROM SAMANTHA CHRISTOPHER

The Spark Within

The Spark Ignites

A Tale of the Hidden Isle

A SPARK SERIES NOVEL

A TALE OF THE HIDDEN ISLE

SAMANTHA CHRISTOPHER

Spark Productions

For my mom,

the one person who has always showed up, whose love never

wavers, and raised me to be a hopeless romantic.

And for all those who believed

Jack could have fit on the door with Rose.

mystery.
Where are the men and women and two babies -- 32 persons in all -- who happily boarded a plane at San Juan, Puerto Rico, and flew 1,000 miles toward Miami? A radio message at 4 a. m. Dec. 27, 1948, reported them 50 miles south of their goal. They never arrived.

This is the most recent news article snippet from E. V. W. Jones AP collected, at Elder Wilder's request, on the subject of what the Nomagi call the mysterious Devil's Triangle. It appears that there are only theories and no concrete evidence about our existence.

1

IZALIA

Recklessness isn't a choice; it's a necessity amongst those with nothing to lose.

One step, and I would be plummeting to my death. I smile from the adrenaline coursing through my veins as I behold the expanse of sea before me. Shimmering aquamarine water stretches in all directions toward the forever-constant dark clouds on the horizon. Only the Protectors could call the storm closer.

My eyes dart to the 150-foot drop. If I fell, I would be spit out fairly quickly, unless I skewered myself on the sharp rocks below. The ocean doesn't often take Divina; it has a taste for Nomagi. It's a terrible saying, but it's true. Those storms have brought down hundreds, if not thousands, of Nomagi boats. And there are never survivors.

A tiny furry hand tugs at the trim of my floral dress, bringing me back to why I'm on the edge of Breakwater Strand's highest cliff.

"Don't worry, Beau. You know I've done this before," I say, peeking at the overprotective squirrel monkey at my feet. If monkeys could roll their eyes, that's exactly what Beau would be doing. Instead, his round, dark eyes are alert, watching my every move as whimpers escape him.

As I twist, kicking off my sandals to lower myself over the edge, I take in my island home of Alohra. Swaying palm trees extend in each direction, the top of Crystal City shines in the distance, and the long-dormant volcano, Mt. Apia, rises above it all. I was born and raised on Alohra, like all its inhabitants, my people, the Divina.

My stomach presses against the rocks as my feet dangle. I begin my descent by bracing the tips of my toes on the rocks underneath and my hands on the crevices of the jagged bits. Beau squeaks and races to the edge as Alohra's landscape disappears from view. My feet find the fissures easily as I lower myself to the platform of rock that protrudes from the cliff. The salty mist from the water hitting the rocks below licks my ankles. I shouldn't look at the angry tide swirling beneath, but I do, and my stomach rolls.

Beau's squeaks grow louder, and I peer at him with an irritated sigh. His black eyes are wide, and his jaw clicks as he hops back and forth. I can barely hear him over the crashing of waves.

"I'm fine!" I yell up, finding another foothold as I near the platform. "Honestly, you're worse than my parents," I mutter. They'd lock me in the house indefinitely if they knew I was doing this.

But Beau, my faithful companion since the incident, knows me inside and out. If anything were amiss, he'd warn me—which is the only reason my parents let me out of their sight. I hoped the coddling would lessen when I turned eighteen, even though being an adult means nothing here, as it does with Nomagi—or so I've heard. I've never seen a Nomagi or been to the mainland where they live. My people haven't left our island for hundreds of years. But no, my parents' insistent worrying about my health will never end. My new false hope is that it will ease once I take the trials. That will be the true sign of independence, no matter the assignment I receive.

"There you are." The bright orange petals are just past the platform's edge.

Before releasing the wall, I test my weight on the rock, which is only wide enough for me and like half another person. My pulse beats loudly in my ears as waves crash into the side of the cliff. Sure, I could have picked a common flower, or even traded for another set of pearl earrings like last year, but then I wouldn't have an excuse to prove myself. Even if nobody else knows I'm taking such a risk—I do. I know I'm more than my messed-up brain. And it will be worth seeing my mother's expression when I bring her the rare avalian for her birthday present, her namesake.

When I step forward, several rocks break off and fall into the frothy mist below. I swallow, focusing on the flower. It's even more beautiful up close. The colors perfectly encapsulate the different shades of a sunrise. The pink center blossoms outward into various hues of orange and yellow. I study it in awe before a cold blast of water reminds me to get moving.

Balancing my weight on the rock jutting over the churning dark waters, I lift my hand toward the flower. Impossibly, it has grown straight from a crevice in the rock, the most unlikely of places to find such a dainty thing. Its existence shouldn't be possible. I'm still a couple feet from it, but that shouldn't be a problem for my Aura magic. I focus on the flower's root and pull it with my mind. Nothing happens.

I take a deep breath, push my dark hair behind my ears, and channel my Sage—my connection to the earth, where our magic lies. My attention is drawn to the roughness of the rock underfoot, the wind threading its fingers through my hair, and the droplets of water plastering the bottom of my dress to my form. The whistling wind, thunderous waves, and Beau's now-quiet whines envelop me.

I inhale and exhale the sea salt air. I pull again. There's movement as the soil around the flowers shifts. Imagining that I'm cutting the roots free from their rocky home, the flowers shudder. Carefully—I don't want to hurt even a petal—I project my touch, light as a feather but swift as the wind, and yank.

The roots release. The flowers, along with a dirty ball at the base, float midair.

"Ooh-ooh!" Beau screeches.

I smile triumphantly. He's bouncing up and down but not stepping toward me. He'd have made this a lot easier if he had just climbed down like a normal monkey, but he wouldn't come this close to water when it's spraying everywhere.

I pull the flowers the rest of the distance. The moist soil settles into my outstretched palm, and the petals tickle my fingertips.

I came across the rare flower on one of my monthly walks of Breakwater Strand a few months ago. I've always been drawn to this place—and not because my parents don't like me coming here. Well, maybe a little bit. It just feels like there is a part of me here, on this beautiful, rocky shore. Like I lost something long ago, but I can't remember what. When I found the flower already wilted, I had a reason to come more often, waiting for it to bloom again, to surprise Mom.

I turn to show Beau, but his round face and pointed, white ears blur at the corners. His eyes are fathomless, and he's utterly still, as if he's sensing—no, no, no, no. This cannot be happening right now.

I clutch the wall and lose my grip on the flowers. A scream escapes me, but they land safely on the ledge between my feet. My hands won't cooperate as I try to grab them. The ground quakes, and I almost lose my footing.

Hold it together.

I squeeze my eyes shut to calm my racing heart. A metallic tang fills my mouth, and the unmistakable feeling of wrongness overwhelms my senses.

My eyes fly open as the world shifts. My stomach rises into my chest. I steady myself on the rocks and wince as one lodges itself into my palm.

Beau's shrieks ring through the air as time slows. I watch in dismay as he climbs down. There is nothing he can do. He can't save me this time.

The cliff face darkens, and I know I'm seconds away from falling to my death. I fight it like I have so many times before, pushing against the black wall of nothingness. But it's useless. I've never been able to control it, and now it will finally claim me.

My legs give out, and my body crashes into the rock wall as my hands curl and limbs stiffen. My mind becomes muddled as if somebody has opened my head and poured mud inside. Darkness overpowers me. This time, I won't wake up.

A shadow drifts over the cliff edge as I slip away into nothingness.

2

THEO

My heart beats frantically in my chest as I blink once, twice, trying to distill what must be a figment of my imagination. She remains close to the cliff edge, peering across the water as the breeze tussles her waist-length, midnight hair around her shoulders. It's her.

I was beginning to think I had imagined her all those months ago, that she was an angel of the ocean from the stories my parents used to tell me—stories about their ancestors who walk the coastline, protecting us from the dangers of the outside world. Those born here die here and remain to watch over their people, giving life to the island and magic to its heart—everyone except for me.

The girl is dangerously close to the cliff edge, peering across the water. The sun is rising in the sky, casting long shadows behind her. She's wearing a long colorful dress, one side tied above her knee. Her other leg has a brown object attached to it—a furry, moving thing. Is that a monkey?

The thing releases her leg and bounces around, tugging at the end of her dress, its long tail whipping through the air. Definitely a monkey, then. She doesn't seem to notice. What could she be doing here?

She's in the same spot she was the last time I saw her, and still, I have yet to see her face. Only in my dreams. I've looked for her in town, even though it's fruitless. Most likely, she's from the city on the other side of the island. It's not like I would do anything if I did find her. I'm much too cowardly.

Now, she's right here. I don't usually come out this early, but today I did. Something made me scan the horizon today when I was supposed to be splitting wood. A magnetic pull emanates from her. I can feel it from my spot on the edge of the trees, just like in the dreams. She drifts through my waking and unconscious thoughts, never turning toward me but always there, looking for something or maybe waiting for someone.

Her head tilts as she studies the cliff face. The wind picks up, and loud squeaks from the monkey reach me as he tries to get her attention. She squats and lowers herself over the edge. I stiffen as her hair clears the edge, and she's lost from sight.

The monkey bounces erratically, mimicking the acceleration of my heart. I know this area like the back of my hand. The platform is right there, but worry grips my chest for this girl. She's a Divina, she'll be fine. I should turn around, get back home, and let her be.

I try to step back, but a weight is tied to my feet, not letting me move another inch.

She's alone.

I exhale and step forward, the sand capturing my sandals, so I shuck them off. I'll make sure she's okay and then return to my duties. The monkey doesn't notice me, even when I'm halfway to it—it's too focused on watching her below the edge, its tail twitching back and forth.

I pause as it jumps up and down in the air with a high-pitched shriek. Is that good or bad?

I quicken my steps, but the monkey stills. I freeze, waiting for it to spot me and attack. Ma tells me to be careful around animals, especially those with Divina, since they can speak with them. It wouldn't be the first time one has sicced an animal on me. I'm so stupid for doing this. Ma's going to kill me.

Unless the monkey does it first. He's so tiny, though, only a little bigger than my forearm. He's even a little cute, with a short grayish coat, bright yellow legs, and big black eyes. My chances are pretty good. With only a few feet to go, maybe I can check on her without it spotting me.

A scream rings out, and the next thing I know, I'm barreling towards the cliff. Vicious monkeys be damned.

I slide to the edge as the monkey disappears over it. My heart lodges into my throat when I spot the girl lying on the small platform, unconscious, her legs rigid and hovering over the side.

I swing myself over the edge and climb down. I keep an eye on her as the monkey reaches her side and tries to pull her legs from the edge. He gets one leg up just as her body begins to shake. The monkey screams and throws itself between her and the drop that will kill her.

My feet hit the edge of the rocky platform when it notices me. He bares his teeth in a fierce glare.

I throw my hands in the air. "I just want to help."

She's shaking harder and inching closer to the edge. As I prepare myself to fight the little thing off, the monkey nods and jumps out of the way.

With my arms underneath her back and legs, I lift her. Warmth radiates from her body, calming my racing heart. Her head lolls into my chest, and I see her face clearly.

My breath catches. The sunlight shines on a delicate dusting of freckles that covers her cheeks and nose. She's breathtaking, even as she writhes against me, making it hard to hold on to her. It doesn't help that her dress is wet and slippery beneath my fingertips, and I have to grip tighter than I would like. I cringe, hoping I won't leave bruises on her bronze skin.

I look at the jagged rocks above us. How am I going to do this? I gingerly shift her weight and place my hand on her face. It's so soft. A tingling sensation travels up my arm.

"Wake up." I tap her lightly.

Her eyelids remain closed, but the shaking dissipates. Holding my breath, I wait for her to wake. I study her smooth, dark features until the monkey yells, and I realize I'm still standing on the platform, the waves crashing much too close. I need to get her off of here.

The monkey continues screeching at me as he climbs the wall.

"Easy for you to say," I mutter.

His large eyes narrow. Is he glaring? I shake my head and carefully reposition her body over my shoulders. It's not too difficult; she weighs less than those sacks of sugar cane I carry from market. Bright orange flowers glisten at my feet. Is that what she was doing? Picking flowers? I pick them up with my free hand.

"Hey, monkey!"

He's almost to the top but stops and looks at me, still with that same glare.

I shove the flowers at him. "Wanna help?" I ask, cocking an eyebrow.

He lets out a sound that I swear is a sigh and climbs back down, only far enough to snatch the flower from me, and then he's climbing again.

Well, here goes nothing.

I ensure she's secure on my shoulder as I grab the rock with one hand. I test our weight on it before grabbing the second one. I grunt as I climb the wall, sweat beading on my forehead.

The spray of cold water beneath us is doing nothing against the blistering sun. The monkey cheers me on, bouncing up and down, as I slowly climb the cliff with the most beautiful woman dangling off my shoulders, still unsure if this is reality.

I grab the top edge, pulling onto my forearms before rotating and lowering her to the ground above me. The monkey grabs her face and studies her body as I hoist myself the rest of the way. I fall onto the sand, panting and wiping the sweat from my eyes.

She's still too close to the edge. If she starts convulsing again, all this is for nothing. I push through my shaking muscles and step towards her. Again, the monkey bares his teeth.

"Really? I just saved her life. We need to get her away from that edge."

He hesitantly hops back. I eye him as I hoist her into my arms and carry her to the trees. Without the risk of imminent death, I marvel at her warmth and beauty. Besides Ma, I've never been this close to another woman. Divina girls want nothing to do with me.

I pause at the edge of the tree line where I was going to put her down. But I might as well take her back to our fale. Ma and Pa should check her out and make sure she's okay.

The monkey squeals as I step into the trees. He jumps overhead, swinging from branch to branch until he places himself between me and home.

"I'm bringing her to my parents," I say, shifting her weight. She's still out of it. He doesn't move. Ugh. I go to step around him, and he blocks my path. "Come on!" I shoo him with my foot.

He dodges but stays put.

"Fine, get stepped on." I continue on the path, and he's smart enough to jump out of the way. I take two steps before he's on my leg and crawling to my shoulder. He places his little hand on her face before turning to me with a vicious glare. He makes a chattering noise. Like I'm supposed to know what he's saying.

"Sorry, don't speak monkey. Not a Divina."

I swear he just rolled his eyes at me. He squawks and points to the ground. I look at him, trying to decipher what he wants me to do, when the girl's eyelids open then close again.

I suck in a breath as she moans and moves her head from side to side. She fully opens her eyes, and I can't help but gasp. Her eyes are a deep, emerald green—the same color as all the Divina, but on her, it's mesmerizing. The whites of her eyes grow as she screams and yanks herself from me. I hold on so she doesn't fall and hurt herself, but end up sending both of us tumbling to the ground.

The monkey jumps out of the way as we land ungracefully in a tangle of legs and arms in the dirt and vines.

"I'm so sorry," I grunt as I try to get free without touching too much of her skin, which suddenly feels much too hot. That can't be a good sign.

She slides off of my legs but sits on my hand. I jump, which makes her jump, and we knock heads.

"Ow!" she yelps.

"I'm sorry," I say again, finally freeing myself and sliding away from her.

She launches to her feet, almost toppling over. I seize her elbow to keep her from falling back into the dirt as I rise. Her eyes dart around as she sways slightly. She blinks and glances at my hand. I release her slowly, making sure she's not going to face-plant into a tree.

"Where am I? I was on the rocks, and then I—Beau?"

The monkey grunts and hops onto her shoulder, holding out the flowers. "You got them!" She smiles, and my breath is knocked from me.

It's as if I've lived in the shadows my entire life and I'm seeing the sun for the first time. Familiarity strikes me, like I've been here before, but not in my dreams—like I've somehow already witnessed that smile.

I can't take my eyes off her as she takes the flowers like they're the most precious pearls we trade in the market.

She moves her gaze to mine, and her face falls. "Who are you?" She tilts her head, her eyes sparking. "*What* are you?"

Oh boy. I know what she's seeing—a nineteen-year-old with weird, light-colored hair and freaky eyes that are nothing like the other guys.

A line etches between her dark eyebrows. What would it be like to press my lips in that spot? The absurd thought pops into my head, and I look away as heat fills my face.

"Are you a Nomagi?" Unlike others, she doesn't say it with disgust or fear, but she seems surprised.

I open my mouth to respond but can't form words. It'll hit her soon that she shouldn't be around me, and she'll run. I'll never see her again.

But the shock on her face settles into curiosity. Then she smiles again—that breathtaking smile that lights up her eyes. I can't talk, move, or even breathe when she looks at me like that. I'll pass out from lack of oxygen soon, then the monkey will have at me. I'll wake up with my face gone.

"I don't know where you came from. But thank you for saving my life. I'm Izalia."

Izalia.

My angel of the ocean has a name, and she's not running away from me.

3

IZALIA

I watch the strange boy talk to his parents. He told me his name—Theo—but not much else as he led me to his home. Typically, I would have brushed him off, but my curiosity got the best of me. I was surprised to find that his parents are Divina, like myself. We all share the same traits—dark skin and hair and green eyes. Does he know they're not his birth parents?

He glances uneasily through the opening of their fale. It's the most unusual fale I've ever seen. The rectangular shape and thatched roof made from woven coconut leaves are the same as the others that line Breakwater Strand, the very edge of our island. Instead of the open layout where there are no doors nor walls, letting the sea salt breeze cool the home, there are bamboo walls erected in the middle. I can't see too many details from where I'm sitting in their outdoor cooking area, and I wonder if that's the purpose—no wandering eyes.

Theo's skin glows a tinge red when he looks at me, and I tilt my head. I've never seen a Nomagi before. He's handsome, in that never-seen-your-kind-but-you're-interesting-to-look-at way. In addition to his tall and lean build, his hair is as bright as the sun, and though his skin is paler than ours, it's tan enough to rival our naturally dark complexion. He could almost pass for one of us—if he wore a hat, maybe—but then there are his peculiar eyes. They are the color of a newborn babe—a dark ocean blue. As we age, they change to a leafy green color before brightening when we come into our magic and begin wielding the elements of nature. But his are still blue. It's quite captivating.

Beau sits in my lap, on guard, eyes locked on the odd family, his long tail wrapped around my arm. I never imagined a Nomagi being amongst us. Could there be more? How did he get here? Too many questions bounce around my head.

They may be arguing, but I can't make out what they're saying. The woman is obviously worried, judging by the huge hand motions she's making, but the man appears rather bored, nodding at whatever the woman says.

I sit up as the family turns to head my way. I pet Beau's head to calm him and myself, threading my fingers through the soft, longer fur there.

The woman's curly hair is cut short around her ears, and the man is balding with a dark, graying beard. They look at me with the same green eyes, the color faded with age.

The woman smiles warmly as they stop a few feet away. "I'm Iris, and this is Boaz." She gestures to the man with a hand towel splattered in pink and purple paint—the same paint that dots the right side of her face, drifting down her neck and continuing onto her colorful apron. "Sounds like you took quite the fall. I'm glad my son was there to help. Are you okay? Can we get you anything?" She looks worried, but not for me. Her quick, uneasy glances at her son betray her.

"No, thanks. And I didn't fall."

"Oh?" she says, her smile wavering.

I cast a look toward Theo, who's looking anywhere but at me. He didn't tell them what really happened. "I climbed on the ledge and had an episode. Sometimes I pass out, and my body goes haywire," I say with a shrug.

The woman stares at me, unblinking, as the man's eyebrows rise slightly. I'm accustomed to people reacting to my condition in various ways. Not many people on the island have defects. Actually, nobody does. I'm the only one. Our pure blood makes it so abnormalities are almost unheard of among the Divina.

The woman's cheeks redden, and she looks away.

I tell them the same thing I tell everyone else. It's been a while since I've had to give my rehearsed speech. Everyone in the city knows who I am. I go through how I fell out of a tree when I was eight and almost died, but instead, I got stuck with this utterly unhelpful condition that causes me to pass out randomly. And that Beau alerts me to the episodes so I don't get hurt.

"It was unfortunate that I was on that cliff. Not something Beau could have helped me with." I flash a smile in Theo's direction. His cheeks change color, his throat bobbing. I smile wider. "But fortunate Theo was there."

They all blink at me a few times before Theo's father murmurs, "How odd."

His mother whips him with her towel. He flinches and scowls at her.

It's the same thing I was thinking about them. I can't help the laugh that bubbles up at his bluntness, scaring Beau. He jumps three feet in the air and onto the grass, which makes me laugh harder. Theo smiles, and his father snickers. Soon, his mother joins in, and we're all laughing, breaking the tension.

His father stutters an apology. "Not…not that you're odd, of course. Just the fact that Theo was there, when he was supposed to be doing his chores." He eyes his son, who sucks in his bottom lip. "The island brought you two together. You must be something special."

A prickling sensation crawls up my spine and into my face. I stand to expel the flush in my cheeks, unsure what's causing the sudden emotion. Beau climbs to my shoulder.

"Thank you again," I say to Theo, whose face is redder than a tomato. "I need to get going, though." I hold up the flower to show them that the petals are starting to droop. "It's my mother's birthday today."

"Let me get you some water," Iris says.

With a flick of her wrist, a jar floats from a set sitting on a table in their home, and with another motion of her hand, a ball of water forms in the bottom of it. I grab it out of the air and carefully place my flower inside.

"Thank you."

"You sure you're alright?"

"Never better," I say, starting for the trees.

Iris clears her throat, and I spin around. "Umm, we were hoping you could use discretion when talking about your incident today." She looks towards Theo, love and worry lining her face. "You can probably tell he's not like us, and not many know about him. We would hate to be a source of disturbance." Her voice lowers with meaning as she levels me with her eyes—eyes of a mother fiercely protecting her child.

I steady myself with a breath. "Of course. I won't say anything. It's the least I can do." I offer Theo a small smile before leaving.

"Ma," Theo whispers behind me.

"I needed to make sure. You don't know if—"

I hear another grunt, probably the dad, and then only silence. I want to look back but, instead, quicken my footsteps. As soon as I'm in the trees, I exhale.

"Sorry about that." Theo's voice comes from behind me.

I jump as Beau scampers into the trees. I glare at him. What a lousy monkey.

My hand flutters to my chest. "By the island, you're quiet."

He frowns. "I'm sorry."

"You know, I think those are the only words you've spoken to me since I met you. Stop apologizing. You saved my life back there."

"I'm s—" he starts but presses his lips together, stopping himself.

I shake my head at him. There's a moment of silence between us before I say, "Come on, walk with me." I have no idea where I'm going. I know it's this direction, and I'm sure I'll eventually find my way out, but he might keep me from walking in circles for a bit. I'm not as familiar with the trees as with the coastline.

He wavers, so I hook my arm into his and tug him along. His arm is cool, so different from the Divina guys, who run even hotter than I do—and that's not counting the ones who have Igna specialties. It's comforting, like drinking iced guava on a hot day.

"You don't talk much." I peer up at him as he moves stiffly next to me. "Come on, loosen up. I won't bite," I say, shaking his arm.

He glances at Beau in the trees, moving with us, and then at me. "*He* might," he says, relaxing his shoulders slightly.

I smile. "Yeah, he would."

"I thought he was going to rip my head off when I tried to save you from that ledge."

"Beau! You naughty monkey," I say, shooting him a look.

He ignores me as he swings fluidly from one tree to another, not missing a vine.

"He was just trying to protect you," he says.

"I don't know what would have happened if you weren't there. I've had some close calls, but not *that* close." Tiny ghost spiders crawl across my skin.

"And all you have is this little monkey to protect you."

Beau screeches.

"He doesn't like to be called little," I lean into him to whisper.

A sweet vanilla scent wafts off him. He chuckles. It's a nice sound I wouldn't mind hearing more of.

"Tell me more about you. I'm most intrigued," I say, wiggling my eyebrows. "You're the first Nomagi I've met, you know. How did you get here?" I try to ask it nonchalantly, but my eagerness to know leaks through my words. I peer at him, and he hesitates. He's battling something behind those ocean-blue eyes.

"You can trust me," I murmur.

Familiarity washes over me, like I've been here before. A vague distant memory tugs on me.

He turns his head, and we lock eyes. The world shifts, and I'm staring into a different set of eyes.

"Here you go, honey," Dad says, placing a mango popsicle in my hand.

"Niko, we're about to go into the dressmaker's shop," Mom *hisses under her breath.*

I pause before licking it. It smells glorious, and the heat of the day is already causing it to melt. But I don't want to get in trouble.

"Oh, let her have a treat. I'll stay outside with her while she finishes." Dad winks at me, and I giggle.

Mom sighs. "I can't believe you're getting out of this."

She says it with a playful tone, so I take that as my cue to lick the delicious frozen fruit finally. The sweetness gathers on my tongue and chills my stomach. Soon, it drips onto my fingers, and Mom shakes her head at Dad. At least I'm not the one in trouble.

We stop in front of the dressmaker's shop in the city. Mom walks in as I lean against the glass building with Dad.

"Take your time, kiddo."

I giggle again and take a bite. That's a mistake. It's too cold for my mouth, and I look up at my dad, whimpering.

"Just spit it out."

I shake my head. No way am I wasting any bit of this yumminess.

"Then swallow, silly."

I try to, but it spews out of my mouth and all over me. Too cold, way too cold. I smack my lips, trying to warm my mouth.

"Izzy!"

"Sowwy," I say, as it dribbles down my chin.

"Stay here. I'll get some napkins from the woman."

Her cart was on the next path over. I try to lick the stickiness off my chin unsuccessfully as Dad walks away.

He rounds the corner and a boy appears out of nowhere, running full speed. He's about to crash into me, but he skids behind the trashcan next to me instead—his chest heaving and his eyes wild.

"Aw you otay?" I ask.

He starts to turn my way.

The boy's face blurs as worry-filled eyes stare at me.

"Izalia! Izalia!"

I blink away the images and sway lightly. Theo's hands are on my shoulders, scanning my face, worry lines tracing his forehead.

"Did you have another episode?"

Shaking my head, I take a steading breath. "No, something else. It's been a while since that happened." My skin buzzes where his hands are. I step away. His arms fall to his sides. "I'm okay—just a flashback. I used to get them all the time when I was little. After the incident, my memories of my childhood were scrambled for a while. I guess there are still some memories hiding away."

I sigh and try to shake off the images. I was so young in the flashback, maybe four or five. It's bizarre that it happened now. What was the trigger? And what happened to that boy? I search my mind, but everything is fuzzy after that moment.

Beau clambers up my frame and points behind us; we must be close. Theo still hasn't answered my question though. The distraction hasn't dimmed my yearning to know more about him. "You were telling me where you came from?"

He studies me for a moment longer before threading a hand through his golden hair. "It's a long story, and the fields are just ahead. Another time." He grimaces. "You sure you're okay? I could walk with…" His words drift off, and we both know that it isn't a good idea.

"I'm fine. I've got Beau, remember?" I point to Theo's chest. "But I'm going to hold you to that. I know where you live." I say it jokingly, but something close to fear crosses his features. I lower my voice. "I won't tell anyone. I promise." He doesn't have much reason to believe me, but I hope he will.

He gives me a halfhearted smile, and I turn to walk towards the filtering light. I leave the trees' safety, and the sugar cane fields open up before me. I feel his eyes on me. But when I look over my shoulder, there is nothing but swaying shadows underneath the palm trees.

I pat Beau's furry, yellow leg under my chin. A part of me is sad that Theo isn't still walking with us, and I almost trip over a rock at the realization. There is something about him that's so…pure, which is unusual, since Divina are the ones with the pure blood. We've been on this island for hundreds of years. Where did he come from?

I hurry through the long grass and along the dirt paths around the small village of Avalon. The huge fale where market is held rises high in the distance, and faint chatter reaches me as people mill about amongst the traders and farmers. It's almost afternoon, peak trading time.

Even though all are welcome at market, I can't help but feel shut out when I go with my parents. There has always been a clear divide between those of the city with specialized assignments and those of Avalon and Breakwater Strand. Although Farmers, a prestigious assignment that specialize in Terra abilities, don't seem to mind living on this side of the island.

The voices from market grow lighter. It's hard to believe Avalon used to be the island's center not even a hundred years ago, before the city was built—before the Craftsmen learned glass-making techniques with their Igna specialties. I don't think our people were always so separated; the divide must have grown with the city.

A flooded green field stretches to my right, and rows of fruit-bearing trees line the left side. The sun grows more stifling. I check on my mom's flower and smile. The ends that had started to wilt have brightened with the water.

Instead of taking the center path, my growling stomach and sweat pooling on the nape of my neck pulls me through the trees. I pluck an apple, and throw it towards Beau, who catches it quickly. He settles on a branch to eat.

I lean against the tree. Picking another apple, I clean it with my skirt before taking a few bites. The shade from the trees is a nice relief from the sun's heat. My thoughts drift to Theo as the sweet and musky fragrances fill me.

"He was kind of cute, wasn't he?"

The words surprise me, and I scan the area to make sure nobody overheard—though it's not like they would know who I was talking about. He's just so intriguing—that golden hair and blue eyes. I've never seen anyone like him. I've always wondered what the mainland would be like. He's a peek into a different world. I would never admit it to anybody, even Beau, but a part of me would love to travel and see what the rest of the world holds.

I peer down the rows leading back toward the forest where Theo lives. I don't know how he is here, but one thing is certain—neither he nor I will ever leave this island.

My eyes trail the blue sky until I spot the dark clouds far off. The storms that the Protectors—who specialize in Aura abilities—create to guard our island and prevent anyone from coming or going.

A chill runs down my spine as I turn away. I don't particularly want *that* assignment. It seems like a difficult task containing those beastly storms.

I take one last inhale of the delicious smells before continuing to the farms. There will undoubtedly be no breathing through those manure-filled fields.

The all-glass, rounded buildings of Crystal City rise before me as I enter the heart of Alohra. I've lived here my entire life, and I'm still in awe when I see it midday. The sun dances off the buildings, making them sparkle like the sea. Mt. Apia blocks out the sky to my left as I take a shortcut around the buildings, through a park designated for small children.

Child-rearers line the benches as the happy sounds of children playing rise. One child-rearer waves at me with a smile. It's Katarina, the only girl given a child-rearer assignment after last year's trials.

I wince. Her youth is obvious around the other older women. I wonder if she's happy. It's one of the lower-class assignments, but she looks genuinely content as she smiles down at the baby in her lap.

I wave back, rounding the trees, and spot my home across from Seaside Academy. It matches the other triangle-shaped white homes lining the path.

Being this close to campus, with my parents as Instructors, is quite convenient, but it makes it hard to sneak away. Although, it won't matter in a week. I'll graduate and prove that my abnormality doesn't limit me, by going through the trials and securing a good assignment on the island. My overbearing parents will finally leave me alone.

Four of the many assignments are considered prestigious—Farmer with Terra specialties, Protector with Aura specialties, Craftsman with Igna specialties, and Fisherman, who specialize in Lympha abilities. Instructor, the *most* distinguished position, specializes in *all* the elements…and is my expected path.

My heart falls into my stomach when I spot the shape on my front steps. I could turn around and go to the beach until my parents return. The idea is tempting, but I stop myself from slinking under the shadows of the tree and, instead, take a deep breath.

I nudge Beau, who jumps down and takes off for the trees. He's not too fond of the man on my steps. I'm already late, and he's going to have questions. I can't hide forever. I'm supposed to spend my free time with a few carefully selected friends, including my—

I swallow when he sees me.

Alexi Wilder, our leader's grandson, stands. He meets me at the bottom of my steps. His hair, as black as night, is slicked back uniformly, just like his nicely pressed sarong and vest that's open to show off his chiseled abs. Oddly enough, he's been leaving his tops unbuttoned lately. Despite whatever intention he has, nothing is relaxed about him. He has an eyebrow raised, and he's trying to control his frustration with me, but it leaks out in the tightness of his shoulders. I wonder if he can smell the fields on me, even though I stayed far away from the animals. I'm not supposed to fraternize with the lower class and keep my eyes focused on becoming an Instructor, just like my parents.

"Where have you been? I've been waiting for half an hour. I almost sent a message to your parents," he says, bristling.

I roll my eyes and walk past him into the house. Alexi is like his grandfather and those in power—pretty much everyone in the city, including my parents, unfortunately—who look down upon lower-class duties. All those who live in fales on Breakwater Strand who could not excel in their trials are now stuck with less-than-significant assignments. And even though I feel that everyone on the island has value, no matter their assignment, I can't divulge where I just was. I can't imagine their reaction if they knew I was not only amongst one of the lower-class families, but a family with a Nomagi son.

Or maybe it would be a little funny.

I smile, imagining my parents' reaction, which would probably involve fire and the uprooting of a tree.

"I've told you before, I don't need a child-rearer," I say, with a little too much venom. I miss the days before my magic manifested, when I could run wild with whomever I wanted, exploring the coasts and coves of Alohra. Falling out of a tree never slowed me down, nor does the short tether my parents think they have me on. Although school lessens the amount of time I can sneak away.

"Hey." He grabs my hand and twists me to face him. His face softens as he pulls a white peony from behind his back and offers it to me.

I sigh—my favorite flower. It's unfair to take my frustrations out on him. He's only doing what he's supposed to.

"Thanks," I say, taking it in my free hand.

He eyes the jar in my other hand. "This is nothing compared to that beauty, though."

"Oh yeah." I hold it up so he can see it better. "It's for my mom."

His eyebrows rise. "Is that a—"

I nod. My enthusiasm breaks through, pushing down my anger.

He places his palms around the jar. I let him take it as his green eyes rove over the beautiful flower. "How is that possible?"

"That's where I was. I found a patch of avalians last year, and I've been waiting for them to bloom." I take it from him and climb the stairs to my bedroom.

He hesitates at the landing. He's not allowed in my room.

"I'll be right back," I say, flashing him a smile.

I open my wardrobe, shove some clothes out of the way, and place the jar on a low shelf, tucking the peony next to it.

When I'm done, I study myself in the mirror and almost laugh at my wild hair. I braid it around my head and startle as I close the door.

Alexi leans against my doorway, his eyes hooded. How long has he been watching me?

"What are you doing?"

"Well, your parents aren't home." He struts forward and wraps his hands around my waist. "And it's getting closer to our ceremony." His eyes rake over my body.

My heart jumps into my throat as he looks at me like a desirable delicacy. "You know we're not supposed to touch until we make the bond," I say quietly. But I don't move away from his hands because I know it'll upset him.

This isn't the first time he's tried something. I've known Alexi my whole life, and I have always known that, one day, I'll have to bond with him. But it didn't become a reality until a year ago when he started to treat me as more than a friend. Since then, there's been a fire in his eyes that's been growing at an alarming rate.

I've been hoping the same feelings would hit me soon. I expected them to. But here we are, a month away from our ceremony, and there has been not even the faintest of sparks.

Not that he's not attractive. Many girls throw themselves at him, even the bonded ones. But I still see him as the little boy who chased me with giant hissing beetles, threw my favorite seashells into the ocean, and pushed me down when nobody was looking. I only managed to get away from his touch the first time because we were in public, but this—we're alone in my room.

My heart stutters. There's nothing I can do.

He looks at my lips, moving his hands to my face.

"Alexi," I say, a warning in my voice.

"You are as radiant as the sun, my Izalia." He moves his thumb over my bottom lip, tying my stomach in knots as my breath quickens.

I've never been kissed.

Heat fills his eyes, and panic settles in my gut as he crashes his lips to mine with a force that makes me step back. He steps with me, threading his hands in my hair, pinning me to his body. Heat wafts off him as he molds his lips to mine. A strong spicy aroma burns my nose.

My eyes widen, and I stare at him, not having the faintest clue about what to do. For a second, I stand motionless as he moves his lips against mine. Then my panic turns into rage. It boils up and moves through my veins into my hand.

I break away and slap him across the face.

We both gasp, and I look at the foreign extension of my arm and then back at him. His eyes are wide, hurt lacing his features.

I pull my eyes away and run for the door and down the stairs. I jump down the front steps and race into the city, away from my destined mate.

4

IZALIA

It doesn't take long for Beau to find me. The negativity radiating off him confuses my emotions as I stare at the same trees I left not even an hour ago.

I could have gone to Freylin's or Natalina's house, but knowing them, they would have been ecstatic over Alexi kissing me, even though it's against the law for such intimate relations before making the bond. They wouldn't have understood.

And it doesn't matter. I've never wanted to confide in them about anything. Our friendships are surface-level at most.

So, when running across the city, I didn't bother going in that direction, but I also didn't plan on coming here, back to the Nomagi.

Beau climbs the nearest tree, whining at me.

"I don't have to meet my parents until dinner; I've got plenty of time," I tell him, stepping into the forest.

The sun shines high in the sky, telling me I've got hours before it sinks behind the ocean, when my parents will be expecting me. Yeah, I'm supposed to spend time with Alexi when

I don't have school, but I doubt he'll be running to my parents anytime soon after what he did. He should be ashamed of himself.

Or should I? Shouldn't I have wanted him to kiss me? I know plenty of other pairs who broke the rules before their bonding ceremonies, and they seem plenty happy. Why am I not happy?

I move dangling vines out of my way as I retrace my steps to Theo's fale. If I'm honest with myself, I know it has nothing to do with the rules.

A rock settles into my gut. We're only a month from our ceremony. I should be feeling *something* by now. He just caught me off guard. That's not what I had hoped for our first kiss.

I kick a moss-covered log. How dare he take that from me. I try to think if any other feelings stirred when his lips met mine, but all I remember is the anger that erupted. I know I'll have to forgive him. He's probably just as upset with himself.

I'll let him stew in it for a while. Then maybe, after I forgive him and we're bonded, and *I'm* the one to initiate it, I will feel differently.

But what if I don't? That small voice inside of me asks.

I sigh. I have to. We're mates.

It takes me longer than I hoped to find Theo's house, but when I do, I hear the strangest, most beautiful sounds coming from within its interior. They're as delicate as a whisper, caressing my ears toward the source.

It begins like the pitter-patter of raindrops falling into pools of water, with each drop creating a ripple of graceful melody. Then the sounds come in waves, building until they crash onto the land, almost like distant thunder—light as a piece of cotton adrift in the air, but firm enough that its vibrations strike me to my core. Warmth spreads through my body as if I were basking in the sunlight on a cool day, watching glimmers reflecting off the ocean waves.

The sounds intensify as I drift closer to Theo's home. The woven blinds that are usually used for stormy weather on traditional fales are all pulled down, except for one opening.

I don't want the mesmerizing sounds to stop, so I slide onto the pebbled floor along the length of a post outside that opening. I close my eyes and let the melody take me to a distant land—a land I don't dare think about unless I'm asleep, with no control over the dreams that overtake me.

The sounds build as a storm strengthens, drawing closer to wreak havoc on Alohra. The waves crash onto the shore, and the thunder intensifies. Voices rise from the depths of the sea, calling louder, louder, louder.

Then silence slices through the air as the voices quietly drift away, and all I hear is my shallow breathing.

"Izalia?"

I open my eyes to Theo's mother staring down at me with a mystified expression that probably resembles my own.

"Are you okay?"

I choke on my words as I realize that tears have escaped my eyes. I quickly wipe them away. "What was that?" I ask breathlessly.

She smiles and eyes the inside of her home. "Theo, somebody is here for you." She holds out a hand.

I take it, and she helps me to my feet. Beau bounces off me. I didn't notice him curled in my lap. He blinks slowly, giving off pleasant vibes. He enjoyed the sounds, too.

"That, my dear, is music."

My eyebrows knit together. That didn't sound like any music I've ever heard before.

"Music from the mainland," she says so softly that I'm not sure she meant to tell me.

5

THEO

I'm lost in the music, far away from the pit of loneliness that plagues me. However, it isn't as wide and all-consuming today. I wonder if Izalia has anything to do with that.

I picture the way her eyes light up when she smiles, meshing the girl in my dreams with the real-life Izalia. She still doesn't feel real, which is best, since I'll never see her again. She said she would return, but in no sane world could that be true. Believing in the possibility would feed that hole inside of me.

How could somebody like her want to see me again unless it's to gawk at my existence? I should return to my mundane tasks, to only seeing her in my dreams. Maybe now I'll see her face.

Market will surely be busy by now, and if I don't leave soon, I won't be able to find all our necessities for the week. Ma will be upset if I bring home the leftover bruised fruit again.

But *music*. Besides my parents' love, it's the only thing that brings me joy. I'm not just a lowly Nomagi when I play. The few times I've played for the people of Breakwater Strand—those who somewhat accept my presence—are the only times I feel I contribute something meaningful to this island. An island where everyone but me wields the elements of nature—water, fire, earth, and air—and want for nothing. Even those here, the certified bottom of the barrel, have much more than I do. But I do have this.

My fingers hit the keys effortlessly, as my emotions flow through the notes, releasing me.

Ma calls my name, saying somebody is here for me.

I sigh as I finish the last few notes of the song. When the music stops, my emotions rush back. I push them down and rise from the piano.

Ainzel, my one and only friend, doesn't usually pause on the threshold, but barges in, loving to interrupt my playing. He says it's because it's what I'm *always* doing. But what do you expect from somebody like me? There's no reason for me to attend school with Divina. I have no interest in going into the city. I can't bond myself to anyone or have children—taint their pure blood by trying to lead a normal life. My instruments keep me sane, but my piano keeps me content. My parents saved a few things for me from the shipwreck, but I will be eternally grateful for this.

I slide my hand along the rough surface of the key lid, pulling it down. It couldn't have been easy to hide the black beauty.

I step around the bamboo slats that block the piano from view, and heat floods my body.

"Hi," Izalia says softly. She's standing on the threshold, her hands clasped and her eyes flitting around my home.

Ma turns and nods towards her with questioning eyes.

I swallow the shock and say, "Come back to turn me in?"

Ma's eyes flare as she lets out a strained laugh, but I wasn't joking.

"Of course not." Izalia looks between Ma and me, her emerald eyes wide. "I just, um, I—"

Ma crosses her arms, studying Izalia.

"Ma, don't you have something cooking?"

She turns toward me with raised eyebrows.

Please, go.

She narrows her eyes before nodding slightly.

"If you'll excuse me, Izalia." She brushes past me with a whispered, "Be careful."

Izalia looks down shyly and shifts on her feet, leaving me to look at her glaring monkey resting on her shoulder. He has one hand on her neck protectively.

I'm about to say something when her head whips up and dazes me, the ability to speak wiped from my memory. Her dark hair is in an intricate braid around her head, and I wish I could sit here all day, counting each freckle on her face.

And her eyes. I could get lost in them forever.

"Your mother said that was music from the mainland?"

"She did?" I glance toward the slats, Ma's curtain of dark hair fluttering past. She's totally spying. I don't know why she's so worried. It's not like the Elders don't know about me.

Izalia bites her lip, and I can't help but stare at the shape of them.

"Were you creating that?" she asks.

My eyes move up her face, still not believing I get another opportunity to study its perfection. "Yeah."

She raises her brows, probably wanting more details. When I don't provide them, she giggles—an incredible, musical sound that takes my breath away, even better than the piano. I could never create something that lovely.

"You're a boy of few words."

Around you, I am, I want to say, but I'm unable to form a complete sentence.

I clear my throat. "It's a…a piano."

Her eyes sparkle. "Can I see it?"

My chest suddenly feels too heavy, and I swallow loudly. She told me I could trust her, and for some reason I believe her. I'm not worried about me but *for her.*

"The things I have, you might get in trouble for seeing."

For reasons unexplained to me, her people are tight-lipped about mainland information. It's not like I know much besides the few things my parents kept for me, but the last thing I want is to get her in trouble.

A smile creeps onto her face. "Oh, now you *have* to show me." She leans down and whispers to Beau, who takes off for the trees.

Based on her stunt this morning, this shouldn't surprise me, but it does. I've never met anyone with such a carefree and daring personality.

I watch the monkey bound up a tree and gesture with my hand. "After you." I wait for Ma to jump out and forbid it, but surprisingly, she's nowhere to be seen.

I study Izalia's face as she takes in our humble abode. Our entire fale is probably the size of one room in her home. I wouldn't know, since I've never been inside one of their rock homes, but I've seen them from afar, and that fact alone tells me they're much bigger than ours.

But she doesn't gawk or run away screaming at our apparent poverty. Her lips pull up sincerely as she glances at the bamboo couch Pa made in the corner, pandanus mats spread on it for comfort. On the opposite side of the room sits a small, colorful table with our ice box nestled against it. Beyond the bamboo slats are our sleeping quarters and my beloved piano. We knew we couldn't entirely dampen the music, but this was the best option to provide the still much-needed breeze.

Even now, sweat gathers along my back, but that could be because of the beautiful woman before me, inside *my* home.

She scans the slats and posts holding up the fale, adorned with hundreds of Ma's paintings—images of me at every age, the ocean, trees, various animals, and portraits of my parents.

She focuses on one and walks towards it, holding up her hand, almost touching it.

Her head tilts. "Is this you?"

She's picked out the one picture that *isn't* me. It's of a baby boy with huge, chubby cheeks and dark hair, wrapped in a green blanket, lying in the sand, the ocean in the background. But it's not my story to tell.

She turns to look at me, waiting for my answer. I clear my throat, not sure what to say.

"No, it's not," says Pa.

We both turn as he enters the room. He scratches his chin underneath his whitening beard. His eyes are on the painting, his face with an unreadable expression.

"Oh," she says, lowering her hand as her eyebrows scrunch. Again, that adorable crease shows itself.

I look away before more absurd thoughts fill my head.

She doesn't say anything else as she looks at the rest of the images.

"That is our firstborn," Pa says, twisting his hands.

The blinds rise, flooding the space with light. I stiffen, not expecting him to tell her such a private part of our life.

She makes a noise and swings his way. "Your firstborn? But how?" Her eyes dart from him to me. Obviously, she knows I'm not their son by blood, but I can't imagine what she's thinking right now.

Her surprise is expected. It's our first and most important law on the island. One child per couple to prevent overpopulation. Couples are sterilized to avoid further pregnancies after the firstborn child. Not that that pertains to me. I'll never be bonded.

Pa collapses onto the couch, offering her the seat next to him. She smiles politely and sits down, back straight, looking like she's about to sprint out of here. Funny, she doesn't mind being around me or illegal mainland objects, but this is where she would draw the line.

I cross the room and sit on the table, moving Ma's painting supplies and dried fruit out of my way. My faded childhood drawings decorate the surface. Izalia's eyes sweep across them curiously before returning to Pa's.

"Our firstborn passed as an infant. A terrible accident."

She places her hand to her mouth but doesn't say anything. What could one say? Death doesn't happen often on the island, and when it does, it's the result of old age. For an infant to die? It doesn't happen.

He reaches for the picture and holds it, looking down at it, not with pain, but with reverence. A son he never got to know. A son that I replaced.

"She spent those months painting him. This is just one of thousands. I thought she would get better over time, but..." He clears the emotion from his throat—from the memories. "That is until Theodore entered our lives." He looks up at me and smiles.

Izalia looks at me, too, eyes full of questions.

"Boaz." Mom's stern voice fills the room.

We all whip our heads toward her. She has a hand on her hip, and if she could shoot fire from her eyeballs, Pa would be scorched.

Izalia immediately stands. "I'm sorry. I'll go. You don't need to tell me these things."

"It is no secret, Iris," Boaz says, ignoring Izalia.

"But Theo—"

"Can make his own decisions," Pa finishes. He stands lazily, turning toward Izalia. "Izalia, you are always welcome in our home." He walks toward Ma, who's growing red in the face, and takes her gently by an arm. He whispers in her ear, and she slowly relaxes. Without a backward glance, he leads her outside.

"I really should go," Izalia says, heading toward the entrance.

"Wait!"

She pauses on the threshold.

"I don't want you to go," I say, standing.

She turns slowly, her face falling. "Your mother doesn't trust me. It's understandable. I don't want to overstep."

It pains me to see her sad in any way. I walk toward her, fighting the desire to touch her. I want—no *need*—to somehow pull her smile back. "She'll come around, trust me."

Her lips twitch upward. "I do," she says almost to herself.

"Then let me show you my piano." I nod toward the slats. Only the outline is visible.

Her eyes light up. She looks toward the wall and back outside. Her curiosity wins out, and she finally obliges.

I lead her around the slats and touch the top of the piano. She doesn't speak as she walks the length of it and back, studying it curiously. I watch her move around it, much too enthralled by the image of her in my room.

Distracted, I hadn't noticed my dirty clothes spread across the space. I scoot toward them and quickly kick them under my bed.

She turns with a grin.

"Wanna sit?" I ask, sitting down and pushing the key lid up.

I shift to the edge as she joins me. Her proximity sends a thrill through me. I ignore how her arm is mere centimeters from mine and start a simple tune, something I learned when I first started playing as a child.

"This is called a nursery rhyme. I have a book full of them."

As my hands glide over the keys, I peer at her. Her eyes are distant as she stares at my hands with a smile playing on her lips.

I finish the last note and sit back.

"Wow," she says. It's quiet momentarily, my last notes still hanging in the air. "It's so…unworldly. I love it."

Her pleasure makes me want to play nonstop for her.

I'm about to play another song when she blurts, "Are there other Nomagi?"

I chuckle. "Nope. I'm afraid I'm one of a kind."

She nods as if expecting the answer. "Do you get lonely?"

I stiffen.

"Sorry if that's a little forward. You don't have to answer." She twists her hands in her lap.

"No. It's a valid question. I have my parents." I was going to stop there, but something about her makes me want to open up. "But I do feel lonely…sometimes. This brings me joy." I gesture to the piano. "I'm content being alone my whole life if I can create music until the day I die." I tap the keys, starting a new song, and add, "And I have a few friends, believe it or not." If a few means one semi-normal person and an old, crazy lady.

We sit together, listening to my music for a while, and I like it. I like it a lot—her sitting next to me while I play. For once, that hole inside my chest isn't that noticeable.

"Where are these forbidden artifacts of yours?"

"Besides the one you're looking at?" I say without stopping my fingers.

Her eyebrow turns up. "Really? Why would a—" she fumbles for the word.

"Piano."

She glances at me, another breathtaking smile on her face. "Why would a piano be forbidden when it creates such beauty?"

I move my fingers to finish the song, debating whether to be honest.

"Theo?"

Warmth pools in my stomach. I enjoy my name on her lips more than I should. I watch her lips as they pinch slightly, causing a little dimple to appear on her cheek, waiting for my response.

I finish my song and let my hands drop into my lap. "Because it's not pure."

It's true. Anything not made by materials of the island and by its people is considered unnatural and has no place here, just like me.

She nods and looks away. By the island, I should have held my tongue. But I don't think I could ever say anything untruthful to her. She has a hold on me that I can't explain.

I've known other Divina girls. None of them affected me in such a way.

It could be that she's been in my thoughts and dreams for months, but that person wasn't her. So far, everything I've seen of the *real* Izalia is so much better.

She presses a note on the piano. It reverberates through the air. "Pure is overrated."

6

ZALIA

I examine the paintings, letting Theo rifle through his things without me hovering over his shoulder. I hope this means he'll tell me where he came from and how he has these things. It's so hard to hold my tongue, but after how his mother made her feelings clear, I'll wait for him to be ready to tell me.

The vibrant colors turn the entire house into a work of art. His mother is a talented artist. I wouldn't ever tire of looking at her work. And to think that this is deemed less significant in our leaders' eyes. I would be nothing but proud to have a talent like this.

There are countless versions of the ocean. She captures every angle and emotion, while watching the sea through its different tides. There are many faces—so realistic, most familiar, as they're members of this family. I trace the angle of Theo's jaw on one and his eyes on another. She painted the ocean in his eyes, perfectly encapsulating their otherworldly beauty.

I return to the painting of their firstborn son that I was immediately drawn to. There's just something about it. It's a little messier than the others, but the detail in the baby's face is astounding. There is such raw emotion in every line and color.

My heart tugs, thinking how awful losing a child would be. For the first time, I get a glimpse of how my parents must have felt when I had my incident. How they continue to feel every time I have an episode.

I sigh. It still doesn't make their over-the-top controlling behavior okay. If they could just see that I'm capable of making my own choices and see that I'm still okay. One more week and I'll be able to prove that to them with the trials. I can last one more week.

I settle onto the couch as a breeze picks up, making the paintings flutter and the scent of vanilla, fresh paint, and bamboo waft through the air. I sometimes wish the houses in the city were still like this—open to the elements. It's one of the reasons I always leave our windows open—the other being so Beau can come and go as he pleases. I could get used to living in a home like this.

Theo returns, holding a gold chest. I slip to the edge of the couch as he sets it on the small table in front of us. The chest is made from pieces of driftwood and painted a metallic gold color. It's chipping in places but sealed tight with a silver clasp.

He sits beside me, brushing my arm when he reaches for the lid. His blue eyes pierce mine. "These are my only connections to the people who brought me into this world."

I put my hand on his, suddenly feeling like an intruder in his life. "You don't need to show me."

His eyes lock on our hands. "I want to."

His eyes travel up the length of me, making me feel oddly vulnerable.

"You're not like the others. I know we've just met, but…" He struggles for the right words. "I want to share things with you."

"Like what?" I draw closer to him, trying to decipher the emotion behind his eyes. My skin buzzes at his proximity.

A knock on a post has us jumping apart. My heart pounds like the wings of a bird in flight.

"Theo, look what I caught just outside your—"

A man with long dark hair tied at the nape of his neck and a seashell necklace around his throat steps around the wall. His green eyes meet mine, lips forming a silent "O" as he looks between us.

A smirk grows on his face, accentuating his sharp cheekbones. "You dirty dog. You didn't tell me you met a woman!" he says without taking his eyes off mine. He's wearing a knee-length sarong, his broad chest bare. In his hand, a long black snake is wrapped around his forearm, wriggling to get free, its pink tongue flicking out.

Theo leaps to his feet. "Ainzel. This is Izalia." He gestures to me.

"Oh. I know who she is," he says with a glint in his eye.

He does look familiar. "You're not in my year," I say. I know everyone in my year and most in other years.

He shakes his head. "Took my trials two years ago. Farmer," he says with a shrug.

That explains it. "I've seen you at market," I say. He trades sugar cane and wheat with his family.

He leans against the post. "And what is a high-class Divina doing on the outskirts of the island, so far from home?"

I cringe at the words. I've never seen myself as higher class.

I shift in my seat as he strides forward, finally taking his gaze off me. He studies Theo.

"A python, huh?" Theo says.

Ainzel seemed to have forgotten that he was holding a snake. The thing is trying to get away from him, wildly thrashing as he grips it by its neck. Fear radiates from the poor guy.

Ainzel holds it up. "Yeah. Isn't he a beauty? I'm going to introduce him to Darlah."

"Who's Darlah?" I ask.

The boys share a look.

"No," says Theo.

Ainzel steps toward me.

"No," Theo repeats, moving in front of me.

Ainzel, sidestepping him with a grin, says, "Would you like to meet Darlah?"

Based on Theo's reaction and Ainzel's excitement…

"My curiosity is piqued."

Theo shakes his head as Ainzel tenderly pets the writhing snake, moving it close to his face. He makes kissy lips at it and says in a high-pitched voice, "Let's go see Darlah."

I stare into the vast hole just outside Ainzel's farmhouse with dread twisting my gut. This is worse than I thought. Darlah is the biggest kingsnake I have ever seen and seemingly Ainzel's beloved pet.

"You're not afraid of snakes, are you?" Ainzel raises a thin eyebrow.

I lift my chin and take another step. Thanks to Beau, my communication with animals is outstanding. "No." I'm not afraid of them per se, but I avoid them. They are not kind animals, especially if they're nervous. I sense that Darlah is anxious about me being here, an unknown human.

"I brought you a present!" Ainzel calls, hopping into the pit.

I choke back a cry and look at Theo. He's watching me, not at all disturbed that his friend just jumped into a hole with a snake twice his length and wider than my torso. I may be reckless, but I'm not delusional.

"He'll be fine," Theo murmurs.

I gawk at him and whip around to watch. Darlah stretches out as Ainzel approaches, her white and black stripes gleaming in the sun. The kingsnake's tongue licks the air, but there are no hostile emotions emitting from her. If anything, I feel excitement from the creature.

The snake slithers up to Ainzel, wraps around his right foot, and creeps up his body. I gasp, taking a step back.

As I watch the snake slink up and over Ainzel's shoulders, I can't conceal the horror on my face.

Ainzel smirks at me before turning his attention back to it. "How are you, sweetheart?" Ainzel coos, not the least bit troubled by the thing.

Could I actually be feeling love radiating from the snake? I shake my head, amazed.

The snake licks the air several times before slithering back to her rocky bed. Ainzel holds his hand out toward Theo. Theo, who has been holding the black snake, places its captured head into Ainzel's hands.

Ainzel's eyes lock on mine. "You see. Darlah is the best judge of character. When I bring her a snake, which is her favorite food, she either eats it or accepts it, in which case I get another snake to add to my collection."

My jaw drops as I eye the rest of the flat field covered in weeds. "You have another snake pit around here?"

He smirks. "Survival of the fittest."

"That's morbid."

He shrugs before letting the snake go. It immediately twists and snaps at his feet, which Ainzel gracefully dodges. It's definitely not happy about being captured and offered as a sacrifice.

Ainzel climbs out of the hole with a giddy expression, loosening a couple rocks that roll toward the snakes. I back up a few steps, not wanting to watch but unable to turn away.

Running into a warm body, I peer into Theo's blue eyes.

"We can go," he says, sensing my mood shift.

I nod, momentarily distracted by his high cheekbones and long eyelashes at this angle, noticing how his eyes crinkle when he talks.

"And miss the best part! No way. Look," the deranged snake murderer calls.

"Is it being eaten?" I whisper, not taking my eyes off Theo.

He looks over my head, and his eyebrows raise. "It's okay."

I slowly turn around. Darlah is circling the black snake, her head reaching the tip of her tail again.

"She would have eaten it by now," Theo whispers. He's very close, and his hot breath causes a shiver to travel down my back. I find myself wanting to lean closer.

I step away, unsettled by my body's reaction, and clear my throat. "Well, this has been great. But I need to get going."

Darlah slithers back into her hole, leaving the black snake to explore the five-foot perimeter of the space.

Ainzel cocks his head. "I think you're good luck. She's eaten the last five."

"Or she's full," I mutter. "So, this is what you guys do for fun?"

The boys share a look. "Come back tonight when the moon is highest in the sky, and we'll show you that Breakwater is much more fun than"—Ainzel splays his arms wide, wriggling his fingertips—"Crystal City."

Theo opens his mouth to say something. A part of me hopes he'll invite me to join. But he closes it and shoves his hands in the pockets of his sarong. I hide the trickle of disappointment by looking toward the sun starting its descent. I need to get back.

I back away, stretching the space between me and the snake pit. "I'll think about it," I say, placing a wisp of hair behind my ear. Once I feel that the snake isn't going to launch out of the pit and slide its fangs into me when I turn my back, I face the trees.

I'm almost to the tree line when Theo calls, "I'll walk with you!"

I smile over my shoulder. Seeing that as invitation enough, he joins me. Beau hops from a tree onto the forest floor before us, scurrying up my frame.

"Now, what have you been up to?"

The tree next to us rattles, and I look just in time to see another squirrel monkey swinging away.

"Oh. Hanging out with your girlfriend?"

Beau blinks and scratches his ear. I laugh, petting the top of his head. Pleasant feelings radiate from him.

"I was wondering if he stays with you all the time," Theo says.

I move a branch out of my way. "He does a lot, but I try to kick him out now and then when I'm around others. He needs more monkey friends."

We walk in silence for a little while. But it's not uncomfortable. I feel surprisingly at ease in Theo's presence. And I get the sense that he's feeling more comfortable around me, too.

"You don't have to come tonight if you don't want to," he says, pushing a branch out of our way.

"Do you want me to?"

"Yeah, of course."

I try not to grin too wide. "I could make a better decision if I know what you're doing."

He rubs his jaw. "Well, according to how you reacted to my music earlier, I think you'll like it."

I smile to myself. A party, then. Those usually have music. "Oh! I totally forgot. You didn't get to show me what was in that box."

He shrugs. "Another time."

My stomach somersaults at the mention of me returning to his home. "Promise?"

He studies me for a moment before nodding.

As the sun sets, light filters through the branches, casting a rainbow of colors onto the palm leaves around us. I place my hand into a light beam and focus on the warmth. The warmth grows as I make a bowl shape with my palms. The beam of light transforms, dancing colorful rays onto us and the trees.

"I've grown up around magic my whole life, but it never ceases to amaze me," he says.

I look up at him. "If given a chance, what kind of magic would you like to wield?"

His eyebrows knit together. "Nobody has ever asked me that."

"Or would you even want to?"

He lifts his chin, his golden hair falling off his face. "Music helps me make sense of the world. I would choose that."

"Musical talent doesn't require magic."

"It could. Music is all around us—the wind whistling through the branches, the melody of the ocean, the sounds of insects, the chirping of birds. Everything is a song. Can you imagine turning all that into a symphony?"

I smile, trying to imagine it. "Okay, but what would that be called?"

He smiles. "Wielding nature's music."

7

AZALIA

I'm opening my front door, still smiling ear to ear, when voices from the adjoining dining room reach me. Mom's birthday.

I race up the stairs but abruptly halt in my room. The memory of Alexi's lips on mine rushes back, leaving me queasy. He'll most likely make an appearance tonight.

I push past the nausea and grab the jar on my shelf, plucking out the peony that Alexi gave me. I study it before crumpling it in my fist. When I open my palm, some of the white petals float to the ground. I expect to feel a little guilty, but I don't. I pull a breeze from the window and let them drift away and out of sight.

The avalian flower is as radiant as a few hours prior, nestled in the dirt and water of the jar. I throw my dirt-coated dress off and pick out a black, shin-length gown with blue floral designs.

Beau squeals, and I turn. He's holding a matching light-blue flower pin for my hair in his little hands.

"You're more chivalrous than any man."

He squawks in approval and jumps onto my shoulder, carefully placing the pin in my hair. I rub his ears and descend the stairs with the jar positioned behind my back.

Dad walks out of the dining room, laughing with two colleagues. His graying hair is slicked back into a stylish wave, and his thin lips pull up, showing off his dimples, when he notices me.

"Sweetheart! Alexi told us you two got caught up. Where is he?"

"Just went home to change," and hopefully get *caught up* with something else. Maybe, if he gave my parents an excuse, that means he's not coming at all. My parents are in such a joyous mood, I doubt they'll notice if he doesn't appear.

"You look beautiful," he says, pulling me in for a hug before striding to the living room.

I cut across the kitchen, looking for Mom, when Mr. Maleko, my history Instructor, intercedes. His voice has a soothing effect that makes falling asleep easy, which is not a good combination when reading out of a scroll for an hour in class.

I spot my mom behind his shoulder, talking to Mrs. Yule. Mom is radiant in a purple gown that flows to her feet. Her dark hair is pulled back, with violet and white flowers entwined within, traveling down to her waist. I know my mom was breathtaking in her youth, but I couldn't imagine her any more beautiful than right now. The faint wrinkles outlining her eyes and smile are the only signs of aging I notice.

She flashes me a wry smile, questions in her eyes.

"Excuse me, but I need to wish my mom a happy birthday," I say, interrupting Mr. Maleko's words about ways to make our Sage connection stronger. Homework for tomorrow, I suppose.

"Oh, yes. Of course! We can finish our conversation later."
Our one-sided conversation.

I keep myself from rolling my eyes and smile, moving around him.

"You look lovely, my dear," she says.

"Not lovelier than you!" I sing as she pulls me in for a hug, her flower scent enveloping me.

Beau grabs my jar with his tail so I can wrap both hands around her torso. She kisses my cheek and pulls back.

"Having a good birthday?"

She smiles and looks across the house to Dad, who's lounging in a chair. "He spoils me."

My dad seems to sense her stare and glances up with a wink. Her smile brightens. Their bond was a match made by the island. I don't know two other people who complete each other so well. Their relationship excited me about my own pairing. But after today with Alexi...my stomach twists.

I push the feelings of unease away.

"I got you something!" I snap my fingers behind me, and Beau places the jar back into my palm. I slowly pull it from behind my back, watching her face.

She blinks a few times before her eyes widen. Placing a hand on her cheek, she says, "Izzy…is that what I think it is?" She grabs it and raises it to her face. "Where did you find this?"

I smile wide and shrug. "It caught my eye on a cliff edge."

She narrows her eyes, and I try to put on the most innocent expression I can muster. "Thank you, Izzy."

She hugs me again, but this one knocks Beau off my shoulder. He throws a little fit on the ground behind us. She squeezes me tighter.

When she pulls back, her eyes are glistening with unshed tears. "This means so much to me. Niko! Come here. Look at what Izzy got me."

Dad and everyone else gather around my mother and me to ooh and ah at the flower.

When I'm entirely red in the face from praise, I squeeze past them to the kitchen. I use the opportunity to grab some food.

I've managed to grab mango sliders, fried bananas drizzled in caramel, and a couple of chocolates when I feel warmth on the small of my back. I sigh inwardly, preparing myself to enter another boring conversation.

When I turn, I find an apologetic-looking Alexi staring down at me.

"What are you doing here?" I hiss and move past him.

"I was invited." He grabs my hand and spins me back to him.

For a moment, I catch what he's wearing—a tight-fitting tunic that accentuates his broad shoulders and muscled abdomen. Somehow, it feels less modest than him showing off his naked chest. Despite what I think of him, he does look good. Again, I'm confused about how my body reacted to his kiss.

I shake him off.

"I came to apologize, Iz." He bites his lip. "I misread the room, I suppose."

I gawk at him. "You misread the room? That's your apology for—" I lower my voice. "Breaking the law."

"Oh, come on. Everyone breaks that one, and you know it." He notices my expression and stutters, "I—I'm sorry." He holds my gaze, and then I see it in his slightly pursed lips and lowering eyebrows—not only shame, but hurt that I rejected him.

"You should have asked. You—you took me by surprise," I murmur.

"Sorry. I guess I don't know kissing etiquette." He chuckles.

I roll my eyes.

"Do you forgive me?" He steps closer, and I stay rooted to the spot, not wanting to hurt him again. He dips his head low, and my breathing hitches. He grabs my chin and tilts it so I have to look into his emerald eyes. He blinks his long, dark eyelashes, and the spicy scent on his breath disorients me as the kiss flashes through my mind. "Do you?"

I give him the tiniest nod, knowing he won't leave me alone if I don't forgive him.

He smiles, releasing me. "I probably need to make the rounds," he says, finally giving me space. His eyes linger on my plate. "Are you going to go hide in your room?"

I force a smile. "Was thinking about it. But you know I won't miss cake."

"That's for sure." He shakes his head, shoving his hands in his pockets. "You should really watch how many sweets you eat, Iz." He raises an eyebrow before turning and heading towards the dining room.

I grumble a curse under my breath before making a break for it to my room. Hopefully, he'll leave soon.

I shut my door and spy Beau curled up on my bed. "I'm going to eat the biggest piece of cake later."

Technically, I'm supposed to limit sugar, because that's the latest thing we're trying to do to lessen the blackouts, but it's just another thing on the list that won't work. Nothing works. We've tried every type of food elimination, natural medicine, pushing my body to its limit, and resting my body for weeks until I almost die of boredom. Nothing works. It's a part of me. I've known that for a long time, but nobody else wants to accept it.

Alexi bossing me around, though, rubs me the wrong way. How can I deal with those remarks for the rest of my life?

Beau blinks sleepily, and I slump onto my bed, offering one of the bananas. He sniffs and blows a raspberry.

I sigh. "Sorry, it's got stuff on it. But honestly, it's good."

He lays his head back down. I shrug and dig in. Maybe these will cause another blackout, and I won't have to talk to Alexi again tonight. I all but lick my plate clean.

Before long, my dad comes to fetch me. "We're cutting the cake in a few."

I pull my face out of my pillow. "Coming."

I yawn and peer out the window. The moon is almost at the highest point in the sky, and I have yet to decide if I'll go meet Theo and Ainzel. It's a bad idea. It's one thing to go down there during the day, but at night? I've heard wicked rumors about Breakwater at night.

But I'd get to see Theo again. Theo, who makes me feel free in a way nobody else does. He doesn't look at me like I'm somebody who needs fixing. Not like my parents and Alexi— always trying to mend whatever is broken in my head.

I sit up at the thought of sneaking out at this hour, my heart hammering. I'll do another round, and then nobody will care if I turn in early.

The thought has me on my feet and down the stairs. The traditional birthday music starts as somebody pats a drum rhythmically, and I can't help but think how Theo's piano could make this sound so much better.

Mom hands me the first piece of cake. "For the best daughter a mother could ask for."

I swallow the emotion and grab the plate of pineapple cake. It's tradition for the birthday person to offer the first slice of cake to whoever means the most to them. Even though it's usually me or Dad every year, it still gets to me.

"Thanks, Mom."

As she finishes dishing out, I find a spot on the couch.

A moment later, Alexi joins me, placing his hand on my knee. "I was just about to leave but wanted to tell you goodnight. Are we good?"

I swallow the piece of cake in my mouth and nod. "I'll see you tomorrow."

He shifts on the couch, his hand briefly sliding up to my thigh before he whispers in my ear. "Twenty-eight more days, my flower."

I try to look excited as he rises. He winks before strutting out the front door. I hope he didn't see the deep-rooted fear in my eyes.

I still have half my cake left but can't take another bite. I stiffly walk to my parents, surrounded by friends, and tap on my dad. He looks over his shoulder.

"I'm exhausted. I'm going to turn in."

"Goodnight," he says, wrapping an arm around my shoulders. He nudges Mom, and she kisses my cheek.

"Night. Thank you again for the avalian."

The flower has taken center stage in the middle of the table. It stands out amongst the other varieties of flowers. Nothing compares to it, just like her. She has always been a person people gravitate to. Everyone wants to talk to her when she's in the room. Her beauty makes others' pale in comparison, even my own.

I lock my bedroom door and glance at Beau, who is completely out of it. I sigh. He's going to hate me. I scan my wardrobe, unsure what to wear to this beachside party. Would I be overdressed in what I'm in now?

After changing five times, I decide on a knee-length, solid white dress, the sleeves drooping off my bare shoulders. I usually wear it as a swim cover. It's a little scandalous, but that's how the beach folks are, always in bathing suits or tiny dresses. I don't want to stick out as a city girl.

Plucking a white plumeria from the plant on my desk, I study it. Should I put it behind my left ear, signaling that I'm taken, or my right ear? It's a silly thing that I've never thought twice of until now. I tuck it behind my right ear and slip my sandals on.

I climb over my bed to the window. The voices drifting from downstairs are even louder now, most of them probably having had one too many Kava. It'll be hours until my parents turn in, and I doubt they'll think to check on me. Just in case, though, I arrange my pillows under my blanket and shrug. Now for the escape.

I throw a leg over the windowsill and Beau jerks awake.

He takes one look at me and jumps up and down on the bed, shrieking—my in-home alarm system.

"Shhh!" I grab him, pulling him against me. "They're going to think I'm having an episode. Calm down. We're just sneaking out."

Beau looks at me oddly.

I gesture toward the tree behind me. "Help would be nice."

He jumps onto my back and hops to the tree outside my window. He wraps his tail around my foot and guides me to the branch. I swing my other foot down. Now all I need to do is—

I push off the window, teeter on the branch for a second, before flailing my arms and grabbing hold of the trunk.

"I'm okay. I'm okay." Scared, but exhilarated.

I look down at our backyard. I'll need to avoid the kitchen window. Climbing down, I aim for the patch of shadow next to the window. But when I jump, I land halfway into the light radiating from the Aura orbs inside. I don't dare look as I throw myself on the ground.

I lay there frozen, waiting. But nobody comes out to drag me back inside. Beau sits on my back.

"Get off," I grunt.

He yelps as I throw him off, and I stand with my back against the house. I run for the neighbor's backyard and walk around their home, keeping in the shadows until I'm far enough away.

My heart pounds as I step onto the path, guided only by moonlight. I wouldn't risk casting an orb.

The city is eerie in the dark, with buildings reaching into the sky and only a few lights emitting from the domed windows. I haven't walked this much across the island in one day…ever. I'm going to be so sore tomorrow. But, hopefully, it'll be worth it.

By the time I reach the fields, my heart has returned to its normal pace. "We did it, Beau."

I let him climb me now that we're further from the city. If anyone were to see him on my shoulder, it would have been an automatic giveaway of who I was.

My hands caress the wheat stalks as I inhale the fresh air; the ocean breeze won't be too far off now. I bypass the trees and take the path straight to the beach. I walk the coastline, my sandals in one hand, sand squishing between my toes, until a faint rhythm reaches me. Drums.

Flames rise high into the night sky, like octopus tentacles, a beacon for me to follow. Shadows sway around them, moving their limbs in odd ways. As I close the distance, I'm lost in the firelight, drawn in by the music and combined voices.

I don't notice the two figures in the sand.

"Watch it, girl!"

I jump back. Two people are sleeping on the beach. No—not sleeping. One is lying on top of the other in a way that immediately has my neck snapping forward.

I scurry away with a mumbled apology.

A tangle of nerves ball into my stomach as I search for anyone I recognize. The drumming grows louder, and there's another noise I can't quite place. I head for it, believing it'll lead me to Theo. People bump into me as they sway and dance around the fire.

What am I doing here? This is probably a huge mistake. I hesitate, looking back toward the city. I don't belong here. But I don't know if I belong there either.

No. I can do this. I take a deep breath and continue to follow the unworldly noise until I see him. A woman and a man are hitting drums with their palms, and in the middle is a smiling, relaxed Theo with a peculiar shape in his hands. It's a piece of wood with strings stretched across a hole, over which he's moving his fingers, almost like he did on the piano. His other hand moves up and down an elongated part resting on his shoulder.

When he sees me, the world falls away and my nerves settle.

His soft smile grows brighter than the fire. He leans into the drummer, murmuring something, before setting down the object in his hands. The two drummers start a new song, the beat rattling my bones. Without Theo's instrument, the light song becomes thunderous and exciting.

"You came! Let me show you around," he says over the music.

I follow him away from the noise to a table—well, less a table and more a giant log that the ocean swept in.

He offers me a coconut with a straw poking out. "These are delicious."

I wriggle my nose. "I've had coconut milk."

He shakes his head. "This is not just regular coconut milk. Trust me. You have not lived until you try it."

I take the rough coconut and place the straw between my lips. A burst of sweetness and tanginess spreads on my tongue— coconut, pineapple, and something else. "Woah."

He smiles as I offer it back. "No, I've already had too many. That's yours."

I continue to sip the alluring sweet drink as we weave through the people. He stops occasionally and introduces me to some who seem to already know me. Guilt tugs on me. They're nothing like the city folk who strut around with an air of superiority and keep to themselves. These people are welcoming, joyful, and full of life.

There are old and young alike, all laughing and having fun with one another. Soon, I sway to the beat, with an inkling to join in, as if the drink sparked something inside me. I watch people intertwine their elbows and spin, delightfully throwing their heads back. A young boy dances with an older lady, who twirls and twirls him. I watch a young couple embracing, dancing to their own rhythm, lost in each other's eyes. I've never embraced Alexi like that—never *looked* at him like that.

I finish my drink, and a wave of confidence washes over me. I grab Theo's hand, and he raises his eyebrows.

"I want to dance."

He looks like he's about to object, but I shove my bottom lip out. He smiles, and I pull him into the crowd around the fire. The warmth radiates from the flames and the many bodies flailing around me. It's not the worst sensation.

I'm unsure how to start, so I begin by copying the movements of the people around me. I spin on my toes and move my shoulders. I grab my dress and sway to the beating drums, letting the rhythm fill me. Theo dances near me at first, and then he takes my hands and twirls me like that old woman and little boy. I'm a feather in the wind as I laugh and spin.

In no time, I'm dizzy enough that I need to hold onto Theo to stay steady. His forearms strain under my fingertips, and I trace one of the veins with my thumb.

His dark-blue eyes capture mine, and the world stops spinning. He centers me like a strong tree trunk in a storm.

I step closer. His hands move from my arms to my back, the touch electrifying. I don't know if it's the music, the drink, or the feeling of nothing holding me back, but I move my hands to his shoulders. The muscles underneath his thin tunic tense underneath my touch, and I suddenly wish he wasn't wearing one, like most of the other men here.

He relaxes and settles his hands around my waist. We begin to sway to our own rhythm.

My heart accelerates at the electric current pulsing between us. His eyes sweep over my face. I study his long, strong jaw and little freckles that frame his nose. His hair is almost orange in the firelight and in disarray, hanging partially in his face, sweat glistening on his brow.

I've known this boy for only a day and feel more comfortable with him than anyone I grew up with. How can this feel so right?

His hand cups my face gently, sending another pulse through my body. I lean into his cool, gentle touch. Our eyes lock, and his breath ruffles my hair as he leans down, smelling of coconut and vanilla—always vanilla.

"Izalia!" comes a strong male voice.

I stiffen, panic clawing up my spine. He found me.

8

THEO

Surprised by our closeness, I blink a few times and immediately drop my hands, stepping out of her space. Her eyes are dazed at first, but then fear shines there as she looks around for our unfortunate disturbance. I ache to touch her again, feel her warmth underneath my hands. Something had been growing in my chest, unyielding and outside my control, but the connection broke before I could figure it out.

I glance at the person who broke it.

"You going to dazzle her with your guitar playing or what?" Ainzel says, cocking his head, an eyebrow arched.

I've never found him so irritating as I do at this moment. Ainzel waits for me to respond, looking between us.

Izalia speaks up. "Yes! I'd love to hear more from your…guitar? And I wouldn't mind getting another of these coconuts." She giggles. The trace of fear I thought I saw on her face long gone. Did she believe Ainzel was somebody else?

The sound of her laugh dissolves my annoyance. I smile and lead her back to the log.

Ainzel bumps my shoulder as Izalia chats with Elenor, who's making the piña coladas. A knowing smile frames his lips. "You sure you don't want to take me up on my offer?"

I shove my hands in my pockets and try to ignore him.

"Come on. You remember Sonya. That girl was all over me."

"I don't need your help." I watch Izalia's long hair tangling across her back in the breeze. She brushes one side behind her ear, and I have an intense desire to reach out and do it for her.

"Man, you have zero experience with the ladies. Do you really want to mess this up? She's totally into you."

Izalia begins to turn back toward us.

"Who knows, maybe at the end of the night, with a little bit of my magic, you'll finally not be a v—"

Ainzel is spread out on the sand before he can finish his sentence, looking up at me with wide eyes.

Izalia peers at him with a suppressed smile. "Maybe I shouldn't be drinking so many of these," she says, frowning at her drink.

Ainzel bursts out laughing and hops back up, wiping sand off his sarong. "There's nothing in there. Now, if you want a real kick, my friend Taz has the good stuff."

I try to shove him again, but he dances out of my reach.

"Ignore him." I shoot him a scowl, but he's not looking at me.

I watch him as he leans and whispers something in Izalia's ear. Her cheeks turn pink, and I grab Ainzel in a chokehold.

"I'll be right back," I say, turning before she can respond.

Ainzel lets me cart him off, even though I know he could outmaneuver me with a flick of his hand.

I release him when we near the water. "What are you doing?"

He rubs his neck where I was holding him and smiles mischievously.

"What did you tell her?" Sparks of anger ignite low in my belly.

"You knocked me to the ground!" he yells, but there's no malice in his voice.

"You have zero self-awareness," I say.

"Whatever. I forgive you. Actually, I forgive you so much that I just did you a huge favor."

I take a step toward him, balling my fists.

He cocks his head. "This is a good look for you. Keep it up." He pats me on the shoulder and walks away.

"Hey!" I try to grab him, but my fingers barely brush against his bare back before my feet sink into the sand, holding me in place.

He turns slowly, his stupid, meddling smile still on his lips. "You should be saying thank you." He points at my feet. "It will release you once you're not so violent anymore."

I fold my arms. "I thought you liked me like this?"

"Yeah, but you're dampening my vibe for the ladies. Can't have you pushing me around. I'm just going to have a quick chat with your girlfriend and then be out of your hair." He gives me a wink and stalks off.

"Ainzel! You get back here right now and release me. Ainzel! You'll regret this!"

I yank my feet, but they won't budge. I curse at his back as he disappears amongst the partygoers. Izalia isn't visible, either.

I sit down and try to free myself, but the sand refills every time I scoop some out. Ugh. I fall onto my back, my chest rising and falling quickly, a storm swirling in my head. I need to calm down.

Counting the stars, I take deep, steady breaths, but all I see is her face, her blush at Ainzel's words, how she looked at me.

Heat crawls up my neck as I wring my hands in the sand. Ainzel can be infuriating. Usually, his tactics are directed at everyone but me, which makes him such a great friend. When he's around, I feel like I could actually belong. He treats me like everyone else but without the practical jokes.

Until now, that is.

I remember the first time I met him. I was playing on the shore closest to my house when some kids kicked sand in my face and knocked me into the water. Luckily, they didn't have their magic yet, or it would have been much worse. I was an easy target. They knew I was different, even with a hat to hide my hair.

Ainzel came running and chased them down—one little skinny kid holding a branch almost twice his size, ready to risk it all. Nothing has ever held Ainzel back.

He told me that he wouldn't protect me next time and that I would have to do it myself. He continued to teach me everything I know. I can hold my own now, and people don't bother me. Some even accept me, but the majority don't. Not even on this side of the island. I've done some embarrassing things because of it. What if he told her? No. He wouldn't do that. Or would he, if he thought he was helping?

I sit back up to try to claw my feet out when a slight noise behind me grabs my attention. I turn, and she's standing there, her white dress swaying in the salt-kissed breeze, her hands intertwined in front of her.

I open my mouth to say something, but nothing comes out. Her presence silences all rational thinking.

She gestures toward the fire. "Ainzel said you'd be out here."

My mind clears, and I wiggle my toes. I'm still stuck, so she lowers herself beside me, delicately tucking her feet beneath her.

"Did he say anything else?"

She shakes her head. I blow out a breath. The bastard was trying to rile me, and he was successful.

"Where's Beau?"

"In the trees. Keeping watch, I'm sure. He doesn't like crowds. This is quite the party. I've never been to anything like it."

I spare a glance at her. She's watching the water. "Really?"

"Dancing like this is forbidden." The side of her mouth lifts as she looks at me.

"Right." Divina are weird about couples getting too close before they're bonded.

"Seems the rumors are true," she says, scooping some sand into her palms.

I arch an eyebrow at her.

The sand falls between her fingers, onto her legs, which are pale in the moonlight. "People out here not following the rules."

She's right. The people on the beaches have never followed the city's strict rules, one of the reasons my parents moved here. If I could be accepted anywhere, it would be amongst the rebels.

"Does that bother you?" I ask.

She smiles wide. "No." She bites her lip like she's said something she shouldn't have and looks away. I wait for her to keep talking, but she doesn't.

"Well, that's probably good, since you're here with me. A walking symbol of breaking the rules."

Her eyes widen, and she lowers her voice. "Is that what your parents did?"

I shake my head, resting my arms on my knees. "My family shipwrecked on the island when I was a baby, and I was the only survivor."

She sucks in a breath.

"My parents raised me as their son."

"How have I not heard about you? People on Breakwater Strand know who you are," she says, waving her hands at the people behind us.

I shrug, not wanting to announce the apparent differences between the people here and in the city. And the fact that I don't have many friends to blab about me.

"So, everyone here just keeps your secret?"

"It's not a secret. I used to visit with the Elders once a year. I guess they assumed I wouldn't be able to acclimate to the island. They seemed to be waiting for me to drop dead or something." I release a strained laugh. I've gotten used to being seen as the oddity. But I'm not going to go out of my way to be made fun of. "I didn't, and the visits stopped eventually. My parents just want me to keep a low profile. They're worried that somebody's going to ship me back to the mainland."

Izalia gasps and places her hand on my arm. "Will they?"

Something warms inside of me at the horror on her face—not as warm as where she's touching me, though. My arm practically catches fire at the spot.

"I'm not a problem for them…yet."

She releases me, and I ache for her to return her hand. Instead, I study her silhouette as she looks across the midnight sea. What is she thinking?

I'm about to ask when a gust of wind blows her hair around her face, and I fight the urge to touch it.

I lose the battle.

Grabbing a wisp, I wrap it around my finger. So soft.

She stiffens and twists. I'm caught red-handed.

"Ainzel said you like me," she blurts, watching me.

"I…uh...yeah." I'm going to find him and punch him real hard this time.

She smiles and hops up. "Then come play for me." She reaches out a hand.

I glance at my feet. They're visible, no longer stuck in the sand. I grab her hand, warmth and electricity traveling up my arm.

Back by the fire, I settle onto my stool, guitar in hand.

I strum the strings. The vibrations instantly relax me. I move my left hand up and down, trying a few chords before landing on the one I want to start with.

Music flows from me into the guitar and out into the world. The notes float through the air. I catch them and turn them into a beautiful symphony. I always hope to evoke in others the same emotions that I feel while I play.

I'm no longer just a Nomagi. I'm something else entirely as the lullaby takes me away from my magicless body. I'm in the grains of sand. I'm in the flames of the bonfire. I'm in the ocean. I'm in the stars. The music flows through everyone and everything. My thoughts are no longer my own.

The drums start up, changing the flow of music. I pat the guitar along with them, the music twisting into something more upbeat. I open my eyes as the people go from swaying to stomping and twirling. My heart fills as they enjoy my music.

I peer at Izalia. She's the only one still watching. Everyone else is lost in the music around her, but her green eyes stay locked on mine.

My hands weave their way over the strings. But the happiness I feel in the music doesn't compare to what blossoms in my chest as she looks at me with wonder, joy, and something else—like she's looking at somebody worth her time, an equal. A sensation full of heat and desire, peace and serenity, acceptance and contentment envelopes my body, spreading through my veins, sealing something in them.

She's the music that thrums through my body—my soul— and I will never be the same.

9

IZALIA

"Miss Rane."

My eyes focus on Mr. Maleko's balding head before traveling to his eyes, which are focused on me with a mixture of annoyance and pity. At least it's not *only* pity, like most other adults who treat me like a wounded animal.

I sit up, blinking, and look around.

Two girls next to me are snickering. Gabriel, sitting to my left, is pointing down at the scroll. Oh!

I study the text in my hand, trying to remember what we were reading. My mind is blank. "Um, where were we?" I ask sheepishly.

Mr. Maleko shakes his head. "Do you need to be excused, Izalia?"

In other words, am I having another episode? I still haven't gotten over the embarrassment after having one at school last month during lunch. Beau hadn't been near to warn me, and I woke up in my bed, with Natalina gleefully telling me how I face-planted into my mashed potatoes, then gave me the rest of the day's work.

My cheeks fill with heat. "No, sir. I'm okay."

He sighs. "We were on section 498."

"Right." I find that section and begin reading.

On the twenty-ninth day of November, in the sixteenth and twenty-second year, the estate of Mahan Alohra of Hawai'i became the focal point of an unexpected and devastating assault. Ill-prepared for the intensity of the violence, Mahan Alohra found himself incapacitated. He witnessed the massacre of his entire household at the hands of Nomagi and was believed to be deceased when the Nomagi people moved on.

Upon regaining physical strength, Mahan endeavored to search for any potential survivors, only to come to the revelation that, not only had the islands of Hawai'i been attacked, but on his return to the mainland, he discovered that the entire nation had plunged into a state of war.

A conflict had erupted between Nomagi and Divina, resulting in a protracted and merciless period of hostilities across the globe.

During this tumultuous period, Mahan sought a safe haven for his fellow Divina and fortuitously stumbled upon an isolated island in the north Atlantic Ocean during his voyages.

Kona raises his hand in front of me. I stop reading, and Mr. Maleko clears his throat, nodding to him.

"I don't understand how a bunch of nothing Nomagi defeated our people."

Mr. Maleko lifts an eyebrow. "Underestimating them is what started this war. And were you not listening to the previous paragraph, Mr. Volaris?" His eyes move to mine and then back to Kona. It looks like I wasn't the only one not paying attention before this section.

Kona's ears redden as he studies the page before him. I take the opportunity to scan it as well.

I come across the term "gunpowder" as Kona begins talking.

"They had some sort of new weapon? So what? We can wield lightning, set them on fire, take the air from their lungs, and throw them into a tree. What kind of weapon could be more powerful than us?"

"Who agrees with Mr. Volaris?" Mr. Maleko looks around the room, and I'm surprised to see half the room with raised hands.

I'm not one of them. How could I agree with somebody who just called Nomagi "nothing"? That's like calling Theo—

Mr. Maleko sighs and places the scroll down. He moves to the chalkboard and draws a picture. "This is called a musket. Nomagi invented gunpowder shortly before the war, and it became our eventual downfall. This lone object could kill us from across an entire field. And this is just the smallest of their weapons. They were very creative in the objects they put gunpowder into. They were able to murder a whole household in one shot with some of them, Mr. Volaris. A weapon that can be continually reloaded to bring down infinite Divina as our energy reserves suffer is the type of weapon that is more powerful than us. Its sole purpose was to murder Divina, and it did its job."

Kona flinches and leans back in his chair.

Mr. Maleko moves his eyes back to me. "Please continue, Miss Rane."

I swallow and take an unsteady breath as I look back at the text. The class is so quiet I could hear a pebble drop.

Discovered our island through his voyages. Right.

"Mahan Alohra, joined by his companions Pristine, Ranelyn, Afa, Avis, and Wilder"—I stumble over the last name, knowing it's Alexi's direct ancestor. All of our bloodlines go back to the founders. Mine goes back to Ranelyn. Their union is the reason for the upcoming bonding of Alexi and me. The purer the blood, the stronger the magic—"made this island what it is through their sacrifice and blood. And the Isle of Alohra was born."

Thank goodness it's the end of the paragraph.

Natalina raises her hand. "What happened to those who didn't come to our island? The Hawai'ian people or others on the mainland? They still aren't at war, right?"

"We believe most of the Divina on the Hawai'i Islands were wiped out since Alohra fled with who he could. Now, on the mainland…" He shrugs. "Nomagi are always seeking war, Miss Savea. If any Divina survived, they likely interbred with the Nomagi to continue their lines."

Gagging sounds erupt around me, and I slump into my chair, biting my lip.

"Do you think there are people like us on the mainland?" she asks.

Mr. Maleko taps his chin. "What do you think?"

Natalina brightens and thinks about it. "Maybe. But they obviously wouldn't be pure like us. They'd be…Impures. The magic in their blood would be dulled by the Nomagi, making them impure, if they still even have abilities that is."

"Impures." Mr. Maleko nods his head. "I like it."

Natalina flips her dark hair over her shoulder and beams. I roll my eyes and try to block out the rest of the lesson.

My thoughts drift back to last night—to Theo and his story. For his parents to take him in after experiencing their child's loss, there is no limit to their love. I understand why his mother is so protective of him. I'm stupid for waltzing into their home, threatening their child's safety, as they try to keep a low profile.

But how do more people not know about him? Do my parents know about him? I can't imagine how anybody could forget a Nomagi ship crashing onto the island—a Nomagi child living here undetected. There's no way the Elders just forgot about him.

I don't care that he's a Nomagi. His people did awful things, but he is not them. He's better than anybody else in this room. I can still feel the warmth of his hands around my waist, the spark of electricity between our bodies. It was extraordinary—not only his world but *him*. I could talk to him for hours. His eyes were always present, soaking in every word I said.

When Ainzel told me Theo liked me, I was surprised by how it made me feel. It was like I was perched on the highest tree, watching the first rays of sun coat the sky.

I wasn't going to tell him what Ainzel said, but when I saw how he looked at me on the beach, it's as if that sunlight caught my skin on fire. And somehow those flames on my skin loosened my lips and I just *had* to tell him.

I smile, remembering how he reacted—delightfully flustered.

Somebody pokes me in the side. Natalina looks at me with narrowed eyes. I shake my head and try to focus on the text.

After a minute, a piece of paper slides under my arm. I look at her.

Open it, she mouths.

I sigh, glance at the Instructor, whose nose is buried in the scroll, and pull it open in my lap.

Daydreaming about Alexi? Did something happen?

I almost gasp at her implication, even though she's right—but also very wrong.

I shake my head without looking at her and fold it back up, placing it on my desk. My pencil rises of its own accord and scribbles more words onto the paper.

Come on. You can tell me. That smile on your face is so—

I blanch at the kissy faces she draws.

I know he was over at your house last night.

I choke on my spit and end up coughing out loud. I clear my throat as Mr. Maleko gives me a pointed look.

I use the opportunity. "Can I get some water?"

"Sure, sure." He waves me off, and I'm out the door in a second.

I walk outside in the fresh air to clear my head. I'm a couple of feet outside when Beau hops onto my shoulder. I barely notice him in my state. Maybe I should tell her something—get her off my trail, at least. But Natalina is the queen of gossip.

I reach the shimmering pond directly in the middle of the school. Statues of our founders rise in the middle, water spouting from the center of the six. I study their faces, all without feeling as they look to the horizon.

Swaying my hands, the water ripples and releases a bubble into the air. It floats in my direction, and hovers above my palm as I watch my reflection. For the first time in my life, my bright green eyes feel abnormal after staring into Theo's for so long last night.

The water fills me, and I shake off the odd feeling swirling in my stomach.

When I turn, Natalina is beelining my way.

"Spill," she says, placing a hand on her hip.

"We've got to get back to class."

She falls in stride with me but nudges me with her hip, which makes Beau squawk.

"Shush it, furball." She grips my wrist. "Us girls are getting together after school. I want you to come."

"Oh yeah. I'd love to hang out, but…" I say the first thing that pops into my head. "I already have plans with Alexi."

She smiles and bites her moss-green lip. I know she means for the color to accentuate her eyes. But she just looks like she didn't wipe her mouth from breakfast. "Okay. Tomorrow then. I know Alexi is training tomorrow. Just us." Her smile grows.

For the first time, it doesn't bother me that she knows his schedule. "Yeah, yeah. Tomorrow." I sigh. It won't be too bad if it's just the two of us.

She releases me and starts singing an off-key tune as she skips away.

At least I have another day to figure out what I'll tell her. Knowing Natalina, she'll keep asking forever. I'll have to give her something. That's it—no more daydreaming in class.

I successfully avoid Natalina during lunch by going to the outer courtyard and finding a fale with a couple of empty tables.

I'm about to bite into my sandwich when a tray rattles next to me. I sigh as Freylin sits down.

"So, what were you up to yesterday?" she asks with a gleam in her eye. Her short, chin-length hair blows in her face. Natalina must have said something. Natalina and Freylin are two feathers from the same bird.

I shrug, taking a bite to bide my time. I almost died, met a boy, snuck out to a party with that boy, and danced with said boy. Oh, and he's also a Nomagi. "My mom had her birthday party. It was…nice."

"Nice?" She eyes me knowingly.

"Okay, it was lame. I don't know why my parents insist on me attending their parties. The cake was good, though."

"I bet. Your mom is an amazing cook. I remember when she made those rolls for solstice with… What was it? Cinnamon, sugar, and…an orange something. Ah." Her eyes glaze over as she plops a honey-coated carrot into her mouth.

Freylin has always been easier to talk to, but I can never tell if she's telling the truth or sucking up. I realized she was using me to get in my parents' good graces when I was fourteen at a sleepover. I overheard the girls talking about me when they thought I was asleep. Freylin had said that I was faking my illness for attention. I stopped trying so hard with them after that. It's not like we ever connected anyway.

I push the memory down when she looks back at me.

"It's how I imagine what kissing must be like." She winks.

Yup. Natalina definitely told her something.

I ignore the slight jab. "Mom always makes those for summer solstice."

I've never needed friends. Beau was always enough.

Theo's eyes float in my mind. But maybe that's changing. It felt so nice to be with him—more than nice. Right. Somebody who truly wanted to be around me. Not just because of my heritage, the popularity of my parents, or who I'll bond to, but because of me.

"I heard Alexi came over for the party." Freylin disrupts my thoughts.

My head snaps up as I swallow the last of my sandwich. Natalina is neighbors with Alexi. Of course, she would have seen him leaving. I should probably tell her to get over her obsession with him. But for Natalina to tell Freylin. By the island. Do these girls really have nothing better to do?

"Yeah. For my *mom's* party." I say, adding emphasis.

She leans back. "So, nothing happened?"

"Nope." I pop the last consonant. I chug the rest of my orange juice. "Gotta go!"

"I'll see you tomorrow at Nat's."

I stop mid-step, about to dump the contents on my tray in the trash, but turn slowly instead. I could ask Freylin why she will be there, but that would be rude. Of course, Natalina lied to me.

"Yeah," I respond lamely.

She flashes me a smile as I leave. I bristle. They are totally going to interrogate me.

The end of the school day is my favorite. Mrs. Tiana waves me toward her. She's one of the six Instructors of the elements, my parents being two of them. All day, we learn about our history, how to harness our Sage, giving back to the island, the dangers of amplified magic and not using enough of our magic, information on the assignments…everything but *doing*. Now, I get to act.

Today, Mrs. Tiana has her hair gelled to stick up at various angles. Every week she has a new eccentric hairstyle. One of the reasons I like her so much is that she's different. She even chose to not get bonded—the only one I've ever heard to willingly make that decision. She doesn't care what others think about her.

A giant glass dome surrounds us. The beach, which is the farthest point of campus, is directly outside. The glass is dull. The surroundings outside are barely distinguishable, but sunlight fills the space, creating a controlled atmosphere that is open to the elements. Benches line one side, rising high in the air. It was one of the first buildings built on the island for the Games of the

Elements our ancestors used to play, but it has long been disbanded because of its violent nature. Now, it's where we practice wielding.

People spread out into their designated groups in the vast space. My parents are on the other side with their groups but pay no mind to me. At school, I'm just another student. Thank the island for that.

I head for my group, containing Gabriel; the Stimez twins, Millie and Macie; and—

"Hello, gorgeous," Alexi says in a deep, seductive voice, as he throws an arm around my shoulders.

Out of the corner of my eye, I see the twins practically swoon. I wish I could feel what they're feeling. Instead, my heart beats evenly in my chest, with not even the slightest of flutters—only annoyance.

I look into his face. He's smiling, showing off his dimples, one on each cheek. His eyes are warm, green like the meadow behind my house when bathed in sunlight. I study his lips, trying to feel something. I remember them pressed against mine, which causes a reaction far from desire. I do know that I don't want him to try to kiss me ever again.

His lips part as he moves closer to me, a longing filling his eyes. *Oh no.*

"Break it up, you two. You're not bonded yet."

I jump out of his grasp, relieved by the interruption.

Alexi chuckles and pulls a hand through his hair. "Oh, come on, Mrs. Tiana. We practically are. Can't I hold my girl?"

Mrs. Tiana eyes him and then looks at me. I have no idea what my expression looks like, but her eyebrows rise momentarily, understanding flashing in her eyes. "Nope. You know the rules."

I hold back from sighing in relief. I shrug at Alexi as I join the twins. They giggle but don't say anything. I wonder how red my face is.

Another reason I love her is that other Instructors treat Alexi like the prince he is, but not Mrs. Tiana.

"You know the drill, Igna warm-ups, go!"

We space ourselves out, and I try to ignore Alexi's eyes on me as I reach for the tiny flame inside my chest. Fire has never come naturally to me. The tiny flames that ignite on my palms are because of Dad. He's been training me nightly for the last month, preparing me for the trials.

I twitch my fingers in the heat of the flames. My own fire can't burn me as it dances inches from my skin, but that doesn't mean others' can't.

Squeezing my hands together, I compress the fire into a small ball. I smile when I manage to do it. I peer at Millie, who's closest, and lose my smile. Flames cover her forearms, and she's bouncing fireballs between her two hands like it's nothing. The others are in various fire-wielding stages, and I sigh internally. It doesn't matter. All of our talents are different. My fire being smaller than everyone else's means nothing.

I'm relieved when she tells us to switch to our Terra.

I place my palms on the earth and close my eyes, feeling the slight vibrations underneath the soil. I grab ahold of the roots and pull them toward the surface. They grow out of the ground, twisting and curving on top of each other, spreading toward the opaque walls of the dome. The vines climb, and just as they droop,

I reach out and touch one, forming tiny brugmansia buds with my fingertips.

I look around. Alexi causes a minor fissure in the ground to open up. The twins work together to grow a bush, sprouting little flowers that will turn into mulberries. Gabriel watches me as he juggles clumps of dirt in his hands.

"Very good!" Mrs. Tiana says, beaming at the five of us. "Girls, I want the three of you to work together to grow something. A vegetable or a fruit."

Easy enough.

She turns to Alexi and Gabriel. "Boys, I want you to use your Igna to keep them from succeeding."

The twins gasp.

"You have until the sunlight reaches here"—she moves her foot to the left of a sunlight shaft hitting the ground, not even five minutes—"to hand me something edible. If not, the boys win."

"Can we use any other elements?" I ask.

She shakes her head. "Only Terra. Begin."

Alexi looks at me with a wicked grin. I narrow my eyes at him and turn away to huddle with the twins.

"We've got numbers on our side."

"Yeah, but we can't even use water. They'll burn down anything that sprouts."

"Not if they can't see it," I say, an idea taking form. "Millie, help me form a wall between us. Macie, you grow the food. Something easy and quick."

They look at each other before nodding, their short black bangs bobbing against their eyebrows.

Alexi holds the same grin, but now his skin burns bright. Gabriel looks almost bored next to him, with a single flame in hand.

"Your move, flower," Alexi says.

Adrenaline courses through me at the challenge. We can beat him. Take him down a few pegs in the process.

I nod at Millie as we reach out, and a wall of gravel and dirt grows before us. Alexi cocks his head as the wall extends higher, until I can no longer see him. We move in unison as the wall circles the three of us.

That's when I feel it—a warm stab to the wall. They're trying to burn it down.

"Hurry!" I yell over my shoulder.

"The strawberries are almost done."

"Heads up!"

I watch in horror as a fireball launches into the sky and slams into the strawberry patch Macie grew. She barely moves out of the way in time.

"Hey! You're going to hit us."

"But I didn't, did I?" Alexi's voice is muffled on the other side of our wall.

I grumble and work on leading the dirt wall over our heads. Macie shoves her hands into the ground again. I realize my mistake as the air heats and breathing becomes difficult, sweat dripping into my top. They're cooking us.

"One more minute!" the Instructor calls.

"Do you have anything?" I gasp.

"Almost."

"We'll be able to serve ourselves up on a platter if you don't hurry, Mace," Millie yells, her bangs plastered to her forehead.

The ceiling breaks above us, dropping fist-sized clumps of dirt. The fire leaches the moisture out of the soil, making it too dry and impossible to hold up. If I could use my Lympha abilities, I could infuse it with more water.

Sunlight leaks into our dirt house. I share a horrified look with Millie as the rest of the ceiling and wall cave in. I squeeze my eyes shut as we're instantly buried. The dirt is in my ears, my nose, my mouth. I can't breathe. I can't think. I can't move.

As fast as the walls crumble around us, the dirt lifts into the sky. I inhale, only to fall into a coughing fit as I dislodge the dirt in my throat. My vision is obstructed and arms pull me up as water douses my face. Somebody wipes the dirt from my eyes.

"Are you okay?" Alexi looks at me worriedly.

I push him off. "Are you trying to kill us?" I shriek.

In the back of my mind, I know this is my fault. It was a stupid idea. I shouldn't have put us into that situation. But that thought is tiny compared to my building anger. All I see is Alexi's face—his arrogant, stupid face. His pompous, winning attitude wafts off him in droves. He always has to win. My whole life, he's been torturing me and throwing in my face how much better he is at everything, and he will continue to do so once we're bonded.

"I'm sorry, Iz."

He grabs me, and I use the force of the wind to throw him from me. He falls onto the ground, right on his backside. It would have been comical if I wasn't seeing red.

"Why do you have to be like this?"

I realize a second too late that it's too quiet around us. I peer around, noticing everyone staring. The twins are caked in dirt, their faces masked in brown, with soil clumps in their hair. I probably don't look any better, and it's all my fault.

Gabriel tries to avoid my gaze, but fails, and Mrs. Tiana clamps her lips together. Even the others glance my way. I can't bear to find my parents in the crowd.

My rage simmers, and I want to crawl into a hole and die to have made such a scene. Even the irony of that doesn't cheer me.

Class isn't over, but I head for the exit anyway.

"Wait," Mrs. Tiana calls.

I hesitate. I can't just walk away from an Instructor.

"I feel dizzy. I need a moment to lie down." I've never used my condition as an excuse, but now is as opportune a time as any.

She nods. "You may be excused."

I leave without a backward glance at Alexi. My face is so hot, I'm surprised I don't leave fiery footprints in my wake.

I lock the bathroom door and fall to the floor. I'm such a fool. It was supposed to be a game. A game! Why did I react like that?

I shake my head when something scratches on the door. I open it, and a tiny furball bounds in. Beau jumps in my lap. I weave my fingers through his silky fur, feeling a little better.

The trials are getting closer, and if I can't succeed at one silly challenge, then how am I going to prove to my parents that I don't need them?

"How gross do I look?"

He sniffs me in response and wrinkles his nose.

"That bad?" Lovely.

I rise and step toward the sink. A wave of lightheadedness hits as I pull the water from the spout. Huh. I look at myself in the mirror. Only the whites of my eyes are visible. I flash my teeth and cringe. It's worse, definitely worse.

I scrub the dirt from my face and then my hair. I look at my dirty clothes. At least it's the end of the day.

Another wave of dizziness hits me just as Beau starts jumping up and down, yanking on my hand, concern wafting off him.

"Now?" I groan and sit on the pebbled floor. My vision blurs.

The knob on the bathroom door rattles, and there is a faint banging sound. My hands curl by their own accord, and everything goes dark.

10

IZALIA

My eyes flutter open. The cracks in my clay ceiling stretch across the room. As I attempt to move, I realize my feet are trapped. I sit up quickly, startling somebody sitting next to me, my feet in their lap.

Blood rushes to my head, and dots blur my vision as Alexi's face comes into focus.

He looks at me, eyebrows raised in worry. "Hey, how do you feel?" His hand strokes my foot absently.

I have to force myself not to kick him.

The memories flood back. I look down at my dirty clothes and fall back against the pillow. "Mortified."

This isn't the first time I've woken up at home after an episode at school, another convenient reason to live so close. But Alexi isn't usually the one that takes me home.

My body feels prickly and a little violated, knowing he held me while I was out. I can't believe the Instructors, especially my parents, allowed it. I guess nobody cares now about us being alone since our ceremony is within the month.

"You guys won," he murmurs.

I try to sit up, but the beginning of a headache twists in my skull. I rub my temples. "What?"

He smiles. "Yeah, right after you left, Macie revealed a strawberry in her palm. That was a good plan."

I laugh without humor. "It was a terrible plan."

He shrugs. "You guys won, so I don't see it that way."

"We could have died."

"Don't be so melodramatic. You were under there for maybe five seconds."

I shoot him a glare.

He laughs, squeezing my foot. "You okay, though?"

"At least I passed out in the bathroom and not under that pile of dirt."

His eyes flare, like he hadn't considered the possibility. I wonder if he's thought much about how my condition will affect our life together.

He interlaces our fingers, meeting my eyes. "I would have pulled you out in a heartbeat." The heat returns to his eyes, and I look away.

He releases my hand. "Really. You don't have to worry about things like that. I will never let you leave my side once we're bonded. I will always be there for you, Iz."

My heart jumps into my throat. That's precisely what I'm worried about.

I step out of the shower feeling a hundred times better. Alexi returned to school after I insisted that I was fine. I have Beau. Alexi isn't usually such a worrier. Can he be annoying? Yes. A tad bit controlling? Definitely. Egocentric? Sure. But caring? He must feel a duty to me with our ceremony growing closer, because Alexi does not do things unless they profit him. Could this be a new side of him I'm not used to seeing?

A shiver runs down my spine. I'll be going from overly protective parents to an overly protective partner—even if I am successful with the trials. My parents aren't the only ones that I need to prove my capability to. Fabulous.

"I swear on the island, if he becomes more needy, I'll…"

Beau tilts his head at me from his position on the top of my wardrobe.

"I'll…" I sigh. I don't even know what I'll do. "I need to get out of this house."

Once I've dressed in a clean sarong and top, I leave out the back and through the forest. The sounds envelop me. The singing bugs, birds chirping, the crunch of twisted twigs underfoot, creatures rustling unseen. The smell of palm branches and dirt with a bit of sea salt from the waves that aren't too far off fills the air. Light dances through the openings. Beau swings through the vines, guiding me.

I'm not sure where we're going until I hear the music. Beau hangs off a branch upside down.

"I thought you didn't like him?"

He scratches behind his ear, pretending not to hear me.

"Ohh, you like him. You like him," I sing.

He squawks and jumps on my shoulder. I giggle. I know it wasn't just Beau. I wanted to come to see him, too. Beau can not only sense my episodes but also my emotions. I was guiding us here as much as he was.

By the time I reach the grass of Theo's property, the alluring music has stopped. I knock on a post. I'm not as hesitant as last time. It's comforting to be under Theo's roof again.

His head pops around the corner with a wide smile. He strides my way, wearing a tight white tunic and black sarong. The tunic outlines his abdomen, and I can't help but stare.

His face lights up before falling as he looks around and pulls me inside. I'm surprised Beau doesn't scurry away this time. Instead, he stays on my shoulder. Maybe he's still on edge from my latest episode. But his emotions are completely at ease. Interesting.

"Am I going to get you in trouble?" I ask.

Theo pulls a hand through his hair and shakes his head, letting the golden locks fall back into his face. "Nah. My parents are out. I don't want to get *you* in trouble, though."

Me?

He studies my face, a smile tugging on his lips.

"I heard you playing. Don't you have school?"

His smile grows. "I'm at Music 101 right now."

I lift the shoulder Beau is sitting on. "Hear that, Beau? We're getting music lessons."

11

THEO

"You could say I'm homeschooled," I say as I lead her to the couch. I turn around and notice her drifting toward the slats hiding the piano. Her eyes are wide and playful, and a smile tugs at her mouth.

"I don't want to disrupt your class." She flashes me an innocent smile and places her hair behind an ear. "I'd like to join."

My stomach flips. I thought she was joking when she told her monkey they were getting music lessons. No Divina—not even my parents—has ever asked me to teach them my music. The people like listening to it, but do it themselves? It seems like an unspoken rule to them not to touch anything that isn't from their island or "pure" enough.

I study Izalia's face, looking for any part of her that's joking. She has a slight smile on her lips, but her green eyes are bright and curious. She's serious. She does want to learn.

I step around the wall, and she settles on the bench, her hands lightly resting on the keys.

"I've never taught anyone before."

She cocks her head, her hair falling into her face, and I resist the urge to push it back. Before she responds, Beau jumps on the piano, his tail curving over the propped-up lid.

She intertwines his tail in her hand in a mindless gesture, something she's probably done hundreds of times, before saying, "How were you taught?"

Beau purrs. Monkeys purr? He settles his head so it's halfway hanging off the piano.

"I taught myself, I guess. When I was young, I would sneak into our storage shed to play with it and the other things my parents saved from the wreckage. They finally brought it into the house when I wouldn't leave it alone." I shrug. "I always have a melody in my head. Over time, I learned which keys to press. Now, it's like an extension of me."

Her eyes widen as she looks at me like I've sprung three heads.

"What?" I ask, touching my face. Is there something on my face?

She smiles and shakes her head. "That's amazing."

"Playing the piano? Not anything as amazing as you can do." I tap a few keys without thinking.

She places her hand on mine, sparking an electric current between us. "Show me," she says softly.

I take her hand and place it on the keys. Hovering my hand over hers, I press down her fingers. She smiles at the simple chord that rings out. I lift her other hand and place it on the other side of the keyboard, then move my hands down a few keys so that she mirrors me.

Her body is so incredibly close that I can feel her heat, and I fight to control my focus and not lean in to smell her intoxicating aroma, a sweet mixture of coconut and earth.

"What now?" she asks.

"Move the fingers that I do," I grunt, trying to pull myself together.

She nods, her eyebrows turned down in concentration. Slowly, I tap a few keys and wait for her to follow.

We continue at the same pace for a few minutes before she says, "It doesn't sound like a song."

"You have to press it faster to be a song, like this." My fingers caress the keys, playing the chorus of one of the first songs I memorized.

Her shoulders slump as she purses her lips. "I can't do that."

I laugh. "Sure, you can."

She looks at me with suspicion.

"Eventually," I add.

She scrunches her freckled nose.

"Try this again but faster."

She copies me but winces when it doesn't sound as fluid.

"You're getting it!"

She bumps my shoulder with hers. "You're just being nice. How did you come up with all these songs anyway?"

"We found a few songbooks in the bench compartment, but I could never figure out how to understand them. So, I used the words and created my own tune."

She tilts her head in question, her hair brushing my arm. I shudder at the touch.

"Books? I've heard you say that before."

"Yeah. They're kinda like scrolls. They have words in them."

She sits up, her hands falling off the piano keys. "Wait, you have a history of the mainland people?"

I shake my head. Of course, that's where her thoughts would go, since Divina reading material is strictly for learning. "Books can contain history, but not the ones I have. Mine contain songs and stories."

"Stories?"

"Yeah, like the ones the Elders tell, but these are from the mainland." I point towards the bookshelf next to my bed.

Her eyes widen as she stands. Her hand travels along the spines until she stops on one. She pulls it out.

I grab it out of her hand. "That one is pretty dark."

I place *The Heart of Darkness* back and pick a different one. She'd probably run away screaming if that was the first Nomagi book she read.

"*Merry Animal Tales*?" she reads.

"You'll like that one. It's stories about talking animals."

"Really?" She smiles and opens it up.

I watch her eyes trail over the words and the pictures, her expression turning to one of fascination. I close it with her palms and press it to her.

"Keep it. I have the thing pretty much memorized."

She wraps it in her arms. "Really?"

I nod, and her eyes light up.

"Thank you."

I look away from her gaze. She could bring me to my knees if I look too long.

"What about the box?"

I bite my lip. I'd hoped she'd forgotten about that. I sigh. "I'll get it."

She perches contently on the arm of the couch to wait. How could she possibly look so…at home, in my home?

When I return, her eyes are scanning the pages of the book I gave her. She doesn't even look up. For a moment, I just watch her. The way her lips squish together then turn upward as her eyes widen—every thought showing on her face. It's nice to see her so open and unguarded.

I clear my throat, and she looks up at me, closing the book.

"I want one."

I tilt my head.

"A bunny. They're adorable with those giant ears and fluffy tails. We don't have such cute creatures on the island."

Beau, who had curled onto the back of the couch, raises his head with a whine.

She grabs him and slides to the cushioned mat onto the bamboo couch. "Other than you, of course. You are much more adorable than this bunny." She nuzzles his face, and he squeaks happily, his big black eyes closing contentedly. "But it would be nice to make new friends, right?"

I can't tell if she's still talking to Beau or me as she looks past him toward the trees.

"I wonder if we could ever visit." As if worried about what she'd said, she sits up quickly and bites her lip, shooting me a sheepish expression.

"You can speak freely around me, you know."

She looks away with a shy smile. "I know." When she looks back, her eyes are on the box, full of curiosity.

I sit beside her, again distracted by her proximity, inhaling her sweet scent. I open the box. It's full of photographs, letters, and jewelry that my birth mother must have worn. "It's all I have of them." I swallow the knot in my throat.

Her hand hovers over the opening. "May I?"

I nod, handing her the box.

She takes it reverently in her hands and picks up the first photo. "It's like a painting but more real," she says, her fingertip hovering over it, as if afraid to touch it.

She flips through a couple more, asking me questions. I answer the best I can, but not even my parents could tell me about the objects in the photographs, so different from what we have on the island.

"I believe that is called a vehicle. Nomagi used it for travel."

Her eyes bulge. "Like this thing could take them anywhere they wanted?"

I shrug as she studies it.

She flips to the next one and pulls it close to her face. It's a photo of a young woman standing next to a house made of small rectangular shapes, nothing like anything we build on our island. I wonder what materials they used. Recently, I decided it must be some type of rock we don't have here. I've pored over these photos so much that seeing these things is normal.

I try to look at it as she would—noting the woman's feathered headpiece and fitted clothing. Her face is similar to mine. I have her eyes and nose.

"You look like her," she says. "Is she your mother?"

"We think so."

She looks at me with raised eyebrows.

"My parents told me which people in the photos were on the boat. I'm not sure who my father was, but the resemblance to this woman convinced us she was my mother. And the fact that her body was wrapped around the box they found me in."

Her mouth falls open, staring at the box like she's seeing it for the first time.

"This is that box. She saved me." I rub a finger on the paint-chipped wood. She must have loved me. That's the one truth I'm sure of.

She returns the photos in the box, and the couch creaks as she rises. "Would you like to do something with me?" she asks.

The change of topic is jarring. I look at her with pursed lips but realize this must be so much for her to process. Death is not a common subject. "I'm sorry if that was too much."

"No, no, no. I want to see. I just—" Her eyes roam over me and then the box, filling with sadness.

I stand. "I get it." I smile. "Let's get out of here."

She takes my hand and leads me away. Warmth radiates up my arm.

She looks towards the couch. Beau is sleeping on the top, curled in a ball. "He'll find me when he wakes," she whispers.

"How does he know where you are?"

"We're connected," she says with a shrug, and that's all the explanation I get.

I shake my head—Divina and their magic.

12

IZALIA

The hike does nothing to shake the pit in my stomach after hearing about Theo's mom and seeing those pictures. It's too real. Those Nomagi were real people who died on that boat. Theo could have died, too.

Protectors send storms out to keep people away, to protect us. But who are the actual monsters? Are we protecting ourselves, or are we just killing innocent Nomagi? We killed his family. It's easy to imagine that we're the only people in existence, that everyone killed each other off in the war three hundred years ago. But that is far from the truth. Those pictures prove that there is life on the mainland, not just theories we discuss in class.

Theo is proof.

What if everything we know about Nomagi is a lie? There is a whole other civilization on the other side of this ocean that I know nothing about. Why can't we leave? Why can't anyone on this island explore the mainland? The scrolls teach us that Nomagi are vicious and war-seeking and that we're safer on our island. But how could that be true? The smiling people in those pictures looked like us and our families, just living life. It could have been true hundreds of years ago, but now? Have things changed? Could we return?

I shuck off my sandals and wade into the water of the falls, hoping it'll clear my head full of questions. I wiggle my toes in the cool sand and look over my shoulder.

Does Theo know about the storms our Protectors send out to sea? That more of his people could be dying right now?

Theo's eyes are closed, and his chin lifts into one of the beams of sunlight filtering through the canopy of trees far above our heads. His unkempt hair ruffles in the breeze.

No, he can't know. He would think I'm a monster. He wouldn't be out here with me.

The steep slope that we descended is directly behind him. I was surprised he didn't complain once on the climb down. My Terra abilities help my feet seek the perfect placement amongst unruly landscapes, but nature seems to work against Theo. I had to stop countless times to help him escape a tricky spot. I hadn't realized what's easy for Divina might not be as easy for Nomagi. When I realized his trouble, I told him we could go somewhere else, but he insisted.

"What do you think?"

He looks at me with a dazzling smile that has my heart skipping a beat. "Beautiful," he responds.

I know he's answering my question, but my heart flutters from those eyes on me.

Then guilt settles in my gut. I should tell him that it's our fault his family is gone.

He walks to me, and I hold a hand out. I'll tell him now. But instead, I say, "Swim with me."

He cocks his head and looks down at himself. "You could have told me to bring a bathing suit."

I shrug. "Whoops." I grab the hem of my dress and lift.

His eyes widen. I hold back a smile as the dress clears my head, revealing my black bathing suit underneath. I giggle as he studies the trees to my right.

"Come on," I say, splashing water in his direction.

His face is beet red, and he's looking everywhere but at me.

I study him curiously. Breakwater Strand is known for having girls that string coconuts as their tops. He couldn't possibly feel embarrassed at my lack of clothes.

I throw my dress at him. He gasps and stumbles back like I threw a boulder at him instead of a thin piece of fabric. A giggle erupts from me, and he finally makes eye contact.

His eyes hold mine, almost as if asking permission to look at the rest of me. I smile as his eyes rake over me, drinking up every square inch of exposed skin. I have swum my whole life with boys who never paid me much attention, but how he's looking at my body feels illegal. It's almost like his eyes are a tangible touch to my skin, warming me to my toes.

"What? You've never seen a girl in a bathing suit?" I was there at that beachside party, too.

He clears his throat and opens his mouth, but nothing comes out.

I shake my head, laughing again, and dive into the crystal-clear water.

The water welcomes and energizes me, pushing away all those terrible thoughts. The beams of light filter through the water and disappear underneath my feet. Rainbow-colored fish swim through the shafts of light, causing colors to dance off their scales.

I have no idea how they managed to get in here, far from the ocean. I swim towards them, and they scatter. My hair floats around me as a blanket of night.

I stay under as long as I can, twirling my fingers through the water, creating tiny tornadoes, giving Theo time to compose himself before finally breaking the surface.

My eyebrows turn down. He's not on the sliver of rocky sand anymore. I swim in a circle, but the shore and surrounding trees are Theo-free.

What the…?

A tug on my foot pulls me under. A scream forms in my chest, but before I can release it, I spot Theo amongst the bubbles, a huge smile plastered on his face. I shove his shoulder and kick myself back up.

He comes up with me, chuckling. "Did I scare you?"

"No," I say, splashing water at him.

He smiles at the obvious lie. My heart beats wildly in my ears as adrenaline courses through my veins. He chuckles again before disappearing back under the water.

Oh no, he doesn't.

I barely get under before he starts tickling my feet. I shriek into the water and reach for his wrists. He moves them out of my reach and swims away, surprisingly fast compared to others. I chase after him and stop. Instead, I grab ahold of the water around his body and pull. The water freezes him in place until I catch up.

I climb on his back and release my hold, giving his hair a light tug. A thrill runs through me when he winds his arms around my legs, securing me to him, and shoots to the surface. We come up laughing, and he releases me.

"You're a pretty good swimmer," I say.

"For a Nomagi?"

I shake my head. "Period."

He raises an eyebrow. "Thanks. I may be unable to control the water, but I've grown up in it. I love swimming. It calms me."

He puts his arms behind his neck and floats on his back, giving me a wicked idea. I kick my feet in the water, gaining the extra energy needed before using the water to launch myself up and directly on top of him. Our limbs tangle together as we sink. Instead of pushing me off of him, though, he pulls me closer. I wrap my hands around his neck, and all my senses awaken. His body heat seeps into mine, and electricity flows through at every point of contact.

His eyes find mine, and they're wide, filled with an emotion I can't name. I feel brave down here, under the water, where nobody can see us. My hands trail his bare back, feeling the tension in his shoulders. His eyes flutter closed at my touch. I continue down his arms, skimming every muscle and vein. His hands freeze around my waist, as if he's afraid to touch my skin. I cup his face, and he opens his eyes. They burn into mine through my barriers, scars, and insecurities. And I know that he sees me. He sees me, and I have nothing to prove. I'm just me—broken and all.

We stay like that for what seems like hours, but I know it's only seconds before my lungs burn and we kick to the surface.

We break the water close to the waterfall. I unwind my legs from his torso and pull his arm towards the falls before he can release me. My eyes close against the onslaught of heavy water that threatens to push me back under. I blink away the droplets and smile as he sputters and comes through the veil.

Behind the waterfall, where nobody in the world can see us, the desire to close the distance between us presses in. The rush of the falls is deafening. We can't speak, only look. I trace the angles of his face and shoulders with my eyes. He's more lovely than any man on this island, with eyes that match the ocean currents and his hair the color of sunlight. It's slick against his sharp cheekbones and neck.

He takes in our surroundings, moving his arms to stay afloat. He nods toward the veil of water, and I shake my head. Not yet. I swim closer to him and point up. He follows my finger, and his lips form an "O." I follow his line of sight.

The top of the hollow cave hosts thousands of twinkling bugs that nest on its ceiling, creating a night sky and our very own constellations. I've memorized the ones in *our* night sky. When I'm here, I can almost imagine that I live somewhere else, with a different night sky and new constellations to study. I can't tell anyone the deepest desire of my heart—to visit other places. Meeting Theo is just that—a peek into a new world. I'm not only drawn to the novelty of it; there's something about him, as if my soul calls to his. Something familiar. I feel complete when I'm in his presence. He fills that missing part of me—the part wrong with my body.

He makes me brave, not the stupid confidence that gets me into unfortunate situations, but the courage to give in to those desires within me that I always push down.

I tug his chin downward to look at me and wind my legs around his waist, trusting him wholly. Without breaking eye contact, he moves us closer inside the cave. His shoulders relax, and his body stops moving. He must have found a foothold. I take his hands and wind them around my waist. I nod sheepishly and place my other hand on his cheek. His hands travel up my skin, breathing life into me. They reach my face and thread through my hair. I stare at his lips. I've never wanted somebody's lips on me so bad.

They form words. I can only make out one word: *angel*. It is so much better than *flower*.

My heart stutters out, extinguishing the flames spreading through my body.

Alexi.

What am I doing? I'm promised to him, not Theo. If somebody caught us alone…I don't want to imagine what they would do to him.

He pulls me closer, and I stiffen in his arms, even though my heart aches to close the distance. He immediately releases his hold. The confusion in his eyes is the last thing I see before I let the water pull me under.

13

THEO

I am an idiot.

I know I'd spooked her as soon as she went rigid in my arms. I moved too fast.

As she slips under the surface, I can still feel her body against mine. An unusual hunger reverberates in my bones to chase after her and mark every inch of her with my lips. For that reason, I hold still, treading water behind the falls until the sensation passes.

Her skin was magic, her hair like silk; I'd never felt anything so soft. I could hold her in my arms forever. And her laugh. The way it transforms her, like nothing could bring her down. My heart warms, knowing I was the one to cause it.

I grab ahold of the rock to steady myself. I've got to be dreaming. There is no other explanation. The way she touched me. Could she like me too? I don't understand how such a perfect, beautiful being could want somebody like me.

I shake my head. I can't get my hopes up. My feelings for her are growing at an alarming rate. I could tell her how I feel.

No.

If my proximity spooked her, then that would *certainly* do it. She's only known me for two days.

But she doesn't know she has taken over my thoughts and dreams for months. She doesn't need to know that.

With control over my emotions, I dive under the falls.

Izalia gives me a tight smile from where she dresses on the bank. "I need to get back," she says.

Right. Of course. A knot forms in my stomach as I swim to her.

Her demeanor changes on our ascent up the cliff. She's quiet and doesn't look at me except when I stumble, but she never looks me in the eyes again. We reach the top, and she hovers, fumbling with her dress.

"That was fun. Thank you for showing me that place," I say.

She nods and smiles, but it doesn't reach her eyes. A terrible feeling that I won't see her again crawls to take hold.

I raise my hand to touch her but let it drop. "I'm sorry."

Her face twists, and she shakes her head. "Don't be. I—I need to tell you something."

She's still not looking at me. I study her as she twists her hands back and forth, battling an unknown force. I can't stand to see her this way. I grab her hand without thinking, needing to do something. I expect her to pull away, but she relaxes and tightens her grip.

"There's a lot you don't know about me...and my family...and my future," she says, finally bringing her eyes to mine.

"So tell me." I want to tell her that I want to know everything there is to know about her, but I hold back.

She frowns. "It's not that easy."

I want so badly to take away her pain that I do what I promised myself I wouldn't. I cup her face, stepping closer. She surprises me even more by leaning into my touch, lifting her hand, and holding mine there.

"I like being around you, Theo."

I can see the truth in her eyes. Hearing my name on her lips, I almost melt in her arms.

"But…I can't be with you."

My heart plummets. Of course not. Who would want to be with a Nomagi? What can I provide for her?

I go to step away, but she won't let me.

Her eyes become frantic as she pulls me closer. "Just listen."

At that moment, Beau jumps between us and shrieks, pulling on her hair. Izalia's eyebrows knit together, before understanding dawns on her face.

"I have to go." She pulls out of my grasp, and before I can take another breath, she's racing through the trees, taking my heart along with her.

14

AZALIA

I study my back windows, trying to catch my breath behind the wide palm branches. My parents pace in the living room. Alexi appears with a glass in hand, giving it to my mother— ever the suck-up. I roll my eyes. I should have expected him to run off to my parents.

Beau prances around my feet.

"Thanks for the heads up." I pat his head, and he grabs my fingers. I pull him up, and he nuzzles into my neck. Fixing my hair, I square my shoulders and open the back door, preparing to lie my face off.

My father sees me, and I pretend not to notice the slice of panic that eases on his face. I simply take off my sandals and move to open the ice box. The most recent layer of ice around it is already melting. It was a scorching day today.

My hand is on the handle when my mother pops around the corner. "Where have you been?"

"Swimming." I shrug, grabbing a juice. Not a lie. "Do you want me to add another layer?" I ask, gesturing to the ice box. It usually only requires one new layer a day.

My mom opens her mouth, closes it again, and stutters. I take a refreshing gulp of sweet pineapple juice from the jar.

"But you had an episode, didn't you?"

"Yeah?" I position my hands on the ice box, concentrating on my Lympha abilities to create another layer of water, then my Aura abilities to freeze it. "It's hot today."

She shakes her head and looks at my father, who's joined her in the kitchen. It's funny that Alexi hasn't made an appearance yet. Good. That overprotective hulk of muscle needs to calm down.

She waves off my efforts before I'm even half done, the lid falling down with a *thunk*, and directs me toward the living room.

"You should have rested and waited for us. You know you're extra vulnerable after an episode," Dad says.

"I got plenty of rest when I was out of it for who knows how long. I needed to clear my head. Beau was with me."

He pulls a hand over his voluminous hair and shakes his head, sharing a heavy look with Mom.

Her eyebrows form a deep V, and she threads her fingers through her long braid.

The juice freezes on my lips. There's more. "What are you not telling me?"

"Alexi, can you come here?" Mom calls over her shoulder.

Alexi strolls into the kitchen, flashing me a guilty smile. I narrow my eyes at him. What are they up to?

"We have another idea to get the episodes to stop. Well, it was Alexi's idea, but both your father and I agree and really think this one will work," she says. "Your blackouts have always happened very randomly. We've tried to pinpoint a trigger, but there doesn't seem to be one. Then Alexi was telling us about the events leading up to today's episode and—"

My face heats, and my eyes widen at Alexi, who's suddenly very interested in his feet.

"It could be an emotional response," Dad finishes.

"We've already discounted that." I take another sip, grateful they don't have some new outlandish theory.

"Yes. But not taking your abilities into account."

I look between the three of them. "Okaaay?"

My mom bites her lip, and Alexi keeps his eyes glued to the ground.

I swallow a lump forming in my throat. "What are you talking about?"

"Think about it," Alexi says. He moves forward and grabs my hands, taking my juice from me and placing it on the table. Alexi raises my hand. "High emotion combined with"—he raises the other one—"an influx of power." He closes my palms. "Too much strain on your brain, and it shuts down." He watches my face.

I shake my head and pull my hands out of his. "You think my magic causes my episodes? That's ridiculous."

My father puts a hand on my shoulder.

I flinch.

"We're just going to try it."

"Try what?" Panic churns in my stomach.

"Stripping your powers for a couple of days," Dad says grimly.

"What?" I shriek, panic exploding from within. "Stripping my powers? But…But the trials."

My mom wears the same sad expression as my father. My mind swirls, and I see red. I turn to stare hard at Alexi. He rocks back on his heels like my glare has a physical effect on him. Good. This isn't my parents' idea.

My mom puts a hand on my face, and I cringe away from her.

"No. I'm not doing it." I face Alexi. "This was your idea?" Fire ignites in my veins.

When I was little, my parents had to help the neighbors put out fires in their home on a weekly basis. Their teenage son had a terrible combination of anger issues and an Igna specialty. For the first time since then, I understand how that boy must have been feeling. They're lucky that I can barely make a ball of fire in my palms or this whole place would be up in smoke.

"Don't be angry with him," Dad chastises.

I can't take another word. I push through them and head for the stairs. I'm grateful that they don't follow.

Upstairs, I slam my door as hard as I can. Beau emerges through my window a moment later. I gather him in my arms and nuzzle him. I wear down a path from one side of my room to the other, unable to stop moving.

What are they thinking? This is unbelievable. Until now, I have always done what they asked, tried all the stupid experiments, and accepted my fate with Alexi—but taking my magic? That's too far. I won't do it. My parents wouldn't force me to.

Would they?

I don't know a lot about the process besides somehow getting cut off from harnessing your Sage, and thus your magic.

Once I've calmed down, I sit. "They want to take my magic, Beau."

He squawks disapprovingly.

I fist my blankets as my face hardens. "I won't let them."

When somebody knocks, I shove *Merry Animal Tales* under my throw. My mom joins me on my bed with a coconut pastry. Her eyes are downcast, and her lips are taut.

I sit up, ready to plead my case now that I've had time to think and compose myself.

Before I can say anything, she sighs. "Hon, we're not going to take your magic right now. You're right…with the upcoming trials and the bonding ceremony in a few weeks. We can try it another time."

I swipe the pastry from the plate, incredibly grateful, but the words "right now" bounce in my head. They won't do it *now*, but they will.

"You guys need to stop listening to Alexi."

She smiles. "He's quite a smart young man, you know."

My parents have always loved Alexi. I roll my eyes, coconut and chocolate flavors exploding in my mouth. If she thought this would help me forgive them—she may be right.

I sit up, an idea sparking. "Let's say he is right, and my magic *is* causing this." I reference my head. "What would be the long-term solution?"

She sighs. "I don't know, baby."

"Take them away indefinitely, make me a Nomagi?"

She flinches, but the word doesn't have the same bite as I was going for. I would be a Nomagi—like Theo.

She shakes her head and places her hand on mine. "No, we wouldn't do that."

"Mom." I sigh, feeling incredibly tired all of a sudden. Tired of all the experiments. Tired of my parents trying to fix me. Tired of going along with it just to placate them. Tired of trying to prove myself constantly. Tired of trying to show that I'm more than my disability. I am so much more than that. "Is there a way you guys can just stop? Stop trying to fix me? I've accepted my fate. Why can't you?"

Her eyes widen and she squeezes my hand. "We're not trying to fix you. We're trying to help you. I don't think you'll understand until you become a parent yourself. You never want to stop helping your children. You'll do everything in your power to give them the best quality of life. I will always fight for you. I will never stop fighting until the very end." She holds my hand tighter. "I love you so much. If I could take this hardship away from you and put it on me, I would in a heartbeat. It rips me apart to see you suffer."

"Mom. I'm not suffering. I'm okay."

She pats my hand and stands up. "I'll never give up on you, hon."

She leaves me alone, and I fall back on my bed. They're not going to take my magic…yet. Icy tendrils climb up my back. I'll cross that bridge when I come to it. I've only heard about it happening to one person. There was a case before I was born of somebody who had killed another. A crime so heinous that the man had his magic stripped away and then was banished from the island, which means certain death with the storms. Nobody, to my knowledge, has had their magic stripped and stayed.

Then there is Theo. The only person on the island without magic. I would be more like him.

My heart squeezes. I can't believe I almost kissed him. Being in his arms is nothing like being with Alexi. That scares me even more than losing my magic. I shouldn't feel like that with him. But all I want to do is find him, let him hold me, and tell me everything will be okay—that becoming a Nomagi is no big deal. I bet he would tell me all those things. Maybe my parents would even let me be with him if I didn't have my magic. No use bonding with Alexi—the one silver lining.

I smile at that thought as I pull the book from behind my pillow, picking back up with the talking ugly duckling, isolated and alone. I really hope his story ends well, because if he can get through it, so can I.

15

THEO

I'm officially a stalker.

This is something stalkers would do. Wait outside a girl's school and catch her as she's walking home. I'll turn around and go home. Give her some time.

But I stay rooted to the spot under the tree, just inside the forest line. Chimes ring out as Divina begin pouring out of the buildings.

It's a beautiful campus. Tall palm trees and vibrant flowers cover the expanse of glass buildings intertwined with traditional fale structures. I've never been this close to the school—never had a reason to come here. It's not my place.

The all-too-familiar stab of not being included comes and goes.

It's a sea of dark hair and green eyes. I can practically hear the whispers in the wind.

You don't belong.

Freak.

Get off our island.

I've only been as far as the city, long ago, as a terrified young child clinging to his mother.

The buildings are tall and sparkly, like the inside of abalone shells. Will Ma let me touch the glass? I could be a Craftsman when I grow up. Making something like this would be so fun.

I reach out my hand, but Ma pulls me to her side and fixes my hat to ensure it covers my hair. I don't see the big deal. Haven't we been coming to the city since I was a baby? At least that's what Ma and Pa tell me. I don't really remember. I think they used to hold me so I couldn't look around. I must not have seen anything. How could I forget this? It's so new and exciting. I don't want to go back to our boring fale. Ma and Pa never let me go farther than the beach.

Two grownups pass and narrow their eyes at me. Ma pulls me closer. I crane my neck so I can see better. I don't want to miss a thing. A strong breeze from behind blows my hat off, and I watch it fly away. I tug on Ma's arm.

"Look, look!" I say excitedly, watching the hat twist and tumble in the wind.

She sucks in a breath and tucks me under her arm, and Pa takes up my other side. Now I can't see anything. I start to complain, but Ma shushes me.

"What is that?" The words come from behind us, and I try to wriggle free to see.

"Hey! You!"

My parents speed up, and I trip over my feet. Their hands keep me upright. Unease spreads over me.

"Get that thing off Alohra," comes a shrill voice.

My parents stop as somebody takes up the path ahead.

The woman's face is twisted in disgust. "Freak," she hisses.

Heat claws at my throat as I fight my parents' hands.

Ma releases me as Pa shouts, "Leave us alone. He's just a boy."

I take the chance at freedom and run down an adjoining path. Ma screams at me to stop, but I turn the corner. There are more people here. I duck behind a trash can, my entire body shaking.

"Aw you otay?" comes a high-pitched voice.

I look up at a little girl with blue-green eyes. She licks a mango popsicle and tilts her head at me. "I like you haiwr."

I flinch as she touches it with sticky fingers. Her yellow dress is also covered in orange stuff.

"Sowwy." She holds her other hand toward me. "Don't be scawed, you can twust me."

As my racing heart calms, I hesitantly take her hand, and she helps me up.

"I'm waiting fo my pawents. Want some?" She angles the popsicle my way, and I shake my head.

"There you are!" Ma yells from behind me. She grips my arm and tugs me away from the little girl.

The girl smiles wide and waves at me as Ma pulls me around the corner.

The buildings aren't bright and beautiful anymore, but ominous and terrifying as I cling to Ma's hand. I hold on to the little girl's smile, reminding me there is good on this island, even as nasty comments whisper past us.

I don't remember that yearly meeting with the Elders that day. But I'm grateful my parents never took me back to the city after that. I never asked them why or what the repercussions were, but I knew they were trying to protect me after what happened.

I haven't thought about that little girl in a long time. Her smile is still engrained in my memory, though, reminding me of the kindness I was shown that day. She sort of reminds me of Izalia.

I blink. Wait. No.

I shake my head. It can't be. Well—it *could* be. The ages line up.

Could it be?

I scan the crowd, feeling a pull from somewhere deep within. She's out there. My eyes immediately find her figure, walking across the field of wildflowers, the wind blowing her hair back, her eyes bright and kind like that little girl. Children's eyes change when they come into their magic. Of course, they wouldn't have been the beautiful emerald green they are now.

I pull up the fuzzy image of the little girl's face in my memory. It *could* be her.

Suddenly, I just know it was her. I feel it in my core.

Warmth cocoons around my heart before seeping into my veins, then my bones, to the essence of who I am. A surety that is as real as the girl walking through the field in front of me.

I love her.

The words rip through me, shattering my heart and then stitching it back together so that every piece is now hers. I don't belong to this island anymore. I belong to her. I love *her*. She is everything good and kind in this world.

I make myself a promise to her, to that little girl who only saw a young boy in need instead of a stranger who was different, to the grown woman who knows of my heritage and still sees only me. I am hers. Her happiness is my new purpose. Whatever that may look like. Whatever she needs. I don't have to be with her to ensure she's happy. But if she'll have me, I won't let her down.

Confidence flows through me, strengthening my resolve. I'm going to tell her how I feel.

I pull a glass shard out of my pocket, find just the right patch of sunlight, and hope it works.

16

AZALIA

Training wasn't nearly as exciting as it was yesterday. Mrs. Tiana probably thought we took it too far when I had my mental—and physical—episode.

I kick a pebble on the dirt path leading to my house when a flash catches my eye. I eye the trees where I think it came from. There's another reflection of sunlight and I squint, searching.

Shrugging, I'm about to turn when a flicker of light hair has me trying to look casual as I quickly stroll toward the trees. The buildings, stretching high into the sky to my left, shine like sea glass erupting from the ground as my feet crunch over fallen branches. I don't see anything as I close the distance. No way I imagined that.

I whip around at a noise. Theo steps from behind a bush covered in large red flowers.

I smile wide, my body instantly relaxing in his presence.

He pulls a hand through his hair and balances on the balls of his feet. "Hey. Thought I'd come to you for a change." His eyes search mine, and something flashes in them.

Before responding, I guide him deeper into the shadows of the trees. Beau swings above our heads.

When we're concealed enough, I say, "You didn't need to do that."

He rubs the back of his neck. "I wanted to make sure you were okay. And I might have been worried that you wouldn't come back, that I scared you off. I'm sorry. I shouldn't have. It's just that—" His words come out all smashed together, and he takes another shaky breath. He's usually not this nervous around me. I immediately feel bad for running off on him yesterday.

I shake my head and step forward. "Stop apologizing. If anyone should be saying sorry, it's me. I'm the one that—" I wave my hand at him—unable to admit to my flirtations out loud.

"But I'm who I am." He looks at his feet.

Does he think I don't want him because he's a Nomagi?

I close the distance between us and place my hand on his chest. "That's not why. I actually love that about you." I touch his face to get him to look at me.

He searches my eyes. "Really?" It's barely a whisper. "I want to tell you something."

I smile and rush on, needing to finish before I lose my nerve. "You're unique. You make me feel...a thousand good things that I can't name."

His lips part again, but I put a finger on them. The softness of his lips does interesting things to my stomach, and I immediately remove my hand.

"Let me just get this out."

He nods, and I take a deep breath, already wincing at what I have to say. "Ever since I was a little girl, I've been destined to be bonded with somebody. A mate…I belong to him. Well, not yet. But at the end of the month, I will."

His face flashes through different emotions—confusion, understanding, and sorrow. "I've heard of that," he says finally.

I step away, needing distance from the emotions swirling inside of me. "That's why we can be nothing more than friends."

"Do you even get a choice? Is he what you want?" His eyes bounce between mine.

I hesitate. Nobody has ever asked me if Alexi is who I want. It's just always been a fact. We're destined to be mates because of our bloodlines.

I don't say anything, and the silence extends between us.

"Okay. Just friends," he says, breaking the silence with a forced smile.

I nod. "Just friends." I want to say so much more—that I wish we could be more than friends. But announcing how I feel wouldn't help anyone. "Now, what did you want to tell me?"

His face falls briefly before he smiles and shakes his head. "It's not important."

"You sure?"

He nods. I want to prod, but I have to get back for my torture at Natalina's. I'll get him to tell me later.

"Okay. I have to go. But I'm glad you came." I give him an encouraging smile.

"You know where to find me," he says, disappearing into the trees.

My chest is heavy as I weave through the houses toward Natalina's. Regret tugs on me like I made a huge mistake. I had to tell him about Alexi, though. He deserves to know the truth. I can't be stringing him along, only to break his heart. No matter if I want him.

And I do want him, probably too much.

I try to push Theo to the back of my mind as I mentally prepare for "girl time." It'll be a nice distraction, at least. Keep me from running back to Theo's house and throwing myself in his arms. Finishing where we had left off yesterday behind the waterfall. His lips felt so nice underneath my fingertips. I can only imagine how they would feel elsewhere.

Izalia, get a hold of yourself.

I can do this. I used to hang out with these girls all the time, or at least when I had to keep up appearances of having friends. I don't care about that anymore. I end up being talked at the whole time anyway, only supplying occasional nods. This time might be different, though. There's information they want from me.

I'm about to knock on the wooden door when it swings open. I stutter a greeting as Natalina leads me in.

"I hope it's okay that I invited Freylin and the twins."

"Yeah, the more the merrier," I say with little enthusiasm. Beau nestles under my hair but dutifully stays with me. He knows I need him.

She looks at me with a lifted eyebrow, sensing the sarcasm, then eyes Beau. "He's not going to poop in my house, is he?"

I scoff as I walk into their sitting room. Even though it's an identical layout to mine, it feels different. Polished ceramic statues of animals sit on various shelves and tables. The furniture is neat and uniform. Stylish black and beige woven tapestries cover the walls.

After greeting everyone, I sink into a bamboo chair in the corner. I pick at the bare threads prickling my thigh. Craftsmen make all the buildings and furniture on the island, but I haven't seen this design before. How did they come across this piece?

The twins smile simultaneously. If I could have chosen who I wanted here, I'm glad it's them. They've always been kind to me…well, when they do talk. But I doubt I'll even get that after our fiasco yesterday. They seem to always be in their own world. I'm surprised Natalina invited them. When did they become friends?

I find my answer within five minutes, when the twins announce they're matched. Natalina beams as if she already knew.

I can't hide the shock on my face. "Who?" I didn't think they would ever get matched. Twins are an exception to the one-child rule. But I have never heard of them getting bonded. They could each have multiples. More children—more people that could lead to overpopulation on the island.

Natalina smiles mischievously. Of course, she knows that too.

"Phillip Anele and Kai Akamu," they say together.

I recognize the names. They must be boys from Breakwater Strand, but not in our year.

"They're older, right?" Natalina leans forward, placing her elbows on her knees and her head in her hands.

I look sideways at her.

The girls nod enthusiastically. It's funny seeing them move together like they're one person, not two separate people. I wonder how their mates will take it.

Natalina lowers her voice slightly. "Like a *lot* older."

Macie's face reddens, and Millie shrugs. "They're in their twenties."

Oh. Well, that explains it. Those guys aren't getting matched if they are that old and still unmatched. What would be the reason to match them with older guys? There are plenty in our year.

"Isn't Phillip like twenty-nine?" Natalina asks, sounding confused, as if she doesn't already know the answer.

Millie straightens. "Yes, and Kai is twenty-seven. Age is just a number."

Natalina smirks, settling back in her chair, but the girls aren't as enthused any longer. The realization hits me—when people don't get matched, they go through the sterilization process, preventing them from having children. Their matches would have had that done.

Neither Millie or Macie will ever have a child.

By the island, I want to slap the smirk off Natalina's face.

Instead, I rise and hug both of them. When I congratulate them, I mean it. Some people never become matched, and these men get a second chance. Even if they can't have children, the twins will have companionship and, hopefully, a lifetime of happiness.

Freylin and Natalina offer less-than-meaningful congratulations. Then their eyes are on me. I bristle and avoid looking at them, still bothered by the way Natalina treated the twins.

"How many more days until your ceremony, Izalia?" she asks.

"Three and a half weeks I think." I pick at the bamboo fibers on the chair again.

Natalina smiles and looks at the other girls. Hooked on my every word, the twins seem to have recovered from Natalina's pettiness. "Alexi went to Izalia's house for her mom's party and got home pretty late." She gives me a knowing look. "Then the next day at school, she was totally swooning."

Knowing her, she's already told them these things, so this must be purely for my benefit. My cheeks heat, and I hate myself. I rub Beau's ears to keep calm.

Millie giggles and says, "And Alexi has been very touchy the last couple of days during training."

I shoot daggers at her, and she blushes, looking down. Traitor. I can't even count on *them*, I guess.

Natalina claps her hands together. "Oh really?"

I study my hand like it's the most interesting thing as silence falls. Finally, I peer up. All their eyes are on me. I sigh. "Nothing happened."

"Alexi wouldn't say that," Natalina mumbles.

My mouth falls open. "What did he say?" I gasp.

Natalina stands with a high-pitched squeal. "So, something did happen! He didn't say anything. But your reaction totally does. Come on, tell us!"

I wince and glance at each of them. "You have to swear not to say anything."

"I swear on the island that gives us our breath." Natalina breathes out the old saying, sitting on the edge of her seat.

I look at the other three girls, and they murmur the same thing.

"He kissed me."

They all shriek, and I cringe. They're all on top of me at once.

"I can't believe it!" Freylin says.

"I knew it. I just knew it!" Natalina screams.

The twins say at the same time, "What was it like?"

"Yeah, what was it like?" Freylin chirps. "Did you faint from the pure ecstasy of it?"

"Does he taste as good as he looks?" Natalina gushes.

I gasp. So do the other girls. And now we're all giggling. I can't help but join in.

Then my thoughts go to what it would be like to kiss Theo instead. I might faint if his lips were on me.

But not Alexi's.

For the first time in a long time, I feel a part of something—like I belong. But I don't. These girls just want more pieces of gossip to share. So, I'll give them something to share.

They quiet and look at me expectantly. I remember being in Theo's arms, imagining what it would be like to kiss him. Theo doesn't have magic, but I know without a doubt that kissing him would be nothing less than pure magic. I could use those feelings to describe the experience, but why give them that? Why give Alexi a confidence boost when it inevitably gets back to him? I can't tell them what actually happened. Even I know slapping somebody is not a normal response to one's first kiss.

"It's as if the earth stopped rotating, and it was just the two of us," I start, watching their expressions before I hit them with the best part. "It was warm, wet, and *terrible*. And his breath was awful. I swear he had just eaten some peppers or something. And fish. Yes! Peppers and fish. Blech."

There is absolute silence as all four girls blink at me. Beau makes a noise that almost sounds like a chuckle, and that breaks the floodgates. Freylin bursts out laughing and the twins snicker. Natalina falls back into her chair with a disgusted expression. I try to keep my face even, but I can't help the smile that breaks across my face. I giggle along with the girls.

"That's awful!" Freylin says once she can stop laughing.

"Yup."

"Do you think they're all like that?" Macie whispers to Millie.

"No! No, they are not. And I don't believe you," Natalina huffs.

I roll my eyes and stand, having had enough. If she's not even going to believe what I say, what's the point? "I don't care if you don't believe me. That was my experience. It was one kiss and nothing more. And I don't plan on repeating it until the ceremony."

Natalina stands with me. "Why not? So what? He ate something foul." Her nose scrunches. "If I were you, I would be all over that man. Hell to the rules. What are they going to do? Push the ceremony up sooner? Like that would be a bad thing. I say try again."

Ignoring the fact that she just told me she wants my mate—like I didn't know—my heart stutters. Could they push the ceremony up? Is that what Alexi is trying to do by suddenly kissing me and being all over me in public? No.

The girls must mistake the dread on my face for worry as Freylin says, "It probably was a fluke. Anyway, I would be more worried about the ceremony night. If the kissing is bad…" She cringes.

I blink at her and slowly sit back down. Beau hops back into my lap.

She eyes me and looks at the others with the same dumbfounded expressions. "Don't you guys know what happens after the ceremony?"

We all stare at her.

"Nobody knows?" She shifts in her seat and tugs on her earlobe. "What you have to do to make the ceremony complete? The joining of two bodies?" Her head whips back and forth. "I can't believe you guys don't know this." She squeals and looks at me. "Especially you. You're three weeks out." She shakes her head in disbelief.

"Are you talking about the cut?" I ask, hopeful that's all she's talking about. We'll each make an incision in the other's palm to bind ourselves together. I'm only slightly worried about that pain, more worried about the aftermath—the *together forever* bit.

Freylin's eyes bulge. "That pain will be nothing compared to what comes after."

I rack my brain for everything my mom has told me about the ceremony and come up empty. "Are you going to tell us?"

She cocks her head with a smile. "I'm not going to ruin the surprise."

"How do you know about it?"

"My mom told me." She shrugs, flipping her dark, straight hair over her shoulder. "There's a reason they don't even want us to kiss."

My eyebrows furrow. "It has something to do with kissing?"

Her shoulders shake in silent laughter. "Yes, and much more. Imagine kissing but times ten."

Natalina whacks Freylin's knee. "Just tell us, Frey."

She shakes her head, waving her hands in the air. "No way. It was so awkward with my mom. I am not going through that with you guys. Ask your parents if you want to know."

"You're insufferable." Natalina huffs and sags into the chair with her lips puckered out.

My thoughts run wild. Something better than kissing? But painful. What in the world?

Once I'm released from the gossipy bunch, I practically run home, but only after I promise to come to Natalina's end-of-the-year party this weekend.

At home, I burst into the kitchen, where my mom is filling coconut halves with sweet potatoes, while banana leaves wrap themselves around fish. My dad is sitting at the counter, a scroll in his hand. Good, they're both here.

"Hi, honey. How was Natalina and the girls?"

"Great. But I have a question about the ceremony."

Mom looks at me briefly as she cuts another sweet potato and the wrapping pauses. "Yeah?"

"What happens the night of the ceremony? Like afterward?"

My mom stiffens, and the banana leaves fall to the floor. My dad makes an unpleasant noise in his throat as his dark eyebrows shoot into his hairline.

"Um. I'm going to go heat the stones for the umu," Dad announces and gives my mom a quick kiss on the forehead, murmuring something in her ear.

She throws daggers at him with her eyes before whipping him with the kitchen towel. He dodges it with a laugh and the backdoor bangs behind him.

That was odd.

With a wave of her hand, the fallen banana leaves return to the table. She turns to me. "Sit."

I do what she asks, and she looks away from me, out the window—probably at Dad, who couldn't even be in the room with me for this conversation. That can't be a good sign.

"What happens on the ceremony night is the same thing that happens when a new life forms," she says slowly.

My eyes bulge. "I'm going to have a baby?" I shriek.

"No! No. No." She rushes to grab my hands and sits in the chair Dad was in. "No. Not yet, anyway. It's the process of how life is formed, but it can also be used for other things. An expression of love, too."

Now I'm really confused and remember what Freylin said. "Like a kiss?"

Her eyes light up. "Yes! Exactly like a kiss."

"But there is more to it?" There has to be. Because if all it takes is a kiss to have a baby, I'm in big trouble.

"I have a scroll!" she announces and rushes out the door.

I notice the coconut halves she left unattended tilt, the sweet potatoes about to spill out. I rush to them. So unlike Mom to make a mess. I settle them against the wall so they can't spill.

She returns. "Thank you, honey. Here. Section sixty-three will have all the information you need." She drops a giant scroll I've seen in Dad's office on the table.

I gawk. She smiles, looking proud, and returns to wrapping the fish by hand instead of using magic.

"Uh. Okay."

"Let me know if you have any questions," she chirps, not looking at me.

I take the scroll and settle onto the couch. What I find in section sixty-three is nothing like I expected. No matter the direction I look at the diagrams, they don't make sense. There are words I don't understand.

But once I'm through with it, I sit back, shocked—no wonder Freylin didn't want to explain this and my dad escaped to the yard.

My hands are clammy, and I can't seem to get enough air in my lungs. It's a literal joining of bodies in the most unlikely of places. And that's an expression of love? Seems more like a torture method.

Suddenly, I gasp and sit up. Do my parents do this? I was born, so they had to have.

My hand flies to my mouth. I think I'm going to be sick.

I leave the scroll on the couch and escape to my bedroom. How am I ever going to look at them the same ever again? A shiver runs through me just as Beau bounds through my window. I look at him and then out the window. Animals do it, too. I've seen it. I didn't know at the time. I thought the wild dogs were simply playing, but no. No. They were *not* playing. And they were not enjoying it either.

I gag and fall onto my bed. No way am I doing that with Alexi. No. Freaking. Way.

I pull the pillow over my face and scream.

17

THEO

"What is it, sweetheart?" Ma asks without turning. I step off the porch and hover over her shoulder. She's sitting on a stool with a canvas in front of her, painting a familiar monkey. Her movements are fluid as she combines different shades of brown and yellow, sweeping her hand across the canvas.

"Beau?" I ask.

"I just had to. That little monkey is too adorable. Do you think she'll like it?"

"Will Izalia like it?" I repeat, a little dazed.

"Yes. Izalia. Who else would I be talking about who has a pet monkey named Beau?"

"I'm just a little confused. I thought you didn't like her."

Ma straightens and places the paintbrush down on her palette with a little sigh. Her hair is pulled up into a bun, a few pieces falling into her face. "Well, you thought wrong. Now, do you think she'll like it?" She searches my face sincerely and that's when I realize that this is an *I'm sorry* gift. She tends to present her real emotions through her paintings.

I take another look at the painting. Even though the monkey takes center stage in the portrait, the profile of Izalia's face is in the background, as if he's sitting on her shoulder. She has a faraway expression, and I reach out to touch it without thinking.

Ma swats my hand away. "It's still wet, Theodore!"

I mumble an apology and tell her I think she'll love it, again lost in Izalia's eyes through the painting.

"It just needs to dry until tomorrow, and then you can give it to her." She peeks at me.

I try to control whatever emotion is on my face. "It's from you, though," I respond.

Brown paint dots her nose and cheeks as she faces me. It would be strange if she weren't covered in color. "Do you like her?" she asks, ignoring my comment.

There's no hiding my emotions as I make a noise in the back of my throat.

She smiles. "Hmm. Pa was right. Don't tell him I said that." She turns back to her painting. "Then it's from the both of us. Give you another chance to see her. You deserve to be happy." Emotion fills her voice on the last word, and my heart falls into my stomach.

For reasons unknown, she's warmed up to Izalia, only for it to be for nothing. I should have expected that Izalia would be matched with somebody. I know the customs, but it still hurts. Even more, now that I know I'm in love with her.

I hate that I've been moping since she told me yesterday. But I do plan on keeping my promise of being friends. Her happiness is the only thing that matters. I wonder if it would change anything if I told her my revelation about us as kids. She may already know, but I have a feeling she doesn't remember, either because she was too young or because of her memory loss. I'm the only one on the island with my colored hair, and she has never mentioned meeting me before.

I scratch the back of my head. "That's what I wanted to talk to you about."

"You have nothing to worry about. Your dear old Ma won't get in the way of you wanting to be…friends with that girl."

I swallow. "What about going into the city?"

Her hand freezes mid-motion, and she slowly leans back with a sigh. "I think this is a discussion that needs to include Pa."

I'm not sure why. He agrees with Ma about everything anyway. Well, except for lately. Was he the one who convinced Ma that Izalia was trustworthy?

"At dinner," she says and returns to her painting. "Which reminds me. Can you go into market and grab some cod?"

"Sure," I murmur and head towards our shed, nestled in the trees.

The shed door creaks open, which is little more than a piece of driftwood, flooding our trading items with light. I fill a sack with potatoes and carrots and grab a painting from the pile Ma saves for market. It's more than enough for fish, but Divina are expert bargainers, and I always leave with more items than planned.

I close the door when a chirp catches my attention. Two yellow eyes blink at me from the dark. I sigh and open the door wider to see what creature is trying to steal from us. A coati is sniffing around the storage bins of food Pa receives from his farm caretaker duties.

I shoo it away with my foot, but with my arms full, I swing off balance and connect with one of the bins. They topple over, almost landing on the creature and revealing a host of yellow eyes.

I inhale sharply, preparing to fight off the coati with some potatoes, but freeze when I notice how small the eyes are. Burrowed behind the bins are a bunch of babies. The mother's striped tail curls around them, eyeing me over her long snout. Typically, I would have scattered them, but instead, I grab a few carrots, replace the lid, and place them on the ground.

I start down the path with a smile, because I know Izalia would have done the same. If I want to be a true friend to her, I need to overcome my fear of the city. I can't stay isolated on this part of the island forever. It's foolish to think, but if those Divina were to get to know me, maybe I could be accepted like I sort of am here. I could have a proper life, a place amongst those who despise me. It's more than foolish, an impossible dream, and hope can be a cruel thing.

The trees part as the village of Avalon opens up. The scents of flowers, fresh fruit and vegetables, fish, and the woodsy aroma permeating every corner of this island waft through the air. The largest fale of the isle hosts market—the thatched roof ruffles in the breeze. Divina line the oval-shaped rocky floor with their tables with various goods. I've been coming to this market since I was a young boy. The Divina in the city might not accept me, but here, among those who were deemed outcasts of their people, I'm at least acknowledged as the son of Iris and Boaz.

"Hey, Dali," I say, passing the old woman who sells flowers fashioned into leis and crowns.

She flashes me a toothy smile and holds a bright purple and orange lei.

I raise my hand. "My mom still has the last one I got from you. But that one is quite beautiful. Very tempting." I'm one of her few customers ever since she tried to trade mainland objects she found washed ashore. Most people forgave her memory lapse, but the city Divina don't take too kindly to such disobedience. As a boy, I would collect things I found washed ashore, none the wiser that some objects I collected were forbidden. I still have them, but they're nothing compared to the treasures Ma saved for me from the wreckage.

She smiles wider. "Such goodness in you. Even the palm trees dance in your presence." Then, her face falls as she leans closer. "Keep your chin high, boy. The stars are speaking, and the sea is hungry. She won't forget, though. The belly of the sea will forthcome anew."

A chill runs through me as I nod. I don't have the faintest clue what she's talking about, but I don't think I want to know. Delusional Dali is the oldest person on this island, over a hundred for sure. The age comes with its quirks. I feel her eyes on me as I pass the fruit stand.

"Theo! I've got your favorites today." Yosef waves me over, holding up a basket of green and red mangoes, my weakness.

"Okay, okay, I'll take a pound. Potatoes or carrots?"

Yosef eyes the painting in my other hand and smiles when I offer it to him instead. "This one is a beauty," he says.

I didn't even look to see what this painting held. Expecting the usual landscape, I jolt when I see a storm-tossed sea, a ship amongst the waves. Huh. Not Ma's typical earthy paintings.

I thank him and drop the bag of mangoes into the bottom of my knapsack, following the scent of fish. I wave at those who say hi but try not to stop again. They'll take all my vegetables before I reach the fish, and Ma will be upset.

"Three cod, please."

"It's your lucky day. We only have four left."

"Oh, good. Ma might serve *me* for dinner, otherwise," I chuckle.

Quill laughs like it's the funniest thing he's heard all day and wraps the fish for me in palm leaves. Somebody throws an arm around my shoulders.

"Where have you been, my man?"

I shrug Ainzel off of me. I still haven't forgiven him for his stunt at the bonfire. "Here."

He leans against the Fisherman's table, narrowing his eyes. "No, you haven't. Could it have anything to do with a special green-eyed girl?" He wiggles his eyebrows.

I'm about to say something stupid when a warm sensation prickles the nape of my neck. A smile grows on Ainzel's face, and I know without looking.

I turn slowly, trying not to seem too desperate to see, but fail. She's as radiant as the sun and more beautiful than any other girl I've seen stand on this dirt-crusted, pebble floor.

Izalia.

In my market.

Staring straight at me.

Others walk around her, as if they don't see what I see. That she's a beacon of light, pulling me home. Her face breaks into a smile as she waves.

"Oh. You've got it bad." Ainzel snickers behind me, but I ignore him as my feet take me to her.

Her eyes dart around us as she meets me halfway. She opens her mouth to say something when a faraway expression washes over her face—like when she had that flashback.

She blinks a moment later. "I was hoping to see you here," she says, but her eyebrows draw together.

I don't think I'll ever get over this woman wanting to be my friend, let alone see me. "Did you have another flashback?"

"Something like that, just a snippet of something." She blinks again before smiling.

"I'm glad you're here." *I'm in love with you, please stay* is what I really want to say

"Well, we're friends, right?" She nudges my side, sending heat crawling through my body.

I remember too well how it felt to have her in my arms. I banish the thought—just friends.

I nod as two people come up behind her. The woman looks like a slightly older version of Izalia, but not that much older. Honestly, they could probably pass for sisters. Her hair is braided down one side, with flowers woven throughout. The dark locks fall into a basket at her hip. The man has a bored expression as he looks around the market. Izalia has his nose. Must be her parents.

Dread swirls in my stomach as I wait for them to look at me disdainfully.

"Izzy. Do you know this b—" her mother begins but freezes mid-sentence as she peers at my light hair and eyes and cocks her head. Her eyes light up. So similar to Izalia's.

"You're the Nomagi boy! Oh, how are your parents? I miss them."

Izalia looks as stunned as I feel.

She looks her mother up and down. "You know his parents?"

"Of course, Izzy. His mother and I grew up together."

Her jaw drops, but she snatches it closed. I sometimes forget that my parents had lives before me. They were city folk and chose to come to this part of the island to shield me from those who would never understand. I don't know what their assignments were, but I'm sure they were much better than a caretaker and trader.

A gnawing in my gut begins, and I feel the weight of the knowledge on my shoulders. What would their lives have looked like if I hadn't come along and ruined them?

"You three must come to dinner. Tomorrow night!" her mother exclaims.

"Oh. Uh…okay," I stutter because how could I say no to Izalia's mom?

"Mom," Izalia says.

She looks at her daughter for the first time. "What?"

"His name is Theo."

She glances at me and back at her daughter. Awareness and suspicion alighting her narrowed eyes. "You two have already met?" She eyes Izalia for a moment before turning to me. "It's nice to meet you. How long have you known my daughter?"

It feels like a loaded question.

"Just a couple days," Izalia pipes up.

Her dad has been silent, studying me—or more like scrutinizing me. I work to keep my hands loose at my sides to appear like I'm not on the verge of an anxiety attack.

"I actually ran into him when I came across your birthday present."

A very loose rendition of the truth.

"Really? Well. You both will have to tell me more about it at dinner tomorrow. We must be going." She grabs her daughter's arm and pulls her away.

Izalia barely gets to wave goodbye. Her dad stands before me. I'm sure I'll melt under his gaze, but before I do, he smiles and pushes out his hand.

"Good to meet you, boy."

I take it, and he squeezes a little too hard before he strolls after them.

I release a breath and hurry home. But first, I swing by Dali, exchanging my few leftover vegetables for the lei. I'm not going to show up for this dinner empty-handed. And I doubt it would be the best time to present my mother's painting. *Hey, Izalia's parents, my parents have already met your daughter, and we've been hanging out secretly. Here's a painting!*

Ma doesn't bring up the whale in the room, so I don't either, as I help prepare dinner. The routine is soothing—cutting vegetables, separating the cream from the coconut milk, mixing it all, and moving my hands repetitively. Before long, my hands itch to return to my piano. I haven't gotten a chance to play today.

Ma notices my longing looks and shoos me away. "Give me something calming, sweetie."

I smile as I place my hands on the keys. I don't have to watch my fingers glide over the keys. I create a new song, combining the gentle rustling of palm leaves and the subtle sounds of seashells clinking together in the tide to make a soothing symphony. The music flows through the room like a warm breeze. Soon, I don't have to think. Images, colors, and melodies fill my mind.

What feels like only a moment later, Ma taps my shoulder. "Dinner's ready."

As the music dies out, the anxieties from earlier return to me like a sharp pain. Strangely, I realize the pit of loneliness isn't there like it used to be. I wonder if that could be from Izalia.

I follow her outside and slump into my chair. "This smells delicious, Ma."

I take a bite. It tastes delicious, too. I savor the tangy and subtly sweet flavors as my mom clears her throat.

She places a hand on my pa's arm. "Theo wants to talk to us about something."

Pa freezes with his spoon in his mouth and then pulls it out slowly.

I sit up, taking a sip of water. Might as well get straight to it. "Izalia's parents have invited us over for dinner tomorrow."

Ma doesn't hide the surprise on her face. I doubt it's what she expected. When I mentioned going into the city, this definitely wasn't the idea. Pa's eyes widen a fraction, but that's the only change on his face.

"I ran into them at market, and they invited us." I shrug nonchalantly and take another bite of fish, hoping that, if I don't make it a big deal, it won't become a big deal.

Ma shares a look with Pa. "What do you think?"

He shrugs. "Well, if they invited us. It's rude to turn down an invitation." Then he digs into his food like we're talking about his morning pruning at the farm.

Ma glances back and forth between us. "That's it?"

We both stop chewing and look at her.

"Oh! Her mom also said you grew up together or something." I smile, hoping that tidbit helps but she frowns.

"It's dangerous," she says quietly.

"I think it's time, Iris. We can't keep the boy hidden forever."

"Why not?" She lifts her chin in challenge.

"He'll be twenty in a few months. He's a man. He doesn't want to live with his parents forever. Do you?" He looks at me, and I stiffen. "This is his chance to meet a girl. Have his own family."

"Boaz," Ma hisses.

She looks at me, then back at my dad. I know what she's thinking. I can't ever have a family, not with children at least. Not here. It would be an abomination. Taint their pure blood.

"I'm sorry," Pa murmurs. "I just wish... Damn." He stands up, rage lining his face. He suddenly looks so much older. Years of bottled annoyance rise to the surface. I've never seen Pa angry before. "Damn, these people. Damn, this island! Maybe we should just leave." His voice rises with each curse.

Ma stands. "You don't mean that."

"I do! Our son can never live a normal life. Let's go. We've talked about it before."

Ma's frown deepens, and her eyes are pained. Pa is red in the face, accentuating his white hair.

I look between the both of them. I could probably count on one hand the number of times my parents have argued, but nothing like this. I'm not sure what to do.

So, I do what any red-blooded male would do and take another bite of food—wrong move.

Ma whips her head at me. I definitely shouldn't have moved.

"Do you *want* to leave?" Her voice is strained.

I look between them as silence stretches between us. "This is my home," I say finally.

"Sit down, Boaz. Let's finish our food."

Pa sits obediently, but his face twists in irritation. The fury fades as fast as it appeared. We all finish eating in silence, the air heavy between us.

"We'll go," Ma finally says without looking up.

Pa and I share a look over our food. *We'll go, but I'm not happy about it,* is what we both know she's trying to say. And when Ma isn't happy, nobody is happy.

18

AZALIA

Setting the table, I try to look like a cool spring morning instead of like the storm raging inside me.

When I convinced my parents to visit the market on the other side of town, I wanted to run into Theo, but this was the last thing I expected. Hopefully, his parents aren't mad at me. They didn't want me to tell anyone about Theo.

This is different, though. My parents already knew. It makes sense that they knew. How would people forget about a ship crashing onto our island and a Nomagi boy living amongst us? They just don't openly discuss it—as if, if they don't talk about it, the problem will disappear.

Then there is the flashback I had in the market. In it, I was little again, standing in the same spot with my parents, looking for somebody in the market. It feels important, and somehow, I know it's attached to the first flashback I had a couple of days ago about me in the city. Every time I'm about to figure it out, the memory slips away again. It's infuriating.

My mom trails after me, fixing the dishes that I set down. I'm so lost in my head, I don't realize I'm setting the table wrong.

"Do you want to do it?" I ask with a sigh.

"No."

I roll my eyes and continue as she follows after me. I purposely start placing the forks sideways and the cups upside down. She chuckles.

"I still can't believe you grew up with Theo's mom."

She looks at me, her smile frozen on her lips. "She was a good friend. I was sad to see her go."

"But she didn't go anywhere."

She shakes her head. "It's not something you'll understand."

"Then help me understand. What makes people who live on Breakwater Strand so different from us?"

"Nothing," Mom says, taking over my duty of setting the table.

"Okay then. So, all she did was move neighborhoods. You could have visited anytime."

A hard knock on our door interrupts us and leaves my mind blank. We look at each other, neither of us moving. Could my mom be nervous? She's had countless dinner parties and get-togethers and has never gotten anxious. If anything, she thrives when throwing a party.

Dad answers the door, releasing us from our frozen state. Mom and I trip over each other to get to the door.

When the door fully opens, my mom has a hand on her hip and a smile plastered to her face.

"Iris!" she coos and embraces Theo's mother.

My dad shakes Theo's and his father's hands, everyone introducing themselves. I stare at Theo, who has his usually untamed golden hair slicked back and a collared tunic on. He offers my mother a beautiful lei. She beams, thanking him.

When he turns to me, my nerves fade. All I want to do is throw myself into his arms. I offer him a small smile instead. He's here, in *my* house.

They step through the door. Theo takes in my house before his eyes settle back on me. I can't tell what he's thinking, probably how grandiose my living conditions are compared to his. How I must be so vain living like this.

I swallow. No. I can't imagine him saying any of that, really.

We all gather around the table.

"Thank you for inviting us, Ava. It's been too long," his mother says.

An actual blush blossoms on Mom's cheeks. "I know. I'm sorry. I should have reached out sooner."

She grabs my mom's hand. "It's okay. I understand."

Mom's eyes water. She blinks them away, recovering quickly. "I hope everyone likes fish!" she announces, turning away from her friend to grab our dinner and place it in the center of the table.

Theo shares a look with his mom before they sit. His dad is chatting with mine, slipping into easy conversation. I sit down and share another quiet smile with Theo. His ocean eyes sparkle. I think this might go better than I hoped.

That is until a knock sounds on the door.

My mom had just asked Theo a question and gestures toward the door for me to answer.

With my mouth full of food, I pull it open. I almost gag, forcing myself to swallow. "Alexi?"

"Hey, flower."

He steps forward, but I block his path, hesitating. "We're in the middle of dinner."

"Great! I'm starving." He flashes me a crooked grin.

"We've got company over." My heart pounds in my ears.

"Oh?" He waits for me to respond, but I don't. "Can I come in?" he asks slowly.

My shoulders sag. I don't know what else to tell him, so I widen the door.

Alexi follows me around the corner. "Room for one more?" Alexi asks.

It's so like him to invite himself over for dinner. He knows how much my parents love him. They'd probably let him spend the night if it wasn't for me.

Theo looks between us, his expression unreadable.

"Of course! Sit. Izalia, grab him a plate," my mom commands.

I drag my feet to the kitchen while listening to my mom introduce Alexi to Theo and his parents. I don't want to be in the room when she announces he's my betrothed, but it doesn't come.

I return, sitting cautiously, and take a few bites before I feel brave enough to look around the table. I quickly regret it, because Alexi is staring at Theo, whose eyes are on me. The conversations have died down, and I could slice the tension in the air with a dull knife.

"So." My father is the first to break it. "Theo. What do you do with all your free time?"

My mom spears him with a look.

Theo ignores the apparent jab and smiles politely. "My parents put me to work."

"When not helping people in town, doing his chores, or studying, Theo makes music," his mother says proudly.

Theo covers half his face with his napkin, pretending to wipe his mouth in a failed attempt to hide his blush.

"Music?" Alexi scoffs with his mouth full of food.

Theo ignores him.

But not his mother. She stares Alexi down. "He has quite the talent. You all should hear him sometime."

"That sounds marvelous," my mom says, too joyfully.

She doesn't love music. She's told me before that it's too loud and disorganized. I wonder what she'd think of Theo's music— his soft melodies on the piano.

The rest of dinner continues without anyone saying anything detrimental, so I relax, despite noticing that Theo hasn't looked at Alexi once.

My mom walks out with her famous fa'ausi.

"Wow, Ava, you didn't need to go all out for us," Iris says.

"Oh, this was nothing."

"She loves to bake and uses any excuse to show off," I tell Theo with a smile.

"I do not!" my mom says, but she cracks a smile as she places the coconut caramel bread on the table.

"Do you?" he asks me.

"What?"

"Like to bake?"

I shake my head, intertwining my hands in my sarong. "No, I never developed her skills in the kitchen."

"Too bad for Alexi." My dad snorts, helping himself to the fa'ausi.

I shoot a glare at him.

"That's not nice, Niko. She just needs more practice," Mom says.

"In three weeks?" my dad says, eyebrows raised.

"What's happening in three weeks?" Iris asks.

My hand freezes as I'm about to spoon a piece of the caramelized bread onto my plate. And here, I thought we could avoid this conversation entirely.

Alexi stands and moves to grab my frozen spoon. He finishes dishing me and then gives himself a helping. "Our ceremony."

I can't help it. I shoot Theo a glance. His shoulders are stiff, eyes trained on his plate. His parents both share the same shocked expression. He must not have told them.

Iris studies my mom. "Isn't that a little young?"

My mom shakes her head. "Not when they've been matched since they were born."

Iris's eyes grow even bigger before she smooths her facial features and nods. "Congratulations," she says with a tight smile.

As she looks back down, I see a flash of disappointment. She barely knows me, and last I checked, she didn't even like me. Why would she have that kind of reaction? Unless it's for Theo's benefit.

My eyes sweep to him. He hasn't touched his fa'ausi.

Alexi thanks Iris and sits. I can't seem to find the words to say the same.

"We should probably get going," Iris says without touching her dessert. "It's getting dark, and we have quite the walk back."

Theo's dad freezes with the spoon halfway to his mouth. One look from his mate, and he shoves the rest in and then stands.

"Oh, so soon?" My mother's face falls. "Did you enjoy the fa'ausi?"

"Everything was delicious. Thank you again, Ava," Iris says as she moves around the table.

Theo and his dad follow after her without a glance at me.

"We'll have to do it again," Mom says, standing up.

"Of course. It was good to see you."

My mom's mouth opens to respond, but Iris stares at me. She gives me a sad smile, and I try to smile back, but it's probably more of a grimace. Theo's back is ramrod straight as the door closes behind him.

"That was strange," Alexi says, licking his spoon clean as he finishes his dessert—the only one of us who has done so.

"They've been away for a while. She'll come around," my mom murmurs, almost to herself. Then she stops and narrows her eyes at me. "You've met his parents before." It's not a question.

There's no use denying it. I nod, and her lips spread into a thin line.

I twist my hair with my fingers. "You know how I told you that Theo helped me find the flower?"

She nods.

"Well, I also may have had an episode. Theo brought me to his house. They helped me."

"And you didn't tell us?" my mom says.

Alexi rises, balling his fists. My dad shakes his head.

"Since when do I need to tell you every time I have an episode?"

"Obviously, when your life is in danger, Izalia," Alexi says.

"I didn't say it was!"

They're close to the truth, though. My cheeks heat as their eyes all train on me.

"Stay away from that side of the island," Dad says.

"Why?" My voice rises.

"It's too far away," Mom snaps, even though her eyes say so much more.

I shake my head. "I'll go where I want. I'm an adult. My trials are in a few days. My ceremony is in three weeks, for crying out loud! When will you stop trying to control me?" I look at each of them.

Their faces show a mixture of anger and pity.

"*Our* ceremony," Alexi corrects me under his breath.

I bite back a rude retort and stomp up the stairs.

When I reach the landing, my mom calls me to return. I ignore her, slamming my door. The tighter they make my bonds, the more I will try to break them.

19

THEO

I stare at my coconut leaf ceiling, hands clasped over my stomach. It's another reminder of the many differences between Izalia and me. Her house was something from a fairytale. It's how I imagine houses on the mainland are—walled rooms and windows. If I didn't know any better, I guess that's where they got the idea for such structures.

I clutch the fabric of my new shirt that I got for dinner and scoff—like I could ever be one of them.

I want to keep my promise to be her friend. It's one thing to be close to Izalia when her bonding ceremony is just some distant event, but now that she will be attached to another man in a matter of *weeks*…

I swallow the anguish, remembering how that guy acted at dinner…like he owned her and was already part of the family. He's a Divina. What did I expect? All the men act like they own their partners. Izalia even admitted to it when she first told me. That she will *belong* to him.

Bile rises in my throat. I promised I would make her happy in whatever way she needs me. I told her we could be friends. But trying to keep up the facade of friendship when I'm so in love with her is harder than I thought it would be. The last thing she needs is me pining over her forever. Maybe her happiness is me leaving her alone. I can't continue to pretend she will ever choose me over him. There's nothing I can give her.

However, my heart cracks at the thought of never seeing her again.

I look at the picture on my bookshelf, the one Ma painted of Beau. I don't know if I can bring myself to give it to her. It may be the only thing I have to remember her by. I can even remain deluded that her faraway look has something to do with me.

Ma peers around the slats. "Can I come in?"

I grunt.

She sits on the end of my bed. "I'm so sorry, sweetie."

"You can tell me 'I told you so' if you want."

She places her hand over mine. "You deserve the world, Theo. I want you to be happy."

"I am happy."

She pulls on my hand until I look at her. "Are you? I've been thinking about what Pa said about going to the mainland."

I sit up, stopping her. "No, Ma. I'll be okay." The last thing I want is for my parents to sacrifice their lifestyle, their people, their everything for me. I couldn't live with myself. "It's my first heartbreak." I shrug, almost wincing at the downplay of my feelings for Izalia, letting my head fall back so she doesn't see my face. I know I'm spouting lies. I'll never not love Izalia. She's it for me. Talking like she's just a brief crush hurts.

She sighs. I don't think she believes me, but she doesn't say anything else on the topic. "Somebody stopped by. They asked if you could play your music."

I push my hands through my hair. "Sure."

She clears her throat. "In the city."

I suck in a breath.

"You're growing up. If you want to go to the city, you can go to the city."

My heart picks up. The only reason I wanted to visit the city was for Izalia. Although I do need to get over my fear of it if I'm ever going to be even a little happy living here. I'll just continue to share my music. I may not be able to contribute much, but I can change people through the talent I do have.

If I can't make a change through loving Izalia, I'll transform this island through song.

20

"Thank you," I say, twirling my midnight black dress for Beau as he jumps up and down. "Who needs a man when I have you?"

He jumps into my arms, and I giggle. He climbs onto my shoulder, grabbing my hair a little too roughly.

"Easy there."

He hops onto the bed with a squawk so I can comb my hair. It falls around my shoulders, blending with my dress, accentuated by white blossoms. I chose it specifically for Natalina's party, something she would like. Showing my parents that I have other friends will placate them enough so I can try to see Theo.

It's been a few days since that dinner disaster, and I haven't seen Theo since. Although I want to visit him, doing it so soon after my argument with my parents isn't wise. I don't want to throw myself into deep water, despite what I told them. Hopefully, Theo doesn't think I've abandoned him like the rest of our island. I'll go to him tomorrow, no matter what. I meant what I told my parents—they can't keep me caged forever.

Beau's tail wrapped around my wrist anchors me as I walk the dirt path to Natalina's house. The buildings of Crystal City sparkle under the fading sun, a full moon already on full display. Knowing many of my classmates will be there makes her house more daunting than ever.

Familiar music drifts through the air as I get closer to the door. I knock, but nobody answers. Slowly, I open it. People are floating around, swaying to the rhythm of the drums. Beau cowers under my arm, looking at me with wide, pleading eyes.

"Go ahead, I'll be fine."

He jumps off me and sprints out the door. I smile, wishing I could do the same, but the music calls to me. I've only heard it once before.

People don't notice me as I slink around them until somebody pulls on my arm. I turn and find Natalina. She's dressed in a long floral gown, half her hair pinned up in a loose braid and the rest falling into perfect ringlets. Her lips are stained a bright red color. She's gorgeous.

"I am so glad you came!" She peers around me. "Is the furball around here somewhere?"

"Outside. He doesn't like people."

She smiles a little too brightly.

"Who's playing?" I look around, trying to get a peek at the musician.

"Ooo, somebody new! Your parents told me about him. I'm not sure if I like the music or not, but it's growing on me. It's got a—"

I tune her out as a pit forms in my stomach. No, no, no. It can't be.

Without me realizing it, she's hooked her arm in mine. She leads me through the room, closer to the music.

Then I see him, fitting in surprisingly well amongst the Divina, his hair tucked under a knitted beanie. Theo's lost in the music, eyes closed. Next to him is the same drummer from the bonfire party, patting on a drum between his knees.

As if Theo senses me, his eyes fly open, locking on mine. Shock crosses his features, but his fingers continue the rhythm. He doesn't miss a beat.

But neither does Natalina.

"Do you two know each other?" Natalina asks, looking between us. I can see the gears rotating in her head and a new piece of gossip itching to burrow in.

I know Theo isn't going to respond, so I say, "Yeah. Our mothers are friends." I don't want her to look too hard into it, so I turn to her and say the first thing that pops into my head. "This party is amazing! You've really outdone yourself."

Flattery goes far with Natalina. It works. She brightens and chats about the different things she did to prepare the house.

A moment later, strong arms wrap around my torso, and my stomach drops. Only one person would touch me like that.

I twist in Alexi's arms to see him smiling down at me. I stiffen as he nuzzles his face into my hair.

"Alexi," I hiss.

He chuckles. "Ugh. I don't want to wait two more weeks. I don't want to wait another minute," he whispers into my hair, his hot breath making my stomach swirl unpleasantly.

I push softly against his chest, too well aware of the presence directly behind me. Guilt bubbles up, and I don't know why.

He leans back, his eyes moving over my shoulder. His face twists in disgust. "What is he doing here?"

I grab his hand, pulling him away from the music. We can't talk about this here, especially in front of Theo. I successfully get him around the corner.

"Did you invite him?" he asks bitterly.

I'm momentarily speechless at his harshness. I didn't invite Theo, but now I wish I had. He hasn't mentioned Theo since the dinner, and I haven't either. Obviously, he's been overthinking possible interactions between Theo and me.

"And if I had?"

He pinches the bridge of his nose, his bicep bulging under his too-tight tunic. "I don't like the way he looks at you."

"He doesn't look at me in any way," I say, even though I know he does. "First of all, he's my friend—nothing more, Alexi. And second, Natalina invited him to play music. I had no idea he was going to be here. But even if I did, you shouldn't be acting all…all territorial." I wave my hand at the tightness in his shoulders and deepening frown.

He nods, face softening. "You're right. I'm sorry." He pulls me against him again, nuzzling into my hair. "The closer we get to the ceremony, the more I feel like I'm going to lose you."

I pull back, surprised. "What?"

He bites his lip. "It's nothing. Anxiety, I guess?"

"You? Anxious?"

"I know, right?" He leans against the wall but doesn't let me go. His hands are too hot against the fabric of my dress. "That episode at school at the beginning of the week really scared me. I haven't apologized for how I reacted, though. I'm sorry. I shouldn't have told your parents my thoughts. At the moment, I was freaking out. What if, one day, you don't wake up, Iz?" His eyes bounce between mine, a crease forming between them.

I place my hand on his chest, and he holds it to him like a precious gift. "That's not going to happen. I've had this for a decade. And it hasn't gotten worse."

"Or better," he murmurs.

"Alexi! Izalia! Come on, we're starting a game." Freylin prances into the hallway. She takes one look at us and falters. "Or you guys could keep doing whatever you're doing."

I step out of Alexi's arms before he takes that as an invitation to sweep me away. "Yeah, let's do it."

I follow Freylin into the room. Everyone is sitting in a circle. Theo is playing lightly in the background. I want to look at him, but I keep my eyes on the group of people.

"Um, what are we doing?"

Natalina bounds to me, nudging somebody with her foot. "Make room, make room!"

They open a space for the three of us, and we sit.

Natalina floats to the middle of the circle. "We are going to play a game of Truth or Lie. Girls inside and boys outside."

Groans echo across the room.

"It's the rules!"

Alexi stands, grazing my arm with his hand. The music fades out.

"Oh no. You two keep playing," Natalina calls.

I glance at Theo. His eyes sweep over me before returning to his instrument, starting a new melody. A part of me is glad that Alexi has to leave the room. I don't think I could take them both in here. I don't want to recreate what happened at dinner.

We move into a smaller circle once it's just the girls and the musicians left inside. Natalina pulls out a glowing crystal from behind her back.

My stomach sinks. It isn't the first time she's pulled it out, and that event ended in lots of tears from more people than just me. But I would welcome *those* tears.

Now I have bigger things to hide.

"I kicked the boys out because I don't want anyone holding back. I'm going to ask you a question, and the crystal will tell us whether your answer is fact or fiction."

"How does it do that?" somebody asks.

"You channel your Aura abilities into it so it glows." She holds it up, and it starts glowing a bright white. "I don't remember the technicality of it, but if you lie, it pulses. Something about your brain and controlling the light." She shrugs. "Here, I'll go first. Somebody ask me a question."

Freylin's eyes light up. "Have you ever been alone with a boy?"

Great, it's going to be that type of game. I swallow loudly.

"Yes." The light holds.

A couple of girls gasp.

Natalina gives us a wicked smile. "But I'm not telling who." The light pulses, and her cheeks pinken. "Here, Frey."

She passes it to Freylin, who bites her lip.

Natalina says, "If you lie or don't respond, you're out of the game. Last one in the circle wins the opportunity to sneak into the boy's game and hear their truths." She giggles, and all the girls start talking at once. "Shh!"

Freylin looks nervously at Natalina, who's tapping her chin dramatically. "Frey, did you steal my lip salve last summer when you told me you didn't?"

"No," she responds with a triumphant smile. The light pulses, and her eyes widen.

Natalina shakes her head in mock horror with a hand to her heart—or real horror if she was that attached to a makeup item, which I wouldn't put past her.

Freylin stutters. "No. I didn't. I borrowed it. Forgot to tell you. And then I lost it…"

"That *is* stealing," Natalina says.

"Semantics," she says with a huff, passing the crystal to the girl beside her.

"Why didn't you get me a new one? You know what? Never mind. Silia," she says, moving her eyes to the next girl who's practically shaking with nerves. I don't blame her. Natalina is a snake when it comes to secrets.

My heart rate spikes with each pass of the glowing crystal. Natalina knows everything about everyone and is using it to her advantage, trying to pull everyone's deepest secrets out. I'm surprised nobody walks out. But that's the power Natalina holds over them. They all want to be her friend despite her nosiness. She has a pull to her that makes it hard to say no. I feel awful for her future match.

The girl next to me is beaming after answering her question, since Natalina doesn't seem to have anything on her. She then plops the crystal in my lap. It's warm in my palm.

Natalina rolls her eyes, and I hold my breath as she studies me. She promised she wouldn't say anything about the kiss with Alexi, so she can't mention that. I feel another pair of eyes on me and, without looking, know Theo is watching me. When I meet his gaze, he raises his brows and motions to the rest of the room with his head. I can practically read his mind. *Why are you playing this demented game?*

It's not something he would understand, though, so I look away, but not before Natalina catches it.

A slow smile forms on her lips as she says, "I want you to kiss that boy if you like him." She points her finger at Theo, whose fingers freeze on the instrument's strings.

"Wha—What? That's not a question."

It's dead quiet in the space, without the music playing. Even the drummer has frozen the rhythmic patting. It feels as if nobody else is breathing, either.

"You don't have to answer a question if you do the challenge instead."

"I want a question," I immediately respond, having no idea what she's talking about. That was not part of the rules.

"Do the challenge if what I said was the truth. You like that boy."

By the island, she's caught me. I can't win. If I deny it, the crystal will show it. And if I do the challenge, that proves it too.

"I'm not kissing him." The crystal remains bright.

"Then you're out of the game."

I stand. "Fine. I want no part of your sick, twisted game anyways." The light shows I'm being honest as I drop it from my hold and it clatters to the floor.

I walk towards the side door to tell Alexi I'm leaving, but Natalina stands.

"You can't go out there. You didn't win."

My anger rises, but I try to calm it before I turn to her. "You didn't follow your *own* rules, so I guess you're out too. Somebody else gets to ask the questions." I fold my arms across my chest.

Her mouth hangs open, and then she looks around. "Who wants to play it with the new rules? You get to pick a truth or a challenge." Her eyes land back on mine. "If you win, you get to kiss the guitar player."

Theo sputters and chokes but doesn't say anything.

I see red. How does she even know what the instrument is called? I put that tidbit in the back of my mind for later. "No way."

She smiles. "Then *you* kiss him. Either the winner does or you do."

I glance around the room. The girls are looking at Theo with fresh eyes. Some look sickened, but others look excited—excited to break the law.

I could walk out right now, but then I'd be leaving Theo to the dogs. But if I kiss him…

I peer at him, hoping he can help in some way. He watches me for a moment before standing, slinging a strap that is connected to his guitar over his head.

"Excuse me. But I actually need to go."

I hold back a sigh of relief.

Natalina narrows her eyes at him. "If you want to leave, then you need to answer a question."

He wavers.

She grabs the crystal and thrusts it into his palms.

She doesn't know.

But how can she *not* know?

He blinks at her as the crystal loses its light. The dark lighting in the house makes his blue eyes lose some color, but if you look closely…

Natalina taps the crystal, confused, and I choke back a laugh.

She looks at him again—*really* looks at him. "Wait. Do you not have magic?"

He slowly shakes his head.

Natalina gasps, stepping back like he's a bug. "A Nomagi?" she squeals. "Get out of my house!"

He dips his head and escapes out the door as the house breaks into chaos.

I slink toward the door, but Natalina spots me.

"You knew?"

I shrug.

"Ew! You get out, too."

No problem. I escape outside but don't see Theo anywhere.

I run to the trees and Beau hops out. "Where did he go?"

Beau races through the trees, and I chase him, trusting his monkey senses. It becomes darker the further I go, the moon unable to pierce the denseness of the trees. A few stars wink at me from the occasional opening in the treetops. I slow down so I don't face-plant into the dirt.

"Beau?" I twist in a circle. He's gone. "Theo?" My labored breathing is loud in my ears.

The air is thick. It's too dark. I look behind me, and it's all the same. I'm lost.

Then there's a squawk to my left. I take off in that direction, trip over a root, and land sprawled on the ground.

I groan and breathe through the pain in my palms and knees.

"Izalia! Are you okay?"

Another groan slips out as I flip onto my butt. Theo's hands slide over my shoulders. The pain ebbs for a moment as I become highly alert to his body inches from mine.

"I'm okay. I just fell."

He takes my hands. "You're bleeding."

"How can you see?" My eyes are only beginning to adjust, and I can barely make out his outline and the shape of his face.

"I can feel the blood."

"Oh, right."

"But can't you make light?" he asks.

The pain is returning as a dull ache across my palms. Of course, I can. Why didn't I think of that?

I wave my hands and wince as a small orb of light appears above our heads.

Theo's face is clear, etched in worry as he studies my palms. "Anything else hurt?"

"My knee," I admit.

His hands move to my calf to look at my knee. There's a small rip on the hem of my dress. I push aside the fabric for a closer look.

"Not too bad. Looks like your hands took the brunt of the impact," he says.

He pulls a satchel from his waist, untwists the end, and water pours onto my hands. For a moment, I wonder if he's somehow wielding water but then realize it's coming from the satchel.

My hands burn, but I talk through the pain, angling my head at the satchel. "That's cool."

"You have to get creative when you can't just make water appear out of thin air." He smiles, even though he had just been made fun of for not having magic a moment earlier.

"I'm sorry," I say as he uses his shirt to wipe my hands. He then rips the fabric at the bottom.

"What are you doing?" I gasp.

He ignores me and wraps each hand with a strip. The pressure makes it feel better, which I try to focus on instead of how my body is humming from the contact of his fingers on my skin.

He looks up.

"I'm really sorry," I say again.

A smile hovers on his lips. "You didn't do anything."

"Exactly. I should have done more."

"That's not what I meant." He grabs the crook of my arm and gently helps me up. "I'm used to stuff like that. No need to worry about my feelings. You should get back."

"I am *never* going back there," I say with as much disgust as I can muster.

He chuckles and wraps an arm around my waist, grabbing his guitar off the ground with his other hand and placing it over his shoulder. He must have put it down to help me.

I don't need the assistance—my knee only feels bruised—but I take the opportunity to lean into him. The familiar vanilla scent wafts off him, calming me.

"It's not okay that people treat you like that," I whisper.

He looks at me with a shrug. "They don't like different."

I put a bandaged hand on his chest. "I do."

His eyebrows rise. The air heats around us as I study the ocean in his eyes. The floating light orb makes them almost iridescent.

I've always loved your eyes.

His smile grows, and I realize that I said it out loud. My cheeks heat.

He brushes my face with his fingertips. "I feel the same way." He blinks, clears his throat, and turns away, as if he said something he shouldn't have.

Could he be looking away because of that disastrous dinner? Because of Alexi?

"I'm sorry," I say.

"Like I said, it's not your fault."

"No, about the dinner. I know it was probably a shock."

He's silent as we begin walking through the trees again. "It caught my parents off guard. And I didn't realize it was happening so soon," he says.

I pull him to stop so I can see his face. "You still want to be my friend, though, right?" I know it's selfish to ask, but I can't imagine him not being in my life.

He searches my face. "I don't know."

My heart sinks, but I nod. It's not fair for me to want him in any way.

After a moment, he asks, "Can you be *my* friend?" His eyes soften, but they're lined with concern.

My thoughts go to Alexi. He's asking if Alexi will let me be friends with him—as if I need his permission.

I bristle. "Alexi doesn't control me." I look toward the few stars I can see through the treetops.

"He *thinks* he owns you."

I grind my teeth, but his hand is on my face, nudging me to look at him.

"I don't want to make you mad," he says tenderly.

My eyes flutter closed, enjoying the cool touch and what it does as it spreads through my body. The coolness turns into heat as the need to be near him intensifies.

I move closer until I have to arch my neck to look at him. His hand is still on my face, the touch sending icy fire down my spine. The light above our heads wavers. An electric current flows between us, my breath catching.

Before I know what I'm doing, I snake my arms around his neck. His hair is so soft and fine as I pull my fingers through it, knocking the beanie off. The golden locks fall around his face. His guitar slides down his arm, and he settles it on the ground, wrapping that arm around my waist.

"Nobody owns me," I say, leaning into him.

Our lips are mere inches apart. His sweet breath whispers across my cheeks. I want so badly to have his lips on mine, as the electric current feels almost tangible now.

I'm about to close the distance when his forehead falls onto mine.

He exhales a long breath. "I don't want you to kiss me in defiance."

I pull back a little.

"I've been wanting to kiss you for so long. You have no idea." He releases a slight chuckle, still not looking at me. "But not like this. Not because you need to make a statement by doing it."

I nudge his chin up so I can look into his eyes. "That's not why I want to kiss you, Theo. You make me feel things that I don't understand. I…I like you. I truly like being around you. I want to be close with you like I've never wanted to be with another person. Nobody has made me feel this way. Not ever. Not even Alexi."

He searches my eyes for the truth of my words, and a smile tugs on his lips—a smile I want to kiss and kiss so it'll never turn into a frown again.

Our bodies collide so fast that I don't know who moved first. His hands trail up my back as his mouth finds my neck. I arch into him, savoring the exquisite sensation. Darkness bathes us as the orb of light stutters out at my lack of control.

The electricity between us reaches an all-time high, and my body sings under his hands. I can't get close enough.

His mouth. *By the island.* His lips on my skin ignite my body. Fire and ice mix where his lips travel up my neck, so painfully slow.

I grab his face, pulling his lips to mine. They crash against me, and I'm gone. I'm floating above the trees, no longer tethered to this world. Only him. It has always only been him. How can somebody without an ounce of magic make me feel everything?

Water, fire, earth, and air swirl and grow inside me—gathering and eating away every rational thought as our lips move against each other.

Somewhere in my body, I can taste him—sweet vanilla and a hint of mango. His hands brush back my hair, angling my head to deepen the kiss. My lips part as I savor every incredible sensation.

He pulls back suddenly, and my eyes open. The elements swirl around us, causing his eyes to widen.

"Don't be afraid." I pull him back to me, even though there is no fear in his eyes, only wonder and deep desire. A painful familiarity to my words slashes through me, but it's gone before I can reach for the memory.

His hands touch the strip of skin under my shirt, and I groan, wrapping a leg around him. He scoops me up. My back hits a tree, and I lock my ankles around his torso. I use the tree to anchor myself to him, letting him explore my mouth as my hands explore his shoulders and back. By the island, I wish my hands weren't wrapped. I need to touch every part of him.

His energy surges into me, through my body, gaining momentum and rushing out as I break the kiss to breathe. The elements swirl faster and faster around us. My hands travel under his shirt, and an actual growl escapes his lips as his mouth explores my cheeks, eyes, the tip of my nose, ears, and neck—cataloging each part of me. I give it all to him. I could never get enough of this. I want to feel everything.

The images on the scroll I was so embarrassed to read about flash in my mind, and I understand. I understand so completely. That's the only way to be close enough—to become one.

His hands travel up my back under my shirt. I need him more than I've ever needed anything.

My hands hesitate at his waistband.

He stops moving.

I stop moving.

He pulls back, panting hard. It's so hard to pull in oxygen. He's my oxygen now. I need him like I need air. I try to pull him back, but he grabs my chin.

"Izalia." My name is like a prayer on his lips.

He slowly unwraps my legs from around him and sets me down. I lean against the tree for support but don't take my eyes off him.

"Theo." It comes out like a plea.

He places his hands back in my hair, and I lift my chin, wanting more. But instead, he fixes my hair, smoothing it down.

The sensation of his hands pulling through it is electrifying, and I scrape my teeth against his chin, unable to control myself.

He stiffens and exhales. "I'm using every ounce of self-control not to throw you down and rip your clothes off right now."

I've never heard him talk in such a way, and it thrills me. "I wouldn't mind," I murmur. I cringe inwardly for speaking such things. But it's the truth. I want to know all of him, inside and out, at this very moment.

"You need to get back before he comes looking," he says gruffly.

And just like that, reality comes crashing back to me like shoving my face into the ice box on an especially hot day.

Alexi.

He smiles a sad smile. "I know." He touches my cheek again.

"I'm sorry," I say.

"I think that's the only thing you've said since you've been out here." He cocks his head, and I remember when I said the same thing to him that day we first met. When he saved my life.

I shake my head and touch my swollen lips. "I'm not sorry for the kiss." I would never take it back. I don't even feel guilty. I just want more. "But I am sorry for everything else. It's not fair for me to…"

I don't know what to say. It's not fair for me to want him? It's not fair that wanting him doesn't feel wrong? That I want him despite Alexi?

He catches a stray hair and tucks it behind my ear. "I'm going to go. Give yourself a few minutes to compose yourself before returning. You look like some wild beast has ravished you."

"Or a wild Nomagi?"

He snickers and touches my cheek with a sigh.

The rush of energy returns, and I plant my feet to keep from climbing him. I place my hand over his, holding it to my face. The gravity of the situation slams into me. "What do we do?"

He pulls back, but I don't let go of his hand. "Not the faintest idea, but we'll figure it out. I promise."

He gives me an encouraging smile and squeezes my hand before letting go to grab his guitar off the ground, placing it on his back. I believe him. I have no idea how, but I know he's telling me the truth.

I let him go, and soon, the darkness is my only companion.

My cheeks are hot. By the island, how will I hide this? I pace around the tree, trying to slow my breathing and fix my clothes. Alexi's going to know. He's going to know I kissed Theo.

I actually kissed him. And it was amazing.

My breathing comes faster. This is not *composing* myself. I close my eyes and lean against the rough tree trunk, inhaling the scent of vegetation around me, slowing my heart rate.

A branch breaks, and I startle.

"Iz! Izzy!" a deep voice calls out.

No, no, no. I hide behind the tree. After a moment, I feel ridiculous. He won't know. There is no way.

As his footsteps grow closer, I yell, "Alexi?"

"Oh, Izalia!" he yells, relief flooding his voice.

I jog towards the orb of light amid the trees above him, wincing at the pain in my knee. It's funny how I didn't feel it earlier.

His silhouette forms in front of me. "What are you doing out here?" He looks over my shoulder into the dark.

For a moment, my heart hammers in my chest. What if Theo came back?

But then he looks at me. "Why don't you have any light?"

Good question. I shrug. "I was upset. I can't stand Natalina. That stupid game! I came out here to clear my head." I harness the anger from earlier and let it build. "I just can't believe her!"

He shrugs and pulls me close. "I heard what happened. Forget about her. It was a dumb game. Wanna go back to my house?"

His house? I never go to his house.

Suddenly, I'm alert to the fact that we're alone in the forest.

He pulls a hand through my hair. I want to slap it away, but I hold still.

"My parents are expecting me back," I say, but it doesn't sound as strong as I hoped.

"I'm sure they wouldn't mind. Our ceremony is so close." He leans into me.

I want to push him away, but I hold still.

I need to think—I need something to get him to stop, to wait until after our ceremony. I need more time.

His lips are on my ear, and his hands travel down my back.

I stiffen. "I'm scared," I say, because it's the truth.

His hands freeze, and he leans back, his eyebrows knit together. Something else flashes in his eyes as he glances over my shoulder again. "Of me?"

Yes.

"No… My parents talked to me about what happens after the ceremony," I blurt out.

His eyebrows rise almost into his dark hairline, where a few uniformed hairs have fallen into his eyes.

"It seems so complicated and…painful."

He drops his hands and eyes the ground uncomfortably. It's working.

I keep talking. "Like, how is that supposed to work? Is yours that big?"

He chokes and steps back. "Okay! Okay." He pulls a hand through his hair. "I think we should get back. We can, um, talk about this as it gets closer. Yeah."

I try to hide my smile as we return to my house. He's quieter than he's ever been around me and doesn't even try to touch me.

When we get home, I stop on my porch and look up at him, hoping I have a look of scared innocence. It's not like I have to fake it.

He grabs my hands, his face pinching. "What happened?"

I pull them away before he recognizes the cloth wrapped around them. I doubt he remembers what Theo was wearing, but still.

"I fell. It's fine. I'll ask my dad to heal me." He's much better at it than Mom. Not like I would ever tell her.

I step towards my door.

"Wait." He grabs my arm, and I'm about to shake him off when he pulls one of my hands to his face. He closes his eyes as he holds it in his palms.

My hand glows bright for a moment before dulling. Then he unwraps the fabric and kisses my palm. He smiles when I gawk. I study my completely healed hand.

"When did you learn how to do that?"

He shrugs. "I've been practicing." His eyes become heated, and I waver. "I'm glad you know about the ceremony night. It'll make it…easier." He takes my other hand, doing the same thing with the light before releasing me. "I don't know what your parents told you. But I promise that…" He clears his throat and licks his lips. He looks down for a beat before he meets my eyes again. "It will be amazing."

He leans into me until his lips are on the shell of my ear. A shiver runs down my spine.

"Don't be scared. I'll make you feel things that you can't even fathom, immense pleasure." He trails his hands over my arms and leans back with a devilish smile before striding down the stairs with a hand in the pocket of his sarong.

I stare after him for a moment, shaken, and then fall into my house, not even realizing I had opened the front door.

Well, that backfired.

21

ALEXI

Where did that damn woman go?

I swear if she acts like this when we're bonded, I'll chain her to the house. Or better yet, our bed. I imagine her moaning my name, begging for me to touch her, to kiss her, to worship her body.

I shake my head and cast an orb of light ahead of me. Those thoughts have been coming almost constantly for the past month since my dad sent me that woman.

That small guilty part of me rises, but I banish it. Everyone knows that men need to explore with other unbonded, sterile women before the ceremony. How else would we know what to do? I imagined Izalia the entire time, anyway.

I have to get my thoughts under control before I find her, or I may not be able to control the desire flooding my body. I deserved her hitting me when I kissed her. It wasn't something I had planned on doing, but my emotions swept me away at that moment in her room. She was breathtaking, and something about the intimacy of being in her room sent me over the edge. I need to find her.

She belongs to me.

When I came into the house after hearing the racket the girls were making, Natalina had said that the Nomagi left right before Izalia did. I swear if she's out here with him…

My hands ball into fists, fire threatening to erupt. She said they're just friends. I trust her. She wouldn't do that to me.

Murmured voices reach me, and I stiffen, looking around. I immediately snap the light off and slink closer to a tree. After a minute, my eyes adjust.

Bile rises in my throat, and rage thrums through my veins. It's Izalia and that *thing*, embracing. It's like witnessing somebody about to die, which I *have*, only once when I was young. My father forced me to watch.

This is what you'll be doing. Do you still want to be a Protector? Hundreds of Nomagi will die in our waters by your hand.

I remember the thrill that ran through me at the idea.

Now, I imagine doing those things to him. I don't know why they allowed the freak to stay on our island.

I can't make out what they're saying to each other, but they are much too close for it to be anything good. He touches her cheek and a roar bursts from within me. I bite my lip so hard to keep it from escaping that it bleeds.

I need to see her reaction first.

She places her hand over his. Has she ever touched me like that? My heart pounds in my ears. If he kisses her, there's no holding back. He'll be dead. But he doesn't; he drops her hand and leaves.

She starts to pace, and I pull myself behind the tree. I'm going to kill him. I will slice off the parts she touched and then tear him apart limb by limb. I knew something was up, knew that he liked her. But never in a million years did I think she could return the sentiment. There has to be another reason.

No. I saw it with my own eyes. She didn't turn away from or slap him like she did me. Her hand had lingered. She didn't want him to go.

Flames build within me, sparking on my fingertips. I step away from the tree. If I give her a wide berth, she'll never know I was here.

My next step breaks a branch. I curse under my breath. She had to have heard that. I'll talk to her, get her home, and then I can intercept him before he makes it back to Breakwater Strand.

I step out from the tree. "Iz! Izzy!" I call.

She's as plain as day, but she can't see me. I throw an orb into the sky and walk towards her.

"Alexi?" Her voice wavers.

She can't know I saw them. It'll be too suspicious when he winds up dead in the morning.

I smooth my features, masking the rage burning under the surface. "Oh, Izalia!"

I smile when my voice comes out tinged with worry. This will be easy. I've been lying to her for almost ten years about the true reason she has her condition. This won't be any different.

22

THEO

The trees blur past. I can't control the air around me, but I swear I'm floating. I'm flying through the stars above, breathless and euphoric. My skin prickles where she touched me. I want to turn around, run back to her, and never let her go. Nature sings around me—the wind whistling blissfully, the ocean humming a passionate tune, the crickets escalating the chorus. A song dances through my mind, music bursting to escape. Something whimsical but electric, joyful, and memorable. A piece that will remind me of the moment I kissed my angel of the ocean. My fingers twitch to work it out on my piano or maybe the guitar.

Tightening my hand on the guitar strap, I find the place I'm looking for on the cliff's edge. Fate intertwined our lives at this very spot only a week ago.

I fall into the grassy area near the edge, letting my feet dangle. I swing the guitar into my lap and settle it on my chest, neck in hand. The song flows easily through me as I strum, the ocean ebbing and flowing with the melody. I get to the final chord and pause, not quite sure how to finish it.

Instead, I place the guitar next to me and lie back to stare at the stars.

Izalia's voice returns to me. *What are we going to do?*

I know I can't be with her, but a small crazy part of me wonders—what if I can? Would her parents force her to be with that guy?

We could go to the mainland. Run away.

No. I can't do that to her or my parents. This is her home. These are her people.

Searching the stars, I study the constellations, hoping they'll give me a sign. With a sigh, I look to the never-ending expanse of sea instead. The moon is bright, and I watch the white caps breaking against the distant rocks. A whole world filled with people like me are out there, possibly even those who share my blood. Usually, the hole in my chest bleeds at the thought, but—

I sit up, grabbing my chest. It's barely there. The pain I feel whenever I think about my biological family is better. Has Izalia filled that hole somehow? Ma and Pa chose me as a helpless infant, and I will forever be grateful for their love, but to be chosen as a man? I didn't realize how much I needed that—for somebody besides my parents to want me, to see me.

I stand with a sudden determination. Am I ready to see it without a massive anxiety attack? To finally move on?

I don't give it a second thought before I'm running.

I only know where to go because Ma and Pa told me never to come here. Pushing down the guilt, I touch the wall of rough rock, taller than twice my height. I can't climb it. There has to be a way around it.

Walking along, I slide my hand, looking for a break. When I stumble, I move the small boulder I tripped on with my foot and find a crumbling hole, probably too small to fit, but if I don't at least try...

I suck in my chest—like that does anything—but it does make me *feel* smaller. Getting on my hands and knees, I knock rocks out of my way with a grunt as I climb through. A part of me yells to turn back, but I ignore it.

The jagged pieces catch and rip my clothes, drawing blood. I think of Izalia climbing down the rock face to get that flower for her mother despite her ailment. She can do anything she puts her mind to, and so can I. I've lived in fear for too long, and it's time to break free.

I shove through the last part of the wall and fall into the sand, grateful for a soft landing. The ocean opens up before me.

At first, I don't see anything but more rocks. I draw closer, the sand crunching softly underfoot until it gives way to rocks and seashells. I try to keep my footing with only the moonlight to guide my way. The last thing I need is a broken ankle. I'd just be a useless sack of potatoes for weeks. I once broke my arm trying to prove that I could do things the Divina can, cliff-jumping into the ocean, but all I proved was how weak I am. Ma tried to heal me with the magic, but it did nothing. Magic calls to magic, and I have none. Coming here in the dark is even more dumb than cliff-jumping.

A shape that looks like the bow of a ship reaches into the sky, and my breathing falters. I head that way, shadows stretching around me like giant fingers. I step carefully, but flimsy shells break under me, causing me to trip repeatedly. Parts of the island can be rocky, but a beach covered in giant fragile seashells is odd.

Climbing over a massive log in my path, I close the distance and stand before what must have been a beautiful ship. I can make out the outline of a hull, broken in two, though the bow seems intact.

This is it. A shudder runs through me. This is where I came from.

The wreckage spreads in each direction. How did I survive this? The impossibility of it is all-consuming. Emotion builds in my chest. A tear runs down my cheek as I place my palm on a piece I can reach. I can't get much closer in the dark.

I close my eyes and think of those pictures in my box and what could have been. I let go of each version of those lives—along with the questions that will never be answered. A life on the mainland wasn't meant for me. I must have come here for a purpose. Because why would I survive when nobody else did?

Could Izalia be that purpose? Could Pa be right when he told us the island brought us together?

I touch my lips, feeling her heat again, and my fingers ache as another song bursts to escape. A song full of hope and love and shared promises.

I need to tell Izalia that I love her.

Turning too quickly, I stumble over a rock or a piece of wreckage, my hands smashing into more seashells. I fist them in frustration, and they crumble into dust.

I stiffen. Seashells don't do that.

Sitting up, I gently grab one nearby. A scream works up my throat as a noseless face looks back at me. No. Not a face. A *skull*.

I jump away from it, taking in my surroundings with new eyes. These aren't seashells and rocks. These are bones.

I gasp, clutching my chest. It can't be. Bones scatter the land, making up the entire beach where there isn't…more wreckage. So much wreckage surrounds me. Parts of propellers and anchors shine in the moonlight—the outline of more hulls, sterns, and bows.

Unable to stop the contents of my stomach from rising, I wretch all over the ground.

I wipe my mouth with shaking fingers. This isn't just where *my* family's ship crashed. This is where they *all* crashed.

This is a graveyard—a graveyard of my people.

I'm running, not paying attention to my surroundings, blind with terror, anguish, and hatred. Branches slash at my face and arms. I don't care. I'm numb until smoke begins to choke me. I don't stop, though, even as dread clenches my heart. A knot forms in my stomach, telling me something is wrong. I need to get home.

But the closer I get, the thicker the smoke becomes as if—

No.

I fall into the clearing with a gasp. Flames billow out from the top of our fale. Half has already collapsed into rubble, and the other half is charred.

I rush toward it, but the heat is unbearable, smacking me in the face.

"Ma! Pa!" What if they're still inside? What if—

My heart stalls. They have to be alive. They have to.

I run around the corner to look for a better opening and spot two familiar silhouettes. Relief floods my body. Neighbors have joined them as they blast the fire with a constant stream of water flowing from a small creek that passes our home on its way to the ocean. The angry flames are eating away at everything in their path, a force to be reckoned with.

More people run down the path that leads to our house. I do nothing but watch in horror, helpless with my lack of water-wielding abilities.

I run to Ma. "What happened?" I yell.

She shakes her head as her face twists in concentration, orange and red reflecting in her dilated pupils. More people join my parents, wielding their power, while I do nothing.

Shame eats at me, because I can't do anything to help keep my childhood home from burning to the ground.

I'm useless.

Finally, after much too long, the flames begin to recede. Everything we own is gone. My mother's paintings, pictures of my brother, my piano, the things they saved from the wreckage, memories of where I came from, and the knowledge of my birth parents. All of it burning away.

I fall to the ground, unable to support my weight any longer. I can't tear my eyes away from the fire until every last flame is extinguished.

Eventually, somebody pulls on my arm.

"It should be safe to enter now. You want to come with us to see…to see…" Pa stutters, not finishing the sentence.

To see what pieces of our family survived the fire?

I nod. Or at least I think I did, as I'm now stepping over piles of rubble, one of which, I realize, is our couch. A flash of what looks like white bones startles me out of my shock. I shake my head. There are no bones in here. My parents are unharmed.

It's all too much. In a daze, I look at the sky. The stars are inside my home. Half the pillars are burnt rubble, but some still stand, charred at the tops. The fumes give me an instant headache, and the ash gathers in my throat. I cough it out.

A tiny bubble of hope rises to the surface when I see the bamboo slats that should have gone up in flames. Impossibly, they are unscathed.

My vision blurs as I trip behind them to my piano. I place a shaky hand on the ashy surface. Remarkably, it's okay, except for a thick layer of ash. I would cry tears of joy if my body weren't so numb.

Pa places a hand on my shoulder.

"How?" I look at him.

His eyes go to Ma.

"While everyone was helping to put out the flames, I focused on keeping these walls moist," she says, her eyes glistening.

Not only did my piano make it, but many of Ma's paintings were attached to the bamboo. They didn't all perish.

My mother bursts into tears as she embraces my father. When she finally releases Pa, she gathers the pictures, leaving black ghostly images of her paintings on the wall. Some around the rim of the space are unrecognizable, the edges curled in black, only a detail or two visible.

Pa places his hand over hers. "There will be time for that."

She shrugs him off. "I have to get them out of here." She sniffles.

He holds his arms to her, and she gratefully fills them with pictures.

I tenderly lift the lid on the piano. The keys are unscathed. I press a few. Sounds ring out, but they sound so eerie in the space that I stop. The phantom of the euphoric song in my head returns. How could I have felt such joy only moments ago? Going from one of the highest of highs to the lowest of lows in minutes is the epitome of human happiness. Joy can be snuffed out so easily.

I close the lid and blow the ash from the top when a breeze picks up, scattering the rest. I shoot a grateful look to Pa, who has paintings stacked to his chin.

"What happened?" I ask again.

Part of me wants to ask about the graveyard—if they knew—but as Ma turns, the sorrow in her face breaks what's left inside me.

"Somebody *did* this," she murmurs.

"What? Who?"

"Now, Iris, we don't know that for sure," Pa cautions.

"Oh? And how often does somebody's roof spontaneously combust?" she quips.

Then her face softens. She opens her mouth again, but Pa balances the paintings in one hand, no doubt using some Aura magic, and palms her face with the other.

"We'll just rebuild. We did it once. We can do it again," he says with conviction.

Ma's expression is pained as she looks at Pa, but she nods.

Anger threatens to overtake me, so I leave the room. I can't stand the smell of burnt memories any longer.

As I step into the trees, I fill my lungs with fresh air. Who would do this? My parents certainly don't have enemies. But me? The Nomagi boy who shouldn't be here?

All those bones flash in my mind, and a frightening certainty settles in my gut. All those ships didn't accidentally crash on the island. The storms around Alohra aren't just keeping Nomagi away.

They are pulling them in and destroying them.

And survivors? Nomagi survivors have no hope here. I'm living on borrowed time and have a terrible feeling that it's running out.

I watch as the first rays of the sun lash across the sky. My eyelids are heavy, and my mind is foggy, but I did it. I stayed up all night to ensure the person who did this wouldn't return and finish the job while we slept.

I take walk number seventy-six around the property, studying the trees and the path, and then head to bed. We'd pulled our beds outside the skeleton of the house last night. The smell was still too overwhelming, and I don't think any of us had the desire to be inside.

My parents are fast asleep, but Pa will be up soon. Always when the sun rises, he's up, and not a moment later. He has been that way my entire life, an incredibly hard worker, never taking a day off from the farms.

I slump onto my bed, and darkness overtakes me before I even pull my blanket up.

When I open my eyes again, the sun is high in the sky. I blink back the grogginess and shuffle out of my bed. It's been a long time since I've slept in like that.

I reach a half-burned pillar before finally looking up, my nose stinging.

I yelp in surprise as the memories of last night slam into me. "Theo?"

I startle at Ma's voice. She's on her stool a couple of yards away, several ruined pictures attached to her easel. At least her painting corner didn't get ruined by an escaped spark. She sits under the canopy of the largest tree on our property, a table with an assortment of painting supplies scattered next to her.

"Are you okay?" She looks at me, her forehead covered in worry lines.

I pull a hand through my hair. "Yeah. Just forgot for a moment." I let out a laugh that doesn't sound like mine.

She nods with pinched lips and turns back to her work.

"You're repainting them?"

"While I can still remember," she murmurs.

I nod, not sure what else to say. "Is Pa at the farm?"

"No. He's rounding up the village."

My eyes widen. "You think they'll help us?"

Without missing a stroke, she says, "They're not the ones that tried to burn down our house."

My throat clogs. "You think somebody from the city is targeting us?" *Me.*

She doesn't respond.

"Mom, what are you not telling me?" I place my hand on her bony shoulder.

She stills and turns slowly to face me, her green eyes bright but tired. "Can you think of anyone who would feel threatened by you? Anyone at all?"

Yes, many.

Her face falls. "I could be wrong." Then she turns back to her work.

She must be thinking of somebody specific. Besides the whole island probably wanting me dead, who would feel threatened by me?

My heart speeds up. Last night, I kissed Izalia. Later that same night, my house was in flames. Did he somehow see us?

But that means if he did this to *me*, then…Izalia.

I take off into the forest. Based on the carelessness with my parents' lives, it looks like anyone who has ties to me doesn't deserve to live. Would he hurt her, though?

"Theo!"

"I need to make sure she's okay!" I yell over my shoulder.

Ma's face is stricken with fear. I send her a silent apology before the branches block my view and I race into the trees.

23

IZALIA

I take two bites of my breakfast before my sour stomach can't take anymore, and I push it away.

"Is it bad?" My mom's eyes widen in panic as she takes a bite of the casserole and then looks at the food in confusion.

I shake my head. "Not hungry. I'm going down to the beach."

"After your training?" my father grunts.

Oh yeah, my trials are in two days. I groan. "It'll be quick, I promise." I flash him my best Beau-like eyes, and he caves.

"Twenty minutes and then meet me out back. We need to strengthen that flame."

"Got it!"

I rush out the door. It doesn't take long for Beau to find me. The familiar salty odor of the ocean intensifies as I get closer to the sound of waves crashing. I break out of the trees, ripping off my clothes and sandals. My feet sink into the sand as water splashes against my shins.

I fling myself into the water and let the warm tide take me out. The water engulfs the worries that kept me up half the night, tossing and turning like the waves. I let the current push and pull my body, while fish swim around me like I'm one with the ocean, sinking deeper and deeper.

But the worries are too big and won't rest.

I remember a training exercise we did to attune ourselves with our Sage and let go of worries plaguing us. It's one of many techniques to help us harness more power by becoming one with the earth, but right now I just don't want to feel.

A golden trunk with flower carvings opens in my mind. The stress of my upcoming trials? I place it at the bottom. Alexi's reaction on the porch last night? I heave that into the trunk next.

My approaching ceremony and the night of—

I push that right in.

Next are my parents and their expectations for me. I throw them over, too.

What's left? I'm surprised to feel a sliver of worry in the corner about my condition. What if Alexi is right, and it does get worse? Or I have to give up my abilities to be cured?

I sprinkle that worry inside.

Then there's Theo, taking up the entire spot in the center of my chest. The way he makes my skin tingle and my pulse increase by his very presence. The way it felt to be in his arms with his lips on mine. That's not a worry. Just pure joy and happiness.

I can't have him, though and that's my biggest worry of all.

I haul it in and close the trunk tight before coming up for a breath. Then I kick to the sea floor and dig my hands in.

Holding onto the feeling of the sand, I imagine I'm burying the trunk, never to be found, as Theo takes the forefront of my mind. His eyes. His lips. His hands. His body. His hair. His everything. I imagine we're together and free to make our own choices…

But I'm surprised not to find us in his house, mine, or even on the island. But somewhere far away from here. A world unknown to me but safe.

I open my eyes and almost gasp before realizing I'm still underwater, my eyes stinging from the salt. I let go of the sand, and the image of us starts to fade, but I hold onto it a little longer and close my eyes as I break the surface and pull in a breath.

We're in this new world with all those strange objects from the faded pictures he showed me. There's a baby. I'm not surprised we have a child. He would be perfect. I don't know how I know it would be a little boy, but somehow, I do. A little boy with the same bright-blue eyes as his father. But what does his future look like in this unknown world? I can't see that far. So, I focus on him and his dad—our little family.

I open my eyes with conviction, blue sky stretching above me. I want it. I want that picture so bad that I'll do anything for it.

I realize I'm far from shore, but it gives me the perfect view of the island. From the jagged cliffs where my friends and I would dare each other to get as close to the edge as possible to the white sandy beaches where I have spent many days in pure bliss. Am I willing to give up this for that picture? My home?

I eye the sun. Twenty minutes have surely passed. I sigh and swim back to shore. I step onto the sand, and the trunk I buried so carefully explodes, scattering my worries all over the place. Gravity hits me, and that perfect little picture gets muddled and skewed. Dreams have to stay where they belong, only in my dreams. I tuck that picture into a recess in my mind and go to meet my dad.

"You're late," my father says when I step into our backyard.

I roll my eyes. "We've got all weekend."

He arches a brow, and I throw my hands out, ready for his onslaught.

"Two days. You have two days until the biggest moment of your life, Izzy."

"I know, I know." I roll my shoulders and grasp my flame, throwing it into my palms.

"Bigger," he orders.

I expand it between my palms, the flames reaching toward the sky, higher and higher. Sweat pools at the nape of my neck, and I hold it.

"Throw it at me."

My eyes widen. What about the target? I waver, and the fire begins to dwindle.

"Now, Izzy! Before you lose it!"

I grit my teeth, trying to gather it into a ball shape, before hurling it toward him. It fizzles out before it reaches him.

"That's okay. Let's try again."

He clasps his hands around mine, his eyes narrowed in concentration, and my new flame grows twice the size. "Now, you can't immediately release the fire when you throw it. It's all about the follow-through. Keep your hands extended. Like this."

He takes his hands away, palming his fire, and tosses it ten feet ahead of us, hitting the wooden target on the edge of our yard, right in the middle.

It takes me several attempts before the fire gets even semi-close to the target. I lean on my knees, feeling like I've just run across the island. It's not fatigue making my heart race, but the heat. It's getting hot outside, and the fire-wielding is making it worse.

"Can we do water now?"

"Yes. But only if you can pull it from the ocean."

My jaw slackens. "The ocean! That's half a mile away."

"The Protectors can wield it thirty miles out."

Welp, I'm screwed.

He sees my face drop. "But you won't need to do that as an Instructor, of course. Come on, you got this. Water is one of your best elements."

Any element other than fire is one of my best elements, but I don't whine. I throw my arms in front of me, focusing on the distant sound of crashing waves, drawing them closer.

Come on.

My arms burn from the stress I'm putting on them, until they begin shaking. After a minute, I release the water as my arms fall to my sides.

"That was close. Try again. Focus on your Sage, Izzy."

I take a deep breath, trying to regain my composure, feeling the salty air fill my lungs. The tide is high, at least. It's right there. I can do this.

I pace forward, closer to the trees outlining our yard. My dad snickers behind me.

I glare at him. "Every inch counts."

"Mmhm," he mumbles, covering his mouth.

I close my eyes, feeling the breeze against my skin, the smells, the sounds. I focus on the sound of distant crashing waves. Gathering the water, I imagine I'm a giant magnet and pull it toward me. It shifts around the branches, getting closer. I cringe when I almost crash the water-filled orb into a tree. Some water droplets fall from my hold. I pull it faster, yanking hard. Maybe if I quicken the speed, it won't fall.

My eyes peel open, and I smile as its hazy outline grows closer. My hands shake, and more water falls from the orb. I reach out as what's left falls into my palms.

I turn to show my father, who's beaming.

"It's a good start."

I gawk as I drop the pitiful handful onto the grass. "A great start," I mumble.

He smiles. "Back to fire?"

I groan and prepare my body for the heat once more.

After a few hours, he finally lets me rest.

Inside, I fall onto my bed, exhausted. Beau bounds onto my stomach. "Oof!"

He screeches and jumps off of me, curling into the crook of my arm.

"Where have you been? I called the whole forest to the yard earlier, and you were a no-show. What does that tell the other animals about me? That not even my best friend will come when I call?"

He blinks his giant black eyes at me, not giving off the faintest of guilty vibes.

I laugh, then something catches my eye. The book Theo gave me peeks out from underneath yesterday's clothes, where I hid it.

I reach for it, cracking it open. "At least these animals talk," I mumble, nestling into my bed.

A knock on the door pulls me out of the story about mice stealing from a farmer, and I shove the book under my blankets. "Come in."

My dad pokes his head in. "Ready for round two?"

My shoulders slump. "No."

He smiles. "You can start with your Aura abilities this time."

I perk up and follow him out the door. We're only a few exercises in when my mother calls me from the house, telling me I have a visitor.

"Tell Alexi to come back later," my dad scoffs at me.

No problem. But I try to look disappointed as I march into the house.

My mom shoots me an odd look before disappearing into the kitchen.

I pull the front door open. "I'm in the middle of—"

The words die on my lips as I find Theo standing on my porch. My heart takes off, and I can't help but look at his lips, the memories returning. My skin heats.

His eyes brighten, a small smile tugging on his mouth. He almost looks relieved. He reaches for me, but I step back. Pain shoots through me as his face crumples slightly, but if anyone sees us—he's dead. I check to our left and right; nobody is outside at the moment.

"Mom! Tell Dad I'm taking a twenty-minute break. I'll be right back." I close the door before she can respond.

I nudge Theo down the stairs and head for the trees' safety. I keep looking back, making sure Alexi isn't lurking somewhere.

Once we're behind a few trees, I relax but can't contain the smile that spreads across my face. He doesn't return it, though.

"Is something wrong?" I shift on my feet.

"You're okay," he whispers.

I cock my head. "Yeeahh. Why wouldn't I be?" A knot forms in my stomach.

He searches my eyes and then shakes his head. "I was just worried about you after the party. That's all."

I smile. I want to throw my arms around him, but I check myself. "Are you sure?"

He nods with a smile, but then rubs his neck. "About last night…"

"I know. I'm sorry."

"Stop apologizing, Izalia."

"I kissed you."

That brings a smile to his face. He folds his arms, and I can't help but notice how his biceps grow larger at the movement. "Didn't I kiss you?"

"It might have been both of us equally…leaning."

"Leaning?" He chuckles—music to my ears.

"It was quite a wonderful lean," I murmur, my ears growing hot.

He bites his lip, and I almost sigh.

"You still don't regret it?" His voice is rough.

I hesitate. "It felt…" I take a step toward him. "Right."

He steps toward me until we're only inches apart, and his vanilla-laced breath tickles my face. He catches one of my stray hairs between his fingers. "It felt more than right."

My heart beats wildly in my chest. There's a reason I shouldn't be this close to him, but all my thoughts scatter. He's the only one who matters right now.

His hand moves to my cheek, sending chills down my spine. I interlock my fingers in his. He pulls it towards him, flips it, and kisses the inside of my wrist.

My legs become jellyfish as I forget how to breathe. He kisses a little higher, and a sigh escapes my lips.

His eyes warm, like the ocean when the sun sets, as they rake over my body.

I'm about to lean into him and finish where we left off last night when a noise makes me jump far away from him. I look around to see Beau hopping from the tree.

I let out a breath, remembering my dad. "I need to get going before my dad comes looking for me. I was in the middle of a lesson. But thanks for checking on me."

He smiles, and I capture it in my mind, replaying it over and over on my way back to my father.

When I return to him, he has an odd expression as he studies me, his anger from earlier dissolving into something else. "I remember feeling like that with your mother."

My eyebrows furrow, but then I remember he had thought it was Alexi at the door. I don't say anything.

He clears his throat. "Now, where were we?"

I make the wind curb to my every beck and call, but I can't get my mind off Theo. He's the wind that travels through the trees, the air around my body, and the oxygen in my lungs.

The sun has dipped below the horizon when Dad finally releases me. I slump into the chair at the table, feeling like I could eat everything in the kitchen. My mom places a massive bowl of warm orange liquid in front of me, and I attack it, savoring every last drop.

"How did it go?" she asks.

I finally look up and find her eyes bobbing between me and Dad.

I look at Dad, since I honestly don't know.

"She's almost ready." He nods toward me.

Mom smiles and reaches for my hand. "I'm so proud of you, honey. How do you feel?"

"Exhausted."

She chuckles. "I mean about the trials."

Right. I haven't thought much about it. A certain Nomagi likes to take up my thoughts. I shrug. "Fine."

She leans back, fidgeting with her spoon as she stares at me. "Do you feel ready?"

"As ready as I can be with you know…knowing nothing."

She chuckles and taps her spoon against her bowl. "You know we can't say anything."

I puff out my cheeks before deflating.

By the time I reach my bed, I fall asleep as my head hits the pillow.

I dream of a golden-haired boy.

24

AZALIA

A cold breeze has me peeling my eyes open.

I pull my blanket around my shoulders and roll over to where Beau is curled. A tapping sound breaks through the space between sleep and consciousness I'm teetering on. Is that what woke me?

The tapping intensifies, and I grumble as I pull myself to the open window at the end of my bed. It's an unusually cold night; goose flesh rises on my arms. I cast a light orb into the darkness, and a person takes form below my window. I jump back before realizing who it is.

"Freylin?"

She looks up, her eyes wide and stricken. Her hair is pulled into a messy top knot that does a terrible job of keeping it out of her face, and she's wearing a green night dress. I've never seen her look so disheveled.

"Are you okay?"

She doesn't respond, just continues to stare at me as if she doesn't see me.

"Hold on. I'll be right out."

I throw a wrap over my shoulders and open my door, tiptoeing to the top of my stairs. The house is calm beyond the pitter-patter of little feet behind me. I slip down the stairs and out the door.

Freylin is sitting against the tree under my window, staring at an object in her hands.

"Freylin?"

She startles and jumps up, fumbling with the object. "Izalia. What are you doing?"

I cock my head at her. "You're under my window."

She looks up as if realizing for the first time where she is. "Oh, yeah. Sorry, did I wake you?"

"What's in your hands?"

She shoves it into her side, tucking her shawl around her. "Nothing."

I look for the brightest star in the sky. It hovers above the south tree line, telling me we have hours until sunrise.

"It's the middle of the night, and we're hardly friends. What are you doing at my house?"

She blinks at me. "We're friends."

I give her a look, and she sighs.

"I haven't been a very *good* friend, but we're friends." She pats the grass next to her, inviting me to sit under my own tree.

I oblige, but only because sleep hasn't fully faded from me yet. She pulls out a large rectangular brown shape with a long skinny, silver thing coming out the top.

"Have you seen one of these?"

I shake my head.

"It's called a handie-talkie. It's how Nomagi communicate on the mainland."

I suck in a breath.

"I found it and confronted my parents. They threatened to send me there if I told anyone, so I ran away." She shrugs.

My jaw drops. Why in the world is she telling me this?

"My parents are pretty open with me, so I didn't see the big deal, but they got really upset. I can only guess they're not supposed to have it and got scared. But still." She rubs the object and shifts uncomfortably. "To actually threaten to send me away?" She shakes her head. "That's too far even for them."

So many questions run through my mind, but I wait for her to finish.

She looks up at me with a sad smile. "I don't know why I came here, but you've always been…different. And you befriended that Nomagi boy. I don't know. I know I'm not your favorite person, but I felt you would understand somehow."

She's quiet for a moment, and I study the peculiar object. "Does it—" I begin to say.

"Oh!" she cuts me off. "There's another thing. Before I asked my parents about this, I overheard them talking about your friend. Theo?"

I nod, a knot forming in my stomach.

"Yeah, his house burned down or something."

I instantly jump up, forgetting all my questions, and run for the forest, throwing a light orb in front of me so I don't face-plant. I don't stop until about half a mile from Theo's house.

I stop and place my hands on my knees to catch my breath. Freylin pulls up next to me.

"What are you doing?" I ask between breaths. She's full of surprises tonight.

She pushes the hair that has completely fallen out of her top knot out of her face. "You're going to see him, right?"

I nod. No use lying now.

"Maybe he'll know more about this." She pulls out the device again, and I have to keep from rolling my eyes. That is the least of my worries right now.

"His house just burned down. I don't even know if he's okay."

"They didn't say anything about casualties," she says.

"Oh. Now you tell me."

"You're the one that took off."

She's right. I don't know what I'm doing. All I know is that I have to see him with my own eyes. He's probably not even there.

"You should go back," I tell her.

Her eyes are wide, pleading. She looks at me earnestly, helpless. I realize she has nowhere else to go. I really want to tell her to get lost, but a teeny tiny part of me feels bad for her.

"Come on. Maybe you can help."

She perks up. I've caught my breath enough to take off at a slow jog.

"How long have you known him?"

"About a week."

"What's he like?"

I look at her, and she seems genuine. But I also don't want to give her any information she can use against me. "He's great."

"Come on. I'm not going to tell anyone. You have something on me now," she says, tapping the bulge under her arm.

I don't respond immediately, but soon we're entering the trees outside his fale. I stop behind a giant palm leaf to survey his home. The roof and many of the pillars are gone, but parts still stand in the center where his room would be. I hope that means his piano was saved.

"Stay here," I whisper before stepping into the yard. I almost reach one of the standing pillars when something clicks behind me.

"Don't move," comes a rough voice.

I swing around to find Theo, holding an unfamiliar object right to my face. I'm staring down a dark tube. I reach out to touch it, and he flinches, almost dropping it.

"Izalia? I almost shot you!"

"You almost what?"

He pulls me to his chest, and I soak in his earthy, vanilla scent. It's more musky tonight, like he's been sleeping in the trees. His heart thrums through my body as he holds me.

I stay like that for a moment longer before pulling back. I examine his face and then his bare arms. I don't see any apparent burns, a few scratches though. "Are you hurt?"

His eyebrows knit together. "You found out."

"Did it just happen?" I ask, looking around the yard to see what else the fire destroyed. Their storage shed still stands at least.

"Friday night."

I whip my head around, almost displacing a muscle in my neck. I narrow my eyes. "I saw you yesterday."

He pushes a hand through his hair. The other still holds the silver, L-shaped object he pointed at me. "I know. I didn't want you to worry."

I think back on what he told me yesterday, how he was worried about me. This happened the night of Natalina's party.

A rock sinks into my stomach. "While you were at the party? Are your parents okay? Was it an accident?"

"They're fine, but no, it was after the party."

I catch that he didn't answer the third question. "After we…" I start, feeling incredibly guilty.

He nods, not looking at me.

Something pulls on my mind—the obvious answer to what I'm looking for. There's rustling behind the trees.

He whips around, pushes me behind him, and raises the silver device, pointing it at the trees.

"Theo, it's just—"

"Show yourself!" he yells. His tone is menacing, something I've never heard before.

Freylin dances out of the trees. "Nice to meet you, too."

His shoulders relax, but he doesn't put down whatever he's holding between us.

"This doesn't look sharp enough to do much damage." She arches an eyebrow and brings her fingers up to touch it like I did.

"Don't. Why are you here?" he says with venom.

She rolls her eyes and looks pointedly at me.

"She came with me, Theo," I say.

He studies her for a beat before lowering the device.

I nudge my way around him. "Theo, why do you keep pointing that at us? What is it?" Freylin's object is strangely similar in foreignness. Maybe he'll know what it is after all.

He flips up the back part of the silver object before lowering it to show me. I can't help but run a finger down the shiny material.

"It's called a gun."

I've heard that before. I suck in a breath, remembering class only days ago. But it doesn't look like Mr. Maleko's drawing.

"What does it do?" Freylin steps closer to examine the object, and I yank her away.

"Does that use gunpowder?" I ask, trying to keep my hands from shaking.

"No, but it has the same effect." He doesn't look at me.

"Then why'd you point it at us?" My voice rises, and the reason snaps together in my mind. It's the middle of the night, and he's out here with a device that can kill our people. He's waiting for somebody.

"I didn't know it was you," he whispers, a muscle jumping in his jaw.

I eye the Divina-killer that he's got clenched in his hand. "Can you put it down?"

He looks at me, his eyes softening. He walks over and sits on a log jutting out of the ground, placing it next to him. His head falls back against one of the standing posts.

I study him more closely—the bags under his eyes, his paleness, his hair more disheveled than I've ever seen, the way his body keeps twitching slightly. I look at the gun one more time to make sure it's not going to jump up and kill me before resting my eyes on him.

"Why aren't you sleeping, Theo?"

He startles, as if I said something surprising. "How did you know?" he whispers, his eyes constantly scanning the area.

"Because you're out here in the middle of the night," I whisper back.

"Right." He rubs his face and releases a breathless chuckle.

"And it looks like you haven't slept since the party."

Since the fire.

Since we kissed.

I raise my hand to touch him, but then I remember Freylin and drop it. He nods.

I begin to assemble the pieces but shake my head, not believing it. Somebody did this. Somebody tried to burn Theo's home down after we kissed. That somebody could have seen Theo and I together. It can't be a coincidence. And he's out here on guard like he thinks they'll come back.

"Why are you out here, Theo?"

He looks at me, exhaustion and pain sketched on every feature. He averts his eyes. "Do you know about the ships?"

I startle. "What?"

He studies my face. "The ships that wreck here."

"Your ship wrecked here. Was there another?" I ask slowly, not knowing where he's going with this and well aware that Freylin is listening.

He shakes his head. "Forget it." He stands, grabbing the gun. "I need to get back to—" He sways on his feet.

"Bed?"

A ghost of a smile crosses his face.

"Somebody did this."

He doesn't respond.

"And you're waiting for him to come back."

His eyes flash to my face, studying me.

Only one person would feel threatened by seeing me kiss Theo. "You think it was him?" I whisper so quietly I can barely hear myself.

He keeps studying me for a moment longer and shrugs again. "I don't know." He does know. I know he knows because I can read him. The realization surprises me.

He does think it was Alexi.

Do *I* think it was Alexi? He's not a murderer, unless he was just trying to scare Theo and his fire got out of control. *No.* Fire is his specialty. It would move exactly how he intended it to.

I shake my head, not wanting to believe it. It could have been anyone. Theo met loads of people at the party.

"What are you two talking about? I feel like I'm missing half the conversation here," Freylin says grumpily, folding her arms across her torso a couple paces away.

I sigh and decide to change the topic of conversation. "Show him."

Her eyebrows raise, but she jumps on the chance and pulls the rectangle out of her pocket. "Do you know what this is?"

He shoves the gun into his pocket, and I wince as he holds his palm out to her. "It makes a weird noise when you press the buttons," she says.

He takes the device, flipping it in his hands. "It's heavy. This isn't from here, huh?" Theo eyes Freylin.

Her eyes light up. "Do you know what it does?"

"I could be wrong." He looks between us, like he's weighing how much he wants to share. "But I think it could be used for communication purposes on the mainland."

She smiles at the confirmation.

Theo tilts his head at her.

"Like we could talk to them if we wanted?"

He shakes his head tiredly. "No, too far."

Her shoulders droop. "Thanks," she says, pocketing it. "Well, I should go. Gotta face them sometime."

"They're not going to send you away. I don't think they can even do that," I say.

"I know. It was an empty threat. Just something they say when they're really mad."

"Have you ever wanted to go to the mainland?" I ask Theo once Freylin disappears amongst the trees.

He looks up a second too late and squints, swaying again even though he's sitting down. "Huh?"

"Never mind. You need to get some sleep." I shouldn't have asked that anyway.

"No, I'm fine." He tries to stand and stumbles forward.

"Sure, you are." I grab him around the waist, the contact increasing my heart rate. "Come on. Are you still sleeping in the fale?"

"My parents are tonight, but—" Panic flares in his eyes as he looks around, like somebody is going to jump out and kill us at any moment.

"I'll keep watch," I say.

He stiffens and stands tall, my arm falling away. "No way. I'm fine."

"I've got plenty of magic inside of me to stop somebody," I say confidently, even though I've never used my magic to fight. I'd probably be useless.

"That's not what I'm worried about."

I study his face as he looks toward the forest with conviction.

"There's something I haven't told you." I avoid his gaze. "Alexi was in the forest that night. He was looking for me but didn't find me until after you left."

Theo grabs my shoulders, his eyes frantic. "Do you think he saw us?"

"It's a possibility." My heart drops. By the island, Alexi did this. I look at Theo's home, shaking my head. "I'm so sorry. I don't know why he would do this."

But I do know. He's staking his claim and removing obstacles, just like how his father and grandfather raised him to act.

"I'm going to talk to him."

"No!" Theo shouts, grabbing my hand and twisting me to him. "Stay," he says softer as his arms circle around my waist.

Butterflies flutter in my chest. "I don't want him to hurt you."

"I don't think talking to him will help."

"Then I'll go to my parents."

"And say what? Are you going to tell them what happened between us?"

I blanch. "I have to do something. You can't just sit out here night after night waiting for him to return. I won't ask him outright. I'll be careful. I promise."

He shakes his head.

I wind my arms around him, wanting to be closer. "But I'll stay tonight so you can get some sleep."

"That's not why I'm asking you to stay." He pulls a hand through my hair. The same heat and desire fills me like the other night. Only his touch has ever made me feel this way.

He trails his other hand down my arm and wraps it around my hand, giving it a slight tug. He leads me underneath a tree where there's a soft patch of grass. "Wait here."

He eyes the property a final time before slipping into the darkness of his destroyed home. My heart beats irregularly as I lean against the tree, pulling my thin wrap closer to my body. I won't admit it, but I'm scared of what might happen if I stay.

Those feelings that overwhelmed me the night we kissed caused me to have little self-control. I'm not here for that; I'm here to support Theo. He needs somebody. He's always needed somebody. It hurts to know he's gone so long without that. If it weren't for Beau, I wouldn't survive the loneliness of being different.

I sit up. Beau. Where is that monkey? He's been disappearing on me more and more lately.

My eyes catch on the charred mess of their house. Is Alexi capable of doing something so monstrous? I couldn't make the bond with him if he did.

And even if he didn't, I still don't want to make it.

The sudden awareness hits me like a tsunami wave. I don't want to bond with him. How I feel for Theo will never come with Alexi. I don't want him.

I'll *never* want him.

For my whole life, decisions have always been made for me. Nobody asks me what I want. I never thought to fight it. But I also never thought I could feel the way I do with Theo. I can't go back. They can't force me to be with Alexi. I want Theo. I may even love Theo.

I gasp and look around like I said it out loud. Is this what I'm feeling? Love? I'm certainly happiest when I'm with him. I only ever want to be in his arms. My body hums in his presence and aches when he isn't near. Even now, with him inside his fale, I miss him.

Theo returns with arms full of blankets, and my resolve hardens as if forged by a Craftsman—something moldable and easily shaped transformed into something stronger and more permanent. First thing in the morning, I'll tell my parents I won't go through with the ceremony. I'll be cut free.

I already feel lighter even as my gut swirls with trepidation. In the right conditions, clay becomes a strong ceramic. But with too much pressure, ceramic can shatter.

25

THEO

She doesn't know.

I didn't plan on asking her, but I held my breath when the question about the ships popped out of my mouth. I hadn't realized how much I needed the relief I got when her face flashed with incomprehension. I told myself it didn't matter if she did know about the graveyard, that I still loved her. She's the only one who looks at me like I'm not a nobody Nomagi, but an equal—somebody worth her time. I want to deserve the way her face lights up when she sees me. I still don't understand how she could feel even a little of what I do, but I'm allowing myself to hope for the first time. The feel of her lips on mine is forever carved into my mind.

She stands as I lay the large quilt over the area. Even though I'm seventy-five percent sure this is a dream brought on by over-exhaustion, I'm thrilled she's staying. Dream Izalia is better than no Izalia.

I leave her with the blankets as I walk the property again, holding the gun carefully in my hand, my finger off the trigger, but poised on the hammer. I try not to think of the fear in Izalia's eyes when she found out what it was. She'll never understand why I need it. Pa gave it to me on my thirteenth birthday, another item from the ship. Ma was against it, but he thought it was important for me to have protection while living in the world of Divina. He showed me how to use it. I still don't know how he knew, but I went along with it—kept it under my bed, never planned on using it.

Until last night.

I've never felt that my life or those I loved were in danger. Now, this gun is all I have to stand up to a fire-, earth-, water-, and air-wielding psychopath that the woman I love is about to bond herself to.

I shake my head. I shouldn't let her stay. I'm digging myself into a deeper hole that I won't be able to climb out of when she ultimately returns to him. Of course, she's going to return to him. Even if she does feel something for me, I can't give her anything. No special ceremony, no magic, no children, no acceptance. Just repudiation and misery.

But I have tonight. One night, and then I'll let her go. I have to.

I catch a shift in the trees to my left and inhale sharply, aiming the gun. A moment later, Beau climbs down a tree and runs to Izalia, one eye on me. I relax the tension in my shoulders. Nobody is out there…yet. I feel sleep pressing against my head, pulling my eyelids down. I try to blink it away as I join her on the blanket.

"You really should sleep," she says softly.

I sigh and look at her, settled against the tree trunk, blankets around her legs and Beau in her lap as she scratches his ears. This is a sight that I could never tire of. I'm even getting used to the little monkey. And I swear I'm growing on him. I haven't gotten a raspberry blown at me once.

The thoughts that I've tried so hard to push down rise through my exhaustion. How am I ever going to tell her the truth about her people? Everything I thought I knew about the Protectors is wrong. I knew that they sent storms to deter ships from visiting the island. I'm not oblivious that these storms might cause some ships to capsize or shipwreck like mine. But that graveyard I beheld was no accident. All those bones tell me there must have been survivors. But I'm the only Nomagi on the island.

Her hand is on my face, and I startle. I didn't notice she'd moved—so lost in my thoughts. She pulls away, and I grab her hand to return it, leaning into her. How am I going to tell her?

She guides me closer, and I don't hesitate. She knocks Beau out of the way, and he squawks, blowing a raspberry. A smile pulls at my lips; looks like I was wrong.

She pats her lap, and I shake my head. "I'm not sleeping."

"Just lay down for a bit. Please."

Her eyes are huge as she looks at me, and I'm putty in her hands. I would give her anything—the very sky—if she asked like that.

I sigh and lay my head in her lap. Warmth, comfort, and her distinct scent of coconut and earth cocoon me. She drags her fingers through my hair, and my eyes glaze over. Her touch is electrifying but so soft and gentle. My eyelids drop. I should tell her to stop, but it feels incredible. Maybe I'll just rest my eyes for a moment.

"I know your backstory but not the little things. Like, what's your favorite food? Color? Time of day? Game? Childhood memory?" Her voice is soothing.

I crack a smile. "Calm down, inspector."

She giggles, and I open my eyes. Her hair is a curtain around us. "I want to know you."

"Same," I sigh. "You go first while I think."

"Or sleep?"

"Just resting my eyes."

"Hmmm."

Her fingers comb through my hair. Lights flash behind my eyelids, forming pictures, and I no longer desire to open them. Her voice flows into my mind from someplace far away.

"I love sweets, but especially anything with pineapple in it."

"No wonder you liked those drinks so much." My words come out jumbled, but her giggle makes me know she understood.

"Those were so good…My favorite color would have to be orange. But like the light orange hue in the sky when the sun sets. That's my favorite time of day, too. Twilight. The time between day and night. It's still light out, but everything is quiet and still—right before the temperature drops. I could live in that moment forever."

Sleep threatens to overtake me, but I hold on to her voice like a life raft, hanging to every word.

"Childhood memory?" I slur.

She's quiet, and I don't know if I said it out loud or not. I'm about to open my eyes when she says, "When I met Beau."

"Wasn't that when you fell out of the tree?" I yawn midway.

"Yeah."

"Your favorite and worst childhood memories are on the same day?" I manage to peel an eye open.

She's looking towards the sky. Her beauty slams into me. My heart beats irregularly as my skin heats. I could admire the shape of her face, the tilt of her almond-shaped eyes, her full lips, and her perfect sun-kissed skin forever. My eyelids are so heavy, though. They slide closed, but I hold onto that picture of her in my mind.

"I guess so."

"Tell'mm about-it."

"I don't remember much, just snippets. Unlike my other childhood memories, I never fully regained my memory from that day. One day, something surfaced—Beau's face. He was just a tiny baby alone in the tree's high branches. I think something happened to his mom. I remember being so angry, but I don't know why. I climbed up the tree to get him. The moment he curled into me and peered at me with such trust in his eyes, I knew I'd do anything for him. And I guess the feeling was mutual since he never left."

Her words grow farther away until I'm certain I'm dreaming the story. I imagine I'm in the tree with her as she gazes at this baby monkey. Then she's falling, and I'm falling with her into the dark abyss.

26

ÍZALIA

The golden-haired boy sleeps in my arms.

My heart is so full I fear that it might explode. I lean down and dare to plant a kiss on his forehead, breathing him in. He doesn't move. His hair is the softest thing I've ever felt. It's fine, unlike the thick coarseness of mine. My fingers slide through as if I'm parting the water. I never want to stop. I'm not sure if I can.

His face is peacefully youthful, only a year older than me. And Alexi tried to hurt him.

Anger pulses through me, making that little flame inside of me leap. I hold it in check, which is a strange feeling since I've never had to suppress fire. It's never been easy to grasp, but I could engulf myself in flames right now. I smile. Maybe that's the trick for me—anger. I just need to get outraged during the trials when I wield fire.

I wish Theo was awake so I could learn about his favorite memories, but he needs sleep. The way he's out here, protecting his home, even though he has no magic…my heart sputters and starts again. He's unlike anyone I've ever known.

My finger lightly outlines his face, trailing down his jawline and stubble. It's light, like his hair, but it's there. I continue back up to his forehead and down the bridge of his nose. He doesn't even flinch.

I lean my head against the tree and look at the stars, never taking my hands off of him. There are only a few more hours until morning. Being here with his weight in my arms feels like a dream. A blazing star shoots across the sky. I close my eyes and make a wish.

I want him. I know I shouldn't, but I want him to be mine. I wish we could be together forever.

I keep them closed as I recall that vision from the other day, thinking about that little child. I fall asleep with more than just Theo in my arms, dreaming of an impossible future.

My eyes fly open as a weight gets ripped off of me.

"What the—?" Theo starts, half crouched on the ground a few feet away. He looks at me and stiffens, his eyes moving to the space beside me.

My stomach drops as I blink away the remnants of sleep. There is a sliver of light on the dark horizon.

Alexi stands above me, his eyes a raging storm.

"Alexi, I—" The words die in my mouth when he grabs me roughly by my arm and almost yanks it out of its socket as he drags me toward him.

"Let go!" I scream.

He squeezes harder, towing me behind him, my feet dragging in the dirt.

"You're hurting me!"

"Hey!" Theo yells. I hear him shuffling to get up and run after us. "Get your hands off of her."

Alexi stills. I freeze as he turns slowly. There's a fire in his eyes, dilating his pupils. His rage is twisted into pure hatred as he stares at Theo.

I swallow, a wild panic growing in my chest. "Theo, go. I'll be fine."

Theo is close behind. There is a glint of silver on the blanket. Theo didn't grab the gun.

A wicked smile spreads across Alexi's face, and my stomach plummets.

"Don't you dare," I murmur.

It's the wrong thing to say. He drops me and goes after Theo. Theo has a dangerous calm about him and doesn't cringe away when Alexi gets inches from his face.

"I can kill you with a twitch of my fingertips." His voice is low and lethal. "Nomagi," he spits. "No magic. You have nothing. You're nothing. You came from nothing, and you will die as nothing."

I gasp and launch myself at them, grabbing Alexis's arm. "Leave him alone."

He reaches back and slaps me so hard across the face that I fall to the ground. My cheek stings, and my eyes fill with tears.

Theo is on him in a heartbeat. My vision blurs, but there is scuffling in the dirt beside me. I scurry out of the way, holding my face. I'm stunned into a frozen state, unable to move or breathe.

He hit me. He *actually* hit me.

Theo has Alexi pinned, and he delivers punch after punch to his face. Alexi blasts him into the sky. He lands a few feet away, near the tree we slept under, with a grunt.

Alexi spits blood on the grass. "I'll admit you've got a good right hook. But sadly, that'll do nothing for you against the very air around you." He twitches his hand, and Theo flies upward and drops hard. "Or how about fire?" He snaps a flame into existence.

Anger flares, finally snapping me out of it. I dive between Theo, sprawled out on the ground, and Alexi, looking at him like he's dinner.

"Stop it. Stop it! It's against the law. They will take away your magic." I'm surprised my voice doesn't waver.

He cocks his head with a smile. "Only if I kill a Divina. He is certainly not one of us."

He pushes past me and panic threatens to envelop me. Theo manages to stand, but he's leaning heavily on his right foot. The beams from the rising sun dance off the silver in his hands.

He got to it.

"You're jealous. It's pathetic," Theo growls.

My eyes widen. Does he have a death wish? But Alexi stops moving.

"I know you saw us that night," he continues.

My pulse is almost deafening in my ears.

"A big, powerful Divina like you threatened by a nobody like me?" Theo smiles. I've never heard him talk like this. His usual quiet and sweet demeanor is gone. He aims the gun at Alexi's chest. "I'm done bowing to your kind. Bring your worst. But just know that she chose me. She preferred me, less than nothing, than to have to be around you. She will never love you." Theo cocks his head. "And you know that. That's why you're so angry. That's why you're despicable enough to hit a woman."

"Shut up!" Alexi explodes, launching himself at Theo.

A force throws me into the air, and I land with a sickening crunch. A loud bang echoes before everything goes dark.

My eyes slowly open, every part of my body throbbing. The air is stifling, but I'm no longer on the hard, dirty ground. I'm lying on something soft.

I sit up quickly, realizing I'm in my bedroom. Panic seizes my body as a pounding headache threatens to take me back under. What happened? How did I get here? Where's Theo?

My door opens, Alexi peeks in. I scramble backward until I hit the wall, narrowing my eyes at him.

"Good, you're awake." He slips in and closes the door. I open my mouth, ready to tell him off when he says, "Your parents know I'm up here."

"Not after I tell them what you did to me," I hiss.

He shakes his head sadly and sits at the end of my bed. I kick out, and he grabs my foot, caressing a finger down the inside.

I wrench away from his touch.

Sorrow fills his eyes. "I am so sorry, my flower."

Panic wraps its hand around my throat. "Where's Theo?"

Alexi's eyes darken, and he shrugs. "I was more worried about you. I went straight to you when I realized what happened, but your injuries were too severe for me to heal on my own. I brought you home. We were all pretty scared. How do you feel?"

My whole body feels like one giant bruise. "*Where* is Theo?"

He sighs and settles against my window, which is shut and locked. That explains why I can hardly breathe.

I curl my feet under me, trying to get as far away from him as possible.

Alexi scoffs. "I think I saw him in a lump somewhere."

"Was. He. Alive?" I grit my teeth, and my chest aches.

He waves his hand in the air. "Maybe. I might have seen movement. I don't know. I was a little preoccupied saving your life." He grabs my hand.

"From you," I hiss, trying to knock him off me, but he holds tight, his hand as hot as a flame.

He smiles. "Semantics."

"Get out."

Surprisingly, he stands this time, releasing me. "I do hope you forgive me soon. Our ceremony is the day after tomorrow."

"What?" I startle. I haven't been out for weeks, have I?

He steps toward my door, but at my question, he turns with a knowing smile. A lethal smile. "Yes, my flower. Isn't it wonderful? They have moved up our date to right after our trials. The council was quite forthcoming after Theo attacked us."

He lifts his shirt and shows a small, healed scar underneath his ribcage. My jaw drops. Theo shot him.

"No need to worry about me. He didn't hit anything important." His lips pull up in a way that makes me want to slap him.

"Darn." It slips out, and his eyebrows rise.

"You don't mean that."

I set my chin and lock my eyes on his darkening green ones. "I do."

He shrugs, pushing up the sleeves of his tunic so his biceps are more pronounced. "You had a few fairly large episodes while you were out. We're worried that your condition is worsening, and the Elders thought my idea about taking your magic away was brilliant. Your parents agreed that it's best for your safety. But, of course, you'll need it for the trials and ceremony, so here we are." He talks nonchalantly, like he's not crushing my entire world.

My stomach twists. "You're crazy if you think I'm going to go through with that."

He puts a hand on his chest in mock hurt after he finishes with his sleeves. "My flower. How could you say such a thing?" He drops his hand and puts it on the doorknob. "You'll change your mind, nonetheless."

"Never."

His eyes narrow. "Oh? Not even if it'll prevent the execution of a certain Nomagi?"

I gasp, and he smirks.

"After this morning's events. He's too dangerous. That's what they wanted to do. But I told the council to grant him mercy and only banish him off the island. I thought it would be a nice ceremony gift for you, but if the ceremony doesn't happen…then I'm under no such obligation."

He leaves with a wink.

My thoughts run wild as I stare at my door. The Elders wouldn't do that. He's just trying to use me. He said so himself. He doesn't know what happened to Theo. If they had him, Alexi would have rubbed that in my face.

I need to warn Theo.

I jump out of bed and hesitate with my hand on the handle. Alexi is probably standing guard, keeping me from my parents, too. They'll believe me. An unsettling feeling settles in my gut. They do love him. They might not believe me. I don't know if *I* would believe me. I never thought he was capable of hurting me like that.

I eye the window that is locked shut. Where is Beau?

I jump across my bed and try to raise the window; it doesn't budge. How did he do this? The seams are sealed tight. No. Fused, like he melted them together.

Movement in the tree catches my eye. Beau walks to the end of the branch, his tail swishing back and forth.

Get the others, I mouth at him.

He tilts his head. I push the thought out of me and into his mind. His eyes widen in understanding before he jumps down and disappears.

I could break the window, but Alexi would hear that. I glance around my room for anything I can use. The candle on my table catches my eye. Fire. Studying my hands, I wiggle my fingers. I could melt the glass.

I place my hands against the cool glass and focus on the anger simmering under the surface. How dare Alexi control me like this? Hurt me and then try to get away with it. Force me to bond with him. Take away my magic. The rage burns brightly as my hands catch fire.

A knock comes to my door, and I quickly pull my hands away. The glass had just started to warp. I shove a blanket against it and move to the other side of my bed.

The door opens slowly. I configure my face into the most lethal glare when my dad pokes his head in.

"Alexi said you were awake. How do you feel?"

I relax. "Like I've been slammed into a tree."

He nods. "Alexi told us what happened." He folds me into his arms, my face pressed against his chest. "I'm so sorry."

For a moment, I feel like a little girl again as my dad's musky smell envelops me. But confusion swirls my thoughts. Did Alexi tell them the truth? Alarm and hurt rises within me. They still support him.

"We didn't realize Theo was dangerous. We're all out looking for him. We'll find him. He has nowhere to go."

Nope, Alexi lied big time.

I shake my head. "Dad, Theo was trying to protect me from Alexi."

Dad smiles sadly. "You hit your head really hard. You even had a couple episodes while we healed you. It's normal to feel a little confused. I'm just hoping things don't get worse." His eyes are full of worry.

Alexi did it. He completely convinced them, and it won't matter what I say. They won't believe me.

But I can't help but try. I grab his rough hands. "Alexi did this to me, Dad! He hurt me."

"I know."

Unease spreads at his words.

"He said he had to throw you out of the way, or you might have been shot as well. He feels awful. Go easy on him."

I drop my hands. Alexi is intelligent. I can't be mad at my parents. There's a reason he's next in line for leadership. It's just too bad that they don't see him as the maniac he truly is.

I try to push down the panic squeezing my lungs, grasping for straws. "Alexi burned down Theo's house."

"He said that's what Theo believes as well and part of the reason he shot him. But it's not true. Alexi would never hurt anyone."

I just stare at him, utterly perplexed by the spell he's under. Of course. Alexi is the son he never got.

I can't take it anymore. I push away from him.

He frowns. "Where are you going?"

"I need some fresh air and to see Beau. Somebody sealed my window!"

I race down the stairs before he can stop me. My mom steps out of the kitchen with worry-filled eyes. I'm about to tear the door off its hinges to get out when Alexi steps out of the living room, placing a hand on my arm.

I grit my teeth, fire burning its way through my veins. I release it to where he's touching me, and he yelps, pulling his hand back. I yank the door open.

"Iz, you need to rest," he says like he's actually worried for me.

"I'm fine."

"Izzy," my mom calls.

I turn. She's standing behind Alexi, coming to just below his shoulder, her hair in its usual braid, concern lining her face. Dad comes down the stairs, watching me like I'm the crazy one.

What a perfect little picture—the three of them, I'm the one who doesn't fit anymore.

"My trials are tomorrow, remember? I need to practice."

My father wavers. I knew that would get him. "Okay, but I'm coming with you."

My mom whips her head at him. "Niko."

"She does need to practice. I'll go easy on her, don't worry."

Mom moves from behind Alexi and kisses the top of my head. "I haven't been that scared since your incident." She whirls on my father with a pointed finger. "Don't push her."

I start for the backyard, ignoring the pain in my hip that radiates up my side. If I can prove to Dad that I can wield fire well enough, he'll let me have the rest of the day, and I can find Theo.

Beau bounds out of the trees and races up my frame, squealing happily. He points towards the trees, where hundreds of yellow eyes blink at me.

I take a step back. "You did that?"

Pride radiates from him.

"Thanks, but I don't need them after all." His little shoulders droop. "Yet," I add in a whisper. I don't know what I was thinking, sending him on that little mission. It's not like they could have opened the window. I smile. It's nice to know they'll come if I need them though.

I wave, and Beau jumps off me, running back to the trees. Slowly, the eyes ease back into the darkness, and once my father catches up to me, only Beau is left, peering at us from the lowest branch.

I turn to him, feeling pretty triumphant.

My dad eyes me. "You sure you're okay? You've got to be sore. Your entire left side was shattered." He places a palm on my temple as if he can feel what's wrong with me.

"Never better!" I make a show of stretching my arms and legs. They're stiff and sore but surprisingly okay—only my hip and head throb. I'm glad I was asleep for the worst of it. "Let's start with fire."

His eyes almost pop out of their sockets. "Okay, I think maybe you should lie back down."

"No. Just feeling more confident is all."

"Really? You want to wield fire?" His eyes narrow.

I roll my shoulders, feeling for my flame, letting it course through my body. With all the rage flowing through my veins, wanting a release, harnessing the fire is much easier.

"Yup," I say as I clasp my palms and open them, revealing a ball of fire.

I push my anger into it and the fire grows, flames traveling up my arms and stopping beneath my tunic. Without looking at the awe-struck expression I know my dad has, I raise my arms and form the biggest ball of fire—a size I've only seen come from Igna specialists—and chuck it at the target, disintegrating the wooden beam into ash.

"Izalia!"

I turn, hoping he's not mad at me for destroying our target. He's beaming.

"I knew you had it in you." He throws his arm around my shoulders and turns me. "Now destroy that one." He points to the target on the edge of our property.

I look at him with my first genuine smile of the morning.

"No problem."

27

IZALIA

I was right.

Once my father saw me wield all four elements to his standards, he let me off early. Besides the pounding headache and the slight pain in my left side every time I step on that leg, the day continues to get better.

When I go inside to change, Alexi is nowhere in sight. Energy surges through me, even though I should be exhausted. I'm going to find Theo. I know it. And then we'll come up with a plan together. Everything will be fine.

I tiptoe down the stairs and stiffen when I find my mom waiting in the living room for me. Her eyes sweep over my long pants and loose tunic. I never wear pants, but I thought it was the best choice, since I may be searching the forest. I had to dig them out from the back of my wardrobe. Mom once gifted them to me, telling me it was a new style that the dressmakers were trying. They're supposed to increase mobility, but they were too hot.

"Come here."

"What, am I prisoner now?" I'm ready to launch into whatever excuse I have for leaving when she shushes me and pats the seat beside her.

I reluctantly sit on the far end of the couch and fold my arms.

"I need to talk to you before your father comes back in," she says quickly. Her tone makes me sit up a little taller, letting my arms fall. "I know you're going to find Theo." I open my mouth to deny, and she shakes her head. "I know what he means to you."

No, she can't.

"I know you don't want to bond with Alexi."

My mouth falls open, and I snap it shut.

She smiles. "I know what love looks like, hon. And I've never seen that light in your eyes with Alexi."

"Theo didn't hurt me." She has to know.

She raises a hand. "Only you know what happened. But I have to say that I didn't believe the nonsense Alexi was spilling, either. However, your father soaked it up." She sighs. "I trust my daughter. I love my daughter more than anything in this world." Her eyes shine with unshed tears.

My throat burns. She believes me.

The doorknob turns, and my mom throws her hand out. A breeze whirls around us, keeping the door from opening.

She draws me close, lowering her voice. "They're going to follow you to try to find Theo." She barely gets the words out before the door bursts open.

"What is wrong with this door?" my dad grumbles, almost falling into the house.

My eyes are still on my mother. Her face softens. "Have fun at the beach, honey," she says, even though I'm obviously not wearing a swimsuit.

I pass my father, feeling a little numb. I glance at my mother again, but she's not looking at me. She's already moving toward the kitchen, her floral dress swooshing around her.

As I walk through the middle of town, Beau catches up with me, bounding up to my shoulder. What's the point of trying to look for Theo now? And who did she mean when she said *they* would be following me? Alexi would be the obvious one. Dad? Maybe.

I peer at my surroundings. I'm at a fork in the dirt path, where one leads into the city, and the other continues past more houses, ending in a dead end. Out of the people nearby—a couple walking from the city, the child playing in their front yard, and an elderly man hobbling his way into the city—nobody is suspiciously eyeing me. But just to be careful I tap Beau's hand.

"Go on, catch up with me later," I whisper, pushing thoughts of his monkey friends into his mind.

He tilts his head at me like he's making sure that's what I want, and I nod. With a squeak, he disappears into the trees. With Beau gone, I'll be less conspicuous. I turn down toward the houses. With one last glance at my surroundings, I slip into the brush.

I quicken my pace and stop every so often to listen. The sounds of the city dampen, and soon, I only hear the forest— chirping birds and rustling branches, but no footsteps. Reaching the lake I used to come to as a child, I skim my hand across the top, pulling some water up with my fingertips. I weave a tiny tornado in the air before letting it fall.

Maybe my mom was wrong, or I lost them. No matter, I still need to be careful. I walk the rim of the lake, taking my time, watching the trees sway, bugs dance on the surface, and coati race across the field between the water and trees. My parents used to bring me here. They didn't trust the uncertainty of the ocean when I was first learning how to swim. They even taught me how to revive a drowning victim—like Divina ever drown. We're born with saltwater running through our veins.

I spot the overgrown path that leads to the top of Mt. Apia. A hundred years ago, people traveled to the top to make sacrifices to the island. It eventually became a wasteful practice. Now, once a year, groups travel up to spread the ashes of our deceased in the breeze. The island created us, and we return to it when we die. I've only been to one such event when Mom's parents died the same year. Papa went first and then Noni not long after, died from a broken heart.

After a while, when nobody shows, I have a plan. Even if somebody is watching, it doesn't mean I can't do some research. My eyes sweep the lake one last time before I melt into the trees. And this time, I run. They would expect me to go to his house. So, instead, I enter Avalon's market, looking for a different familiar face. The place is busy, and people from both the city and the strand are here. Good. I'll blend in. The breeze ripples through, carrying with it the familiar smells of market mingled with the ocean.

Finally, I spot him.

Theo's best friend sits behind bags of sugar cane, drawing something on his arm with a black-tipped feather. I grab a mango from the basket next to the bags. It must have been something they traded for but didn't need.

"What do you want for one?"

"For one? You can have it," he says without looking up.

I sigh. "Ainzel."

He lifts his head, eyes widening. "Ma, I'll be right back," he says over his shoulder.

His mother is a large woman, elbows deep in a bag of wheat. She waves him off. He nudges his head toward the back flap of their tent. I follow.

He turns on me when we're out of sight. "You shouldn't be here."

"I'm trying to find him."

"So is the whole island because of you."

I step back, feeling like he punched me in the gut. He's right. It is my fault. None of this would have happened if Theo hadn't met me.

He sees my face, and his voice softens. "You need to leave."

I shake my head. Tears prick my eyes. "Do you know where he is?"

He shakes his head. There goes that plan.

"This is all my fault. I need to find him and—"

"And what? Get him killed?" His voice rises.

I cringe.

"It wasn't nice to play with his heart when he can't be with you. And now everyone on the island is hunting him down because of your little teasing act."

I shake my head, tears spilling down. "You don't understand."

He throws his hands in the air. "Oh, I understand perfectly. I know how our people like to play games, especially you city folk. Woe is me, my life is perfect." He scowls at me.

"My life is not perfect!"

He scoffs. "Are you kidding me? Do you know what it's like to live on *Breakwater Strand*?" He says it the same way the people in the city do, with a bit of disgust. "To have your own people look down on you? Which doesn't even compare to how they look at Theo. I have nothing to complain about compared to what he's gone through, and you *definitely* don't."

"I'm not complaining. I—I just—"

"Leave Theo alone. He's not some charity project to make yourself feel better."

"No, that's not how I see him! I love him!" My hands fly over my mouth.

He blinks a few times. "You what?"

I can't deny it. It doesn't make sense. I've only known Theo for a short time. But saying it out loud…

"I love him," I say again, stronger.

But as I do, something breaks in me. I am in love with a man that Divina despise. I am in love with a man who is missing. I am in love with a man my people are trying to hurt. I am in love with Theo, and it terrifies me because it will get him killed.

I fall into Ainzel's arms. He stiffens and then slowly places a hand on my back.

"I'm so sorry! I didn't mean for any of this to happen. I didn't know I was falling for him. I just really liked being around him. I wanted to be his friend. But then he kissed me, and it was wonderful. And Alexi saw and tried to burn down his house. Then I went looking for him to make sure he was okay, and I stayed. I shouldn't have stayed! Now everyone thinks he's violent, and they're going to punish him, and it's all my fault. They should punish me, not him. I'm such an idiot!"

The floodgates have opened, and I can't seem to get the words to stop. Ainzel awkwardly pats my back as I slump into him more. He lets me soak his tunic in my tears before gently pushing on my shoulders. I sniff and look up at him.

He studies my face. He has warm, friendly eyes. I can see why he makes such a good friend to Theo.

"You're in love with him."

I nod.

"Well, that changes things." He hoists me up by my elbow with renewed energy, his entire demeanor shifting. "I need you to get a hold of yourself. You're ruining my tunic."

"Are you going to tell me where he is?" I sniffle again. The tears don't seem to want to stop.

"I already told you I don't know."

"Oh, I thought you were lying."

He raises his eyebrows. "I do not lie. Sometimes, I withhold the truth, but I don't lie." That brings a small smile to my face. "What did his parents say?" he asks.

"I thought it was too risky going to his house."

"You haven't even gone to his house to check?" He rolls his eyes at me. "He could very well be snoozing in bed."

I cock my head at him.

"Okay, that's probably not true, but still."

"You don't even have any guesses where he could be?" I ask.

"Of course I do," he says indignantly. "I just don't think it's plausible that he would be there."

I furrow my brows.

"He's smarter than that. He would be somewhere that even I don't know about."

"I'm never going to find him."

He eyes me. "Maybe that's a good thing."

I sigh. "Fine, I'll go talk to his parents."

I wipe my eyes to ensure they are good and dry and start for the trees.

"Wait, I'll join you. Give me a sec," Ainzel calls.

I hesitate at the edge of the fale. Ainzel knows him better than me. If anyone can find him, it'll be him, even if he claims Theo won't be anywhere Ainzel knows of. I just don't see how that's possible. The island is only so big.

I don't have to wait long before he guides me to the path that leads to Theo's fale. It's barely noticeable amongst the trees. The rooftop comes into view—a new roof. That was quick. I look behind us every so often, but still, nobody follows.

"You seem jumpy," Ainzel comments, looking at me sideways, his long ponytail swooshing behind him.

"My mom said they would follow me." I take a couple more steps before I realize that he's stopped. I turn. "What?"

"That would have been good to know before we entered this trap." His hand is on his hip, a stance similar to my mom's when she scolds me. It makes me smile. "You find that funny? Because they won't hurt *you*. But *me*…"

"Nobody is hurting anyone. They just want to see if I'll lead them to Theo. And it doesn't matter anyway. I haven't seen or heard anyone since I left my house."

"You don't think that's suspicious? What if your mom just said that so you wouldn't go looking for him?"

I throw my hands up in the air. "I don't know! But I'm talking to his parents. With or without you." I start down the path again.

I reach the end of the narrow, dirt path, the clearing opening up. I hesitate when I see a bunch of people, wood and bamboo flying through the air, palm leaves being sewn together by a couple of old ladies, and men carrying furniture and household objects. I look for a familiar face, but his parents aren't among them.

The air shifts next to me, and I glance at Ainzel, who has a huge smile. "Call, and they shall come."

"Huh?"

He looks at me. "My people. They're amazing."

I notice how he says *my people*, as in the people of *his* town, not the ones in the city, who burn down people's houses in a jealous rage. These aren't the people trying to hurt Theo. These are the people that accept him.

Just then, Boaz rounds the corner, his arms full of more wood to shape, his balding head glistening with sweat.

I run up to him. He startles when he sees me, shifting his weight under the wood. "You came."

"Do you know where he is?"

"Iris has a message for you," he says, tilting his chin upward toward the back of the house. He moves past me.

Ainzel shrugs as he follows me to the back, where I find his mother settled on a stool with a canvas in front of her. A small, faded picture rests on the back corner. When I get closer, I notice it's one of the pictures from their walls.

My heart drops. How many paintings did she lose?

"Hi," I say, coming up to her side.

"I knew you would come." She breaks out in a smile.

"Why do you guys keep saying that?"

She looks around before gesturing to come closer. I obey, and she leans in until her lips reach my ear. "Before he left, he told us he knew somewhere safe and said that when you came, to tell you that he's under the stars."

My eyebrows knit together as she pulls away. Her eyebrows rise expectantly. I smile like I know what she's talking about, but I'm even more confused.

She grabs my hands, her face growing serious. "I know you will do the right thing."

The right thing? What is the right thing? I have no idea what to do. I want to fall to my knees, beg her forgiveness, and ask her what I should do. But I don't. I caused this. I need to fix it.

She flashes me one more hopeful smile before returning to her painting.

"What did she say?" Ainzel says as we walk away.

I shake my head. "I have no idea."

Under the stars? That could be anywhere. I roll her words in my mind. We were under the stars together at the fire party, but there's no good hiding spot over there. Could he have meant where I fell? Maybe where he saved my life? Yes, that has to be it.

Thinking about him hiding down on that ledge makes my stomach flip, but it would be a good spot.

We stroll to the beach. Ainzel remains quiet, as I think. Finally, I turn to him when we reach the water. "I think I know where to look, but I don't think I should do it now."

He taps his chin. "I'll do it, then, after it gets dark."

I nod as the salty water tickles my toes. I peer around. A couple of yards away, a group of people hover on the forest's edge where the sand meets the trees.

Déjà vu hits me and suddenly I'm freefalling.

I land on my knees in the warm saltwater. Embarrassment blossoms on my face as I try not to look at the group of kids that distracted me. He's not amongst them, I'm sure of it. If I hadn't been looking so closely, I wouldn't have tripped over that stupid log the tide brought in.

As I stand, somebody grabs my elbow. A young boy with long, dark hair and a seashell necklace around his throat grins at me. I'm pretty sure he was with that group of kids near the trees.

"Oh, thanks," I mumble.

"No problem!" he says before running back.

I take one last look along the shore of Breakwater Strand before heading off. He has to be here somewhere. Three years is too long to not have seen him again on an island of only a few thousand. How have I not found him already?

I dig into my pocket and pull out the shark tooth. If not for this, I would have believed I had imagined the whole thing. He's here somewhere, and one day, I'll find him.

My heart hammers in my chest as I blink away the memory.

Ainzel is holding my elbow. "Woah there. You almost face-planted into the sand."

"I know you!"

His eyebrows knit together. "Yeah…"

I shake my head. "You helped me when I fell." His lips pinch. "Never mind." It was such a long time ago, and it's not like anything memorable happened. Not for him, anyway. "I was going to tell you where to look."

He tilts his head, letting the confusion stay a moment longer before sighing. "And?"

I roll my eyes, leaning into him, and tell him about the cliff in a quick whisper.

"Please get word to me as soon as you find him. And tell him…I'm sorry."

He nudges my shoulder. "You can tell him yourself."

I shake my head. "I don't want to put him in danger again."

"He can't stay hidden forever."

"I know. I'm going to convince them not to banish him."

He raises an eyebrow at me.

I lift my chin. "I'm going to use my power for good. The council wants me to bond with Alexi? Then they better give me what I want first."

Ainzel tugs on his ear. "I don't want to speak for Theo, but I don't think he would like that plan."

My shoulders drop. I know he wouldn't, but it's his only chance. Alexi played his hand, and now I'm playing mine. He's not the only one who can wield threats as if they're elements.

28

THEO

The flickering stars steady me as my emotions threaten to crash into me once more.

I work to keep my eyelids open and focused on the stars. If I don't, I'll see her face or the bones. I've been planning on asking my parents about the shipwreck graveyard but hadn't built up the courage before this disaster. And now I may die here, never knowing the truth. But don't I already know?

I swallow those deep, dark, twisted thoughts.

My teeth chatter against the cold. I don't know how long I've been here. My worry for Izalia grows. It could have been days or hours. What if she's not okay? I saw Alexi take her away. He's a bastard, but he cares for her in his own twisted way, even if it's just for his profit. I have to believe he wouldn't let her die, or I'll follow through on my overwhelming desire to check on her despite the risk.

The slap rings through my head for the fiftieth time, and I wince—that bastard…

A growl from my stomach distracts me. I should have brought more food. I suck on one of my last pieces of mango leather, which dulls the ache slightly. I pull my arms around myself, creating patterns in the lights above me.

She's okay. She'll come.

And if she does come? Then what? The only way we can be together is if we leave the island. I could never ask that of her. This is her home.

But could I let her be with *him*? A man who hits his partner?

I bristle and move toward the bamboo I collected. I rub them together, trying to create a spark. Nothing happens. I'm useless. I throw them against the wall. I'm useless to this island! I'm useless to her! Why did I ever think I could be with her?

My head falls into my hands. *You're nothing.* The bastard's words won't leave me, but he was right.

I am nothing.

29

IZALIA

I wake the following day filled with determination. I'm going to tell Alexi off, and then I'll prove my capability by excelling in my trials today. I'm ready.

I slip out of bed, and something flutters to the ground. I snatch the paper off the floor, noticing my window is back open. Ainzel. My heart sinks as I read the hardly legible sentence scribbled onto it.

Theo wasn't there.

I fall back onto my bed. Beau stretches and hops into my lap. I rub his ears as I stare at my wall. I was sure that was it. Where else could he be?

When I got home yesterday, I looked for the shark tooth from my flashback, but came up empty. I have no idea what it means or why I keep having these memories. Just another thing to add to the ever-growing list of *things that Izalia is confused about.*

I dress quickly and eat, absorbed in my thoughts. My parents left early to prepare for the trials that take place after school. They gave me their pep talks before bed. Telling me to focus on my Sage, do my best, and that they'll be right there when I get out.

They could have at least told me what to expect, but they kept their mouths sealed against my questions.

I'm not as nervous about the trials as I am for Theo. What if something happened to him? What if he fell?

My heart squeezes, and it stops me in my tracks. I place both hands on my knees in front of the main building. I breathe, keeping myself from spiraling. He's fine. He's a great swimmer. He proved that to me when he—

I straighten, my eyes bulging—when he swam with me under the stars. The cave. How could I be so clueless?

I turn, wanting to head down there this very second. No. Not now. Maybe I could sneak away during lunch. We have an hour, and Freylin could cover for me. I never in a million years would think to ask for her help, but after the other night, she owes me.

But first, Alexi.

I march across campus to where I know he hangs out. I catch sight of the back of him, lounging on a palm tree near the fountain, surrounded by a bunch of Alexi wannabes.

I walk straight into their circle. "Alexi, I need to speak with you."

Their eyes land on me, and I catch their shocked faces and smiles in my peripheral vision.

"Now?"

"Oh, Alexi's whipped," one of the guy's murmurs, and the others start oohing in unison.

Alexi's cheeks pinken, but he straightens. I look at him coldly, not bothering to hide my disdain. He hesitates.

I fold my arms. "You wanna talk right here?"

"I'll be right back, boys," he says, placing a hand on the small of my back. He leads me into an empty fale for a facade of privacy. More oohing and whipping sounds die in the distance.

"Was that necessary?" He cocks an eyebrow.

I launch straight in. "You made yourself very clear yesterday, but now it's my turn."

"Oh?" He smirks and leans into me, entering my breathing space.

I step back and curse myself. I can't let him get to me.

I place my palm on his chest and move him back. "You will march back to the Elders and tell them the truth."

"And why would I do that?" He tilts his chin, looking at my hand with a hunger in his eyes.

I quickly remove it. "I've got evidence of you burning down Theo's house."

His smile falters. "No, you don't."

"I do. Somebody saw, and before you ask, no, I will not tell you who. I'll go straight to the Elders with them and refuse to bond with you if you don't let Theo off the hook. He has just as much right to be here as we do. This is his home." I stare him down, hoping he doesn't call my bluff.

He leans back, rubbing his jaw. "You're not exactly starting our lifelong relationship on good footing."

"Are you kidding me?" I lower my voice. "You obliterated any chance of me being happy with this union when you hit me."

A muscle in his jaw jumps, then his face softens. He reaches for me, and I cringe. "I'm really sorry about that, Iz. I was just so angry to see you with him. It was a mistake."

"Nothing happened. Like I told you before, we're just friends."

"You did not look like 'just friends.'" His eyes flash.

I want to yell at him that Theo is more of a man than Alexi will ever be, that I love him, and that, of *course*, we're not just friends. But I keep my mouth sealed. I need to keep the facade up, or all this is for nothing.

His voice grows heavy. "Prove to me that you want me and not him."

I raise my eyebrows. I know he won't believe anything other than the truth. "I *don't* want you right now."

"Fair point. But you'll need to change your mind by tomorrow." He takes my hand. And only to save Theo's life do I not rip it from his grasp. "Allow me to change your mind."

I arch an eyebrow at him. "Show me you can be good. Leave Theo alone."

He takes a deep breath and blows it out. "Fine. But not because I believe your whole somebody-saw-me-burn-down-his-house garbage."

I gasp. "So, you admit to it."

"That's not what I said."

I rip my eyes from his to control my emotions. Fire runs through my veins, and I fight to force it back down. Theo. I can do this for Theo.

My gaze sweeps back to his when he cups my face.

"I did not burn down his house." His eyes bore into mine, and I almost believe him. How can he be such an excellent liar?

A wave of fear runs through me. What else has he lied about?

"Then why were you there?"

"I was looking for you." He doesn't miss a beat. It's quite eerie.

I decide there's no use in arguing with him. I've got what I wanted. I pull away. "I need to get to class."

He nods. "Good luck with your trials."

I don't respond as I walk away.

Freylin isn't here during the first hour. I force myself not to worry. When she doesn't show up for the second hour, I'm fighting to keep from breaking into a panic attack. Can I get away without her?

Not only that—I'm worried for her. She wouldn't miss the last day of school. Did her parents really send her away?

I'm tapping my nails on the desk repeatedly when Natalina faces me. "What's wrong with you?"

I had already asked her if she'd seen Freylin, and all she did was shrug, tell me she probably slept in, and then study me with those meddling eyes.

"Nothing."

She smiles. "You're nervous about the trials, aren't you?" She leans in over my table. "Nervous you might end up as a farmer's hand? Or worse, a child-rearer?"

"Technically, we're all going to be child-rearers."

"Bearing a child and raising them are two totally different things." She flips her hair over her shoulders.

I roll my eyes. I'm grateful to have a mother who took a considerable part in my upbringing instead of shoving me off with a child-rearer. It doesn't look like it'll be that way with Natalina's child. I feel bad for the little boy or girl already.

I tune her out until the third-hour chimes ring. I could still fake an episode, but who will pretend to watch over me? It can't be Alexi. I round the corner to our next class in a fale that overlooks the ocean and almost cry in relief. There she is.

Freylin is standing before the class's entrance with Natalina, locked in what seems like a heated conversation. I stroll that way, hoping to catch her once they're finished. They notice me, and Freylin turns with a smile. Natalina turns with a less-than-hostile expression.

"I need to talk to you," I say to Freylin.

Natalina looks between us, not holding back her surprise.

"Notes, remember?"

Besides a slight tilt of her head and a minor pause, she jumps onto it. "Right! I'll be right back, Nat."

We leave her in the middle of the path with her jaw hanging open. I can't help but feel a little satisfied.

I shuffle through my bag to keep up the facade. "Are you okay?" I say once we're out of Natalina's hearing range.

"Not really, but at least I'm not being shipped to the mainland."

"I need your help with something."

She grins. "Look at us, turning into besties."

I scoff. "Will you help me?"

She sighs, lowering her voice. "Is it true that Theo attacked you and Alexi?"

"Of course not," I say a little too loudly and peer around to ensure nobody is listening. "Alexi saw us together."

Her eyes flash. "You stayed the night?"

I don't respond, and her face lights up with mischief.

"Oh." Then it twists into worry as her lips turn down. "Oh."

"I need to find him. The only opportunity is right now while everyone is in school. I'm going to have a near episode. I need you to cover for me."

"How am I supposed to do that?" she asks with her hand on her hip.

"You're smart. You'll figure it out. Just make sure Alexi doesn't find out I'm gone." I take her hand to make sure she understands. "He will kill Theo if he sees us together again."

She flinches and opens her mouth, but something in my face stops her. She squeezes my hand. "Okay."

I smile and want to hug her, but that would be too suspicious. "Thank you, Frey Frey."

She cringes at the mention of her childhood nickname. "Yeah, yeah. Surprisingly, I like Theo, so you better find him."

Once you get to know him, you can't help but like him. I hand her something from my bag, and her face twists. "Notes."

"Oh. I thought that was a charade."

I shrug. "It was, but that doesn't mean I still can't give them to you."

She takes them with a smile. "Only you would still be taking notes on the last day of school," she says, bumping me with her hip.

Halfway through the next class, I stand, faking a dizzy spell. Freylin doesn't miss a beat, immediately offering to take me to lie down.

As we near the outside grounds, I squeeze her hand, then escape around the restroom building. Everyone is in class, so I don't meet a soul, but just in case, I go toward my house before disappearing into the forest.

Then I run. I don't stop when Beau finds me. I don't stop after I trip over a root and then another. I run and run and run.

When I reach the slope to the waterfall, I almost collapse down the thing, sliding down most of it, scraping my arms in my rush to get to him. I pant, looking around the cove and at the glistening water under the falls, but there's no sign that he's here. He *has* to be here.

I shuck off my clothes so I'm only in my undergarments and hide everything behind a bush.

"Keep watch," I tell Beau before entering the warm water. My heart pounds and my stomach swirls as I swim across. I part the waterfall, not wanting it to crash on top of me. I need to see him. He has to be here.

It's dark, and I wait for my eyes to adjust. The stars blink above me as I swim deeper into the cave. The sand squishes between my toes, and I walk up the small embankment, shivering. It's so much colder in here than outside.

"Izalia?"

I freeze. I don't see him, but his voice bounces off the rocky walls. He steps out of a dark corner, a flash of silver in his hand. I stare at him for less than a second before throwing myself onto him, burying my face in his neck. He holds me tightly against his chest, lifting my feet off the floor.

"You came," he mumbles.

I lean back and realize I'm getting his clothes all wet. I try to step away, but he doesn't let me go.

One hand stays on my waist, and the other trails up to my face, raising it to his. "You came."

"Of course, I came." My voice comes out barely as a whisper. I glance at his lips. The electricity amplifies between us, and I can't hold myself back from rising on my toes.

He stops me a mere inch from our lips meeting, rubbing my cheek with his thumb. "Are you okay?"

"I am now." I crash my lips into his, not giving him another opportunity to speak. The need to have his lips on mine is too great.

He kisses me softly, but I nip at his bottom lip, encouraging him. His hands are in my hair, and I'm the one pinning him to a wall. I explore his mouth, and with my hands, I explore his body. A soft moan escapes his throat, and I break the kiss as a wild desire fills me.

Suddenly, I'm very aware that I'm wearing almost nothing and he has too many clothes on.

I slip my hands under his jacket, and it slides off, hitting the cave floor. We're both breathing hard when he places my face between his hands.

"Izalia. I—I—"

I place my finger on his lips. I know what he's about to say, but I can't hear it just yet. "Kiss me."

His eyebrows raise.

I bunch the front of his sweater in my hands. "Please."

We embrace again, our bodies intertwining as his lips run down my neck. I arch into his body, holding tightly to his shoulders. I slip my hands under his shirt and explore the ridges of muscle. He makes a noise that has me pulling the sweater over his head. He briefly breaks the kiss to tug it off and pulls me into his arms, pressing me against the wall, the stone cold against my bare skin. His skin is hot, or it's my heat seeping into him, because I'm completely dry now. The fire in my veins warms both of us. The feeling of his skin against mine is a pleasure like nothing else I've felt before. I want him closer still.

I grab his face and pull it back to mine. My hands trace the outlines of his back before returning to his hair. He is my air, and I can't survive without every breath.

"Angel," he murmurs against my lips.

I am undone.

The thread that keeps me together unravels, and I am but loose string in his palms. He can do what he wants with me. I am his.

He pulls back, and I whimper. He presses his forehead against mine, but I can't stand even an inch of space between us. I cling to him.

"Angel. I would love to worship your body. But you're not mine."

My breath comes out rough. I am, I want to scream. I can only be yours. But it's not the truth. He wipes something wet from my cheek. Only then do I realize that I'm crying.

"Oh, Izalia." He pulls me to his chest.

I pull my arms into my chest so he can cocoon me. I let loose the rest of the tears I had bridled until now. "I don't want him, Theo. I want you."

He pulls my chin up and gently kisses me on the lips. I lean in for more, but he pulls back. "I've been thinking of a way out of this. But it's selfish of me to want. I could never ask it of you." He looks toward the waterfall.

I tug his face back to mine. "Tell me."

"What if we…" He takes a deep breath. "Leave."

I bite my lip. "You'd run away with me?"

"In a heartbeat."

My heart beats erratically. Could I do it? Leave? "What do you think the mainland is like?"

"I'm not sure. I've only seen pictures from books."

"Show me."

He looks toward the waterfall and back at me. "I'm kind of stuck here."

"No, you aren't!" I realize that I haven't told him, yet. I was too busy ravishing him. "I got you off the hook."

He pulls back so he can see my face. "You're kidding. What's the catch?"

I smile, but it quickly fades. I pull away and walk toward the water. I can't tell him while in his arms, but being away from his body raises goosebumps on my arms and sends a chill down my spine. It's really cold in here.

I hug my arms around my torso. Warmth wraps around my shoulders. I twist to see it's Theo's jacket. He's putting his sweater back on. I take one last longing look at his muscled abdomen.

"You've got to be freezing," he says.

I notice some sticks on the floor in a small pile. "Were you making a fire?"

He rubs the back of his neck with a wry smile. "Trying."

I smile and snap my fingers. Flame pulses above them. Pride fills me. I've gotten so good at that. I let it grow and flick it toward the wood. The fire catches, and we both settle around it.

I wrap Theo's jacket closer, watching the flames dance off his skin. "I'm to make the bond tomorrow."

His eyebrows raise, but surprisingly, he doesn't get angry, as if he was expecting it. He only nods. I wait but he doesn't say anything.

"You're not going to ask me not to do it?"

"This is your life, Izalia. Your choice."

Unrighteous anger fills me. I want him to fight for me. Didn't he just ask me to run away with him? I tell him I'm going to be with another man tomorrow, and that is it? It's my choice?

"What do you want me to do?" I have trouble keeping my voice steady.

I want him to say it, to convince me to run away with him and leave this all behind, and to tell me he loves me. I want him to give me a reason. But he just pulls his knees up and looks away.

"It's your choice."

I close my eyes, trying and failing to control the disappointment churning in me. The small, sane part of me knows he's just trying to do what's right. But I want him to fight like he did yesterday. Where's that guy with the sharp tongue and deadly glare? I want him to do something. Would he really let me go? Just like that?

I open my eyes, stand, and throw the jacket at him in one quick movement. By the time he realizes what I'm doing, I'm back in the water.

"Izalia, is something wrong?"

"Oh no, nothing at all!" I throw my hands in the air. "I'm just about to give up my life to another man who had the audacity to hit me. Remember that? And you would just let me? You would just lie down and take it?"

His jaw drops.

"Whatever. I've got to go. I have trials to *excel* at."

"Izalia!" he calls as I dive into the water.

I swim as fast as I can to the bank, throwing the water off me with my magic as I shove my clothes back on.

I'm almost to the rocks when I hear his voice again.

Some of the anger is starting to ebb, but embarrassment replaces it. I race up the wall, knowing he can't follow as swiftly.

When I reach the top, he's still calling for me, apologizing, which makes it so much worse.

I run away from the only man I love. If only I had the guts to tell him. Maybe then he would fight for me.

30

THEO

By the time I reach the top of the cliff, she's long gone. I throw my pack against a tree. It ricochets, the contents spilling on the ground.

"I am an idiot!"

I thought it was the right thing to say at the time. It is her decision. I could never ask her to leave her home for me.

You're nothing.

Alexi's words pierce me again. I can't get away from them. I have nothing to offer her.

When I reach home, I pause momentarily, awed by how much has been rebuilt. The pillars are back up, the roof is covered with freshly woven coconut leaves, and several furniture pieces have been replaced. The smell of newly chopped bamboo and fresh paint reaches me from the grassy edge a few feet away—no more stale, burnt smells wafting through the space.

As I enter the threshold, a strange feeling stabs me. It doesn't feel quite like home anymore. The indentions on the post closest to the couch that held my measurements as a growing youth are gone. All the familiar clutter of painting supplies, Pa's tools, and the random collection of seashells and odd objects littering the space are absent. Our table, which used to be covered by my childhood paintings, has been replaced. The space is a blank canvas, ready for new memories. Will I be in those memories?

Ma stiffens as she enters from the opposite side, beyond the slats, the only thing of our original home left. Her face lights up. "Theo!" She rushes toward me, holds me at arm's length, and inspects my body. "Are you okay?"

"I'm fine. Is it true? Have they let me off the hook?"

Ma's face falls. "I haven't heard anything, Theodore. But don't you ever do that to me again! I wake up to the city folk barging into our home looking for you, and you're nowhere to be found."

"Didn't you get my note?"

She whacks me with the painting towel she's always holding. "Of course, I got your note. But you should have woken me up and talked to us." She moves a hand to my face. My cheek warms. "You are all I have. I will support you in your choices. But please tell me before you go running off again."

I nod slowly, struck by guilt, thinking of the risks and sacrifices my parents have made because of their love for me. Of course, they'll do everything in their power to protect me. But that also scares me. They've already given so much for me.

"Promise me," she says, her green eyes piercing mine.

"I'll come to you."

She holds my gaze for a moment longer before smiling and pulling me into her arms. Her warmth and familiar smell of citrus and paint wrap around me, making me feel young and free of worry—like I only need one of her hugs and a mug of warm tea to ease my pain.

"Now, get some dry clothes on, and I'll make you something to eat. Where have you been, in the ocean?" she says, pulling back and wiping her arms off with the towel.

"A waterfall."

She cocks her head, her eyes sparking. "The cave." She pinches my cheek. "My smart boy."

"You know about it?"

She scoffs, pulling me forward and pushing me into my room. "I was a teenager once. Where do you think Pa and I—"

"Don't want to know!" I yell, covering my ears like a five-year-old.

I hear her soft chuckle as she walks away. A shiver runs through me. I did not need to know that. My room is the only familiar space in my home, and my eyes are already closing as my head hits the pillow.

Warm hands shake me awake. I look around my room, dazed. Darkness greets me.

"What time is it?" I groan. How long have I been asleep? There's only a bit of light shining through the slits. Must be close to sundown.

"Somebody is here to talk to you." Pa's face comes into view, worry lining his brow.

They're here for me.

I sit up, instantly wide awake. I breathe in, preparing myself. It was bound to happen. I shouldn't have run away the first time—a cowardly move. I did shoot the poor excuse of a man. It's time to own up to my actions, even if I don't regret it. I would do it again, maybe aim a little higher after what he did to Izalia.

"Where's Ma?"

"She's out there with him."

Great, she's already putting herself between me and them.

Ma has a hand on a pillar, looking toward the yard. Her face is strained, but her words are cheerful. I walk up next to her, preparing myself for somebody official.

Alexi stands in the unscorched grass, hands in pockets, with a slight smirk on his lips. He looks me up and down. "So, he lives after all," he murmurs.

The shock must register on my face because his smile grows. He rubs his side. "All healed up, in case you were wondering. Or, you know, wanted to apologize."

I pull my lips into a thin line, trying not to grimace.

"Ma, I've got this." I step toward him and push her lightly into the fale. I walk past him and toward the side of our shed, which is not in direct view of our home.

Without seeing if he followed, I say, "Come to finish me off?"

I wait, keeping my hands loose at my sides. Maybe, it won't hurt as much if I don't see it coming. It's not like I can defend myself. My gun is still in my pack. I didn't think of grabbing it after Pa woke me.

"You're the one that tried to kill me," he grunts from directly behind me.

The dirt crunches beneath my feet as I turn to face him. It looks like he wants to play with his food. "Oh. And what do you call burning down my house?"

"Why does everyone think I did that?" He chuckles and shakes his head. His hands are still in his pockets, his shoulders relaxed. But I don't trust him. "And before you go into what happened the other night. I found you with my girl. How else was I supposed to react?" A muscle ticks in his jaw. He can't keep up this nonchalant facade forever.

"I don't know. Maybe act like a sane person who asks questions instead of serving up threats and beatings."

His jaw tightens, and his eyes flare. "I didn't beat anyone."

"I think Izalia would say differently."

He takes a step towards me, and a fisted hand slips out of his pocket. There he is. "Don't you say her name."

I don't know what it is about him, but I want to make him angry. My emotions are hard to control in his presence. For the first time in my life, I want to be destructive. I want to hurt. Him hitting Izalia and then her collapsing to the ground flashes in my mind. Fury runs through me, wanting to consume. I wish I had brought that gun with me. It's not a fair fight at all.

He calms himself quickly, flexing his hand. "I didn't come here to fight with you."

"That's funny, because that's exactly what I want to do."

He smiles at me, one filled with teeth. It's not pleasant. "I don't need my magic to beat you down." He looks me up and down. "Pathetic."

I take a step towards him, my fist itching to connect with his smug face.

He puts a finger up. "I came here for Iz."

I stop. She sent him?

"I mean, I'm happy to fight you, but I don't think she would be happy with me, and I'm trying to stay on her good side…for now." He rubs his chin, a sly smile forming on his lips. "This time tomorrow, I'll be on a different side of her as she moans my name."

"You son of a—" I'm on him without realizing I've moved.

I give him a swift punch to the face before he flips me, and I'm eating dirt.

He grips my wrists tightly, pinning them behind my back as his breath burns my ear. "You're nothing, remember? She's mine. You're just a little distraction. I can't blame her for wanting to explore a little. Not like I haven't done it. And if she's anything like those women… Trust me. She'll never think of you again once I'm finished with her."

My blood boils as I struggle under his weight. "You sick bastard!"

He has me locked in place. "Wanna know why she chose you? She feels sorry for you. You're not the first orphan she's taken in."

I buck against his hold, but it feels like the very ground has me encased. I knew he wouldn't fight fair.

His breath is hot against my skin. I taste acid on my tongue.

"Stay far away from her. If I see you again, I won't hold back," he hisses.

His weight is gone. I flip over, my fist ready, but he's gone.

I punch the ground instead. It looks like Izalia will get her wish. I'm going to fight. No way am I going to let that bastard deceive her.

The sun lowers over the horizon, twilight setting in. A calmness settles over the island as I get my breathing under control. Even the cicadas stop their music. Izalia was right; this is the most peaceful time of day.

My breathing slows, and a quiet determination fills me. I need to convince the woman I love that, if she still wants me, I will follow her until my last breath.

31

AZALIA

The view from the top of Crystal Tower is breathtaking yet frightening. The never-ending ocean stretches out all around, making me feel small and insignificant. The sun lowers over the horizon, a thin slice of orange floating on the blue expanse. I think about Theo asking me to leave, to go into that unknown. My chest is still heavy from lashing out at him. I should emulate him, not denigrate him, for wanting me to make my own choice.

I look away from the expansive windows to my hands.

Freylin nudges me. "It's pretty up here, isn't it?"

"Do you come up here a lot?"

She shakes her head. "Just once. I'm just as in the dark as the rest of you."

I'm unsure if I believe her. Her parents create the trials. Wouldn't I want to give my child a leg up?

"I don't understand what we're doing in the tallest building on the island. We're as far as we can get from water and earth. How are we going to wield them?"

She chuckles. "Maybe they're going to push us off the top and see if we can use the elements to stop ourselves."

My eyes bulge out, and my heart kicks up in rhythm.

She snickers. "Kidding." She places her hand on my knee. "If they were doing that, there would be a lot more casualties."

"There are casualties?" I squeak.

The nerves didn't catch up with me until we entered the foyer. Everyone in my year seemed just as confused, as the caretakers directed us to this room lined with hard chairs to wait.

Our Instructors don't disclose the specifics of the trials. They only tell us to strive to be efficient in the four elements and that if we gravitate towards a specific one, we should do our best to cultivate it. Now that I've unlocked my Igna, I feel pretty confident in all four, but being here without knowing what I'm getting myself into puts my nerves on edge.

There is no reason to worry, I remind myself. Everyone on this island has gone through the trials to get an assignment.

"Of course not," Natalina scoffs, leaning from her chair so I can see her exaggerated eye roll. "Stop being a child."

Freylin shoots me a look. Natalina is becoming increasingly nosy about our sudden closeness. However, it's nice not to be on the receiving end of whispered gossip for once. Freylin helping me get back to school unnoticed went smoothly. I honestly wasn't sure if she would follow through with helping me. I give her a secret smile. It's nice to have a real friend.

Suddenly, the door swings open, and a woman in a long white dress, her hair buzzed short, calls my name. There have been a few before me, and it feels like forever since the last person went through.

Everyone turns to look at me. I pull my shoulders back and stand. Freylin whispers *good luck*, and I meet the lady with the clipboard. She looks me up and down once and ushers me inside, her face blank.

I walk behind her into a dark hall, where she casts an aura of light ahead of us. Doors line one side of the never-ending hall.

"Room three," she says, gesturing to the left. "But first"— she pulls something from her clipboard—"hand me your arm."

I barely lift it before she grabs it, and something pinches the inside, behind my elbow.

I yank my arm away. "What was that?" For a moment, I'm afraid this is a ruse to steal my magic.

She doesn't respond but gestures toward the white door with a giant three on it. I rub my arm at the sting, but the pain slowly subsides. My flame pulses as I search my body for anything amiss. I swallow when I still feel my magic—a swirling living thing that nestles into all the empty spaces—and place my hand on the knob.

I glance at the woman with the clipboard. "I just go in?"

"Hurry now, your year is quite large."

I step inside and am assaulted by darkness that absorbs all light from the hallway. I look back at the woman.

"Hope you're not scared of the dark," she says, shutting the door and sealing me in obscurity.

My heart pulses in my ears as I look ahead. "Hello?" My voice echoes.

There is no response.

Hmm. I guess the trial starts now. I breathe in and out and thread my fingers through the air to create an orb of light. There are a few sparks in the space before me, but nothing else. Every spark gets sucked back into the abyss.

My breathing intensifies, and I fight the urge to bang on the door behind me. I focus on my other senses. There is a distant sound of water, maybe a stream nearby? That's odd. The familiar earth smells of the forest saturate the air.

I step forward, pushing my arms out, not knowing how that could be possible.

I feel nothing as I take another hesitant step and then another. On the fourth step, my hand grazes something soft. After shrinking away, I steel myself and reach in that direction. Leaves. Water sloshes over my feet as I take a small step toward it. The ground slopes as I walk, the water deepening and the brush thickening as I have to hold branches away from my face to prevent them from slicing into me. Soon, it's too dense to walk any further. Maybe this isn't the right way.

I retrace my steps until my back hits a wall. My hand runs over the rough texture. I set my palms against the wall and follow it as it curves. Keeping one hand on the wall, I thrust the other in front of me. Rough bark grazes my fingertips. My chest tightens. What am I supposed to do?

Think. What do I know? This is a challenge to test our skill level with our magic, to see our strengths and weaknesses. If I'm in total darkness and can't use my Aura abilities, then…fire.

I snap my fingers, and a flame appears above them. The light stretches a few inches ahead to the tree in front of me. I'm a fool for not thinking of it sooner. I grow the flame, expanding my circle of light by a few feet. Trees stretch up before me, with no ceiling to be seen. The only noticeable entrance is an opening between a bush and a tree. The water is from a small stream to the side. A cobblestone path runs beside it. I follow it as it winds in front of me. Thunder rolls above my head. By the island—

I peer up, but of course, I don't see anything. A raindrop lands on my forehead. I wipe it off as more fall. The fire sputters out, and darkness envelops me again. Ugh.

I strip my sandals off and cast them aside to feel the path. As the rain soaks through my clothes, I shut my eyes and focus on my Sage. There isn't a reason to close my eyes, but the action still helps me center myself. I should have done this the first moment I walked in here.

The stones are smooth and hard underneath my feet. My fingers graze the large palm branches hanging into the path. I listen to the *pitter-patter* of rain on the trees, the stone, the stream beside me, and something else.

I stretch, listening intently. *Plink. Plink. Plink.*

Heading towards the sound, I listen closely, keeping on the path until it veers off in a different direction.

I could use my Aura to stop the rain, but then I wouldn't have my only clue. I stay on the path, hoping it'll wind back, but it only goes further from the sound, so I backtrack. It looks like I'll have to traverse the forest blind. I step off the path and immediately regret it, slipping on a muddy slope and falling onto my tailbone.

A shriek slips out as I slide downward. I try to grip anything around me, but I slide faster and faster. I reach for my flame and push it outward, using my panic as fuel. Trees race by before the rain extinguishes the fire. But I get an image of what's below me.

Nothing.

I'm freefalling. My scream is plucked from my throat as panic crawls to take hold and render me useless. Using the air to my advantage, I wrap the wind around myself, slowing my descent. My stomach is in my throat. Have I managed to slow myself enough to keep from dying upon impact?

The air shifts, becoming unmistakably humid. I sense water rising fast beneath me, my body preparing itself before my mind registers what's happening. The water swallows me, my feet and spine aching. I must not have slowed myself enough.

My senses dampen, but my body awakens. I swim upward, breaking through the water and inhaling fresh air. A bit of light shines from afar, as if I'm in a tunnel. I swim towards it. The ground slopes, sand sliding between my toes. I gather the light in my palms and send an orb into the air. The light dances off the walls of a cavern.

Once out of the water, I pull the droplets away from my body, and I'm dry. I follow the direction of the light, walking on a thin bank of sand. They must be watching me from somewhere. I have no idea if I'm doing what I'm supposed to or passing this trial. Am I on the next one now?

The tunnel brightens, and I no longer need the orb as I step up to the mouth of the cave.

A smooth wall stretches up, moonlight bathing me. I look towards the stars, where tree limbs stretch far above my head. Dirt walls encase my surroundings. Did I go the wrong way?

A shiny object embedded in the wall catches my eye. I feel along the space and dig my fingernails into the dirt. Physical pulling does nothing. Instead, I focus on the soil around it and pull it out with my Terra abilities. A hard, metallic pole slides out. I grab it, but it doesn't budge. I test my weight on it, bouncing lightly.

Observing the wall above me, I notice more shiny objects. I place both palms on the wall and pull forward as many poles as possible.

I grab hold of the first one and heave myself up. Pretending it's the tree branch outside my window, I balance on it and place my foot on the next. I slowly climb, using the metallic poles as holds.

I'm halfway up when I make the mistake of looking down. Far below me, water has gathered and is rising. Adrenaline floods my veins. Based on the moon's position, it's high tide. I need to move faster. My energy is fading from using so much of my magic.

I concentrate on pulling more poles out but can only manage two simultaneously. At a slow pace, I reach the top and heave myself up onto the land. My chest rises and falls as my muscles scream at me. The hole I crawled out of is half full of water. I look around myself. Besides the trees hanging over the side, the rest of the landscape is bare. Where am I? No part of the island looks like this. There are trees in the distance and nothing to do but walk. I really wish Beau was with me.

I walk until my legs ache and my throat burns, but the distant trees aren't getting closer. I look back. The trees at the edge of the hole are gone, and the bare landscape stretches on. The realization that I'm lost hits me like a falling boulder. Everything hurts, and my magic has dwindled.

My Sage. Focus on my Sage.

I close my eyes and reach out with my senses. I walk without looking where I'm going, remembering what it felt like to be in the pitch dark with only my senses guiding me.

When I open my eyes again, a person with golden hair stands in the distance. Theo! I gasp, breaking into a run.

"Theo, what are you doing out here?" I pant, getting closer, but he doesn't respond. He just stands there looking at me.

Something moves from my right.

Alexi steps out of the shadow of a tree. "He will die if you don't choose me."

I shake my head. Not this again. "But you said—"

"He will die if you don't choose me."

I step toward Theo, and Alexi's arm rises. I look at him. "What are you doing?"

"He will die if you don't choose me."

The three of us are an equal distance apart. I look at Alexi, back at Theo, and break into a run. I scream at Theo to get down as fire erupts from Alexi. I throw water at him with the force of a tsunami, which extinguishes the fire and knocks Alexi down.

I grab Theo by the shoulders and shove him. "Move! You need to move!"

His eyes are glassy and transfixed on the space behind me.

"Theo, please!" My voice breaks. What's wrong with him?

Alexi is moving towards us. I stand between them, but I'm not tall or big enough to cover Theo's body.

"You'll have to kill me first." Rage and fear burn in my veins. I'm not as powerful as Alexi, but I can hold my own. I have to.

"He will die if you don't choose me."

"I will never choose you!"

He stops walking, and with a flick of his wrist, I'm flying through the air. I hit the ground, pain radiating through my right side.

I look up in time to see that Alexi has Theo in a chokehold. "No!" I scream.

I gather the elements—fire, water, air, and earth. They consume every fiber of my being, and I throw them at Alexi, directing the air to pull Theo from his hold, the water to surround his face, the fire to burn his arms, and the earth to smash into him over and over again. I limp, my entire body trembling as the elements swirl around them. The intensity of my fear threatens to swallow me whole.

As I close the distance, the elements dissipate, leaving a lump on the ground. My entire body slackens. I wasn't fast enough.

I collapse onto Theo and pull him into my lap. His eyes are closed, and his face is slack. "Theo! No, please." I sob, shaking him, but he doesn't move. I feel for a pulse, but there isn't one.

His skin is too cold. *No, no, no.*

"Please come back to me. I can't lose you. Theo!" I gasp as tears blur my vision. An intense pain spreads through me, and I can't breathe. "Theo." I choke, caressing his beautiful face.

I'll kill him. The pain turns into a boiling rage as I scan the area for Alexi, but we're alone.

I glance back down to Theo, and he's gone, too.

I jump up. "Theo!" I scream as my surroundings shimmer and sway. I blink, and I'm in a room.

"But...he...I..."

"Brava! Brava!" comes a voice behind me.

Tears stream down my face as I turn towards the voice.

"That was quite the show, Miss Izalia."

"A show?" I slowly look around the white room. There's a wild woman with tear-stained cheeks, bright green eyes, dark hair in disarray, and torn clothes. A second later, I realize it's me. Mirrors cover the wall before me.

"You were marvelous!"

"You killed him," I choke.

A woman steps towards me, her smile fading. "That wasn't real, my dear."

"It wasn't real," I repeat, feeling dizzy. "He's still alive?" My pulse pounds in my ears, and hope gnaws at my heart.

"Who?"

I hold my tongue. What did she see?

"What was that?" I hiss.

"Your worst fear, of course. But I am so curious. Who died? Your parents? Your mate?"

She doesn't know.

My heart settles into an erratic beat. "My dad," I respond.

She nods and writes something down.

"Was it all fake?" I ask.

She holds out a hand, and I realize that I'm still sitting on the floor. I fight the urge to slap it away and grab it instead. She pulls my shaking body up.

It wasn't real. He's not dead. He's not dead. It wasn't real.

No matter how often I think it, my body doesn't believe me. I can't pull enough air into my lungs, and my eyes dart around, looking for him.

"I can't reveal that information."

My eyes widen, and I glance around. Is this the same room that I entered at the beginning?

She chuckles. "It can be quite disorienting to come out of a hallucination. Your parents are waiting for you outside."

I walk towards the door in a daze. I enter a lobby with bright-colored couches and chairs—a separate room, then. Some of it was real.

My parents see me before I do. I'm in my mom's arms, my dad on her heels.

He reaches me and pushes my hair out of my face. "How are you?"

I want to tell them everything that happened, but I can't. Another part of me wants to yell at them for forcing me into something like this without warning.

My mom leans back and studies my face. "I know, hon, I felt the same way. Let's get you home."

I don't remember going home. But suddenly, I'm changed out of my hopefully burned, grubby clothes and am sitting in front of a hot meal. My mind is still spiraling. My parents ask me questions, and I find my voice enough to tell them mostly everything. I don't reveal Theo's death. I wince at the memory, the pain returning to my chest. I don't bother with the charade of eating, and I walk up to my room soon after, feeling numb.

I stare at my wall with Beau in my lap. I notice too late that he's trying to get my attention. I pat his head. "I saw him die, Beau. It felt so real."

Beau whimpers, his eyes wide, as he nuzzles my arm—my distress radiating from him.

"I'd rather be attached to a jerk for a lifetime than to lose Theo." I swallow the knot of emotion building in my throat, fighting against the horrible realization. I pull Beau into my arms. "I have to go through with the ceremony."

32

IZALIA

As soon as that cocky grin spreads across his face, I almost turn around and walk back down the stairs. Almost. Instead, I take an unsteady breath and keep my eyes fastened on Alexi's sharp cheekbones, not really looking at him.

"You want me to convince you?" he scoffs, shaking his head. When I keep my icy stare on him, he loses his smirk.

"You let Theo off the hook, didn't you?" I ask.

As soon as my mom woke me, telling me the Elders weren't going through with Theo's trial, that Alexi had explained that it was a misunderstanding, I came here, knowing if I gave it much more thought, I would lose my nerve.

Even with his gunshot wound, Alexi can pull strings for Theo. It sends an icy chill down my spine. What else is he capable of?

Beau squawks anxiously at my side, unable to settle since he realized where I was going.

The smirk returns as Alexi leans against the door frame. "I sure did, my flower. But I gotta say, I didn't think you would keep your end of the deal."

I try to calm my racing nerves and fail. I'm doing this for Theo. So he can live. "You told me that you could change my mind. I want you to convince me to bond with you."

He looks at me for a second longer, trying to decipher my thoughts before his eyes light up. He grabs my hand, pulls me into his house, and pins me against the wall in one swift movement.

Alarm bells ring in my head, but I seal my mouth shut against the yelp. That doesn't stop Beau. He climbs up Alexi and fists his hair with a screech. Alexi goes to knock him off, but I grab Beau before he gets the chance. I push him outside and close the door.

"Sorry, you know how protective he gets."

Alexi grumbles and leans into me, his grimace melting into eagerness.

For Theo.

Alexi pushes my hair back with the tip of his finger. His warm breath caresses my face, smelling like coffee beans with a hint of mint. I stare into his eyes, trying not to let him see the tribulation I'm battling. I had hoped he'd want to talk it out, but of course, he would use the chance to be physical, thinking this would be the best way to convince me.

Well, maybe it will. Some biological feeling has to be there if he's my match. I *have* to feel something for him deep down. The first time he kissed me, I was too shocked to react appropriately. I wasn't ready. But maybe if I try to want it.

Warily, I place a hand on his arm. His bicep flexes at the touch. Then I place the other on his face, the stubble prickling my fingers. I ignore the feeling of wrongness in my gut. His eyelids flutter against my touch. It's the first time in my life that I've touched him so tenderly. It takes everything in me not to yank away. I hold my ground, determined to follow this through.

There is only a second of hesitation before a fire erupts in his eyes, and he pulls me against him, smashing our lips together. I close my eyes. His hands are everywhere, forcing me closer, traveling through my hair, down my back, and cupping my chin to deepen the kiss. He slips his tongue inside, and I work hard not to bite it as he explores my mouth.

Bile rises in my throat. I can't do this.

I break the kiss, and he moves his lips to my throat, pulling me into his arms.

"Alexi."

He feathers kisses down my neck, and I feel nothing—absolutely nothing. He pulls back with a lazy smile, leaning against me.

I'm too confined.

"I know. I know. You're just so—" He runs his hands down my waist.

He's too close. I need space.

"—amazing. I want to touch you everywhere, Iz. Ugh. I can't wait for tonight."

I step out of his embrace before the claustrophobia gets too much. "We need to talk about that."

"Oh, please don't ask me how we're going to fit together again," he chuckles, his eyes gleaming. "I promise it'll work." He steps closer, trailing a finger down my arm.

I shake my head, warmth spreading up my neck, and move to sit on the couch. "The trials took a lot out of me, Alexi. Could we postpone our ceremony?" I didn't come here to ask him for this, but I need more time to accept that I'm bonding with a man I will never love.

He shoots me an analytical look. He thinks I'm up to something.

"Just a day. The trial. I—I—" And then the tears fall. I'm so horrified by the fact that I'm crying in front of him that I cry harder.

Concern flashes across his face as he sits beside me and awkwardly rubs my back. "What happened?" He says it so soothingly that my crying stops as I look at him. "Did it not go well?"

That's what he's worried about? I bite back a snide remark and look out the window. A movement of gold catches my eye, but it's gone by the time I look back at it.

"I don't know. How do you even know if it goes well? It was freaking sensory deprivation and hallucinations. What's a win? That I got out?" I shake my head. "No, that's not what I'm upset about. It was just a lot. I need some time to recover."

He hesitates, and without thinking, I press my lips against his again. "Please?"

It feels like I'm kissing Beau. Actually, kissing him is much better. I have to keep from wiping my mouth when I pull away.

He leans into me with a sigh. "Okay. We'll do the ceremony tomorrow."

Wow. I didn't think that would honestly work. I've seen my mom do that move countless times, witnessing my dad unravel, but Alexi is not my dad.

He leans in to kiss me again, but I jump out of his reach and head for the door. "I should get going."

"Hey, wait. Are you okay?" He stands to follow me.

"I told you. That trial really messed with me. And I didn't get much sleep last night."

"Do you want to talk about it?" He takes my hand in his.

My eyebrows pull down. Since when does he want to talk about stuff? I look down, staring at the pink floral designs on my orange dress. "Who did you see?"

"What?"

"Who did you see die?" I look up, and his face is pinched. "At the end of the trial?"

"I didn't see anyone die." His eyebrows lift. "Did you?"

I bite my lip. Maybe not everyone's worst fear is somebody they love dying. "I did. It was horrific." But I don't say anything more about it. "What did you see then? At the end?"

He shifts on his feet, letting go of my hand. "It's kind of embarrassing."

That is not a word I would use for a worst fear. But I wouldn't put it past him to not fear anything.

I watch him as he plays with the top button of his dark tunic. He sighs and looks toward the far wall. His house has similar furniture to mine, the only difference being a painting of his grandfather front and center. Elder Wilder's expression is stoic as he sits behind a massive desk. No other pictures of Alexi or his family are on the walls.

"I was on the other side of the island on Breakwater Strand. It seemed like I was living with those people." He shakes his head in disgust. "I tried every way to get back to the city, but it didn't matter what path I took. I'd walk straight back into that nasty market each time. I then resorted to trying to destroy the thing. It didn't matter if I called in a storm or set it ablaze, it would appear every time I turned around." He shrugs. "I couldn't figure it out. I guess I failed that one."

I blink. He didn't know it had shown his worst fear. He thought it was just a simple maze he couldn't solve.

Awareness washes over me. His worst fear isn't losing somebody he loves—if he even loves anybody—it's becoming weak. He sees those people—even though they are us, but with different assignments—as weak, as below him. His worst fear.

I almost laugh at his lack of empathy. No wonder he thinks so little of Theo.

Theo. His face brings back the memory of me holding his lifeless body in his arms. Alexi killing him. My chest aches, the air ripping from my lungs.

"I'll see you tomorrow, Alexi." My voice wavers.

He grabs my hand before I can escape, pulling me into another agonizing kiss. I launch myself out of the house before he can do anything more.

I don't stop running until I reach my bathroom. I take the soap on the counter and scrub my face and lips, but it doesn't help. I can still feel him on me, his hands touching my body. I strip and fall into the shower, wielding the water from the tube jutting from the wall.

When I've scrubbed everything, including the inside of my mouth, I collapse onto the pebbled floor. Once I lose the ability to pull the water, I let my tears douse me.

He will die if you don't choose me.

I let myself feel it. Feel the insurmountable loss of Theo dying. I need to feel it everywhere—in my veins, in my bones, in my muscles, in my every aching breath. Because if I don't, I will run back to Theo.

And I can't do that. His life is too precious.

33

THEO

I'm just in time to see the psychopath pull her into his house. I pace, trying to decide if I should barge in or wait. He's not to be trusted, especially around her. Before yesterday, I probably would have turned around and left after seeing her willingly go into his home like that. Convinced she chose him, and that's it.

But not today. Today, I'm fighting. It doesn't matter that I'm a Nomagi. I am worthy of love. I am worthy of her.

Last night, I had come, but she had looked past exhaustion, on the verge of collapse. The trials must have taken a lot out of her. And even though I wanted to comfort her, I knew I needed to wait and let her heal. One time, I asked my parents about their trials. The way their eyes hooded, I knew it wasn't anything pleasant. I hate that she had to go through something that took so much from her, the strongest person I know.

I step out of the brush when something soft wraps around my foot. Big brown eyes peer up at me. Beau holds me back with his tail. Well, not really. I could easily walk with him attached to me like that. But the way he's looking at me makes me pause.

"You don't think I should go in there?"

He blinks, keeping his tail tight around my ankle.

I sigh. "Why not? You like him better than me?"

He squeals. I laugh at the look of disgust on his face. Does he understand me somehow?

"So, you *do* like me?"

He doesn't respond, but his tail loosens, and he scales my body to sit on my shoulder. It's a weird sensation; I don't know how Izalia handles it.

"I don't want her alone with him."

He purrs in what I imagine is agreement.

"Then why aren't you in there?"

I sigh when he doesn't answer and then shake my head. I'm talking to a monkey. I'm going in there.

I'm about to take another step when Beau leaps off my shoulders, crawling down my arm, and grabs my hand as he lands on the ground, yanking me back. I try to shake him off, but he pulls harder, digging his nails into my palm.

"Ow, stop it!"

His eyes move past me, and I glance back at a group of Divina men coming down the path toward Alexi's house. They haven't seen me.

I step back into the shadows. Alexi told me I was off the hook, but I shouldn't risk it if I want to talk to Izalia.

Beau looks at me, his nose turned up smugly.

I roll my eyes. "Thanks."

I wait for them to pass, but they hover between houses. I have no chance of getting into Alexi's without being noticed. They probably won't take kindly to me busting down his door. I shift uneasily under Beau's weight. Just when I'm about to risk it, the door opens, and Izalia walks down the stairs, her eyes wide. I leave the tree line, but she doesn't see me. She takes off in a run. I chase after her, Beau at my heels, but she's too fast.

"Izalia!" I call as she rounds a corner and disappears into her house. I slow as Beau blurs past and climbs the tree, hopping through the window that must be her room. I scoff, contemplating doing the same thing. But when I look around, I notice others staring at me.

The door. I should try the door. As I climb the stairs, anger coils, ready to spring. The way she sprinted away from that house…

If he did something to her, I'll kill him—no matter the ramifications.

I knock on the wooden door and stand back. It swings open, her father taking up the doorway. Was he always this big? I swallow. "I would like to speak with Izalia."

"No."

I bite back a retort. "I'm sorry, sir, but shouldn't that be up to her?"

His eyes pierce mine, but I won't bow down. I'm done bowing to these people.

"She's unavailable."

I don't believe him. I just saw her. But it's not like I can contradict him. Tell him that I had been following her. "When will she be available? I can wait."

"Theo, I'm going to be blunt here. Her ceremony is this evening; after that, you will need to go through Alexi, since he is her mate. I don't believe he will be as forthcoming as I am. I believe it will be best for you both for you to leave and never come back. Let her be."

I wince, and his face softens.

"I wish you well." He closes the door in my face.

My heart hammers in my chest. Tonight? That can't be. Didn't she say she still had weeks?

I trip down the steps and stare at the house for a moment. My eyes go to her window, and I wait to see if her face will appear. It can't be. She doesn't want to be with Alexi. I know it. I just need to talk to her. But how?

I jump as a hand lands on my shoulder.

"Theodore. It's been a long time." I turn to a man with wrinkled, dark skin and even darker hair cascading down his front, staring at me with hostile curiosity. But something about it is familiar. "Do you not remember me?"

"I'm sorry, I don't. I don't often come to the city."

He smiles, but nothing about it is pleasant. "I'm Tauvagna Wilder. Alexi's grandfather."

My eyes widen. The high elder is Alexi's grandfather? I should have known he'd have such bad blood in his veins. Nothing I've heard of this man has been pleasant. It's his fault that my family's ship wrecked here. And even though I have yet to confirm it with my parents, I can't shake the sinking feeling that they were alive when it happened. He's probably the one that murdered them.

"Nice to meet you," I stutter a minute too late.

He tilts his head. "You've met me. Your parents used to bring you to me every year. You've grown into quite the...man." He seems to struggle to find a word for me.

I swallow but refuse to let him see my fear. This man could turn me into a pile of bones at the flick of his fingers. And I shot his grandson. I'm tempted to flee but hold my ground and push back my shoulders, comforted by the fact I'm a little taller than him—like that would help.

He looks me up and down, and I try not to bristle during his inspection. He nods. "I was surprised when Alexi came to me and pleaded your case."

I wait for him to continue, but he doesn't.

I step away awkwardly. "Well, thank you then."

"I've let you live twice now," he says softly, his eyes darkening. "Your days are numbered here, Nomagi."

I take another step, clasping my hands together, waiting for him to release me from that look of abusing darkness.

With a slight nod, his eyes leave mine, and I can't get away from the man fast enough. When I'm down the path, I chance a look behind me. He's gone. A chill runs through me as I lengthen my stride, shoving my hand in the pockets of my sarong.

My steps waver when I make it to the edge of the city. I can't leave her. If she is going through with the ceremony tonight, it's my last chance. I can't live on this island without telling her how I feel.

I look back at the towering glass buildings I used to fear, realizing they're no longer intimidating.

34

IZALIA

My mother finds me under a pile of blankets. At this point, I've done my best to piece myself back together. Beau fidgets uneasily on my legs.

"Izzy! Why aren't you ready?"

I glance at my nightdress that I put on after my shower, which I was planning on staying in all day since I convinced Alexi to postpone our ceremony. I was looking forward to becoming one with my bed.

She throws open my wardrobe and starts tossing dresses onto my bed. "Closing ceremonies are starting in twenty minutes!"

Right. I'll be getting the results from my trials. I can't find it anywhere in myself to care, though.

I let her dress me like a doll and do my hair as I stare blankly at my reflection. I try to feel excited. But it's as if all emotions have filtered out of my body, leaving an empty shell.

Her eyes fill with concern as she finishes her work and finally looks at me. "Are you okay, honey?"

"Yeah, never better." My voice comes out monotonic. I rise and brush past her before she can ask me more questions. Beau hops on my shoulder and nestles into my hair, worry radiating from him.

She walks me across the path to campus, casting uneasy glances at me now and then. "I have such confidence in you, sweetheart. You have nothing to worry about."

I kind of wish I was feeling worried right now—some sort of emotion—but I continue to feel nothing. This is my life now.

People in my year who have never talked to me before greet me with enthusiasm as I find my seat in the front with the other graduates. The grounds are transformed. Beautiful flowers decorate the fales and around the fountain in the center. The glass from the other buildings reflects the charming scenery. A podium has been positioned in front of the fountain, and people from all across the island gather behind us. All are invited to the closing ceremonies, but I can't help but notice the absence of many faces from Breakwater Strand. I probably wouldn't have noticed before I met Theo. A sense of guilt stabs me, but I'm still beyond feeling for it to bother me.

I stare past the podium to the ocean as the seats fill around me. A familiar voice talks to me, and I nod politely in return. The voice stops before too long.

Another voice booms over the space, and I blink, trying to pay attention. But I can't. I slump into my seat and focus on keeping my eyelids from drooping.

I pay attention enough to learn that Alexi got assigned Protector, which is exactly what he wanted, despite his Igna specialty that should have placed him with the Craftsmen. Why did he even bother with the trials? He pumps his fist in the air, and I go back to watching the ocean.

A nudge on my shoulder raises me out of my stupor. I glance at Freylin, whose eyes are wide and apprehensive.

"It's almost your turn to go up."

I smile, hoping it looks realistic.

Her eyebrows knit together. "Are you okay? You've been uncharacteristically out of it, and that's saying a lot. Did something happen?"

I shake my head. "I'm fine."

"Izalia Rane!" My name echoes from the podium.

Freylin shoves me up as people whoop and cheer behind me. I focus on putting one foot in front of the other until I stand before Elder Wilder. I swallow as he places a wrinkled hand on my shoulder.

"You did very well, Izalia. The results showed us that you have a well-rounded grasp on all four elements, perfect for that of an Instructor." The last word is said loudly for all to hear.

The cheering is almost deafening. Has it been like this the whole time? I look around at the crowd. My eyes catch on my mom and dad, whose faces are the picture of proud parents.

My eyes move past them to a head of golden hair in the back. Theo smiles, and my heart squeezes. But when I blink, he's gone.

As I step out of the spotlight, my parents wrap me into a warm embrace. They congratulate me and tell me how proud they are.

I feel nothing.

35

IZALIA

om says the shock will fade—that she felt the same way when she got her assignment. I know it won't, because what I'm feeling isn't shock. It's a sadness that seeps into my very bones. I'll forever be this empty shell of a person, going through the motions.

I stare at myself in the mirror with the dress I picked out months ago for my ceremony with Alexi, the white fabric flowing to my feet and the sleeves hanging off my shoulders. It's strange and unfamiliar, as if the dress isn't meant for me anymore. I chose this fabric and loved the designs the dressmaker drew out. It's my dream dress. I should love this dress.

But that nothingness continues to drag me down, like I'll never feel joy again. The girl in the mirror is not me. The real me is on the other side of that mirror, banging with her fists to be released. I turn my back on her.

With my new dress hanging over my arm, I wait for my mom to finish her conversation with Mrs. Zuri. Is this where I will be in twenty years? Talking with the dressmaker about my child's ceremony? Will I be excited for them? Will this gut-curdling feeling have passed by then? Will I ever find happiness with Alexi?

I do know that I will never force my child into a ceremony with somebody they despise. I wonder what my mother would say if I told her the truth. But then, what about Theo? If I tell her, there is a possibility she could side with me. She did warn me about Theo's capture. But that's what I'm worried about. Even with my mother's support, I can't stop Alexi from going after Theo if I don't follow through…unless I could…

If I…

I can't finish the morbid thought as a face in the window claims my attention. The same face that I thought I had imagined in the back of the crowd at the closing ceremony only an hour ago, before my mother dragged me to the dressmaker, despite me telling her we had another day to prepare.

The face is gone before I blink, but I would know that face— that hair—anywhere. I excuse myself to go to the bathroom. My mother doesn't notice as I walk in the opposite direction and slip out the back door, my heart hammering in my chest as I face the back of the building.

For a moment, as I stare at Theo's physical form, all I can think is that he's not dead. *He's not dead.*

I throw myself at him, and he catches me, cradling my face to his chest. The last time I felt him, I was holding his lifeless body in my lap. That wasn't real. But it could be.

Abruptly, I remember where we are and pull away from him, wiping my eyes. He doesn't let me get far.

He cradles my face. Fire burns in his eyes. "I'm going to fight," he announces boldly, as if the words have been fighting to escape for a long time.

My heart falls into my stomach. I wanted to hear those exact words yesterday morning—a lifetime ago. But now, I can't stand the thought of having him put himself in danger. He's vulnerable as a Nomagi. Fear strikes me again, and I scan the small space between buildings, pulling him deeper into the shadows.

I open my mouth, but he places a finger on my lips. "I need to tell you this. Please."

I nod slowly, captivated by his touch. He leans against the wall, sliding his hand over to cradle my face. His eyes skirt over me. "I will do anything, go anywhere. I am all in. If you want to get off this island, I'll do that. If you want to stay and keep us a secret, I'll do that too. If you want me to hunt Alexi down, I'll gladly do that. Just tell me what I can do, and I'll do it." His hands find mine, squeezing them with promise.

My heart soars into the blue sky but then comes crashing down like a meteor. "Theo. I—I can't."

His face falls, but only for a moment. He closes his eyes and opens them again. His determination shines so brightly that it's blinding. "Izalia, I am utterly and hopelessly in love with you. Tell me you don't feel the same, and I will go."

My heart stutters and restarts. He loves me, and he knows I love him too. Or he at least suspects.

I close my eyes and see him dying in my arms behind my eyelids. I hold the image there. "I don't want you to die." A hot tear slips down my face.

His cool touch wipes it away. I open them, and he's so achingly close. "I have not been given many choices in my life.

But you. This choice. This choice is mine. I want you. I'd die over and over again if that means holding you in my arms for only a moment. Life isn't worth living if you are not in it, my angel. You have plagued my every thought—my every *dream* from the moment I saw you months ago. I have been in love with you since before I even saw your face."

He smiles, moving closer until he's only a breath away. "As long as my heart beats, you're my existence. You are all I have ever wanted in this life. That is my choice. *Mine*. I am yours if you want me or not."

His lips brush mine, the slightest touch, but enough to erupt a fire inside of me that I know I will never be able to quench. I lean into him as footsteps come our way.

Just before the door opens, I manage to push him to the side and stand in front of the door. I hold it steady with Theo on one side and my mother on the other—two decisions before me.

Theo glues himself to the side of the building, his heated gaze still on me. Those ocean-blue eyes have only ever been on me. *Months*, he said. He has loved me for *months*.

"Mom." I'm surprised my voice doesn't waver.

Her brows wrinkle. "What are you doing out here?"

"Oh, I just needed some fresh air."

"In the back?"

"Yup. Are you finally done gossiping?"

She rolls her eyes as she steps out. I press my left shoulder into Theo, and the door widens. Electricity courses through my body at the contact. He's still blocked, but not for long.

"I left my dress inside," I choke.

"I got it," she says, indicating the dress in her hands and stepping fully into the alleyway.

In a split-second decision, I grab her arm and let the door slam closed. I lead her down the alleyway toward the path in front of the shops, hoping she doesn't look behind us.

She startles when I push her into the sunshine. "What's gotten into you?"

"Just want to get home!" I say a little too exuberantly, tripping over a trash can and knocking over the lid. I bend to pick it up and freeze as my vision blurs and a face takes shape.

A little boy with blue eyes and hair like the sun blinks at me. He's shaking. Why is he shaking?

"Aw you otay?" I lick my mango popsicle nervously. I've never seen anyone like him before.

He doesn't respond, but his shaking lessens. His hair is so bright. Is it real?

"I like you haiwr."

I reach to touch it, and he flinches, so I pull back. Then I realize how sticky my fingers are and trade hands.

"Sowwy," I say, holding my other hand out. "Don't be scawed. You can twust me."

I smile as he takes it. His hand feels nice. "I'm waiting fo my pawents. Want some?" I angle my popsicle toward him.

He shakes his head.

"There you are!" comes a voice from down the path. A lady with wild eyes scans us and grabs his arm, yanking him away from me.

He glances back at me before he rounds the corner. I smile wide and wave. A hesitant smile forms on his lips before he disappears.

The rest of the popsicle melts off the stick and plops on my foot. I look down, shaking off the cold liquid. Who was that boy?

"Izzy, how could you have made an even bigger mess? I've only been gone for a moment," Daddy says as he washes me up with a ball of water forming in the air and the napkins he must have gotten from the popsicle lady.

I stare down the path where the boy disappeared. I take off for the spot as Daddy yells at me. I look down the alleyway, but he's gone. My heart falls.

Daddy grabs my hand. "What has gotten into you? Let's get you inside before your mother throws a tizzy."

"But I love him."

"Who?"

"The boy with sun haiwr."

We pass the trash can and a shark tooth lies where the boy was crouched. I reach for it and barely grasp it in my small hand before Daddy pulls me inside the shop.

The images shift, and I'm in the market with my parents. I'm looking for the boy, but he's not there. Colors swirl and I'm on the coastline, shark tooth in hand. Day after day, I explore the beaches on Breakwater Strand, looking for the boy with the sun hair.

I gasp, fully coming out of the flashbacks.

My mother has me around the shoulders, her eyes frantic. "Izzy, are you okay?"

I nod, glancing back at the trash can. He's the reason I've always been drawn to those beaches. Goosebumps travel down my arms as a burning sensation crawls up my throat. I've been searching for him my entire life.

I found him and didn't even realize it.

I look back into the alleyway, but it's empty, as if he was never there. But he was, once as a young boy and now, declaring his love for me, as everything inside me lit up hotter than if I were wielding real fire.

Something other than nothingness finally fills me. The same thing that I have felt countless times since meeting Theo as a young child and even more in the last week. Something deep, unyielding, and undeniable. Something that may get us both killed.

I'm pacing my bedroom as the dress watches me from my wardrobe and Beau watches me from my bed. I clutch the shark tooth that I found after remembering where I had hidden it ten years ago, right before my accident—underneath my wardrobe covered in dust.

It's been hours since I saw Theo, and I've held myself back, countless times, from running to his home. Dusk settles over the island, the treetops turning into orange-red shadows as I fight with my heart.

I fall onto my bed, pulling Beau into my arms. I close my eyes. My fear for Theo battles with the undeniable feeling that has taken over my body.

One finally wins out as I drift into the dark.

I jump as a sound awakens me, almost knocking Beau off the bed. Blinking away sleep, I jump again as something hits my window, and Beau squawks in protest.

With a strange giddiness, I lift the window. Theo is standing under my tree, wearing a hesitant smile. I scan the area—the land is swallowed in darkness, hours must have passed—before pushing the window further up, clambering onto the tree branch, and swinging down to meet him.

He looks at me in awe and a hint of nerves as he sways from side to side. "I wasn't sure if you'd want to see me, but since we were interrupted earlier and you didn't get a chance to give me your answer, I thought—"

I pull his face to mine, unable to stand another moment of not having his lips on mine. I've been craving his touch since we parted, and I've tried not to want it—I really did try— but I can't deny it. I am irrevocably and helplessly in love with him. He's not dead. What I saw was just a hallucination. That's it. It wasn't real. Theo is real, and he loves me.

He kisses me carefully, but I wrap myself around him, passion burning in my limbs. He reacts, pulling me into his arms and pinning me to the tree.

I thread my fingers through his hair. I pull back, breathing hard. "You're the boy from my flashbacks."

A smile grows on his face. "You remember."

"You knew?" I gasp.

He chuckles. "Of course I know. I've been waiting for you to remember."

I point to my head. "Brain injury, remember? Some help would have been nice." I kiss him again, biting his bottom lip. "That's for not telling me."

His eyebrows flash. "Hmm if that's what I get when you're angry with me. I'll have to find more ways to get on your nerves."

"Theo!" I giggle, and he nibbles on my earlobe. "Theo, bond with me."

He pulls back, his eyebrows disappearing into his hairline.

"I've been looking for you my entire life. As a little girl, I used to look for you in the market and walk Breakwater Strand searching for the boy with the sun hair." I thread my fingers through his hair and pull out the shark tooth that I wrapped with twine and placed around my neck. "With this. I found it after you left."

His eyes widen, and I drop it back onto my collarbone.

"Even when I couldn't remember you, I was still looking. I always wondered why I was drawn to the coast. I have loved you for a long time, Theo." My breathing hitches. "And I'm never letting you go now that I found you."

He smiles as bright as the sun, my own personal Aura light. I pull him into the cover of trees, not being able to get my hands on him fast enough. We pull apart as I pant against him. His hands are in my hair, and mine are up the back of his shirt, feeling the lines of muscles.

His body shudders. "I've been dreaming about you for months," he mumbles against my neck.

I pull back, my heart wanting to burst.

"But I've been yours for longer. Once I made the connection that you were the little girl who showed me kindness on those city streets, I made it my mission to make you happy, no matter if you chose me." He fingers my makeshift necklace. "You're my life now."

I kiss him with the force of a thousand waves.

When we break apart, he asks, "So, how do we make this bond? I'm ready to tie myself to you in every way possible."

I shrug, and he chuckles, pulling my mouth back to his.

"Do you think your parents will help us?" I say in between kisses.

He leans back. "Yes." His mouth suddenly twists down. "But aren't you supposed to bond with Alexi tonight?"

I wrinkle my nose. "I was able to push it back. Nobody will interrupt us tonight." I kiss him one more time and tug on his hand.

He eyes me. "Tonight?"

I nod and bite my lip. "You said you're ready."

"Absolutely!" He lunges for me and twirls me under the stars until my cheeks hurt from smiling so wide.

"Your laugh is sweeter than any music." He sets me down, tucking the necklace back into my tunic. "And I'm glad you found my shark tooth. I've been looking for that thing for thirteen years."

I squeeze his fingers as I pull him through the forest, my giggles trailing us, and soon, he's the one pulling me along.

And I know I will follow him anywhere.

36

THEO

I keep checking over my shoulder, even though her hand is in mine. My beautiful angel of the ocean with a monkey perched on her shoulder, looking at me, smiling at me, wanting me. She can't be real. How can any of this be real? I don't know how she could love me as much as I love her, but somehow, it's true. I am worthy of her love. My entire life, my parents have been telling me that I'm loved, intelligent, and capable, despite not having magic. Izalia is my confirmation. I am not nothing. I am worthy of her.

The gravitational force that brought me to her on the city streets, then again on the cliff's edge, also brought me to the shop window. It was easy to figure out that graduation was happening today, with everyone flocking in that direction, but afterward, everyone dispersed. Like those other instances, I can't explain how I found her again. It had to have been the island.

She was breathtaking in that flowing white dress, the way I pictured her in my dreams, a similar white dress flowing behind her, never turning to look at me. But there she was, beauty incarnate. Right then, I decided I'd rather be fed to the sharks than not be with her. She is everything good in this world and more.

"Wait here," I say, capturing her chin and planting a light kiss on her temple.

I savor her warmth on my lips as I make my way to my parents' bedroom. I feel like I'm six years old, waking Ma up in the middle of the night because of a nightmare. But now it's because of an unbelievable dream come true.

I gently touch her shoulder, and she stirs, blinking up at me before sitting up so quickly she almost knocks me out.

"What is it? Are you okay?" she gasps.

"Just keeping my promise."

Her eyes focus in and out as she searches my face and then looks around the room, back at me, then understanding clicks into place.

"You're leaving."

I smile. "I'm getting married." That's not quite the word Izalia used, but it's what it is—what Nomagi call it in the books, anyway.

Her jaw drops, and without looking behind her, she shakes Pa awake. "Boaz, you need to wake up."

He grunts and rolls over.

"Izalia?" she asks.

I chuckle. "Who else?"

She shakes her head. "Are you sure?"

"Can you do the ceremony?"

"I can't," she whispers.

My heart drops.

"I can," Pa mumbles, rolling out of bed. He strides over to me and clasps me on the shoulder. "We're here for you, bud."

"She's right outside."

"Now?" My mom exclaims, sharing a look with Pa.

"Now or never," I say, rushing toward my room for one last thing.

37

IZALIA

Theo's Mom gently pulls and winds my hair into a braid as I sit on a low stool. I told her I didn't want to waste time, but she insisted, saying you only get one ceremony. No regrets.

My chest warms. I know I'm doing the right thing. The dress in the shop didn't feel right, not because I didn't like it anymore, but because I was doing the wrong thing. Now, preparing to bond myself to Theo, I could be wearing a bathing suit and wouldn't care. This feels right. I love him.

I can't completely ignore the tugging at the back of my mind, though. What kind of repercussions will we face when everyone finds out? What will Alexi do? A shiver runs down my spine and I push the worries down, down, down, into a little box to think about later. I want to give this moment all of me. Whatever the consequences, we'll handle them together. We'll be bonded and there's not much they can do about it. He's my choice.

She hands me a mirror, and I look into it. My wildly untamed hair from before is now beautifully crafted into a halo braid with loose dark curls draped around my shoulders. I smell the coconut oil she used, giving the curls a shiny, soft look. She tucks little peach and white plumerias into the braid. I'm in complete awe as she finishes and pulls out something else.

She glances at Beau in my lap, the same flowers she put in my hair, fastened into a mini crown.

"And for the best little paranymph."

I haven't heard that word in a long time. Paranymphs were close friends who accompanied each person getting bonded as witnesses to the ceremony, an old tradition. They aren't needed anymore, since ceremonies are widely attended now. I guess that is what Beau is since it's just us.

I swallow a lump in my throat at her kindness. A pain blossoms in my chest, knowing my parents aren't here. It's for the best, though. They would stop it in a heartbeat. And I've never been so sure about something my entire life.

Iris sets the crown between Beau's ears. He immediately grabs it, studies it, looks at my hair, then sets it back on his head. I chuckle in surprise that he didn't try to eat it. Iris beams and disappears around the corner.

When she returns, she has more flowers in her hands. I turn to her and quickly realize they're not just flowers. She lets go, and a sheer white fabric flows to the floor. Plumerias cover the fabric, the same color as the ones in my hair.

I stand, palming the garment. "I thought these were real."

"I painted them. I want you to wear it," she says, biting her lip. "If you want, of course."

"Wear it?"

She fans it out, showing two thin straps at the top and a heart-shaped neckline.

"It's a dress," I say, announcing the obvious.

She smiles. "I don't have a daughter. I had no idea why I made a ceremony dress, but the design wouldn't leave my mind until I created it. Now I know it's for this moment. It's for you."

Tears prick my eyes as she hands it over. The fabric glides over my hands. It's luscious. I've never touched anything like it. It's ten times better than my other one.

"I don't know what to say," I choke.

"Say yes."

I give her a slight nod, and she smiles, pulling me in for a hug. "Thank you."

"No, no, no. Thank you. This is the most beautiful dress I've ever seen," I tell her as soon as I pull away.

She touches the fabric. "I used to love making dresses as a child, but my parents insisted I get a higher assignment. I hated being a Protector. Theo truly was the best thing that ever happened to me. Moving out here, I could do what I truly loved—paint. It's not looked down upon here." She shakes her head, as if expelling the memories. "And you are the best thing to happen to him. Thank you for loving my boy." She wipes a tear from her eye.

My throat becomes thick, and she leaves me alone to change before I can respond. I had no idea that Iris was a Protector, one of the highest assignments. Is that how she was able to save Theo? I've never heard of a ship crashing onto our shores before Theo mentioned it, but if they do, Protectors must have a hand in it. I'll have to ask her more about that later.

The dress hugs my curves and flares at the waist, landing just past my knees. The flower work is impressive. The dainty things look so authentic. I feel different in this dress than the other. Lighter. Freer.

I peer around the corner but don't hear anyone. I find them outside as I step near an opening between posts. I'm still astonished by how quickly they rebuilt their fale. It's similar to before, but the fresh bamboo and palm leaf smell is potent.

Theo is talking with his parents. He's changed into a white sarong and a matching linen top, with the sleeves pushed up his forearms. His mom breaks into a smile.

Theo turns as I descend the small slope to where they stand. His face goes from shock to wonder to pure joy. I've barely stepped onto the grass when he runs towards me and sweeps me into his arms. I giggle as his lips meet my neck.

"You are the most radiant beauty I've ever laid eyes on."

"It's all your mom," I say with a blush.

He leans back to rake his eyes over me again. "You are beautiful in pajamas. You are beautiful in a dress. You are beautiful bathed in mud and upside down. You are exquisite, always."

Heat flares in my cheeks as the look in his eyes turns into something else. Something that definitely needs to be saved for later when we are not in front of his parents.

"Okay, you two lovebirds, it's almost daylight. Come on," his father says, but I'm pretty sure I saw him wipe something from his cheek.

Theo holds me tightly around the waist as we weave through the trees toward the beach. The sky has begun to lighten.

When we step out of the trees, I smile at the familiar outlook. "This is where we met."

He grins back, his blue eyes sparkling. "The second time, yes. Most importantly, this is where I fell in love with you. It seemed only fitting that this is where I give you my heart for the rest of our lives."

I plant what's supposed to be a quick kiss on his lips, but he doesn't let me pull back. My pulse quickens, and I'm about to climb him and do something indecent when he pulls back.

He guides me to the edge of the cliff where his father stands. I don't take my eyes off Theo. He's going to be mine—this darling, sweet, perfect man.

There is a faint pink glow on the flat horizon. The brightest stars still dot the sky, a sliver of the moon peeking overhead. The silhouettes of palm trees blow in the wind as the glow spreads, reaching the farthest corners and signaling the sun's imminent arrival. A ray of piercing blue, the same as Theo's eyes, shoots from the horizon. Boaz raises his voice above the sounds of the waves crashing against the cliff.

I face Theo with Beau at my feet. There's a tug on the bottom of my dress and I peer down. It's not just Beau; another monkey, smaller than him, has joined us. He licks and nuzzles her.

My eyes widen. *Is this why you keep disappearing on me?*

A feeling of happiness settles over them both, and I turn back to Theo, who squeezes my hands. My smile widens when Theo notices them, too. He winks at Beau, then looks back at me. I'm lost in his eyes. Peace, as I've never felt before, settles over me.

This is right. *This* is everything I want. Everything I need.

Beyond Theo, the ray expands into the blue sky that is so familiar above my head. Black sea birds fly over the water, diving into its depths to collect their breakfast. The world brightens around us. Bright pink and purple wisps scatter the horizon. The sky turns a faint violet blue. The gray clouds whiten as pink and orange splatter the horizon.

Boaz hands me a knife, and I do as he instructs, slicing into my palm without hesitation. Theo follows, never taking his eyes off me. My pulse leaps as we join our hands, warmth, and magic radiating from our palms and seeping into my bloodstream, traveling up my arm and into my heart, sealing our love forever.

A radiant, bright orange sphere rises from the ocean, ascending towards a dark storm brewing far at sea. This tiny orb brings light to my world as a new day begins—as my new life begins.

38

THEO

I gather her in my arms. "You are my life now."

Her eyes widen, and her smile grows impossibly wide, making my heart stop as if struck by lightning. I kiss her long and slow, savoring her taste like the sweetest dessert. She wraps her arms around my neck, and I dip her at the waist with our lips still interlocked.

As I'm about to lose balance, I pull her up, Ma clapping enthusiastically in the background. I hold back my desire to touch the rest of her and break the kiss. Her cheeks are flushed, and a beam of sunlight illuminates her emerald eyes, swirling with a faint blue that I swear wasn't there earlier. My body hums, warmth flooding my veins.

"And you are mine." She pulls me against her for another kiss. This one is different, rougher, and more eager, with a promise for more.

"I love you so much," I tell her against her lips, and her body slackens against mine.

The feel of her in my arms is what I imagine wielding magic would be like—a euphoric high. I want her closer still, but I pull away to take something out of my pocket. I slip it onto her finger. She blinks and peers at her hand. A gold band with a sun positioned in the middle wraps around her middle finger. Light dances off the tiny crystals embedded in the sun, sending hundreds of dazzling beams bouncing off her bronze skin.

She inhales sharply. "Theo!"

"It was my mother's. I thought you might like it."

"I love it!" Tears burst from her eyes, and I quickly kiss them away, savoring the salty taste. She untangles the twine from her neck and places it around mine.

"Technically, it's not mine, but—"

I used to collect all sorts of sea trinkets as a boy. The shark tooth must have been one and knowing that she's held onto it for this long makes it the most precious object in the world. I swallow the heat gathering in my throat.

"—since I've had it longer than you, and it was my only proof of your existence." She places it against my chest and closes her eyes. A light glows from her fingers. "I hope it always guides you back to me." She pulls her hand away, and the shark tooth has taken on a whiter and shinier texture.

"Thank you," I breathe, placing my forehead against hers and tucking the now-warm necklace into my tunic. I'll never take it off.

I'm finally ready to face my parents and thank them for trusting my decision. But when I turn, they're nowhere to be found. I look around the deserted beach, confused. Even the monkeys are gone.

"I think they're giving us some privacy," Izalia whispers.

I look back at her. Oh. Her eyebrows rise, and she studies me with raw emotion. The last part of the ceremony is our joining. *Oh.*

A wild excitement thrums through me, but I squash it. I want her to take the lead. I don't want to do anything she's not ready for.

I push my hand through her hair. She looks towards the ocean for a moment and then back at me. "Come."

She grabs my hand, and I follow her. I'll follow her anywhere. I'll follow her into the very ocean in the middle of a storm if that's where she wants to go.

We walk on the beach in a peaceful quiet, with only the salty breeze between us. The warmth from her hand that radiates to the rest of my body is its own euphoria. If we were to stay exactly like this forever, I would be okay with that. She tugs on my hand, and we find ourselves in an alcove of rocks, hidden from the rest of the beach but not the ocean stretching before us. The sand is cold, having not yet been warmed by the sun.

I wind my arms around her waist and nuzzle into the back of her hair, breathing in a floral coconut smell that's uniquely hers.

She twists so we're face-to-face. "I would love to hear your music right now," she says, burrowing into my neck. When she plants a kiss on the hollow of my throat, my knees weaken.

"Close your eyes," I tell her. "Listen."

Can she hear nature's music around us? The ocean's rhythmic whooshing, the sound of seashells clattering, birds singing, the wind rushing through the palm leaves, whistling its tune. The cicadas' buzz doesn't disturb the melody as they're not yet awake.

I hum along the island's rhythm, adding another layer.

He saw her on ravine's brink.
A beauty from the sea.
Her eyes like emeralds.
Her hair wild and free.

An angel of the ocean.
Magic in her blood.
He'll love her forever.
Never be apart.

She danced on the edge of his heart.
As dreams of her swirled.
Always hoping and waiting.
Though she's not of his world.

An angel of the ocean.
Magic in his heart.
Their love is forever.
Never be apart.

39

AZALIA

The song echoes around us, caught in the breeze and the sea. Warm fingers brush tears from my cheeks. I keep my eyes closed, memorizing the lines of the song, never wanting to forget. My love for this man is so full that it's bubbling up and spewing over the edges.

I open my eyes, letting him see the longing there that I can barely contain. Grabbing his hand, I pull him onto the ground with me until we're lying side by side in the cool sand. I study the lines of his face, his lips, the blue in his eyes, feeling too many emotions—stunned and full of joy by the song he created for me, a powerful yearning to kiss every part of him, and a bit of sorrow knowing that I missed out on a whole life of knowing him because of my damaged brain.

He gently threads his fingers through my hair as if trying to catalog each strand. Electricity courses through my veins, and I lean into him like a cicada to a flame, feathering kisses up his jawline.

A sigh escapes him, and his hand on the back of my neck pulls me to his lips. The kiss starts slow but builds as our bodies tangle together. His hands ignite a fire in my blood and an overwhelming desire to have his skin against mine. My hands shake against his buttons, and I curse my naivety. He places both hands on my face, guiding me to look at him. He searches my eyes, a heated question in his gaze.

I nod, and in one graceful move, he flips me over so my back is pressed into the sand, and he hovers over me, his shirt gone. His hips pin me to the sand, but none of his weight is on me as our chests rise and fall as one.

I marvel at the beauty of his light skin. Unlike before, I'm not shy about touching the curves of his chest and muscled abdomen, lowering my hands to the indents just above his sarong. He's mine now to touch. He shudders, his breathing becoming rapid as his eyes flutter closed. His hand tightens around my waist and the arm holding him up strains. My eyes follow the protruding veins on his bicep, my pulse jumping as I continue to tease that sensitive area of his body.

"Izalia." A barely audible moan heats my skin.

I pull him down to me, and our lips crash together, more hungrily this time, as I fumble with the fabric of his sarong; my dress hikes up around my thighs. He pins my hands together and pushes onto an elbow, his lips only a breath away.

Tracing the lines of my face with his free hand, he stares at me, eyes full of love and yearning. "Are you sure, my angel? We don't need to rush this."

I have never been more sure of anything in my entire life. I want him. I need him. I love him. A smile plays on my lips as I wiggle my hand up to his shoulder and give him a slight shove. He lets me take control as I straddle his body.

Gently, I pull down my straps, tugging my dress down until it pools at my waist, giving him my answer. His eyes widen but don't leave my face as his hands slide over my hips, up my arms, and to my neck, leaving an icy fire in their wake.

"You are perfect," he murmurs.

My hands travel up the plains of his chest as I lean into him. I kiss the indent at his throat and then higher on the stubble of his chin.

When I reach his ear, I whisper, "We are perfect together."

The sun is rising higher in the sky as I open my eyes against the sleep threatening to take me under again. I'm curled against Theo's body, his arms wrapped around me in a warm cocoon.

We are perfectly made for one another inside and out. I've been born again—remade from pure bliss, rays of sunlight, and the salt of the ocean after our union.

I trace designs on his abdomen, his chest rising slowly. We both had fallen asleep, and even though I want to relish this feeling forever, I know we must face the rest of the day. I kiss his relaxed lips. He stirs under my touch. I kiss him harder, threading my fingers through his hair. He responds, kissing me back greedily. I feel closer to him than I ever have. No wonder they call it making love. Love blooms in my chest, threatening to overtake me.

He pulls me on top of him. "Ready for another round?" he teases groggily.

I giggle. Oh, how I wish we could remain in this blissful state forever. His eyes open, a lazy smile spreading on his lips.

"I would love to, but—" Reality threatens to crash into me. The worries that I've pushed down so that this moment can be perfect are building under the surface.

He blinks sleep from his eyes and sits up. We need to do the inevitable. There's nothing the Elders can do now. We're bonded, and the ceremony is officially complete. But still, my stomach does somersaults as I rise and grab my dress.

He watches me. I thought it would feel strange to be so vulnerable with a man—for anybody to see me without clothes. But it feels natural with Theo.

His gaze makes me rethink wanting to dress. I settle the straps of my dress over my shoulders and straddle him again. He wraps me in his arms, burying his face into my neck. Heat flows through me once more, a desire settling in my core.

"Maybe if we made it quick," I murmur into his silky hair.

He swings me around, pinning me to the sand. A giggle escapes my lips. He cocks an eyebrow. "You sure?" He studies my face.

I bite my bottom lip. I don't know what the future holds for us. But right now, here with him, I want to make the most of our time. I nod enthusiastically, and he chuckles.

He fingers the strap on my dress. "I can be quick," he says with a boyish grin.

How lucky am I? That he's mine.

I smile, wrapping my legs around him and pulling him down.

I'm panting and trying unsuccessfully to fix my dress, which is somehow backward.

Theo chuckles as he finishes dressing and reaches for me. He wraps his arm around my waist, tickling my sides. "I think I prefer it this way."

I swat his hand away with a giggle. "Help me."

In one quick move, he has the dress in the correct position and threads his hand through mine. It's still pretty early for anyone to be on the beach, but I check carefully around the corner before slipping into the trees, hand in hand. Thunder sounds in the distance, and I turn.

"Does that seem closer than usual?" I ask.

Theo looks behind me and shrugs. "There are always storms out there."

"I know, but it just feels close." An uneasy feeling buries in my gut, and I try to ignore it. It's just a storm. The Protectors must be busy this morning.

When we reach his house, Beau bounds for us and unexpectedly climbs Theo instead of me. Theo smiles smugly.

"He approves," I say, squeezing his hand.

Beau bounces from his shoulder to mine. Theo's parents wait for us on their couch just inside their fale. Heat fills my cheeks, and I make sure my dress is still in place. I didn't even think about my hair. My whole face bursts into flames as Iris stands.

"I have a gift for you!"

I look at Theo, and he shrugs. A smile tugs on his mouth, and I can't help but kiss it hungrily. He has to know.

She returns with a canvas in hand. She looks excitedly between us before giving it to me. I flip it over and gasp, tears filling my eyes. Theo has the same expression. It's a picture of us from this morning. We're facing each other, hand in hand, the sun rising behind us. All my favorite colors of the sunrise decorate the sky. The expanse of ocean that matches Theo's eyes. The expressions on our faces so full of love. Even Beau and his little girlfriend at my feet. She captured everything. It's perfect. Our love is palpable.

I shake my head. "How?"

"I was painting it during the ceremony." She laughs. "It's okay. You two only had eyes for each other at the time."

"It's beautiful. Thank you." I throw my arms around her, and she stills for a moment before wrapping her arms around me.

"Welcome to the family," she tells me, voice heavy with emotion.

Then I embrace his father, because none of this would have been possible if it wasn't for him. He pats my back and lets go.

"Thank you," I say, holding his gaze.

"It was my honor," he replies.

Theo is in his mom's embrace, and she murmurs in his ear. He pulls back, and his dad pulls him in. There are tears in both their eyes. They look at their son with so much love, it makes my heart ache.

That feeling in my gut doesn't leave me, though. What if my parents don't accept him? What if something terrible happens? I shake the thoughts away. My parents won't cause me pain, and that's what would happen if something happened to my mate—inexplicable pain. Our very souls are intertwined now. If anything were to happen to either of us, the other wouldn't be able to recover. My body may live through it, but not my mind.

"I'll be right back," I announce.

Theo releases his father and turns toward me, wariness lining his face. "I thought we would tell them together?" He gestures toward his parents. "A united front."

I nod and try to smile. "I know, but I think I should give the decency of warning my parents first."

Theo grabs my hand, searching my eyes. "Are you sure?"

"Yes. I'll be right back. I promise." I kiss him, and he holds me to him momentarily before releasing me.

"If you aren't back within the hour, I'm coming to find you."

I nod. "Deal."

"We'll round up more friends in the meantime," his mother says, patting her son's shoulder. "The more people to vouch for you, the better."

He nods warily, but his eyes stay on me. "One hour." He kisses me again. I can feel his worry radiate off him. It is as if our bond amplifies the emotions we feel from one another. I hope he can't feel mine—my fear.

40

THEO

It physically hurts to let her walk away, but this is our life now. Though we are bonded, she is still a Divina, regardless of whether her people accept me. She is her own person, and if she thinks she should break the news to her parents privately, I trust her.

The reality of my new life weighs on my shoulders. Will she want to move out here to Breakwater Strand or stay in the city? Crystal City has grown on me. I wouldn't mind having a home there, living in one of those beautiful, strange houses. Either way, I'll be happy if I have Izalia by my side.

And what if she wants a child? I shake my head. She chose this life with me, whatever that may look like. If she wants to leave to go to the mainland and raise a family, I'll make it happen. If she wants to stay and is content with me spoiling only her for the rest of her life, I can do that.

Ma pulls me out of my thoughts. "Let's go. We don't have a lot of time."

Right. I start to follow but hesitate. I need answers about the ship graveyard. Now that I'm bonded with Izalia, I already feel the guilt starting to eat me alive, not having told her. And I can't talk to her without first confirming the truth.

"Wait." My hand shakes, and I shove it in my pocket. I can't stay ignorant forever.

My parents turn toward me.

"The other night, I wanted some closure, and I went to the place you told me never to go." I swallow as Ma sucks in a breath, and Pa's face falls. Ugh. Why am I doing this now? They're the happiest they've been in a long time.

"Theo," Ma says, her voice pained.

"I need to know the truth."

Pa places a hand on her shoulder. They share a look, and with a solemn nod from Pa, she begins.

"I never wanted to be a Protector, but my parents were like Izalia's and all the Divina in the city. They wouldn't take anything less than perfection from me. I learned quickly that the assignment was mostly about keeping secrets—secrets about the outside explorations of our Elders, secrets about the true role of Protector of our island, secrets about our way of life."

My mind whirls, so many questions rise, but I focus on the most important one at the moment. "Secrets about shipwrecks?"

Her eyes blink back from her memories, and she nods to me. "Yes. During one particularly dreadful night, when the storms were raging outside our control, one ship escaped through."

Mine.

She nods again with tear-filled eyes. I didn't know that I said that out loud. "Your ship crashed along the barrier reef, the most brutal side of the island, which is why the people are warned to stay away. But you've seen that that's not the only reason we don't go there." She takes a deep breath to steady herself. "We are told to direct all ships that make it free from the storms there."

I gasp.

She shakes her head. "I didn't know." She steps toward me. My feet are sewn to the ground. She grabs my hand. "I didn't know, Theo. I—I didn't know." Her words come out faster than I can comprehend. "We went to look for survivors. It was my first time going. Nobody told me what we would have to do if there were survivors." She sobs. "There was a woman with a box in her arms fighting off our advances. She clung to that box as if her life depended on it, like something more important than her was inside. I know that look, because I felt the same way when Lucera died. I stopped the others' advances long enough for her to plead with me with her last breath to save you. And when I looked at you in that box with your big blue eyes and golden hair, I became her—an enraged, fighting mother. But I had what she didn't, my magic. I used it to flee. I knew I couldn't hide you, so I went straight to the Elder Tauvagna Wilder and told him that, if he didn't let me keep you, I would reveal all his secrets because, you see, he was the worst of them all. His voyages to the mainland were not explorative but held much darker objectives. I knew this, and I used it against him."

My feet unglue from the ground, and I step away.

She doesn't release me. "Please forgive me, Theo. I was only trying to keep you safe. I have loved you since I first laid eyes on you."

"What about the others?" My voice comes out hoarse, not my own.

"The ocean has a taste for Nomagi," she whispers, repeating words I've heard before.

It's why my parents never wanted me to play in its waters as a young boy—why storms ravage the borders of our island. Because Divina kill them. And Nomagi who do survive, are murdered in cold blood, and it will never stop.

I fall to my knees, and Ma falls with me, pulling me into her chest. Pa wraps his arms around us.

"I'm so sorry, Theo."

I shake my head. "You have nothing to apologize for. You saved me. You were the only good one amongst them. That's why she trusted you."

My mother. They killed her.

Suddenly, I stand, shaking from head to toe. "Who killed her?"

"I don't know. There were so many of them."

Red-hot rage boils through me. "I can't stay here."

"You have nothing to worry about. Divina can't hurt you. It's part of the deal that I made with—"

"No. I can't live on this island knowing that Nomagi are being slaughtered on its shores."

"It's about damn time," comes a voice from behind us.

We all whirl as Alexi Wilder, grandson of the man Ma made a deal with for my survival, strides out of the trees. His stance is casual, like he's not here to break his grandfather's deal and try to kill me for bonding with Izalia.

Wait. How would he have found out about us?

Izalia.

"If you hurt her, I'll—" I start, but he cuts me off with a laugh.

"You'll what? Shoot me again? That won't work. Now that I know you have the thing, I'm better prepared." He thrusts his arms out wide. "Try me!"

"I think I will," I spit, even though the gun isn't much use at the moment…under my bed.

"Calm down, boy. Nobody is shooting anybody," Pa says, stepping forward.

Alexi holds up a hand. "It was just a suggestion. I came here to voice the same thing your *boy* just said. You want to leave? I've got a ship for you. Just say the word."

"Theo isn't going anywhere," Ma says, stepping forward with Pa.

Alexi puts a hand over his heart as he paces the tree line, a hungry animal readying to make the kill. "It was his idea, Mrs. Ali."

"Let's go." Ma grabs my hand, but I don't move. "Theo." She looks at me, waiting for me to tell her that I don't actually want to leave the island. I can't lie to her.

"I don't belong here, Ma."

She leans into me. "And what about Izalia?"

My words ring true, I don't belong here, and I certainly shouldn't live here amongst those slaughtering Nomagi. But I'm more than some nobody Nomagi who got lucky as a babe. I have Divina parents who love me and have risked everything for me. I have the most beautiful Divina partner, who chose me and believes in me. I've promised to follow her anywhere and to always make her happy. I don't intend to ever break those promises. Izalia and I could bring change to these people—our relationship as a symbol. Or we can at least try. If we fail—they could choose to send us away or kill me—but I won't die a defeated man.

I don't say any of this to Ma. Instead, I say, "I'm going to talk to her."

Alexi stalks closer. "Oh, you're not taking Izalia anywhere."

"My *mate* can go wherever she wants." The words are out before I realize what I said.

Alexi stops mid-step. I watch as the realization washes over his features. He didn't know. I assumed he knew because why else would he be here? Ready to throw me into the tempest-strewn sea?

"What did you just say?" he says in a lethal whisper that seeps into my bones. I really need that gun.

He takes another step, and Pa blocks his advance, a hand raised in warning. "Stop right there, boy. It's done. Izalia and Theo made the bond. I'm sorry you had to find out this way. I know it can—"

Alexi explodes.

The air is knocked from me as I land in the dirt. I try to get my lungs working, but I can't get air into them. My vision is spotty, but I watch with a mixture of admiration and horror as Ma fights against Alexi.

Fire and rock swirl around them as Ma dodges his advances, sending them right back or throwing up water shields.

I landed near the edge of our fale. Where's Pa? I look over the landscape, but I don't see him anywhere.

Ma is graceful as she sends a tornado of fire his way. He dodges with a wicked smile on his lips. I gather my strength, my chest aching, and stumble into our home for the gun.

I reach for it under my bed, but it's not there. Panic seizes my body as a high-pitched scream echoes through the fale and curdles in my stomach.

Ma.

I dash out of the fale. Alexi is standing over her crumpled figure, a fireball in hand. I launch myself at him, tackling him to the ground. With rage igniting in my veins, I pound into him. With my next punch, he grabs my fist and twists me, throwing me off. I crouch low, energy buzzing through me, my knuckles cracked and bleeding. I prepare for him to launch another fireball, but instead, he smooths back his hair and dusts off his gray tunic with a frighteningly calm demeanor.

"I didn't come to fight your family. But you are coming with me." He gestures to Ma on the ground. "If you want them to live."

The fight in me dissipates as I watch her shallow breathing. I don't even know where Pa went.

I straighten, a wild, crazy idea taking form. "I will, but first, heal them."

He arches a brow. "You are in no position to ask favors of me."

I step toward Ma, my heart breaking. My sweet, selfless, passionate mother. "You said so yourself. If I want them to live, I come with you. So, heal them so they can live."

He studies me, and then his lips turn down in disgust. "I've tried to understand it. But I don't have a clue what Iz sees in you." He starts toward Ma. Relief washes over me.

"I'll be right back."

"Excuse me?" he says, pausing.

"I need to grab a few things to take. You know, with leaving the island and never returning?" Like I actually believe he's going to let me sail away into the sunset.

"Whatever," he spits. "But if you shoot me in the back, you're dead. I don't care if Izalia never forgives me for it."

When I know that he's trying to heal her instead of hurting her more, I escape into the house. I scrawl a quick note to my parents, hoping they understand or will forgive me if I fail.

When I'm done, I inhale, trying to capture the scent of home to keep with me in case I don't return. My hand drifts over the keys on my piano before grabbing a book from my shelf. This will work. It has to.

When I walk out of the house, a satchel in hand, the contents burn a hole through my side as I pray Alexi doesn't check it.

Alexi is finishing with Pa, who I can see now under the trees. My parents are passed out still. It's for the better. They'd only get themselves killed trying to fight for me. I'm done letting other people fight for me.

I kneel next to Ma, placing a hand on her cheek. Her heart beats strong. He's a psychopath, but at least he keeps his word. "I love you, Ma. Thank you for being the best mother a boy could ask for." I plant a kiss on her temple as an ache grows in my belly. She's sacrificed so much for me. No more. This ends today in one way or another.

I stand to say goodbye to Pa, but Alexi grabs my arm.

"After you."

I shake him off, taking one last glance toward Pa. He taught me what being a man looks like, and I will honor that to my last breath. *Love you, Pa.*

A strange calmness settles over me as Alexi trails me through the trees…and a feeling that I won't return. But I'm not afraid. I am Theodore Ali, Nomagi son of Iris and Boaz Ali, mate of Izalia Rane. This island is my home, and I will not bow down.

41

AZALIA

By the time I reach my house, my vision is cloudy, my brain is a jumbled mess, and I can't stop sweating. I clench my shaking hands. Fear wraps itself around my heart like a python. *Theo is safe.* I repeat the words over and over. They can't hurt him, only me. At least, not right away. My parents love me. That has to be enough, right? My mom will come around, but my dad…

I blow out a breath and open my door.

The house is too quiet. There should be smells of food cooking permeating the air. My mother has cooked breakfast every morning for the last eighteen years.

A glance to the spotless kitchen deepens my worry. I take careful steps to my parents' door and give it a slight knock. It's possible they slept in. There's a first for everything. No response.

I open the door and peek inside. I bite back a sickening feeling and step onto the stairs to look in my room. The realization hits me like a boulder in the stomach during Terra training.

I was not here when they awoke.

They would think the worst. I race to my room, taking two stairs at a time. My room is trashed. The book Theo gave me is wide open in the middle of my bed. I pick it up with shaky hands. Beau bounds into the room a second later, squawking.

I'm out the door before the book thuds onto the ground.

I don't stop knocking on Alexi's door, holding myself from barging in as it opens too slowly.

"Izalia?" Mrs. Wilder says, her dark eyebrows raised, wrinkles framing her eyes. Alexi got his high cheek bones and full lips from her. A beauty back in the day, now she just looks extremely tired. How could she raise such a terrible person?

"Where is he?" I ask.

"Looking for you. When your parents—"

My heart drops, and I leap off their porch before she can finish. I know what she's going to say. My parents came here to get Alexis's help in finding me. I don't need to guess where they would have gone.

I race through the trees. I'm going to be too late. I can only hope that Theo and his parents went to the market. If my parents and Alexi find them, it's not like they'll know immediately what Theo and I did. They would have to tell them, and they won't without me. They won't. But if they do—

They won't kill Theo. They can't. But if Alexi is alone…

I push myself faster. I stumble on a tree branch and right myself quickly. I get turned around in my panic and have to stop myself before I cause myself to have an episode. Beau screeches at me, leading me out of the trees and into the opening behind Theo's fale.

"Theo!" I race through the opening, peering into each room, but nobody is here.

Minutes later, I sprint into town, gasping for air. I haven't run full out like this in a long time, and my lungs are screaming at me to stop. A few people are setting up their booths under the community fale. They shrug when I ask about Theo and his parents.

I twirl in circles, ready to pull my hair out. He's not here, either. No, no, no. This cannot be happening.

My pulse pounds in my ears as the wind picks up around me. My senses sharpen and explode. There are suddenly too many smells, too many noises. I close my eyes against the too-bright sun. I throw my hands over my ears. The world is spinning faster and faster, and I can't stop it. They weren't supposed to go for him.

It's me. I did this, not Theo.

The ground trembles under my feet. Fire erupts along my skin.

I hold pressure on my head because I will shatter if I don't. How can I still hear everything? Shouts and screams intensify as water barrels burst around me. I can sense every water particle racing through the air.

"Theo! Theo!" I scream and scream and scream until rough hands are on my shoulders, pulling me backward.

I thrash, directing my fire at them, but the hands are like steel and continue to yank me away. My feet hit the sand, and water surrounds me, not of my making, extinguishing my fire. The person twists me towards them, but all I see are flashes of white amongst the world quaking around me.

"Izalia, control it! You need to control it!"

The flashes mold together into dark clouds. Lightning strikes through them. It dazes me for a moment, and the air clears, but everything is still moving too fast.

"I can't," I cry.

The ground cracks under my feet, the trees sway roughly, and bushes uproot. Embers kindle in my veins as cold water crashes into me, keeping the fire from igniting.

The world shakes again. No. *I'm* shaking. Long dark hair, green eyes, and a seashell necklace materialize in front of me.

Ainzel's hands are on my shoulders, shaking me roughly.

"Theo! Where is Theo?" I choke.

"Calm down and I'll tell you!"

My heart beats wildly in my ears as the shaking lessens. I close my eyes and focus on my Sage—the feeling of the wind, the fire burning inside my body, the cool water wrapping around me, the earth beneath my feet. I breathe through it—in and out, in and out. Theo. I can do this for Theo. The wind slows, and the earth stops vibrating.

Ainzel releases me. "There we go." He leans back, eyeing me. His hair flows to his waist—dark silky locks that would make any girl jealous.

I take stock of the wreckage around me and a path of uprooted trees that probably leads to market. I gape.

"Did I do that?" My hands tremble.

He nods. "Is it true? Did you and Theo bond?"

I grab his shoulder. "Where's Theo?"

His eyebrows rise, and he blows air into his cheeks. "I don't know."

My eyes bug out. I'm about to start shaking him.

He pushes his hair behind his ears. "But I know where his parents are."

"Then what are we doing here!" I throw my arms up and start walking.

"You needed to calm down, girl. Did nobody tell you how your magic would be amplified after the ceremony?"

I stop. "But he's a Nomagi. No magic to amplify."

He looks me up and down. "Guess that myth is false."

"Myth?"

"You see anyone bonded to a Nomagi around here?" He pulls a strip of fabric out of his pocket and twists his hair behind his head.

I shake my head and keep walking. "Where are we going?"

"His parents went to the city." He avoids my gaze as he finishes re-tying his hair. There's something he's not telling me.

"Why did they go to the city?"

He side-eyes me. "I don't want you to blow up again."

"Ainzel! I will hit you."

He waves away my aggression. "All I know is that there was an incident. His parents came to market looking for Theo and then went into the city. I was still in bed." He rubs his neck. "I knew I shouldn't have slept in."

"Did you hear anything else?"

He nods cautiously. "They were also looking for Alexi."

No, no, no. Alexi took Theo?

My vision blurs around the corners, and I can't dislodge the lump in my throat.

Ainzel places a hand on my shoulder. "Do you still feel him?"

I search my mind, rubbing the incision in my palm that's starting to scab. What is it supposed to feel like? Like the tiny flicker of flame in my chest? I move past that, and there—a spot in the middle of my heart that has Theo written all over it—his smell, his smile, his music. There is a slight humming sensation there. The connection is there. My body warms at the feeling.

I nod slowly.

"He's still alive then."

He's still alive, but that doesn't mean he's well. Alexi could be torturing him for all I know.

My chest tightens. I can't think like that, or I'll spiral again. Alexi is keeping him alive for a reason—to get to me. He wouldn't need to torture him for that. I wish the connection could tell me where he is.

"My parents realized I wasn't home and told Alexi, but he must have come alone, because my parents wouldn't have let him harm Theo."

"You sure?"

A chill runs through me, but I nod. My parents are good people despite their misgivings. "You said that Iris and Boaz were looking for Alexi, not my parents."

"And how do you think he found out you two bonded?"

I shrug, imagining him coming upon Theo and his parents and what that conversation would have been like. By the island. I should have followed our original plan, but I got scared, and now Theo is missing.

"Maybe Alexi followed you and saw?"

I shake my head as I dodge a tree branch and breathe through the panic, crawling to retake hold. "No way. He would have stopped the whole thing. My parents definitely told him that I was missing. Alexi's parents said—"

Actually, I didn't stay long enough to hear what Mrs. Wilder said. I assumed she would tell me my parents had come and got Alexi, but maybe he had already left. I don't think he could have held back if he saw me with Theo. Not with his anger issues. No. He came after, but maybe before I left, biding his time.

But how did he know?

It's silent between us for a beat.

"Could the Elders have known a ceremony was taking place?"

He looks toward the city as a muscle in his jaw ticks. "They are very much connected to the island, but no, I don't think they would be able to know that."

"You knew."

He looks at me with a raised eyebrow.

"You asked me if it was true that we were bonded."

He nods. "Theo's parents."

"Right. That was after Alexi took Theo." I groan, not feeling any closer to figuring this out.

The city comes into view as we walk through the grain fields, not bothering to go around. "We'll find him," Ainzel says confidently.

I hold on to that, willing myself to feel the same, but the pit in my stomach grows.

"You're lucky I came upon you. You could have blown the whole market apart."

I glare at him, but he's looking forward as we half-jog toward the rising city. "I haven't heard of others losing control before," I say. I would probably be embarrassed if I wasn't so worried right now.

"Well, usually they are more…" He looks at me. "Prepared beforehand. And the whole host of people there to witness the ceremony help absorb the excess energy."

I avert my eyes, thinking about what happened after our ceremony. A whole lot of energy was dispersed, that's for sure.

He clears his throat. "You guys at least…um…finished the ceremony, right?"

My cheeks flare—not just my cheeks—fire crawls up my neck and face as if he guessed the direction of my thoughts.

"I'm not trying to be nosy. It's just that you'd have almost no control over your abilities if you didn't. You'd be in a limbo state. It's very dangerous." He clears his throat. "You know what? Pretend I didn't say anything. You were able to gain control of yourself back there, so I'm guessing... Ugh. I'll shut up."

I train my eyes on my feet. "You don't have to worry about that," I mumble.

He grunts in response. Silence hangs between us until we hit the dirt path leading to the city, where the wind picks up, throwing my hair forward.

Ainzel shoots me a sharp look.

"It's not me!" I look toward the sky and gasp.

Ainzel follows my line of sight. "What the…?"

The sky is swirling with angry black clouds.

We look at each other and break into a sprint. It makes no sense. The Protectors keep the storms contained at sea. They shouldn't ever get this close.

Ainzel directs us to the second-tallest building on the island. By the time we open the doors, rain is falling. The bottom level is empty, so I race after Ainzel up the steps until voices meet us on the third level.

We open the doors to an office larger than my house. Glass walls cover two sides, with a couch and two chairs in the center. A desk made of dark wood I've never seen, takes up an indigo-colored wall. A giant painting of our island hangs above it. Seven people stand in the vast space, half of them yelling. My parents are shouting at Theo's parents. Theo's parents are shouting back. Alexi's grandfather is standing between them, whipping his head back and forth. If the situation weren't so dire, I'd laugh. My parents, who have never even raised their voices, are in an actual yelling match, with Elder Wilder as referee. The other two, an older guy and a middle-aged woman, who look familiar but I've never formally met them, look like they would rather be anywhere than here.

Ainzel clears his throat, acknowledging our entrance.

Everyone turns to us at once. The atmosphere is so charged that one spark would make it burst into flames.

My parents' faces soften as they wrap their arms around me. Iris and Boaz hover just behind them.

Iris hugs me, and my mom watches uncomfortably. "I'm so glad you're okay."

"Where's Alexi and Theo?" I ask the room.

Iris turns on Elder Wilder, shoving a finger into his chest. "Give me my son," she hisses.

Her ferocious stare has him blinking, but he quickly composes himself. "I already told you I do not know the whereabouts of my grandson. This is not my problem. I gave Theo to you at great cost to our island nineteen years ago, and your actions have brought this upon yourselves." His voice rises. "And then again, I let him stay after he wounded Alexi. Whatever happens to him now is out of my hands. I told you it would be better for him to return to the mainland, Iris."

"Oh, don't pretend you did that for anyone but yourself," Iris spits.

Boaz puts a hand on his mate's shoulder, but she steps closer to Elder Wilder, her face inches from his. My mouth drops open at the flash of fear in his eyes.

His face hardens. "Don't," he warns.

"What? You don't want anyone to know about your activities off the island?"

The room goes silent as Elder Wilder's face reddens. He pushes back his shoulders. "You don't know what you're talking about."

"Oh, I'm going to—" Iris launches herself at Elder Wilder just as the wall of glass behind them shatters.

The wind throws us all off our feet. Things are flying everywhere, inside and out.

"Get the Protectors!" Elder Wilder shouts to the woman over the roaring current of air.

She flees the room as he stands and brushes himself off.

He throws a withering look at Iris, who is helping the other man up, and says, "Get to the bottom floor." He waves us forward as we make our way down the steps.

More glass crashes somewhere else in the building. I wince, automatically latching onto Ainzel, who hasn't left my side. My mother is on my other side.

"What was that about?" I ask her under my breath.

She leans into me. "There are rumors that Elder Wilder has a secret life on the mainland. It's so outlandish none of us took them seriously, but now I'm not too sure."

I suddenly think of the foreign device Freylin had. Do her parents know? Could that be how they got the device?

"I believe it," I murmur.

Her eyes widen. A couple of weeks ago, I wouldn't have believed it. But now, something tells me that Tauvagna Wilder isn't the man he says he is.

"Mom?"

She looks at me as we round another set of stairs. So many questions buzz through my mind, but I can't voice them because her bewilderment turns into sorrow. I see the questions forming in her gaze.

"We thought you could have been with Alexi when we realized you weren't in bed this morning. I mean, you guys were supposed to get bonded today."

I bite my lip. They know.

"But when we went to his house, his parents told us that he was out looking for you."

So, he did leave before my parents got there.

"I knew I should have trusted my gut. When we were looking for you and Theo, we ran into his parents, who told us everything." She winces again. "It hasn't been pretty since." She squeezes my hand. "I'm sad you couldn't trust me enough to tell me, but I understand."

I look into her tear-filled eyes and feel like the worst daughter on the island. I open my mouth, though I'm still unsure what to say, when the doors to the building slam open.

"Sir! It's too strong. I did my best."

I twirl to see a young man barely above my age at the bottom of the stairs, his clothes soaked and hair windblown.

"Where are the others?" Elder Wilder asks.

"They're coming. I was on duty this morning. I switched with Tia just before sunrise, and all was calm. The storm was plenty far off. I had no hardship in controlling it, but it's as if…" He looks around for a moment, realizing he has an audience.

"Spit it out, boy!"

"It's as if one of *us* purposely pulled it here. Somebody powerful." He shakes his head. "I don't think any of us has such power, on our own at least. I—I don't understand."

Elder Wilder looks us over and settles his eyes on me. "I think I may know who."

My heart drops. There would only be one reason that Alexi would bring a storm here.

Time slows as my parents reach for me. I twirl out of their grasp and Ainzel grabs my elbow. I yank away from him, blasting him with air and launching down the stairs. I'm out the doors before their shouts can reach me.

The island is in turmoil. Trees sway violently as debris and objects fly through the air. The sky has opened up, angry that we've held it back for so long, as it pours without mercy.

Like a streaked shearwater, I fly into the typhoon to ride the wind, rain stinging my face. I concentrate on the connection inside me, feeling a pull I hadn't felt before. It's subtle, but it's there. I ignore my name being called faintly behind me, pushing my legs faster. They will only slow me down. I need to get to Theo. I've already wasted too much time.

The path winds toward the school. I shoot my arms out as a tree branch hurtles my way. It arches over me. I race across the front of campus. I strain my muscles to open the door, but it's sealed tight against the wind. It takes all my energy to focus on the direction of the wind and pull it away from the door. I yank it open at last.

The instant quiet inside is eerie. The only sound is the clicking of my sandals and the water dripping off my soaked dress as I race down the wide hall of the main building that holds the Instructors' offices. They're not here.

I catch my breath and turn toward the nearest doors to brave the storm again. They could be in any of these buildings. I dodge flying trash and branches until I reach the center of campus. The once beautifully decorated space is hardly recognizable. The statues of the six founders stand eerily in an empty pool. Pieces of them litter the ground.

"Theo!" I yell. A piece of paper flies into my mouth. Gagging, I spit it out, and familiar print catches my eye. The text looks just like the one from the book Theo gave me—like somebody ripped a page out of it. But this is not *Merry Animal Tales*. At the top, it reads *Heart of Darkness*. The page could only have come from one person.

I flip it over and stiffen. One sentence is scrawled on it. It doesn't make sense. I shove it in my pocket to think about later. I need to find him. They're here. I know it.

Think. Think. What would Alexi do? I know he wants Theo gone—

The boat dock. The Fishermen cast off on the other side of the island, but there's a boat here for educational purposes. I've gone out on it a few times for class. I race around the next building and see the dock extending into the ocean.

The sailboat is gone. Alexi sits on the sand with his hands in the water.

"Alexi!" I scream, but my voice dies in the wind.

I run, using the wind against him, throwing him backward. He sprawls onto the ground briefly before hopping up and twisting around to face me. He flashes me a wicked smile, his unbound hair slick down his face.

"Where is he?" The wind dies down just where we are. I'm not sure if it's him or me causing the calm.

"Who, Iz?"

"Theo. You psychopath."

He shakes his head sadly and raises a hand to me. "My poor wilted flower. What did you do?"

I fold my arms, ignoring the slight jab. "I'm guessing you already know, or we wouldn't be here."

"We're supposed to be preparing for our ceremony." Rage flashes in his eyes, but he cools it quickly. "Not to worry. It shouldn't be long now." His eyes travel towards the ocean.

I follow his gaze. There's a boat on the horizon, heading directly into the heart of the storm.

I splash into the water, but he catches me, wrapping his arms tightly around my torso and pinning my arms, throwing me to the ground with him. He lands on me as my face hits the sand, and warm saltwater flows around my legs. I kick out, connecting with something, but he doesn't let go.

"We're bonded. Kill him and you kill me!" I scream. "Then what *precious flower* will you have left to bond with?"

"You don't understand, do you?" he yells, twisting me so my back is in the sand, and he's sitting on top of me, my arms in his hands as I struggle against him. "You are mine," he growls. "He's nothing! His death will do nothing to you."

I spit in his face, watching in delight as his face changes colors, mucus traveling down his cheek. He slaps me. Then all I see are stars—no—sparks pulsating around me. Sparks that kindle the embers and ignite in my body.

Using my free arm, I blast him in the chest with a fireball. He stumbles away, patting away the flames.

I stalk towards him. "He is *not* nothing. He is more of a man than you will ever be—a man that I love with every fiber of my being. I have never felt anything for you, and I never will. I hated kissing you. You disgust me. With how much I love Theo, I loathe you tenfold."

I watch as the daggers hit home. An iciness settles over his features.

I prepare myself for his onslaught, but he lowers his voice. "I should have finished you off for good."

"What are you talking about?"

He smiles. "When I pushed you out of that damn tree."

I shake my head. "You've never—"

I stop as his smile grows. He stalks around me like a predator, and I'm his prey. I turn my body, keeping him in front of me with one hand up, ready to defend myself if needed.

"Only because I made sure you wouldn't remember. Maybe I can jog your memory."

He snaps his fingers, and a fire ignites above his palm. It grows as pictures form and dance in the flames. He's even more powerful than I thought. I don't know of anyone that can do that.

There's a picture of me as a small child in a tree, baby Beau cupped in my hands. It was the day I found him. The image pans out, and I see eight-year-old Alexi in the tree with me. I'm yelling at him.

"You were telling me off for killing his mom."

I gasp, looking up at him. There's no sympathy in his eyes.

"It threw poop at me. It was disgusting." He shrugs. "You saw and saved the baby monkey. Told me that you would tell my parents and that you hated me." He cocks his head. "Similar to what you were saying earlier, actually." He shrugs again. "I didn't want to get in trouble, not for killing the monkey but for making you hate me. My parents were so insistent on me being your friend that I had to get you to like me. I needed you to forget. So, I—"

I watch the flames with horror as Alexi pushes me out of the tree, and I fall onto my head. He climbs slowly down, tilts his head, and pokes me with his foot, no compassion in the little boy's eyes. Then he takes off, leaving me as a crumpled heap on the ground, with Beau crying in the crook of my elbow.

The flame snuffs out.

I place my hand over my mouth. "All this time."

"It actually feels nice to get it off my chest," he says with a smirk.

Bile rises in my throat. "Why are you telling me now?"

He shoves his hands in his pockets and backs away from me, eyes on the raging storm at sea. "Because your darling Theo is about to die, and you're going to go try to save him. You won't make it in time, of course. Which means you won't return either. It's a shame, really. We would have been powerful together." His eyes narrow. "But I don't need you."

He raises a hand, and lightning strikes the ocean just past the dock. I jump, glancing at how close that was. How could I compete with power like that?

Movement catches my eye at the edge of the tree line, and I look back at Alexi. He thinks he's won.

My blood heats, and I try to control my breathing. "You always underestimated the creatures. Sure, they're not much on their own, but together?" Rage makes my heart take off. "Now, Beau!"

Confusion crosses Alexi's features, but he doesn't get a chance to move before they're all on him—every monkey on the island. Beau had gathered them all for me, waiting for my command.

Alexi falls to the ground, yelling and thrashing, trying unsuccessfully to throw them off. Every time he manages to get one off, another pounces.

"Looks like monkeys hold grudges. I always wondered why Beau hated you. And little me was a great judge of character, by the way. I never liked you either."

I place my hands on the ground and roots shoot through the soil and wrap around his wrists and ankles. He throws me a dagger-filled glare, but I turn on my heel and head toward the ocean.

I pause when a giant kingsnake slithers in my peripheral. I can't fight the smile that pulls at my lips. "Darlah is a great judge of character, too, and I don't think she's going to like you," I say over my shoulder.

I leave him to the animals and focus on the boat, which is drifting farther and farther out as the waves toss it side to side. My chest heaves, and my pulse is deafening in my ears as wave after wave crashes into it. It's still upright, and I can still feel Theo.

I take a deep breath and harness my Sage. I've only done this a few times, lasting only a few seconds. Theo never saw weakness in me. Alexi, my parents, and everyone I grew up with always saw my disability first. Theo only ever saw *me*. I can do this. I have to do this.

I step onto the water. It's like trying to balance on—well, water—but it holds. I take another step and stabilize myself, but then somebody pulls me back.

I look up at my mother's face. "What are you doing?" she screams. She's sopping wet from the rain, her hair plastered to her makeup-smudged face, and her eyes are wild as they take me in.

"Theo is out there!" I say, pointing at the boat getting farther away by the second. I yank out of her arms.

"You'll get yourself killed, Izzy."

"And I will die if I don't do it," I snap.

She looks at me with a mixture of sympathy and fear. "If you make it, you won't be able to return."

"You already told me that."

"No! Because of the bonding. You're both…banished. That's what we were yelling about when you came in earlier."

My senses hone in on the water at my feet, where they sink deeper into the wet sand with every wave, bonding me to the earth of this island as the man I love drifts farther away. The ocean is constant. The waves consistently crash onto the shoreline day and night. They are as consistent as a heartbeat.

But unlike a heart that will stop beating at the end of one's life, the spangled waves will continue on, unbothered by our earthly existence. The white caps of the water will appear day in and day out. I can count on them.

Home. This is my home.

I look past my mother at the landscape. The island is all I know. How could I leave it?

"But if you stay and he—" She can't even say the word. "Maybe you'll be okay. You've gone through worse."

Theo.

The island may be perfect, but the people aren't. People are corruptible. Theo is my home, the rope that tethers me to the ground. If that requires a different setting, as long as I have him, it'll be worth it. My new constant. Always by my side.

I pull the page out of my pocket, finally understanding, but completely sickened. I push it into her hand. Her eyes widen as she reads it.

"It's true, isn't it?"

Her silence is my answer.

I shake my head, stepping back into the warm water. "We can be better. Make it better, Mom. It can be your new purpose. You don't need to fight for me anymore. I'm okay." I smile.

Her eyes are still wide, still trying to comprehend. I glance over her shoulder at Alexi, who's managed to get his feet. He's limping and bleeding badly. He deserves worse.

I grab her hand. "Alexi is the one who pushed me out of the tree. That entire family is rotten to the core. But I guess we all are a little if we're allowing *that*." I indicate the paper and turn.

"Wait!" She throws her arms around me. "Not you. Never you. You have always been the best of all of us. You're right. We need to be better." She smooths my hair. "I promised that I would fight for you until the end."

She pushes me into the water. I stagger, but then realize I'm on top of the waves.

She smiles at my realization. "Be happy, Izzy." Tears stream down her face as she closes her eyes in concentration.

I run, not wanting to waste a second of her help. There may be hope for my people after all.

Every footstep is more solid than the last. Her magic dissipates, but energy pulses through me, keeping me from sinking. I push myself, racing faster across the massive waves. The boat is so far, though. Lightning strikes not too far away.

But then, suddenly, the clouds clear above me, and the waves lessen. I glance up. The dark storm clouds are retreating. Maybe the Protectors are doing something to combat Alexi. It does nothing for the storm out at sea, though. They wouldn't worry themselves about that.

I'm getting closer, but I don't know how much longer I can hold this. My magic is declining. A huge wave crashes onto the boat, almost capsizing it. I push myself harder, ignoring the pain in my legs, the burning in my lungs, and the dizziness of pushing the elements to the extreme. I feel myself waning. Maybe I'm close enough to swim now.

I release the control incrementally and begin to sink, but there is a shift in the water. My attention is pulled back to shore, where three figures bend down. I can only guess it's my mom, but the other two? I squint. Theo's parents? Guilt ripples through me. They didn't get to say goodbye to him. I wonder if they hate me for causing all this.

A large wave going in the wrong direction surfaces behind me. The water is up to my knees now, and my body slackens as it rises higher, speeding me toward the boat. I lurch upward, trying to balance on the wave like when I'd surf as a little girl. It reaches its peak, throwing me into the air. I'm weightless above the black waters.

A feeling of wonderment and terror envelops me. I'm invincible.

But the water is rising faster than I can stop it. I barely get a breath in before I'm spinning under the surface. Dizzy, I don't know which way is up or down. I swim, pushing myself to what I hope is the surface, but I'm knocked sideways by another wave.

My lungs burn as they beg for oxygen—the edges of my vision blur. It's too dark. I'm in a black abyss where I will never breathe again.

THEO

As the storm wreaks havoc around me, tossing the boat like a leaf in the wind, I feel that strange calm again. My only regret is not that I failed to get away from Alexi, though that does sting a little. I regret not reaching Izalia in time.

I hold the warm shark-tooth necklace in my palm. I felt it pulling me to her, but I couldn't go. I couldn't bring her into this. I planted the seeds, which will blossom on this island like a rare flower. And when they pick the flower, the truth will unravel. It will fester inside their hearts until the effects can't be undone, and the island will finally breathe. Divina will have a new reality, and I can only hope that it will bring harmony in the end—that Izalia will have a better life for it, even if I can never experience it.

Despite my peace, I ache to hold her one last time, kiss her, and tell her how much I love her and that I'll always be with her. I can't imagine being far from her side, even in death.

A wave crashes into the boat, knocking me into the wall of the tiny cabin I've taken shelter in to wait for the inevitable. The storm is growing angrier, waiting to devour me.

The sea has a taste for Nomagi.

I look out a window, back at the island one final time. And there, like a beacon of everlasting fire, my angel of the ocean has come for me. She walks on the water—unaffected by the storm raging around her—my beauty of the sea, its conqueror.

For a moment, I swear it's a vision or another dream brought on by how close I am to the end. But I blink, and she's still there.

I throw open the door and catch myself on the railing. "Izalia!"

Wait. She can't come here. There is only death out here, and that is not her fate—only mine. "Izalia, no!" I scream, but the wind rips the words away before they leave my mouth.

Water sprays me, the salt stinging my eyes, but I won't close them. A huge wave ascends behind her. I can't breathe or move as I watch in horror, my hands gripping tightly to the railing, preventing me from launching toward her.

But the wave is moving the wrong way. Waves move toward land, not from it. The wave picks her up, launching her to land only yards from the boat.

I blink, and she's gone.

I dive.

IZALIA

Arms wrap around me as I take my first breath of air. I cough the salt water out of my lungs and fight the sting in my eyes as Theo guides me toward a ladder attached to the boat. With impressive strength, I'm hoisted halfway up. I climb the rest of the way. I sprawl flat on the deck, trying to suck in as much air as possible but it's not long until I'm back in his arms. His eyes are wild, searching my face. There's a cut above his left eye, but he's otherwise unharmed.

"Izalia! What are you doing?" Theo asks.

"I'm coming with you," I choke, my throat scraped raw.

"No! That's so stupid!" He shakes his head and grabs my face. He's angry, but terror fills his eyes as he smashes his lips into mine. I melt into him, but he pulls away too quickly.

"So stupid!" he repeats and kisses me again. This time on my temple. "It's a death sentence!"

"I don't care. I'd rather die with you on this boat than live on that island without you."

He kisses me again and touches my face. "You're really here. I didn't think I'd ever see you again. But that was very stupid."

I roll my eyes. "You already said that," I say, trying to sit up. The intense rocking of the boat makes it hard, but with his help and cautious eye, I'm finally on two feet.

"Not only could you have had an episode out there doing that, but—" His eyes widen. "We have to turn the boat around."

It didn't cross my mind that I could have blacked out and drowned. It's been a while since I've had an episode. Then I register the second part of the sentence.

"Wouldn't that have been the first thing you tried? Turning the boat around?"

"Let me show you the problem."

Another wave crashes into the boat, throwing us into the railing, which keeps us from falling back into the ocean. Pain shoots up my side.

He holds tightly to me, and we make our way to the door of the small cabin. There's barely enough room for the two of us. Once we're safely inside and Theo wrestles the door closed, I gape at where the steering wheel should be.

"That does pose a problem, but we can't go back anyway."

"You'll never be able to return. Your family…" he says, voice laced in pain.

I search the small space for anything that might help us, but I don't know much about boats. "I know."

He lifts my chin until I meet his gaze. "You haven't thought this through. Come on. With your magic, I'm sure we can figure out how to steer this thing without a wheel."

"I don't want to go back," I say, touching his jaw. "I saw one of the pages. There are more, aren't there? You released the truth."

He smiles. "You found one?"

I nod, leaning in to kiss him again. "The island is built upon bones and lies. Bring back the light," I say, repeating the words he wrote. "I wondered why you asked me about ships the night I stayed with you. The barrier reef, I'm guessing?" It's the only place on the island that is off limits.

He nods solemnly, his eyes taking on a faraway expression. Another wave knocks us into the glass, and my body presses into his.

"I went looking for closure and found a mass graveyard. Ma said that my mother was still alive when they shipwrecked."

I suck in a breath and close my eyes. His mother was still alive. She was murdered by my people. He cups my face, wiping away a tear that escapes. It's even worse than I thought.

"We need to go back, Izalia."

For the first time in my life, I'm ashamed of being a Divina. I shake my head without opening my eyes. I'll never go back.

"Izalia, we won't live through this storm. Let's first live, and then we'll figure out the rest."

I open my eyes to his bright-blue ones, filled with determination.

He's right. We need to live, because a world without Theo is not one worth living in.

"What do you suggest?"

He points to the gaping hole. "What do you think the wheel connected to?"

"Umm, something in the water?"

He nods. "Exactly. Maybe if you can control where that goes, we can turn ourselves around."

"But I don't know what I'm looking for, and I need to know how it works in order to try to manipulate it—*if* I can manipulate it."

My chest aches, pain radiating up my side and into my ribs. My limbs feel heavy all of a sudden as I rest against the wall. Running across the ocean completely drained me. Theo catches me as I slump to the bottom.

"Izalia!"

"I'm okay, just exhausted," I say.

He pushes my hair behind my ear. Even though this is not the time for it, a spark runs through me at the contact, his closeness, and his body heat. "Okay, forget my plan. Maybe we can hunker down and wait it out."

I look at him. We both know there is no waiting it out. This storm is going to kill us.

I grab his tunic—the same one he wore this morning when we performed the bonding ceremony—and pull him close. The memories of our blissful, euphoric morning return, and I want them back. I'd do anything to get those moments back.

"I can do it…or at least try. I just need a minute," I say, our lips inches apart. Heat floods my veins, and I want to intertwine myself with his body and never let go.

He seems to sense the shift of my thoughts. "I thought you were tired?" he says, raising an eyebrow.

My lip twitches upward. "Maybe you can fuel the fire in me."

He flashes a boyish smile and runs his fingers down my face, sliding them against the nape of my neck to my collarbone. Heat trails after his fingers.

"I think it's helping," I murmur. It actually is, though. The spark inside of me grows. "Did you know you made me stronger?"

His eyebrows rise as his fingers hover over my throat. "What do you mean?" His breath raises goosebumps along my skin.

"My magic. I've been stronger since our ceremony. They said that wouldn't happen with a Nomagi, but it did. You made me…more. There is something inside of you." I place my hand against his chest, over his heart.

His Adam's apple bobs. "I did?" he says slowly, studying my face.

"How do you feel since we…?" I start.

He smiles. "Happier, more fulfilled, euphoric. I feel…more, too. But not like you, obviously. But I thought it was just because I was happy, not that you physically gave me anything."

I brush my lips against his. "We complete each other."

Our lips meld together just to be immediately thrown apart. My head hits the wall, and Theo slams against the door so hard it flies open. The door rips from the doorframe and is lost to the black void outside.

Theo holds onto the doorframe as he slides toward the boat's edge. My vision is fuzzy, but I reach for him, and he grabs my outstretched hands. My muscles scream, his hands slippery, but I hold tight. Together, we pull ourselves underneath where the steering wheel should be.

"I'm going to try it!" I yell, placing my hands on the floor and closing my eyes.

I center myself and push the boat to follow my will. Water surrounds us. I don't know which direction land is.

"Where's land?"

Theo doesn't answer, but the warmth from his palms around me, holding me against him in the cramped space, helps. My strength and energy return, and I force it into the boat, flexing that distant muscle in my mind. There's a churning darkness to my right, so I choose the opposite direction.

With a jolt, I think we're moving. I'm doing it. We're doing it.

I open my eyes and twist my body to look over the helm and out the front window where the glass has long since shattered. There is the tiniest sliver of light ahead. I smile and glance at Theo. His eyes are closed, and his face is surprisingly pale. My heart accelerates. Did he hit his head when he flew out? I shake him, and his eyes flutter open.

"Theo, we're doing it! Look!" I point to the sliver of light, but he can barely move his head. I feel his cheeks. They are ice-cold, but his palms are warm.

The realization hits me like a punch to the gut. I leap away from him, pressing myself against the opposite side, making sure I'm not touching any part of him.

"What are you doing?" He reaches for me, but his hand falls as his eyes flutter closed. "I was helping you, right? I could feel it, Izalia. I could feel it," he slurs.

I shake my head, horror-struck. "Theo, I was depleting you. Don't ever do that again."

"What? No." He weakly shakes his head.

"Promise me you won't do that again." But as I say the words, the sliver of light on the horizon dims. The storm is pulling us back in.

I crawl to Theo and grab his face. "We live together, or we die together. You got it?"

His eyes close, and I shake him.

"I'm okay. I'm okay. I feel…okay."

"I wonder if I can help with that." I press my palms into his cheeks, and he works on keeping his eyes on me. Taking the excess energy pulsing through my body, I push it into him. My hands warm, and color returns to his cheeks. "There. How do you feel?"

He straightens, nodding, but lays his head against the wall. "Izalia." He grabs my hand, and I eye it. He lifts one side of his mouth in a lopsided grin. "Worried I'm going to sneak-energize you?"

"I mean it, Theo. We're in this together. I'm not going to kill you in order to get back to the island."

Pain flashes across his eyes. "It may be the only way."

"No, I've got this." I point at him and give him a look. I close my eyes, ensuring he's not touching me first. I had no idea that was even possible, but like Ainzel said, nobody has bonded with a Nomagi before.

Pushing my magic back into the boat, I find more resistance, but after a moment I feel the boat move to my command again— away from the darkness. I got this. The air thickens, and it's hard to draw breath, but for some reason, the boat is moving faster, almost like it's doing it on its own now.

Theo shakes me, and I open my eyes. His face is panic-stricken as he looks past me. Dread fills me as I turn my head.

A wave twice the size of our tallest building on the island is looming ahead, dragging us in. And I can't stop it.

"Izalia, please." He raises his palms to me. "Take it. Take it all. Please. Live. Please." Tears stream down his cheeks. Sobs break through as I shake my head.

"Theo, not even that will help us now."

He can see the truth in my eyes and nods slowly, opening his arms wide. I bury myself in his chest, and he holds me, crushing me to him.

"We're going to have a beautiful little boy," I say, my daydream suddenly becoming bright and clear.

He stiffens, but I don't stop.

"I thought he'd have your eyes but he won't. He'll have mine, but your golden locks."

"He'll have your attitude. He'll get into all sorts of mischief," he responds, playing along.

I smile. "And your musical talents."

"Your love for animals."

I look up at him. He's smiling down at me. I outline his lips with my finger. "Your gentle, kind heart."

He rubs my cheek with his thumb. "Your ability to love deeply."

"I love you, Theo," I choke.

"Until my very last breath," he whispers across my lips.

I lean into him, and he kisses me softly. The turmoil all around fades until it's only the two of us. Our lips melt into one, and I close my eyes, cataloging every inch of him—his sweet vanilla taste mixed with the salt of the ocean, his soft lips, the feel of his sun-kissed skin against mine, the tingles that run through my body when his hands are on me. This love is forever. No matter what happens, it will always be him.

44

THEO

er lips are on mine, and I can picture it so easily—the two of us growing old together with our beautiful little boy. We continue to live on the beach, unable to be far from the ocean. We tried, but we couldn't fall asleep without the sounds of the waves nearby. Our island-bred hearts will always bring us back.

Despite how often she says he looks like me, the boy is an image of his mother. He'll have her radiant smile, blinding me with it every time we practice piano and he gets the notes just right. His hands are so small on the keys, but he picks it up quickly. Izalia watches it all, one proud mama. I envision her eyes getting those little wrinkles, the first signs of aging. But she's just as beautiful as the day we met.

She asks me to play her song often, and I do, adding more verses as the years pass. Our son becomes a marvelous young man with a heart of gold. Like his mother, he likes to wield magic, and he has a talent for it, too—almost as good as his talent for music.

He's happy.

She's happy.

I dance with her on the water's edge, the waves lapping onto our feet. She asks me to sing to her. So that's what I do. My sweet, beautiful Izalia. My forever love. My angel of the ocean.

45

AZALIA

I'm tumbling through the water, ripped from Theo's warm embrace, the hum of his chest, his lips against mine. Water wraps around me, my forever companion.

I open my eyes as needles stab into them—a good sign that I'm still alive. The water is a dark chasm, reaching forever in all directions. I kick and swim to what I hope is the surface, but something crashes into my stomach, pulling me down and down and down.

Bracing my hands against it, I throw the force of the water, blasting it away from me, and kick for the surface. I gasp, pulling air into my lungs, and look around. Taking in the absence of the boat and the debris floating on the rough waters, I don't see Theo.

"Theo!" I grab onto what looks like the door to the small cabin and cling to it, coughing out the water in my lungs. "Theo!"

Taking a huge gulp of air, I return to the watery depths. I clasp my hands to create a ball of Aura light and push it through the water. Everything beneath and around me lights up.

Just as the light starts to dissipate, it shines off something golden. Theo.

I kick towards him, using the force of water to bring him to me as I swim. I wrap my arms around his torso and launch upward. His head lolls against my shoulder as we break the surface. I swim under his weight to the door, hooking my arm onto it. Holding him with the other, my heart pounds in my chest. I'm not strong enough to lift him. I let go of the door to pat his face.

"Theo," I choke.

I reach for our connection but am greeted by a widening hole. The door drifts away, and I paddle with one arm to get it, almost slipping under the water again. I focus on the water and pull to create a wave beneath us. It hits us, and I shove Theo halfway onto the door. I sink into the water and push his legs the rest of the way, the muscles in my arms screaming.

I pause to catch my breath before climbing up after him, careful of my balance so as to not send us back into the ocean's embrace.

I grab his face. "Theo!"

There's only a hint of my magic and energy reserves left. I seal my mouth against his and blow. Water shoots out of his nose. He's still unresponsive. I blow again and again. This isn't working. Sobs work their way up my chest. I can do this. I can do this. Don't panic.

I straddle him, careful not to tip us over and start compressions the way my parents taught me, with two hands over his heart—his non-beating heart. I swallow the fear and hysteria trying to bubble up, pushing into his chest over and over again, then plug his nose and blow. His chest rises.

It's been so long since they taught me, I don't even know if I'm doing it right, but I keep going. Compressions and then breaths, over and over again. I push the last of my strength and magic into those compressions, hoping our bond can revive him somehow. This has to work. It has to.

"Theo, please live. I can't go on without you. Please, Theo. I love you so much. What about our little boy? Remember, he needs you. Please, Theo." My hands are numb as I fall onto his chest, sobbing into his too-cold neck.

With one hand in a fist, I hit his chest. "Theo, Theo, Theo," I say the words with every hit of his chest.

A slight flutter in his chest makes me sit up. I return to the compressions, even though my arms are about to snap in half. Water dribbles out of his mouth as his chest rises at last.

"Theo!" I cry in relief.

I turn his head so any water can come out easier. I carefully lay next to him, placing my ear against his chest. His heartbeat is soft and erratic, but it's there. His heart is beating.

I stay like that for who knows how long. Clouds still darken the sky, and rain is my constant companion, but we're floating away from the worst of the storm. I tell him more about our future and steal kisses on his cheek, which is still too cold. I squeeze his hand occasionally, waiting for him to squeeze back, but he doesn't.

Eventually, I settle half on top of him so he can't accidentally slide off without my knowing and close my eyes. Feeling the exhaustion of pushing my magic and my body to the limit, I let the heaviness of sleep drag me under.

A loud horn startles me awake. Theo is still underneath me. A large white ship floats close by, nothing like the Divina have on the island.

The Nomagi found us. We must have drifted outside the perimeter of the storm.

"Theo, wake up, somebody found us!" My voice is rough, barely above a whisper. I shake him, but his body is much too stiff. "Theo?" His skin is ice-cold. I shake him again. "Theo!"

I place my ear to his chest. Nothing.

I shakily remove my head from his cold, too-still chest. I stare and stare and stare at his beautiful face. Not comprehending. Not understanding. His heart was beating. Wasn't it? I heard it.

But…but I fell asleep. No. I did this. I did this to my Theo.

My blood turns into ice. I palm his cheek, pushing back his hair and tracing the outline of his face like the night he slept in my lap. He's only sleeping. This isn't real. I'm dreaming. That's it. I'll wake up and find him at his house, face full of color, a smile on his lips.

I lay back down and close my eyes. And wait to wake up. Just a dream. Just a dream.

I'm wrapped in a blanket when I wake again, lying on my bed. I sit up, but when I look around, I'm not in my bedroom. I'm in a strange place where all colors have melted away. The walls and ceiling are white, white blankets are draped from the ceiling, and even the bed is white. The light is peculiar and unnatural, giving me an instant headache.

Where am I? How did I get here?

I kick the blankets off. Then I remember the storm splitting the boat apart and the aftermath, being on a door. The awful dream. Theo.

"Theo?" I choke out. My voice doesn't sound like my own. I try again. "Theo?"

Footsteps sound out, and I slide off the bed. The floor rises too quickly, and I'm suddenly in somebody's arms.

"Theo!" I say, my voice full of relief. I look up and see the light curls and immediately burst into tears, wrapping my arms around him. "You're alive. You're alive!"

A smell stings my nose. He smells all wrong, like pesticides on sugar cane. And come to think of it, his chest is too small. Did he lose weight? It doesn't matter, as long as he's okay.

He helps me to my bed, where I can finally get a good look at him.

But it's not Theo. This face is thinner and all wrong.

I jump back, scrambling to the other side of the bed, putting as much distance between me and this Theo look-alike.

"Woah there." The man's voice sounds strange.

A woman appears next to him, holding a clipboard. Her hair is bright red. It's so odd, yet beautiful, like fire.

"Where's Theo?"

Her eyes are wide and blue—both their eyes are blue—but not the same as Theo's. No, nobody could have eyes like his.

"Please lay back down. I don't want you to pass out again," the woman with fire hair says. She enunciates the wrong parts of words.

"Again?" I ask.

"Do you not remember?"

I'm feeling more and more confused by the second. But between the too-bright lights, the terrible smells that burn my nose, and the pounding of my head, if I don't sit, I may soon see the contents of my stomach.

"Please just tell me where Theo is."

The man clears his throat. "What does he look like?"

The woman shoots him a look, but he doesn't take his eyes off of me, so I tell him. He nods, his face falling. He and the woman share a look.

She steps toward me. "May I check your vitals?"

"Huh?"

"Your heartbeat, blood pressure, body temperature, that kind of thing. Just want to make sure you're okay."

I stifle the questions those words cause and say, "Only if you tell me where he is."

She blows out an exasperated breath and opens her mouth. The guy places a hand on her shoulder and steps toward me. A little too close. I scoot back until my back hits something hard.

"Some fishermen found you in the ocean outside the Devil's Triangle. Did your ship go down in there?" He shakes his head. "It's a miracle you survived. Nobody has gone in there and returned."

I stare at him, and the woman nudges him. "Too soon, Maverick." He ignores her, studying me.

Devil's Triangle? Is that what they call our island? "I just want to know where Theo is."

"There was a man with you. Is that Theo?"

I sit up. "Yes! That's him!"

He nods as if he expected me to say this. "He's gone." His voice comes out rough.

"What do you mean gone? Like he left? He wouldn't do that. Not without me." I look around. This place must be bad. I need to get out of here and find Theo.

He opens his mouth to respond, but the woman sidesteps him. "We will tell you what we know. Please just let me get your vitals. And maybe a name?"

I hesitate. "Izalia."

She nods and moves her pencil against the clipboard.

She pulls a silver rope from around her neck, closing in on me. I cringe away from her. Her face softens as she touches the end of it to her palm. "All this does is let me listen to your heartbeat. I'm going to put it on your chest."

I look at the guy, and he nods, so I nod warily. It's not like I can trust either of them. She places it on my chest, and that's when I realize that I'm in a light-blue paper gown, and I think I'm naked underneath it.

She writes something else down and pulls out another device. This one is blue and flat, made from some strange cloth. "I'm going to wrap this around your arm. It'll give you a light squeeze."

I let her, and she scribbles more notes.

"What are you writing?"

"Just your information."

"What are you going to do with it?"

"Oh. Well, we need everyone's information in order to treat them."

"Treat me? Is something wrong with me?" I move my limbs and take a deep breath. My body is sore, and my ribs hurt, but I think I'm okay. "Did I have another episode?"

She cocks her head. "What do you mean?"

I hesitate but tell her. "I randomly black out, and my body shakes."

Her eyebrows lift, and she writes down more things. "Epilepsy?"

"I don't know what that is."

"Where are you from?" interrupts the guy—Maverick.

I can't handle the questions anymore. I just want to know where Theo went. "Please tell me where Theo is, and then I'll tell you everything."

Maverick looks at the woman, and she nods. "When the fishermen found you, they said the man with you was already deceased. He had been gone for a long time. They couldn't peel you off his body. You even threw some of them into the ocean. They had to restrain you until they got to Cape Canaveral."

I cover my ears, shaking my head. "No, no, no, no. They're lying. I didn't do those things. He's fine. His heart was beating."

"We have him in the morgue, if you want to see."

"He's here?" I gasp. "Yes! Yes, I want to see him. Bring me to him right now."

The two share a look, and the woman sighs. She must be in charge. The guy reaches out to help me, but I swat him away.

They lead me down white corridors filled with people dressed similarly to them and me. Everyone's hair, even their skin color, seems to be a different shade. I can't help but stare at a guy whose skin is as black as night. I have so many questions but push them to the back of my mind. I just need Theo, and then we can figure out all this together.

I follow them into a metal box and hesitate at the opening. "What is this?"

"An elevator."

I cock my head. "What does it do?"

"It's going to take us down to the morgue."

I take a deep breath and step into it, feeling too closed in. But I walked on water. I can do this for Theo.

They push buttons that light up on the side of the metal box, and the ground moves from under my feet. I grab Maverick's shoulder, holding too tight. But he doesn't try to push me away. When the thing comes to a stop, I let go. The woman steps out, and I follow her, with Maverick trailing behind me.

The space is darker, but the light resembles the other rooms we passed. They remind me of light orbs but are long and stuck to the ceiling—another question to add to the list.

We walk to a glass-embedded wall, and they slow.

"Wait here."

A door slides open in the glass, and Maverick enters. There looks to be a bunch of tables with more white cloth draped over them and lumpy things underneath. Maverick chats with another man inside what seems to be a tank. There is glass on all sides. He nods and grabs one of the tables. It has wheels. That's pretty ingenious. He moves it close to us.

Where's Theo? I look around, but there are no other people in the room.

Maverick joins me and the woman again. "Are you sure you want to see?"

I stare at him. "Theo is down here? I don't see him."

He clears his throat and shifts uncomfortably on his feet. He looks behind me at the woman. She places a hand on mine, and I yank it away.

"You said you would show me him. He isn't here!"

"Izalia, he's right there." She points to the table on the other side of the glass—to the lumpy object underneath the blanket.

I stare and stare at it. The lumpy object does kind of look person-shaped. But it's not moving. "He's under the blanket? Why on earth is he under there?" I can't do this anymore. I push past the guy and reach the door.

He grabs my arm, and I launch him away from me. He lands hard against the wall. I wince, but there's no time to worry about him right now, not when something could be wrong with Theo.

I move into the room. Dread fills me as I walk to the blanket. The other guy blocks my path.

"You can't be here."

I wave my hand, and he slides out of my way. I reach for the blanket and throw it off.

I freeze. I can't move. I can't breathe. I can't. I can't. I can't. I can't. I can't look away.

It's Theo. Or it used to be him.

Whatever is on this table isn't him anymore. It's the shape of him. It has his hair and high cheekbones and even wears the shark-tooth necklace that I gave him. But it's not him.

I grasp onto the necklace as a high-pitched wailing sound that I can't place takes over the room. The walls shake. The lights blink. Sharp things fly through the air. I don't care if I get hit. Any pain is better than this sickening pain that is wrapping around everything in my body.

There's a tearing sensation in my heart, in my head, in my very bones. It's pure, unadulterated agony. And it's ripping me apart from the inside out. I will be dust soon, and this will all be over.

Something sharp pricks my arm, and everything goes black.

I wake back in the white room in the white bed with the people dressed in white watching me. The only color is their hair. More have joined the two that were previously with me. I can't look at Maverick's curls. I try to sit up but quickly realize my wrists and ankles are attached to the bed.

I shake them but feel so weak. I lie back down. Fine. Let them watch me. Let them watch as I cave into myself and die. I want to die. *Please kill me,* I want to shout, but I can't form words. I just look up at the too-white ceiling.

He's gone. I can't think his name. It's too much.

That tearing sensation returns, and I want to finish the job. Maybe I could. Lighting myself on fire wouldn't do anything. Could I suck the very air from my lungs? It might be worth a shot. But no, I'd probably just pass out, and my body would breathe on its own. I can't do it by fire or air. Earth? I could break open the earth, let it swallow me whole. No. That would take more people than just me. I don't want others to die—just me.

That leaves water. Yes, water. I'll go the same way he did. Then we can be together again. I just need to convince them to let me use the bathroom, and the rest will be easy.

I take a deep breath, about to say the words when somebody's cool hand presses against my forehead. I flinch, but they don't pull it back.

Ready to bite their damn hand off, I scowl at the person—not like that would help my predicament. But the throbbing in my head fades, and my mind clears. A young woman who can't be more than a few years older than me looks at me curiously. Her hair is dark like mine, but so are her eyes, the color of earth.

"She's an Aura, all right," she says.

Aura. How does she know that word? There are murmurs around her as she smiles at me.

"Now, if we release you, will you be good and not make any more knives fly through the air?"

I don't respond.

"Izalia, right? You don't need to be scared. I'm an Aura myself." She flicks her wrist, and the thing wrapped around my right foot unclenches, and I can move it. She flicks her other wrist, and the other one releases me.

I sit up warily, pulling my feet under me, not taking my eyes off her. She's calling herself an Aura, not a Divina. How odd. Does everyone here have abilities?

I look around the room with new eyes. They aren't all Nomagis? Natalina was right. Huh. What did she call them in class? Those Divina who came to the mainland and mixed with Nomagi? The name is somewhere in the recesses of my mind but I'm too tired to dig.

The woman seems to read my mind. "I'm Anna, the only Elemental currently in the room. There's nothing to worry about, though. We only want to help you. I know you've been through a lot, and we actually have some good news for you."

Elemental. I'm so confused that I don't know what to say, even if I could speak.

Theo's dead.

That tearing sensation returns, and I want so badly to wrap my arms around myself. I'll never hear his voice again. It's only fair if nobody hears mine, either.

So, I stay quiet. Quiet and utterly confused. It doesn't matter. I'll be gone soon enough. But I pull at my wrists and quickly realize that, if *she* can release me, I can release myself. So that's what I do. The chains fall, and I pull my arms in.

A few people step forward, and I shrink back.

Anna stops them with a hand. "Just give her a moment. She just lost somebody very significant to her."

The tenderness and understanding in her eyes snap something in me, and the tears fall. "Theo."

She brightens. I didn't mean to say his name. "Yes, Theo. I am so sorry for your loss, Izalia. You loved him very much."

It's not a question. She can see it in my face. I can't handle this anymore—the looks, the pity. They don't know me. They don't know that I'm the one that killed him. It hurts. It hurts so much, and I can't stand it any longer.

"Can I use the bathroom?"

She looks at the others and then nods. "I'll accompany her."

The woman, Anna, leads me down the hall to a door, opens it, and goes to step inside with me.

"Please, just give me this," I say, pleading.

Studying my face, she nods. "I'm right here." She says it as a warning.

I look away so she can't see my expression. Her dark eyes are way too observant.

As soon as the door closes, I look around. There's the toilet water. Ew. But it could work. Then there's the sink. I'm about to siphon the water out but notice handles. I tap them, and nothing happens. I squeeze them. Nothing. I hit them, and finally, a drop of liquid slips out. I keep hitting them until they turn slightly. Oh! Twist. I twist both, and the water rushes out.

For a moment, I'm awed as the water flows freely without me having to do anything. There are so many questions I will never have answered.

But then I look at the monster in the mirror. Her hair is wild, and her eyes unforgiving. I wonder if Theo will forgive her when he sees me—if he sees me again. I don't know much about the afterlife, only what the Elders would say during releasing ceremonies on Mt. Apia. Our magic returns to the island to give it life and continue to support our people. But we didn't talk about what happened to our souls.

I'm reminded of one story the Elders passed down to us. A story I heard as a child about angels walking our coastline—our ancestors protecting us. Will our souls return to the island? Or will we be lost forever because we didn't die on the island?

A shiver runs through me. Did Theo think I was one of those angels when he first saw me? Is that where the nickname came from? His song flows through my mind, and I gasp from the pain that erupts inside of me. I need to do this now and join Theo wherever he is. Even if we're lost souls wandering forever, we'd be together just like we promised.

I touch the ring on my finger one last time before weaving the water before my face. It's inches from my mouth. I just need to breathe it in instead of swallowing. I can do this.

It shoots down my throat, but the door bangs open, knocking me over and causing me to cough out the liquid.

The woman slams onto my back, and I heave up the water in my lungs. Then she twists her fingers in front of my face, and I throw up the rest of it.

She grabs my face, forcing me to look at her. I gaze into her odd, dark eyes.

"Izalia, please don't give up. I know it's so hard right now, and it will be hard for a long time. I can't tell you that the pain will go away, but it will become bearable. If you don't want to live for yourself, please try for your unborn child."

I freeze.

She presses a hand to my stomach. "It's early, but another nurse who is a Lympha sensed its presence with her abilities. You're going to be a mother."

Something other than pain blooms in my chest. It doesn't cover the pain but settles right next to it. Something strange and unknown to me. Hope.

So I do the most reckless thing I may have done yet—live.

46

AZALIA

I roll for the third time in bed, heaving my large stomach. There is no such thing as comfort these days. My legs wrap around a pillow longer than my body, my hips ache, and I already need to pee again.

I gasp as he kicks me in the ribs. "I know you don't like this side, but my hip is numb," I mutter. He shifts, and my belly protrudes upward. I pat his bottom or head, unsure which is jutting out now. "Not too much longer. Anna says only a couple more weeks."

I close my eyes and see the island. I miss the sounds and the smells and the vibrant colors. Florida is nice. Some things are similar, like the trees and the bugs. But not the animals. I miss Beau. I hope he has his own little monkey family by now. My heart aches, knowing I wasn't able to say goodbye. I miss my parents. They probably think I'm dead. I wonder if my mom regrets letting me go.

My hand goes to my throat, to the shark tooth wrapped in twine. I miss him.

My chest physically hurts when I think of him. Anna was right when she told me the pain never goes away. If it weren't for this piece of him inside of me that gets to live on, I would have followed through with my dark thoughts that day at the hospital. But I chose to live for him.

I rub my belly, and the babe stirs again. He is my life now. I hum an off-key tune. My voice is nothing like his father's, but I know he'll need it as much as his dad did. Music was Theo's life. My lessons to prepare for his arrival have been nothing short of comical. I was terrible at the piano and the guitar. Some other instruments I tried were okay. But it wasn't until I struck the strings on the harp that I felt like I did when Theo played. He would like it. I bet he'd be proud of me.

Sleep begins to take me under, the island coming to life around me. When I'm swimming in the ocean, I can almost imagine being there. The people here know nothing about the Isle of Alohra. I assume it's inside what they call the Devil's Triangle—where they found me eight months ago. They have many theories on why sailors never return. Some hit too close to the truth. I don't believe my people will ever let up on those storms that keep the Nomagi away, but I hope they don't continue to slaughter Nomagi on the shores and that Theo's legacy will live on.

Maybe I'll dream of him tonight. I've only dreamt of him once since his passing, the scars inside my soul feeling fresh when I realized it wasn't real. But it was so nice to see him again. I worry I might forget the little things about him—the feel of his hair, his lips against mine, his smell, his smile. I'm terrified I'll wake up one day and have forgotten it all. It's worth the pain the memories bring.

I worry how I'll keep his memory alive for his son. I have nothing of Theo's, just memories. So, every night, I think of the moments we had together, trying to burn them into my brain forever. Tonight, I'm at the waterfall. Tears run down my cheeks as I remember him tickling me under the water and wrapping his arms around me for the first time. I can almost hear his laugh, feel the mist from the falls, and smell his intoxicating sweet scent. He's so graceful when he swims. He grins over his shoulder, and I lose myself in that smile.

The most intense pain overtakes my stomach, and I wake up screaming, holding my belly.

Anna barrels into my room. "Iz! Are you okay?"

"Something is wrong." I shake my head, feeling for the baby.

No. If something happens to him, I won't survive. The intense pain radiates from my pelvis and up my back. I throw my head back, releasing another scream. The window cracks.

Anna turns on the light and pushes the blankets off of me. Her face transforms from worry to joy.

What is she smiling about? I'm about to strangle her, but the pain lessens, and I can breathe again. My legs and back feel soaked, and I look down, preparing for the worst.

"You're in labor! The baby is coming!"

"What? Tonight? I thought I still had a few more weeks," I pant.

She shrugs as she helps me from the bed. "Looks like he wants to make a grand entrance."

I smile at her. It's the first time she used that pronoun. I've told her for months that he'll be a boy, and I even know what he'll look like…but she forced me to choose a girl's name just in case. I did—only to appease her. Thea. I thought it would be a nice variation of Theo's name. I love it so much that a part of me hopes it's a girl.

Water drips down my leg as I stand. "Ew."

"Your water broke." She laughs.

"This is not funny! Somehow, this giant thing has to come out of me." Suddenly, I'm terrified.

She grabs my hand. "Women have been pushing babies out for thousands of years. You'll be fine." She snatches the bag I packed from next to my bed as we pass the bassinet one of the nurses gave me.

Panic courses through me. I don't know how to take care of a baby.

"Just try to rein in your abilities," she says, glancing toward the cracked window. "The OBs hate dealing with Aura women. We always break something."

I've gotten remarkable at my Aura abilities, trying to embrace the title of somebody with only air-wielding magic. Of course, nobody can know what I truly am.

I realized pretty quickly that Anna only has one type of ability. And so do all the Elementals here—either air, water, fire, *or* earth, not all of them, like my people. The Elders never told us that there were more of us on the mainland. Our history books conveniently left out the fact that we weren't the only ones to survive the war.

From scouring the library—which I could live in for days, weeks, months, and never tire of—I learned that other Divina integrated with the Nomagi after the war hundreds of years ago. Over time, our abilities went away, separating the elements. They live together here as one people. It's remarkable. Nomagi aren't savages like the scrolls taught us. They have things like automated lights and cars.

Cars are amazing. As Anna guides me to the door, I'm relieved I don't have to walk to the hospital in such a state. We get to drive. It was terrifying the first time I experienced being in a car, and now I can't imagine life without one.

"Anna, you promise to help me with him, right?"

She looks at me like I've grown three heads. "Of course. I can't wait to do all the things for this precious angel!"

I stifle a gasp at her word choice but quickly recover. "You're the best roommate."

She shrugs. "I know."

After I was released from the hospital all those months ago, Anna quickly realized I was different and took me under her wing. She was pretty understanding about me not telling her everything about my past. She thinks I grew up in Bermuda, the closest island I could find on a map.

She's taught me everything and gave me a home and a job at the hospital. I owe her my life. After learning that our magic can help sick Nomagi, there was nothing else I wanted to do. My parents had wanted me to become an Instructor, and I could have grown to enjoy teaching, but healing people after being seen as broken for so long brings me immense joy. I can't bring back the people Divina slaughtered, but I can help these people live.

There are so many that come in every day with the most mundane of things. I laughed the first time somebody came in with a broken bone. And the *illnesses*. We never got sick on Alohra. I seem to catch some new germ every other week now. There are also loads of people with disabilities like mine. Epilepsy is what Anna calls it. I've only had a few episodes since coming here because I can manage them with medication. And meeting people like me—it's remarkable. I'm not broken, and I have never been broken. My whole life, I was looked down upon because I was different, but here, everyone is different. Theo would have liked it. He would have thrived here.

I squeeze her hand to get her to look at me. "No, really. I'm grateful for you and everything you've done for me. I'm scared. Scared of being alone through this. Scared I won't be able to be a good mother and father." I choke.

She looks at me, eyes full of sympathy.

"You've been there for me. I've never had a friend like you. Thank you."

She smiles and pulls me in for a hug.

But then the pain returns in my stomach, and my grip tightens. "By the island, it hurts!"

She looks at me oddly. I've been careful about using certain expressions around her, but sometimes, it slips. Luckily, this time, I'm in too much pain for her to ask questions.

"Breathe through it. You got this." She rubs circles on my back as I do what she instructs.

Once the pain ebbs, I stand straight. "Let's go."

She opens the front door and steps back with a sharp intake of breath.

"Hello? We were wondering if Izalia lives here?" comes a familiar high-pitched voice.

No. It can't be. A boulder settles into my stomach.

"Um. Who…who are you?" Anna stutters.

I walk around Anna, and my mouth drops open at the people standing before us, emotion burning my throat as tears fall.

Their faces light up when they see me, and then, when I hobble toward them, they see all of me.

Theo's parents' expressions mimic mine.

I fall into Iris's arms as sobs break through my chest. She clings to me, and his father wraps his arms around the both of us.

"Oh, Izalia."

They smell like home. Pain slices my heart—too many memories crash into me. Not now. I can't deal with that kind of pain now, not when he needs me.

I pull back, wiping at my face so I can see them. I'm surprised they're wearing Nomagi clothes like mine—gone are the days of sarongs and tunics.

"What are you doing here? How?" I ask, blinking to make sure they're real.

"After you and Theo disappeared, the island was in chaos." She smiles. "Good chaos. It was time for a change. Much came to light, new leadership was called, and we left shortly after."

So many questions swirl in my mind.

"We have been looking for you two for a long time."

Oh no. They don't know. How would they know? I can't be the one to tell them.

"Congratulations," she says, placing a hand on my belly. "Is Theo here?" She looks around me with a huge smile that makes my heart fall into my stomach.

I open my mouth, not knowing how I'm going to tell them, when pain slices through me. "Oh!" I double over, and all three of them catch me.

"She's in labor! We got to go!" Anna says.

I almost forgot she was there. She grabs my elbow as Theo's parents' hands fall away. We hurry down the hall, his parents trailing behind.

We pile into the elevator, and there is a stretch of silence between us as the elevator lowers us to the ground floor. I don't meet Iris's eyes, worried she'll see the truth in my face.

I wish he were here.

A different pain erupts from my chest, nothing to do with the baby, and I have to use all my strength to stay standing.

Oh, Theo. I grab my stomach—our child—as close to Theo as I can get.

"I've got you. Good thing we got this apartment so close to the hospital," Anna says, mistaking the twist in pain on my face for another contraction.

She loads me into the car in the parking garage. Anna awkwardly tells his parents they can ride in the backseat, and then we're off.

"Izalia?" Iris's voice wavers.

Boaz shushes her. I twist and twist the ring Theo gave me around my finger. I can't stand it. I need to tell them.

"He's gone," I whisper.

The car is silent. All I hear are the cars rushing past us and the purring of the Pontiac's engine. Anna keeps her eyes straight ahead. At least she has something to do. I can't stand the too-loud thoughts and emotions piercing the air.

"I'm so sorry. I couldn't save him. I tried—" I feel a hand on my shoulder, and my words fall away as I turn around.

Iris has tears in her eyes, and Boaz's face is grave. His hand rests on my shoulder.

"You don't need to tell us right now. Focus on that baby."

"But you deserve—" Another contraction rips through my stomach, and I double over, breathing through it. Once it passes, I look back at them. "You need to know."

"We knew." Iris's voice comes out strangely calm.

I stifle a gasp.

"We felt it when he passed. We shouldn't have. He's not even our blood. But he's my son, and I knew the moment his heart was no longer beating."

"But then why—" I start.

"Why did we come anyway?" Iris asks.

"Because you're our daughter, too," Boaz answers.

Silent tears run down my face, and I bite my lip so I don't completely break down with ugly sobs.

Iris gives me a watery smile. "When we saw you, I thought maybe—impossibly—I could have been wrong. It was strange. I didn't realize I was still holding on to that hope. I'm sorry for putting that on you."

I shake my head, full-on crying now, my chest heaving. I'm about to tell them they don't need to apologize for hoping when another contraction seizes me. This one is even closer than the last.

We pull up to the hospital, and Anna climbs out of the car. Boaz is the first at my door. He helps me out. There is a wheelchair already prepared for my arrival. I fall into it as I look at the faces around me. Somehow, impossibly, I will have my loved ones around me for this. It can't be a coincidence for them to find me on the night I go into labor, just like it wasn't a coincidence for Theo to save my life on the cliff's edge.

There is no doubt that Theo's spirit is here. I can feel him racing along as the nurse pushes me through the opening doors—

like, if I look back, he'll be there, an excited smile stretching on his face.

I push one last time, the pain at an all-time high before relief wraps around me and a wail pierces the room. A weight is placed on my chest as the words, "It's a boy!" rings through the air.

I breathe a sigh of relief; the pain finally gone. I lay my head back, one of my hands in Iris's, who isn't squeezing as tight. Or maybe that was me squeezing her. It's all a blur as I catch my breath.

She moves my hand, and I hold something warm. I peer down as two blue eyes take me in. An overwhelming love, close to what I felt for Theo, flows through me like molten lava into every crack and fissure, connecting me to this child and forging our bond in stone.

He's mine.

The babe stares at me with all-knowing eyes. No. Not at me. At something behind me. I glance over my left shoulder, but there is nothing there.

He's still looking at that spot when I feel a faint touch on that shoulder. I stiffen and choke back a cry when that place in my heart that held mine and Theo's bond, a place I thought I would never feel again, gives a slight flutter. *Theo.* He's here. He really is here.

The baby hiccups and then smiles over my shoulder. Tears run down my face as I pull the baby up to nuzzle him, inhaling the smell of heaven.

When I pull back, the babe looks into my eyes. For a moment, we stare at each other, unblinking. Theo is in the shape of his eyes and the arch of his nose, and just like that, our memories together no longer bring pain and sorrow but joy and solace. Our love created this perfect little human.

His little nose scrunches, and he starts wailing again. I can't help but laugh. I peek under the cap to see a full head of blond curly hair and smile. I knew he'd have his father's golden locks.

"He's perfect. My little Theodore."

Hours go by. I stare at the moon for the passing of time, even though there are clocks here, where you never have to look at the sky again. But it makes me sad to lose that connection to the sky, even if it's for something minor like telling the time. Too many things here cut us off from nature.

I start to nod off, but then jolt awake, not wanting to take my eyes off Teddy. He's sound asleep in the bassinet after moving from one set of arms to the next in constant rotation. He seems to enjoy mine the most, though. He always wants to be on my chest, looking over my shoulder.

My eyes become heavy when I hear a soft, musical voice. My heart skips when I realize it came from that spot over my shoulder. I twist, and there he is—my Theo. I can't breathe or move. I stare up at the impossibility. But that spot in my heart—our connection—warms and spreads through my body.

We're still bonded. Even death can't separate us.

Impossibly, he's even more beautiful. His skin has a faint glow, and his hair is truly as bright as the sun, making it hard to look at. But I don't dare look away.

He smiles and leans down to kiss my temple. A current of electricity sparks at the spot, and I gasp. The damn breaks.

"Theo, Theo! How are you here?"

"I only have a moment. I've stayed much too long. I've been waiting for you to fall asleep."

"I'm asleep?" I look around, and there is a haze around the edges of my vision. Indeed, I am. But it feels so real.

"He's perfect, angel. I've been here this whole time."

I knew it. "I miss you," I sob and then immediately steady myself. I don't want to waste this time crying, unable to see straight.

He threads his hand through my hair. "I miss you too. So much."

I hesitantly touch his cheek. He's really here.

Even though I know better, I ask anyway. "Can you come back?"

He looks at me sadly. "I'm always here. Or at least I try to be. There's a lot of work to do on this side."

My eyebrows squeeze together.

He shakes his head. "Oh yeah, you wouldn't believe it. There is so much to do in the afterlife. They never give me a break. I kind of had to sneak away for this."

I blink in disbelief but decide to go with it. "So, you're really okay?"

He smiles, and I touch the outline of his lips. "I am. Everyone is very kind. They—" His lips spread into a thin line. "Sorry, I'm not supposed to say too much about it. I just wanted to tell you that I love you. You're going to be a phenomenal mother. Don't worry about me."

I swallow back the tears. "I'm so sorry."

He grabs my face, and I lean into him. "My death is not your fault." He pierces me with those light-blue eyes. "Say it."

I shake my head. "It's my fault you were out there. My fault that I couldn't save you in time."

"Izalia, that was my choice. I knew what would happen if we went through with the ceremony, but I did it anyway. Like I told you, I would gladly die over and over again as long as I got the chance to hold you in my arms. Look what our love created."

I smile since I was just thinking the same thing. I glance at Teddy. He's awake and staring straight at his father. He can see him.

"I don't regret any of it, and we'll be together again before long. A lifetime is almost nothing up here, angel. We'll have an eternity together. Just hold on, okay? Live your life. Be happy."

He leans down, whispers a kiss on my lips, then steps back, releasing me.

I try to hold on, but he's starting to fade. "No, please don't go."

"I'll always be around. I told you I'd love you to my last breath, but I was wrong. I will love you for an eternity."

My heart threatens to burst.

He looks at our son. "He is so beautiful. Just like you said he would be."

"Can he see you?"

"Seems so."

I smile. "I love you, Theo. More than life itself."

"I'll love you forever." His whisper echoes off the walls.

I open my eyes, looking around, my eyes adjusting to the dark. Teddy is fast asleep in the bassinet. Anna is on the pull-out couch. Theo's parents left when it got late, but they'll return in the morning.

They told me they had a few surprises they brought from the island. Iris and Boaz aren't planning on returning—banished the moment they set foot on the mainland. They did that for me.

My chest aches. Too many sacrifices. Theo and now his parents. I'll make them count and return the favor one day. That is for certain.

We discussed getting a house together and that Anna is welcome, but I don't know if she'll take them up on the offer.

They answered some of my more dire questions. Elder Wilder and the others involved were stripped of their titles, and all the people—even those on Breakwater Strand—voted for new leadership. Voted. I can't believe it. There were high hopes that that would change the division between Divina. New guidelines were placed for the Protectors. Iris mentioned they were still arguing about what to do with surviving Nomagi when she and Boaz slipped away on Elder Wilder's personal ship—not like he needed it anymore.

Then there's Alexi, who unfortunately, survived his injuries. He had his magic taken—a small victory. Not enough, though, for what he did to Theo. But at least he'll have to live in that misery of never being able to wield again—a punishment worse than death in Alexi's eyes.

I didn't ask about my parents. I'm not quite ready to have that conversation. But it will come. We have all the time in the world now.

My head falls back into the pillow, and I look at where Theo stood. I don't know if it was real or a beautiful dream, but I have to believe there is some truth in the vision, that part of him still exists out there somewhere, that he's still with me. I'll hold on to that hope and do what he asked. I will do my best to be happy.

EPILOGUE

"So, was it real?"

I blink back the story as it fades into the recesses of my aging mind. My great-granddaughter sits across from me, her strawberry-blond hair cascading down her thin frame. "What?"

"Was it real? Theo being in the hospital room?" she asks, her emerald eyes watery.

"Teddy was always looking off somewhere as a baby. He'd be playing with blocks on the ground and randomly smile into the corner, or he'd chat in his baby language to absolutely nobody. Even as a toddler, he was always lost in another world. So, yes, it was real to me. Of course, Teddy eventually grew out of it and didn't remember any of it. But I like to think that his father was with him throughout his childhood as his guardian angel. It's funny. Theo always called me his angel. But Theo was—is—the true angel."

I look past her, over the treetops and the expanse of snow-capped mountains. I'm so far from the ocean now. I think Theo would like it out here, though. It's peaceful and full of magic, like where we grew up. I look down at my hands, wrinkled from age, spinning the little golden sun ring he gave me. I've lived my life to the fullest, just like Theo told me to. But now I'm ready. I'm ready to return home.

I can feel it in the void in my heart dedicated to him, a warm familiar pulse. I'll be reunited with him any day now. My soul longs to be threaded back together with his.

My other half. My one true love. My angel of the ocean.

Author's Note

Thank you for reading Izalia's story! If you want more of her, her story continues through her granddaughter in The Spark Series trilogy, starting with The Spark Within. The first two books are out, with the third and final installment coming in 2026. If you don't want to miss any announcements and updates on these books, make sure to follow me on Instagram or Tiktok @samchristopherwrites and join my email list through the QR code below.

Every review helps me reach more readers. If you feel so obliged, please leave a review on Amazon, Goodreads, B&N, or social media.

About the Author

Samantha Christopher is a mother to three boys and lives in the Pacific Northwest. When she's not wrangling her wild children or two dogs, you can usually find her hiding in her bedroom with a bag of Sour Patch Kids and a good book or typing away at her next story. If you want to follow Sam, you can find her on Instagram and TikTok @samchristopherwrites or visit her website for all things reading, writing, and the joys/chaos of motherhood by following the QR code on the previous page.

Acknowledgments

What started as a fun new hobby back in 2021, after having my third child and feeling consumed by motherhood, has turned into something bigger than I could have dreamed with this third book. A late-night Titanic watch with my husband brought on this particular story idea. I was writing the second book of The Spark Series at the time and had barely introduced Izalia's character. And it just hit me, the vision of Izalia telling her and Theo's story to Maya, her great-granddaughter, a story of true love and heart-wrenching sacrifice. I knew it would destroy me to write but aren't the best stories the ones that make you cry?

My husband, Alan, who is my number one cheerleader and supporter, thank you. Thank you for helping me achieve this dream and making it possible to publish three books in thirteen months. And thank you for never having watched Titanic, so I just had to make you watch it and spur on this story idea for me.

I couldn't have written this book if it weren't for my three boys, who encouraged me during NaNoWriMo. If you don't know, NaNoWriMo is a challenge to write a book, or 50K words in a month. I turned it into a family activity by creating a chart that my boys would color in. Every time I reached 10K words, we celebrated as a family with a special treat or activity. This made my boys so excited for me to write. And I did accomplish my goal! After about six weeks, this entire novel was drafted.

I would also like to thank all the other writers doing NaNoWriMo in November 2023, specifically Rogue Writers and my overseas accountability partner. Everyone helped and inspired me to stay on top of my daily writing goals and make my favorite story that I've written so far a reality.

I am always grateful for my editor, Shannon Cave, and my cover designers, Maria Spada, and the people at Miblart. You guys do amazing things!

And you! I can't do this without my readers. I am forever grateful that you choose to read indie books and help make my dreams a reality. I'm thankful for all my readers I find through social media and for my street team full of amazing people. Thank you from the bottom of my heart for your support.

My friends and family, thank you for the love and support you continue to show me. No matter that this is my third book, you're still here, still reading, still showing up. I love you guys!

Izalia and Theo's story may be fictional, but there are many tragic love stories out there. And I am forever grateful for my knowledge of God's plan, which gives me comfort in knowing that this life isn't the end. People like Izalia and Theo will get their happily ever after. Not even death can keep them apart. And if you don't believe those things, that's okay! I hope, at least, that this story will inspire you to choose love over hate. Peace over contention. Friendship over intolerance in a world that is eager to split people apart.